THE SIXTH DIMENSION

© May 2018

Mark Cupit

Grosvenor House
Publishing Limited

This book is published by
Grosvenor House Publishing Ltd
Link House
140 The Broadway, Tolworth, Surrey, KT6 7HT.
www.grosvenorhousepublishing.co.uk

A CIP record for this book
is available from the British Library

ISBN 978-1-80381-293-9
eBook ISBN 978-1-80381-294-6

CHAPTER ONE

When we were younger, in our early twenties, the long February evenings were always hard to fill. It wasn't the lack of things to do, rather the lack of money to pay for entertainment. Although we were all in good and promising employment, disposable income is scarce when you're just starting out in the employment world.

This particular Sunday evening was no different from many others. It was late in the month, which usually meant we were broke. Not wanting to waste another evening in front of the box, we spent a lot of our time playing cards. The group had naturally gravitated to my second-floor flat. It was normal that we would all be congregated in my living room. We were playing rummy; however, after an hour or so, our interest in the card game waned. Pushing the cards away I declared, "This is getting boring, anybody got any ideas?"

With me that night was Patricia Cummings, my girlfriend of three years. Trish, as everybody called her, was five feet two of vivacious personality, full of laughter and mischief. Just turned twenty with, as she saw it, an exciting and adventurous life ahead. Trish had always tried to experience life to the full. When Trish entered a room, she could energise it, simply with her enthusiasm for life. Wedded to this, she occasionally had a temper which could blow hotter than a volcano, but afterwards, I've never seen her sulk, or hold a grudge.

Trish's dark brown hair hung in the then fashionable pageboy style, framing a cute pixie face that hid an inner demon; not an ounce of excess fat adorned her agile figure; clean, soap-scrubbed, pale skin completed the picture of my own angel.

I knew the real pleasure of knowing Trish was being able to look deep into those olive green hypnotic, laughing eyes. Eyes which would return the stare determinedly, seeming to look deep into my soul.

Also, with us that night was Trish's sister Sue and her boyfriend David Ball. Sue was very much like her sister in features, though ever so slightly larger in size at five feet four, and one dress size bigger. Sue had blue eyes with honey blond hair, cut in the same style as Trish. However, where they were similar in features the two girls were very different in character. As you got to know the sisters, the differences between them became apparent. Trish was the talkative, excitable, bouncy personality. She would gravitate to the centre of any gathering, whereas Sue was much quieter, more reserved. Initially Sue would be shy with strangers, able to drift into the background of any group. It was hard to remember that Sue was the elder by two years. Nevertheless, when you got to know Sue well, then the enormous depth of her compassion, her caring, maternal nature would shine through. Sue had chosen nursery level teaching as a career, a profession which she seemed perfect for.

At five feet nine inches tall, with a wiry figure and brown curly hair, David Ball had been our friend since we'd all been at Westfields Primary School together. David was the comedian of our group. Any group has someone who enjoys a joke, and David could never resist a laugh, always ready with a wisecrack, usually at my, or his own, expense. When he was only ten, David's father had walked out of the family home, leaving his mother Annie to cope alone. Ever since, from necessity, David had become the man of the house, spending a large portion of his childhood helping out, caring for his younger siblings and the family home, while his mother went out to work, keeping her family afloat with two jobs.

I sometimes thought that David had real reason to hate life, to be resentful, but David was always laughing and smiling.

Then myself, Martyn Holloway. I was then twenty-three years old, short brown wiry hair, a six-foot, well-built, but trim, athletic frame, and what some people would call a boyish face. I'd created for myself the image of laddishness, playing rugby for the local town club and indulging in general middle-class rowdiness, most Saturday evenings after a game. Despite my carefully self-engineered roguish image, for the rest of the week I was a responsible model citizen, working hard and owning a small modern immaculate two-bedroomed flat, close to the centre of town.

During the day, I could be found toiling away in the technical drawing office of Price Brothers, a small family run firm of architects, whom I'd joined straight from university.

Even with the monthly mortgage drain on resources, I loved my flat, it was a place which I could call my own. A place where I could meet up with my friends when we had no money, a place I called home.

Accepting a helping hand from my parents, I had secured the flat six months previously. Young and broke,

I was still trying to develop a personalised themed décor, but the two grey worn leather couches, which dominated my lounge, did match, having been bought as a pair through a local charity shop.

Every evening, during the first three months of ownership, I could be found toiling away with a paint roller in hand, as I sought to add my own personality to my new home. Light grey walls in the lounge complemented the couches. A chrome and glass occasional coffee table, taking up position in the centre of a rose-coloured, deep-pile Chinese rug, a welcome hand me down from my parents. The rug went some way to disguising the threadbare beige carpet, left by the previous owners, a carpet which badly needed replacing. The remaining furniture in the lounge, table lamps and sideboard, had been purchased from a famous Swedish flat-pack furniture supplier, when need was identified and monies available. Furniture chosen for its simplicity. Pictures and ornaments were rare in my home. I preferred a minimalist, masculine aspect, rather than the available clutter of mismatched hand-me-downs. Ornaments and pictures would only arrive when funds and desire collided.

Now, six months after buying, I was justly proud of my small flat. It was a place where I felt comfortable and safe, a place where my friends and I could congregate and seek out our own entertainment.

Trish answered my appeal. "Why don't we do something different? My friend Lucy was telling us the other day about how she experimented with the Ouija board. She said it worked really well. She wouldn't stop talking about it for days." Trish was quite animated.

"She said it was quite scary, that there was no way that it could be faked."

Trish managed to make it sound exciting, different, and just a little risky. "It's obvious," she concluded triumphantly. "We have to have a go."

I looked across with mild surprise at my grinning girlfriend, then at David and Sue. David spoke first. "I'm game if everybody else is."

"Okay," I said, only slightly reluctantly. "I doubt it will work, but why not."

After discussions on what to do, we set about making our own home-made board. Trish cut card into small squares and wrote the letters in her precise neat handwriting. All the while she chattered excitedly as we prepared for this unusual experiment.

Under Trish's instructions, I wrote the words YES and NO on separate cards, before clearing the coffee table of its accumulated detritus. On the glass surface of the table, we set out the letters in the prescribed circle, the YES and NO sandwiched between the A and the Z.

Fetching a small glass beaker from the kitchen, I placed it upside down at the centre of the circle.

Somewhat nervously, we seated ourselves around the table, cross legged on the floor. David, Sue and myself turned expectantly towards Trish, waiting for her to take the initiative.

"Go ahead, Trish. It was your idea. What do we do now?" I prompted, wanting somebody else to lead the experiment.

Even now, I can still remember the thoughts going through my head at that time. I was laughing and joking with David, expecting failure, mocking Trish for her belief, but it was just possible to see slight foreboding in David's eyes. I have no doubt, the same could be said for myself. I didn't expect this to succeed, but I was definitely uneasy, just in case it did.

"Put your index fingers on the bottom of the glass," Trish instructed, placing her finger there. "Lightly. Lucy said you don't need to put much pressure on it." Following Trish's guidance, we obediently did as we were told, four fingers on the upturned glass, waiting for Trish.

"Is there anybody there?" she intoned, projecting her words towards the upturned glass. Nothing happened. We stared at the glass in silence. Trish repeated her words with greater conviction. "Is there anybody there?" I glanced sideways, my eyes meeting Trish's. We waited, expectantly, unsure if we were hoping for a sign from the other side, or not.

The seconds passed slowly. I'd begun to relax, feelings of relief forming.

Releasing my pent-up breath with a loud sigh, I spoke. "Looks like it's all codswallop as I thought, nothing in it whatsoever." As if to prove me misguided, as the last syllable left my lips, the glass abruptly responded, giving a slight jerk. Just a tiny movement under my finger, almost imperceptible, but then slowly, very, very slowly, it began to move, sliding across the glass tabletop, towards the word YES. Dry mouthed, I instinctively looked towards David, expecting laughter revealed by the eyes, an indication signalling this was a joke, that this was David having fun.

David was staring down at the glass, transfixed and wide-eyed, a look of incomprehension etched upon his features. He understood my glance and gave a slight shake of the head. "Not me mate." Whoever was moving the glass, I knew it wasn't David.

It continued its jerky motion, halting by the word YES, all four index fingers still in contact with the glass.

It had been Trish's idea; we were content to allow Trish to continue talking.

"What is your name?" Trish asked the glass while staring at the base. Again, the glass began to move slowly, an unsteady, slightly jerky motion, moving firstly to the letter P, then on to A, T then R, until finally the glass spelled out the name Patrick, once again halting at the centre of the circle. Trish's eyes were bright, dancing with excitement, happy to do our talking.

She asked, "Have you lived on Earth in a previous life? Are you a spirit?" The glass immediately responded, moving again, beginning to spell out its message. Travelling slightly faster now, gliding easily across the glass tabletop, it gradually revealed the tale of Patrick, who claimed to have lived in rural England, existing as a poor peasant during the early nineteenth century.

We became acquainted with Patrick's life story, that he'd married at twenty, lost his wife in childbirth, only a year later; Soon afterwards, his son died in a state-run orphanage. Then of the man himself, succumbing to typhoid fever before he'd reached twenty-five years of age. The tale of Patrick moved us all.

Time passed unnoticed; we had been at the table for over an hour. My arm was beginning to feel the strain of constant contact with the glass.

Sue groaned out loud. "Wait until tomorrow. This is killing me." With relief, we readily agreed, saying our goodbyes to Patrick, until another time.

A qualified exhilaration replaced my earlier caution. I'd never considered myself a spiritual person, but it looked like we'd found an exciting and cheap way of filling the evenings.

Trish was enthusiastic insisting, "Wow, that was brilliant. We've got to do it again, tomorrow night, that was beyond belief."

I was both intrigued and fascinated by what I'd just witnessed, if not yet convinced. "I'm perfectly happy to give it another go." But, I pointed out to Trish, "It's all very well you being eager, but what we've seen is proof of nothing; the story of Patrick wouldn't be difficult to invent."

"Then give it another go tomorrow, see what happens," Trish responded with a cheeky grin, knowing she had her fish hooked.

Sue was the only one to raise doubts. "We shouldn't risk it; it's dangerous," she stated firmly, pouting. But Sue, and ourselves, knew she would be there the next evening, if that's what David and the rest of us wanted. Sue wouldn't stop it.

The next day, while seated at my drawing board, I reflected upon our experiment, wondering what it all meant. Had we really contacted a spiritual world, a world which I hadn't had the time to consider before? My logical brain began to plan, wondering how I could test this phenomenon, ascertain if there was any truth in what we'd seen. Suddenly I had an idea; I was going to set a test for our next visitor.

Monday evening, the group was once again seated, cross legged, around the circle of letters. However, this time

I wasn't part of the circle. I was seated several feet away, perched on the couch. At my suggestion, the group had agreed to try and test the authenticity of our alleged spiritual visitor. Trish, David and Sue were going to make contact. I was to be the questioner, though not present in the circle.

When they'd arrived, I'd seated the group in the lounge and suggested my plan. "We're going to ask to speak to my auntie Rose, the one who died from cancer, two years ago," I told them. "If Rose, who was my mother's sister, claims to be answering, I'm going to ask several questions that only I know the answer to. I figure if the Ouija board can answer these, then maybe it is just possible we've reached a spiritual realm," I said, looking around the group. Knowing my need for logical evidence, the others quickly agreed, all curious to see the outcome.

Waiting, as Trish prepared, I carefully scrutinised the rest of our group. Sue I could tell was jittery; David would always hide any nervousness by being louder and more cheerful than usual, joking when none was needed. I had known David longer than anybody. I could sense any slight anxiety; but tonight, he wasn't too far from normal. He would always be up for an adventure. David, I was sure, would be intrigued rather than fearful; he would let it run, waiting to see the result of our meddling.

As expected, Trish was displaying the most excitement, seemingly the least sceptic. Trish has always been a girl who, once she accepts something, she will unquestioningly give it her whole heart. Coupled with Trish's vivacity came recklessness and little thought for consequences. It had been Trish's original idea. She, I could tell, was simply thrilled with what we were doing, Trish was happy to let it run. "We're going to have fun tonight," Trish said, as she primed the table.

Watching her animated preparations, I drifted back to our first meeting. I'd seen her around, in the street plenty, and spoken to her occasionally at school, until, on one of my rare visits home from university, she'd collared me at my garden gate. I remembered how she'd crossed the street demanding, "Where have you been? I haven't seen you for a couple of months?" Trish had quickly captivated me with her beguiling charm. No longer some gawky kid from along the street but an enchanting young woman, who delighted me simply by agreeing to join me for a drink. Ever since, the enthusiasm and energy she'd brought to our relationship never ceased to amaze me.

"Is there anybody there?" Again, Trish took the lead. I studied her expression as she spoke, eyes bright and intense, focusing on the glass. As soon as the question was completed, Trish bit her bottom lip, a trait that I'd noticed she did when she was excited or nervous. This evening there was less waiting; several seconds passed before the glass began to move. Beginning with a little judder, it slowly glided across the table aiming for YES, before returning smoothly to stop at the centre of the table.

"Can we speak to Rose Horton, please, Martyn's aunty?" Trish enquired quizzically, her voice rising by an octave as she spoke. We waited. Several seconds passed with no movement. The glass remained stationary.

David glanced towards me, the beginnings of a relieved expression, revealed by his eyes.

"Nothing happening tonight," I whispered, suppressing a grin, not knowing if I was pleased or not.

Twenty seconds passed. The thought occurred, that's it, it's all a fake.

However, during this time, the three protagonists still maintained contact with the base of the glass.

Abruptly the glass gave a small jerk; its sudden movement startling them, so much so that Sue momentarily lost contact. Trish and David managed to maintain enough downward pressure. Quickly, Sue replaced her finger, as the glass began slowly moving across the circle.

With an uneven motion it travelled across the circle, stopping by the letter H, then on to the E, before completing the message, "*hello Martyn*". Once more, the glass stopped, halting at the centre of the table.

I briefly forgot why I was there, taking a second to recompose myself, before inquiring limply, "Is that you, Auntie Rose? How are you?" Not realising how daft I must have sounded.

The Ouija board responded immediately, spelling out, "I'm dead. How do you think I feel?" My three friends twitched, expressions shocked until they realised I was smiling. This was typical of Aunty Rose's dry and caustic wit. The glass moved again, spelling out, "I'm happy, and in a place of peace with no pain."

Remembering the reason for my request to speak to my so-called maternal aunt, I continued with our experiment.

"Can you tell me the maiden name of your mother?" I demanded, of my spiritual relative. Again, the glass began to move, faster this time, yet still with the same jerky motion. Spelling out the reply.

"Woodhead." Bingo! This actually was the maiden name of my maternal grandmother. I knew it was very unlikely that the three in the group would know this; deliberately, I hadn't pre-warned them of the question. Doubts that one or some of my friends were playing an elaborate trick began to recede.

For the second evening running, we remained on the board for over an hour once I'd joined the table after completing my questions.

Aunt Rose, as I now secretly suspected it was, managed to answer all questions, without any difficulties. She also managed to tell some amusing stories, concerning her childhood with my mother and grandmother.

Despite the now jovial atmosphere, every time we asked Rose a question about the nature of the afterlife, the glass would stop abruptly; she refused to answer. Nonetheless, she did manage to put me at ease, telling us, "I am comfortable. There is no pain. I'm in a good place." I wished I could phone my mother and tell her what we'd learnt, but I was in no doubt, my mother would be horrified if I revealed our source. My mother was very unlikely to believe in the existence of the afterlife, and even less likely to accept our meddling in it.

Once we'd finished, I withdrew to the kitchen to make the coffee, listening through the open door. A loud and excited chatter was coming from the lounge. Trish, positively bouncing after this successful outcome, came through into the kitchen, hugging me as I worked, announcing, "I'm more convinced than ever, we're on to something unusual and exciting." I hugged her back, squeezing her tight, using the moment to bury my scepticism. I was unsure how I felt about it.

Only Sue still showed reluctance. "It's dangerous!" she asserted. "The danger is the unknown. If we continue, we have no idea what we're letting ourselves in for. It might have dire consequences." She may as well have tried to turn back the tide. Sue did her best, but already we were confident and reckless. The consensus was three to one, we would carry on. If only we'd listened to Sue!

We talked, drinking coffee deep into the evening until, finally, thoughts of the next day and work focused the mind. Leaving the clearing up until the following day, I said my goodbyes to Trish and the others, David giving both girls a lift home. After they'd gone, I went for a late evening run, an activity I found great for clearing a lively mind.

The words were mine but, to this day, I do not know what induced me to say them. I had no conscious plan to say anything. The words had no earthly reason to be in my head, or in my mouth, but the voice which broke the silence was mine.

"Can we speak to Jesus, please?" I was as surprised as the rest of the group. They all stared at me in disbelief. I guessed they were wondering if I had gone mad! Deep down, I tried desperately to understand the reason for my petition, but there was none; even I, the questioner, had been totally caught by surprise.

As a group we stayed in silence, staring at the motionless glass, all four fingers still in contact with its base. Since I'd spoken, maybe thirty seconds had elapsed. I didn't repeat the question. I couldn't gauge the time, possibly thirty seconds, maybe a whole minute. I don't know, but we sat there, never breaking contact with the glass, not daring to move, wondering what had just happened.

The glass moved, provoking a small yelp of surprise from Trish. Instinctively, I sneaked a peek at Sue. She was ashen faced, lips tight, but her finger still maintaining contact, as we waited for an outcome. Now, the glass had an altogether different motion. Moving purposely, it lacked any of the stop-start, jerky movement of previous visitors. Consciously, it spelt the message. "Why do you wish to speak with Jesus?"

An unanswerable question: I could only mumble in reply, "I don't know, my words were involuntary. I have no idea where that came from!"

The glass moved, again with the same faultless and positive action. Its speed made it difficult to maintain our tenuous, one-fingered contact.

"I am Luke," it announced. "On Earth, I was known by the teacher, the man you call Jesus." Before we had the chance to grasp this, it was followed with the instructions, "Be here at half past seven tomorrow. Ask to speak to the disciple Luke." Following this bombshell, the glass instantly froze.

We remained sitting, thunderstruck and motionless, staring at the glass. Finally, Trish reacted, angrily. "What on earth were you playing at?"

"I don't know. I didn't plan that. It just happened. The words fell out of my mouth!"

I defended myself from the unexpected anger and accusations of stupidity, but there was little I could really say. I had no idea to my motivation.

"This has to have some meaning. I've never heard of anything so weird," Trish stated with certainty.

"It could well be thrilling, but I'm still unsure," I responded. I'd instigated this contact, but I was very uneasy about its outcome.

We finally parted, having agreed to continue the next night. I hugged Trish, kissing her and whispering "goodnight, I'm sorry I had no idea what I was saying."

"Don't worry. It'll be fine," she replied, confidently. Having forgiven me for my stupidity.

After they left, I went for my usual late evening run, but with the complexity of the situation flooding my thoughts, I didn't sleep until the early hours. As I dozed, it dawned on me – we had been ordered to be there the following evening. This was a situation in which we were the ones now being controlled. Still, I reasoned, there's absolutely no way we're not going to do what's been asked.

At last, the working day was over. I scuttled from the office and prepared for the evening. David, Sue and Trish arrived punctually at seven. But our half hour of preparation did nothing to lessen the nerves. I could feel the butterflies as we arranged the circle.

I was responsible for the present situation so, reluctantly, I'd been nominated as our spokesman. Trish had agreed to take shorthand notes, recording any messages with her free hand.

"Is there anybody there?" I uttered the words slowly, hesitantly, lacking confidence. Instantly, almost as if we were expected, the glass began to move. Travelling with the same swift and accurate motion of the previous evening, it spelt out an amazing message.

"I am Luke, disciple of the man you know as Jesus." He gave us no time to react; the glass continued moving.

I'm sure that Trish never thought she would take such an unexpected dictation as the one she recorded.

"YOU HAVE BEEN CHOSEN. YOU WILL BE FORMED INTO A SYNDICATE OF GOD, ON THE EARTH."

This drew a collective gasp. I glanced around with astonishment, seeing David open mouthed, as we began to digest the enormity of this amazing and completely unexpected message. A message which caused immediate confusion.

"Oh, my Go..." My words tailed off. We had fingers on the glass and bewildered expressions on our faces. However, there was little time to dwell before the glass continued its movement.

"YOUR RESPONSIBILITIES WILL BE TO PREPARE FOR THE GREATEST EVENT IN THE HISTORY OF THE FATHER AND MANKIND."

The glass stopped, but only because we'd broken contact in surprise. Once we'd replaced our fingers, instantly the glass began moving, the same powerful and smooth motion as before.

It was fortunate that we'd had the insight to prepare, utilising Trish's shorthand for this initial contact. We were given lots of instruction, with very little chance to ask any questions.

Firstly, Luke explained, "You were chosen before birth." He told us this was the reason for our friendships. Luke warned, "You are going to be instructed and trained. Your training will progress with a preliminary series of tasks. Do not worry. I will be with you as you prepare for your destiny."

He further warned, "There are inherent dangers involved in the use of Ouija boards. It is easy for the devil to intercept communications of this type." Luke finally promised, "There shall be a new method of communication. I will use this soon to contact your syndicate."

Heartlessly, he then refused to elaborate further to what this unknown method of communication was.

With absolutely no chances to ask any of the myriad of questions which had occurred, the glass spelt out, "Be here, on the board Friday, seven thirty." Again, the glass abruptly ceased all movement.

We'd been there well over an hour. My arm was aching but in my adrenaline-charged astonishment, I'd hardly noticed the ache until after the glass stopped.

There followed several seconds of total silence; then, simultaneously, we erupted with a babble of noise. At that moment, I found it almost impossible to articulate a reaction. I guess excitement, confusion and incredulity all rolled into one is the closest I can come to articulating my emotional response.

Trish was evidently the most excited, a huge beaming smile across her face, hugging us in turn, asking, "Is this really happening?"

Eventually, the conversation rolled on, aimless babble, as we each tried to absorb the reality of what we'd just been part of.

We stayed talking into the early hours before they left, and I fell into bed exhausted. Previously I hadn't given religion much thought. I'd always prided myself that I possessed a logical mind, but now religion and the spiritual were front and centre. There was nothing logical about the experience we'd just undergone. So far, all it had left me was totally confused.

Secretly I resolved to seek evidence. I wanted to devise a test for Luke before we met on the Friday evening.

During my working Friday, I avoided most of the banter and chatter that would normally occur in the workplace. I had trouble concentrating and keeping my thoughts from wandering, but slowly I was developing a plan.

After missing out on the usual Friday night, post work, trip to the pub with my colleagues, I hurried home. I'd remembered somewhere at home I had my old Bible; it had been given as a present by a godparent at my christening, twenty-three years earlier. Since then, it had remained unopened. The book was eventually located in a storage box, one which had sat untouched since the day I'd moved into the flat.

The most important plan for the evening was to try to establish if Luke was for real. Consequently, I refused to open the Bible; I just hid it in the living room before filling the kettle and making my evening meal.

The three arrived together, punctually at seven, even Sue seemed eager to continue, though we were all slightly nervous of whatever fate awaited. Quickly I described my plan, receiving nods of encouragement in return as I'd explained my need for corroborative evidence.

On the dot, at half seven, we were seated in the customary circle. "Are you there, Luke?" I enquired with trepidation.

Instantly the glass moved the now familiar assured motion of two nights previously.

Trish began to record in her shorthand notebook.

"Martyn, you wish to test my validity. You wish to ask me a question!" I sat there motionless, completely gobsmacked. The concept of an omnipresent spiritual world, observing constantly, hadn't even crossed my mind. Without even launching into my devised test, I began to accept, just a little bit more.

"Yes," I said, "I have a proposal to test your knowledge of the Bible." Breaking the circle, I retrieved my concealed Bible. Reaching for it I couldn't help wondering just what kind of situation we were really in, where it would end.

If only we'd known!

The glass continued, spelling out the message, "I will answer your question, and put your mind at rest."

Beforehand, I'd explained for the benefit of Trish, Sue and David that I planned to ask Luke to recite a line from the bible. Only then would I look up the particular verse.

None of us were proficient bible scholars; this would at least eliminate any human element. I have a constant desire to validate. If the spirit of Luke was able to recite a text, which I would pick at random, then at least this would be a partial authentication to Luke's spiritual identity. Beyond this I could think of no other scheme to test the integrity of our visitor.

It now seemed that Luke was ready and fully prepared but there was no choice. I had to persevere, though I guessed we knew the result even before we started.

I opened the Bible at its contents page. With my eyes shut, I touched my finger to the page. "ISAIAH, chapter

51." I spoke, aiming the words at the glass. The glass started moving swiftly, faster than we had ever seen it move before, spelling out these words:

"*Hearken to me, yea that follow after righteousness, yea that seek the Lord.*"

Appropriate words, I thought, almost as if chosen for us, but it was random. Passing the unopened Bible to Trish, I watched attentively as she searched through the pages to find the right chapter and verse. Smiling she began reciting the already familiar verse, "*Hearken to me…*"

It was bewildering, the sheer scale of events which were overtaking us. I hadn't known if I'd wanted this test to be a success or not, but there was little doubt, it had. We were on the brink of an adventure, which was beyond comprehension. I knew then that we would be unable to curb our curiosity and harness restraint. I would continue to seek whatever the cost.

During the second visit Luke allowed our questions. We were desperate to know, so we kept on asking, "What is the great event that we're preparing for?"

But still, Luke refused to be drawn. "You are impatient. All will be revealed in due time, my children."

However, Luke did divulge that he was only the first of our spiritual teachers. He said, "There will be many teachers, not all are as patient as myself."

"So much for the patience of a saint," David replied, with a grin.

Through the glass Luke reiterated that the calling table, as Luke called it, was dangerous. He said, "It is a conduit for evil." Then once again Luke promised. "Be patient, there will be another method of communication, very soon."

We were taught that a group chosen to serve was called a syndicate, and this is what we were. In fact, he revealed, "You are one of only three in Britain. The other two have the sole job of protecting you." This stark warning made Sue go pale as she recognised the significance of the announcement. Her lip quivered, but she remained in the circle.

In amongst the warnings of danger and jeopardy, Luke had some small comfort. He instructed white acts as a partial barrier to the evil entities which exist in the spiritual dimension of the planet. He commanded, "Use white sheets, surround the calling table. This will ward off the evil spirits which observe from the spiritual realm."

After about an hour, Luke left. There was so much more that we wanted to ask but an hour seemed about the average time limit for the calling table. I guess in the spiritual world they can suffer fatigue, just as we did.

After raiding our bedding collections for as many white sheets as we could hang on the walls, the next evening, again, saw the four of us around the table. We made ready for another visit from Luke.

There was so much to find out. Firstly we asked him, "Why did you pick us? None of us are particularly religious; it doesn't make sense. How can we be suitable?"

Luke replied, "You were all chosen before birth. You aren't religious, but this makes you a blank canvas for my Lord's masterpiece." He went on to inform us, "However, you are all Christians at heart; you have the capacity for love and forgiveness." Disturbingly, Luke added, "Also, you will need your youthful energy to see you through the times ahead."

During these times together, Luke revealed many exciting secrets, but not our reason for being there. He would go as far as promising, "When the time is right, you will be fully prepared. Your training may continue for years. It will consist of many small tasks which require completing and eventually you will be ready to participate in the Lord's plans."

After that Friday, we were given the weekend off. Another essential rest day, as we came to terms with our surreal situation.

In those days, when we could afford it, we would usually congregate as a foursome in the bar of our local pub. That Sunday was no different. We were in the lounge bar of the Wellington, our local of choice, although the bar was strangely quiet for a Sunday.

I liked the Wellington, I was glad that it was our local. It would never be a fashionable pub. Ken, the landlord, didn't want a jukebox, so most of the town's youth stayed away. The Welly, as it was known, was a good old British pub, even if it was owned by a chain and made to look artificially like a traditional country pub, mass-produced horse brasses on the walls. The sepia photos of the local area of yesteryear and a log fire, which Ken would light on winter's days, gave the pub a cosy ambience. That and good beer denoted the Welly as a great place to chill out, relaxing with friends.

That Sunday evening there was obviously only one topic of conversation. We were in a secluded alcove; nobody could overhear.

Luke had ordered that his visits remain secret. He'd asserted, "There is far too much evil in the world for you to announce the existence of your syndicate to an unsuspecting population." When he'd said this, I considered the reactions of my friends at the rugby club. I, for one, was glad, I told the others. "I guess I would be visiting a psychologist reasonably fast if I turned up at training and announced the physical appearance of the apostle Luke in my life."

David grinned, declaring, "Yeah, I guess Slumbertron electronics would be sending me to the company medical centre pretty quickly if I did the same, and just when I'm making a career for myself."

I stood alone in a darkened room. I could just make out a tiny speck of light. The light seemed to move closer to me, surrounding me with luminescence, From the heart of the light, I could make out the figure of an old man, hunched over, as if years of living lay behind him. His countenance serene and genteel, radiating love and peace, evoking a love within me. He was dressed in a white flowing robe, which glowed as bright as the light itself. I felt absolutely no fear, only a warm quilted cocoon of love and peace.

Then the peaceful stranger began to recede, back towards the light. Desperately, I stretched out my hand, distraught at the loss of this stranger's love, but to no avail; the distance between us began to grow. Then there was nothing, only the oppressive, all-embracing darkness enveloping me. I felt the overwhelming devastation of love and loss. I cried out loudly, calling for this stranger to return, with his presence of peace and love.

As I jerked awake, I found Trish was staring down into my face, revealing concern. "What's the matter, why were you shouting, you sounded pained, what have you done?" Her eyes showed alarm because I had been thrashing around, crying out in my sleep. Now I was awake, but I could still feel the pain of my loss. I explained my strange dream, drawing her attention by stating, "I think I've met Luke."

In those days it was normal for Trish to stay over on the weekends. I was glad that she was here now. We laid there, talking in the darkness. I mused, "I wonder what it means if anything. It was very vivid. Could this be the other method Luke had to contact us? I vaguely remember something about dreams being biblical, or at least they can be!"

"Honey, that sounds so wonderful, yet painful at the same time." She gave my arm a squeeze, letting me know she was there. Once her concerns had evaporated, Trish's voice betrayed desire. She wanted to share the emotional intensity of my experience. We cuddled together under the quilt, Trish eager to get back to sleep, just in case.

I'd had the dream on the Friday night after we'd spent Monday through Thursday being coached by Luke. He'd given us Friday as a rest day, instructing us to return and contact him again on the Saturday evening.

When I was a younger, Saturday was always my favourite day of the week. Saturday was a day of hedonism. If Trish stayed over on the Friday, we could get up whenever we liked and potter around the flat, have a slow read of the newspaper and maybe a couple of pints over lunch. Or during the season, if I was playing, I would make my way over to the rugby club, spend the afternoon on a muddy rugby field trying to knock down strangers, then have a hot shower, a good meal, and a few welcome beers with the same guys I'd been trying to flatten an hour earlier. For me days like this are the embodiment of my early twenties.

However, this particular Saturday was different, much to the surprise of my teammates. I finished a second pint, announcing, "That's it. I'm off. Things to do, places to be."

Back at the flat, Sue and David arrived early, both eager to contact Luke again.

After contact was initiated, the first message the glass imparted was aimed towards me.

"Did you enjoy your dream last night, Martyn?" Digesting this information, I experienced a fleeting sense of disquiet. I recognised that even my inner thoughts and dreams were not private or hidden, but even then, I still knew the dream had been a special experience.

Luke explained, "When your minds are receptive, you can all be contacted in this way." But he emphatically denied that this was the new method of communication. I'd been relaxed after a visit to the Welly so, while I slept, it had been easy for Luke to reach into my inner subconscious mind. He disclosed, "It was myself who visited you last night; you are the first human in nearly two-thousand years to actually see my face." This astonishing fact left me totally gobsmacked.

Trish asked, desire evident in her voice, "Will we all get a dream? I want to meet you."

Our heavenly host eased her fears, clarifying, "Martyn was the first; you will all receive a dream visit soon, at a time when your minds are the most receptive."

Finally, Luke explained, "This is how your training will progress. You are to be given two more weeks of instruction via the table; then another method of communication awaits."

It was so frustrating not knowing what form this method of contact would take but I guess Luke had his reasons.

Luke was very forthcoming on other matters. So far, the instruction had taken a course of us asking countless questions, which would then be answered promptly. He'd divulged many aspects about the life of Jesus and Luke when they were on Earth together, a time when Luke had been a follower of Jesus.

We were also full of questions about the nature of heaven and God. Luke would answer all of our queries with patience and understanding. He was fast becoming a friend to the whole group:

And so, it carried on. For a further two weeks we continued to live outward lives, pretending everything was normal, while leading a bizarre secret life.

During that time, we learnt some of the secrets of the earth and heavens. He taught of the existence of man in the scheme of things. Of the plains of existence, Luke schooled us, "There are seven plains of existence. The Devil alone occupies the first plain and then upward to God, who is alone on the seventh plain. Mankind occupies the third. The spirits of the dead, who had lived and died on Earth are on the fourth plain, while the angels are closer to God on the fifth plain." Luke then illuminated, "Myself and the other apostles and of course Jesus, are closest to the Lord on the sixth plain. While the Devil's demons are closest to their master on the second plain."

On the Saturday, seven days after my dream visit, Trish's relaxed mind state allowed Luke to pay her a visit. Ecstatically, she woke me at four in the morning. "He came. I've seen him. The love and serenity exude from every pore. Oh Luke," she sighed dreamily, as she dwelt on the man whom we knew to be the apostle of Jesus Christ.

Sue and David also received their dream visits during those two weeks. The common theme reported by all was the peace and love they experienced during their encounter.

We'd been educated on the wonders of heaven, a place that was love and serenity, where time had no meaning and pain and worries no longer existed.

As part of our education, alongside heaven and Jesus, Luke also warned of the existence of evil, and Satan. He gave chilling warnings. "The Devil knows your whereabouts; he seeks ways to help you to fail in your task!" A sobering thought when we realised, we were expected to confront the most dangerous adversary of all.

We still had the promise of our new method of communication. On the Friday evening as the two weeks came to a close, we passed a relaxed hour seated around the table, asking questions of Luke. By now, even Sue seemed totally at ease in Luke's company, eager and willing to ask whatever came to mind. That evening, Luke tutored Sue after she asked, "Tell me about the love of Jesus and how his compassion drew everybody to him."

Luke explained, "As their divine creator, Jesus drew all around him; even the fish that were caught on the first day were drawn to their creator."

Interrupting, I asked the question which was at the forefront of my mind. "When will we know this new method of communication? You promised it would be soon. You have to tell us sometime!" The glass stopped for a short moment, then continued.

It spelt out, "Today is your last visit to the table! You are to enjoy your time off. Rest this weekend. You must all be here at five on Sunday evening. Do not use the glass. I will reveal my new form of communication." With that electrifying message, the glass came to an abrupt halt.

Once we'd decamped to the Wellington, a mood of relaxed euphoria prevailed. Obviously, one topic dominated our conversation. As the drinks flowed, gossiping excitedly, we tried to second guess this proposed route of contact.

"I think it's dreams or visions," guessed David, sipping his pint.

"No, he's already said it's not that. We might get a ghost like visitation," retorted Trish, anticipating the forthcoming encounter.

Our new interaction with the spirit world. What this new method of contact was, we had no idea. None of the suggestions even came close.

We'd previously planned the day. Trish and I met up with Sue and David for a Sunday lunchtime drink. With the unknown ahead, we were content to remain on shandy instead of our normal beer.

On that Sunday, Trish and Sue's parents, Lynda and Richard, had invited us for a Sunday roast after our lunchtime drink, an event which wasn't uncommon, as Lynda enjoyed cooking and entertaining.

Richard was an electrical engineer, who'd done very well for himself. Over a twenty-year period, through hard work and dedication, Richard had built up his own business. With the success this had brought, he found he could finally afford to move from the small, terraced house, where the girls had been brought up, to a large four-bedroomed detached house, situated in a quiet, leafy suburb, on the edge of town.

I liked both Richard and Lynda. They always made me feel welcome in their house and I admired Richard's commitment, both to his career and his family. They had done well from the days of the two up, two down terraced house. The newly built modern house they now lived in was large and spacious. The décor in the lounge attained to the tasteful Asian influence, which Lynda had set out to achieve. Chinese silk drapes and throws gave a pleasing aesthetic elegance, coupled with teak furniture, which Lynda had persuaded Richard to purchase, soon after they'd moved in. A few too many ornaments for my liking but I understood Lynda and Richard had attained the style and sophistication that I would like to achieve in my own home, one day.

After a splendid lunch of roast lamb, the four of us spent a pleasant afternoon playing Monopoly, relaxing in Richard and Lynda's company. Then it was time for us to thank our hosts and leave.

Once at the flat I made the coffees. Drinks in hand, we seated ourselves nervously in the lounge. There was no preparation required. Luke had been insistent, none was needed.

Luke had always been punctual so, as the second hand of the clock moved towards the hour of five, the conversation subsided. We held our collective breaths in expectant silence. We watched as the second hand on the clock continued its sweep. Nothing in the room changed. Collectively we exhaled trapped breaths.

Beside me, I felt Trish stiffen. At that moment Sue let out a small gasp of horror! "What the…" Her voice trailed off. Swivelling, I followed the direction of her gaze. Sue was staring at David, whose head was lolling sideways. David's eyes were wide and staring, but he wasn't seeing. Involuntarily, I sprang towards him, as his eyes slowly rolled up into his head. Without uttering a sound, David pitched forwards into my arms, unconscious.

CHAPTER TWO

Pandemonium ensued. Sue threw herself forward, yelling, "David." Instinctively she'd rushed to him, her maternal reflex reacting. My mind raced. Was this Luke, or had the tension somehow caused David to faint?

Sue, as a nursery teacher, had been taught first aid so she began to examine the lifeless form of David. I wondered if this situation might be beyond her level of training, reaching for my phone, I tried to take control. "I'll call for an ambulance. How can we explain this one?"

"Wait," Sue commanded. "He's probably just fainted with the suspense and anticipation, the stress of the moment." She gave David a rapid check-up, pronouncing, "All outward signs are normal." That is, all except the fact that David remained totally comatose. Sue spoke again. "I think we should wait; his pulse is regular and steady."

"More than can be said about the rest of us," Trish replied, laconically.

Sue continued checking David's vital signs. Except for breathing, he remained totally lifeless, even when Sue pinched him hard, trying to elicit a reaction. Tersely I let the phone drop. "OK, I'll wait your instruction."

Under Sue's instruction, I gently moved him, leaving him lying in the recovery position on the sofa.

Sue let the training kick in; she was efficient and calm, assuming the mantle of command. "We should monitor

David for a few moments, call an ambulance if there is no change within five minutes. It's only seconds since he fainted; his breathing and pulse are normal."

A voice said, "I'm sorry my friends. I didn't wish to cause you so much fear and anxiety." Instantaneously I span towards the voice, my hands involuntarily clenching into fists ready to ward of the threat. I'd turned away from David, towards Trish. At that moment the voice came from behind me. I didn't recognise this voice; it came from David, yet wasn't David. I'd never heard the voice before in my life.

David's eyes were now open wide. He raised himself into a seating position, staring straight at us.

Looking into the eyes, the windows to the soul, I realised it wasn't David within his body. Of that I was certain.

I still find this hard to explain, even now. We had the certain knowledge that the body of our friend didn't contain his soul, whatever a soul is, the essence of his being. But that's the truth, David's human form didn't contain his soul.

I wondered, is this Luke?

Fear gripped. I wanted to turn and run but we couldn't. It just wasn't fair on David. Time slowed to the point where those few seconds seemed like hours. The entity within David, returned our stare. A stand-off, lasting several seconds. In the void, I felt my heart pounding against my ribs. Behind me, magnified, I could hear Trish or Sue's rapid breathing.

Suddenly the occupier of David's human form spoke. Instinctively we edged one step backwards. "Do not be afraid. It is me, Luke." The same voice from several seconds earlier. In the context of the almost expected, the voice had a genteel and reassuring quality. I hesitated, wondering what do next, relieved but unwilling to take any chances.

"Prove it!" Trish demanded from behind, sounding very suspicious.

Luke replied, "*Hearken to me yea that follow after righteousness, yea that seek the Lord*" Isaiah chapter 51."

We relaxed slightly, but only slightly, daring to believe the possibility that we were indeed talking to Luke, the apostle of Jesus. But it still felt very surreal, even after so much preparation.

Again, Luke spoke. "I'm sorry for not warning you; you were unprepared for my arrival but if he'd known beforehand, David's spirit would have been ready and fighting to deny me access." He continued. "I can only remain for a short while. This is the first time I have entered David's body; it has undergone a huge amount of stress. For now it is dangerous to him, for me to inhabit for too long. Housing another spirit is stressful for his human form. It will be very tiring for David to begin with. He will feel like he has had a virus. Initially, David will require plenty of rest and recovery time; that is, until his frame becomes adapted to accommodating my spirit."

Sue spoke in a shaky voice, asking, "Where's David's soul now?" Typical of Sue, her first thought was for the well-being and safety of her boyfriend.

Luke responded quickly, "David's spirit is with us. When he awakes, he will remember nothing of his ordeal, but he will be exhausted. You must allow him time to recuperate."

Worried for my friend I asked, "Will it become easier for David if you continue with this method of communication."

Again, Luke assured us, "With the passage of time David's body will become accustomed. The risk to David is much greater during the early stages; after tonight, contact will become easier!"

Before we could continue our questioning, Luke announced, "I must go now. David needs time. We will have more time in the future; for now, let him sleep." With that David's body relaxed, his head falling back onto the sofa, eyes slowly closing.

For several seconds we remained motionless. Trish still held my arm. I hadn't noticed but her fingers were pressed so tightly that I would be bruised for several days.

Finally, Sue muttered, "Wow, what just happened?"

David lay peacefully on the sofa. Sue, then Trish, slowly approached the sleeping form. Once Sue reached him, somehow sensing she was there, David visibly began to relax, his breathing eased, as he seemed to settle into sleep.

Sue remained cross legged by the sofa, holding David's lifeless hand in her own.

Absently I glanced at the clock, ten past five. "Amazing, the whole incident took a mere ten minutes."

Every few minutes, Sue would check David, but he never moved, sleeping on peacefully while we watched over him, and waited, drinking enumerable cups of coffee.

David slept for a total of four hours before finally coming round. "Where am I. What happened?" he said, yawning and rubbing the sleep from his eyes. David was uncomprehending, still not fully awake.

Gently, we tried to explain what had happened, but a still confused David found it hard to follow. One moment he had been sitting with his friends, expectantly waiting for the apostle Luke to appear; the next thing David knew was waking up several hours later. Sipping a cup of hot tea, that I had thrust into his hands, David just sat there, shaking his head repeatedly, a quizzical look expressed on his face as he repeatedly mumbled, "What happened, what's happening?"

The next day was Monday. All of us had a working week ahead, so when Trish and Sue made moves to go home, he jumped up, asking me. "Can I use your spare room tonight?" A note of pleading in his voice.

I understood. I said "yes" nervously, inwardly worried about a repeat during the night, but I reasoned with myself. I hadn't come to any harm the first-time round.

We drove Sue and Trish home, David babbling continually. I guessed the constant chatter meant he didn't have to stop and think about what had just happened to him.

Monday morning arrived, leaving me still feeling drained, deprived of my night's rest by an active mind. I had to shout in his ear to rouse David. We both needed the stimuli of strong coffee before confronting the forthcoming day.

The evening eventually arrived and with it a gathering of the syndicate. Luke hadn't left any specific instructions, but by now we were expectant that something might happen. I was unsure if he would but looking drained and very apprehensive, David arrived bang on time.

Luke didn't hang around; we'd hardly had time to sink into the sofas, with coffees in hand, when things began to happen. David was obviously under very close observation. His eyes rolled into his head, then he slumped forwards. Seated closest, I reached out to stop him falling, but even before I made contact, David's body jerked backwards, the head turning towards me. "Thank you, my friend."

This time we knew what we were expecting. The voice was the same calming lilt of the previous evening. I willed myself to calm down and relax.

Luke spoke, addressing the group. "It was easier to displace the soul of David from his body today. The strain he is undergoing is considerably less than yesterday."

I studied the spirit in my friend's body closely. Over time we realised that, when Luke appeared, there was only a very minute physical change to David's demeanour. Apart from the voice, the noticeable changes were only detectable to those who knew David well; watching closely, his different mannerisms were clearly noticeable to us.

It is said by some that the soul can be viewed through the eyes; we knew this to be true. We would look deep into those eyes, seeking the inner person. When he looked back at us, we'd know, instinctively, another spirit resided. The spirit of David didn't dwell within David's body.

Sue asked, "Where is David now? What does, *with us* mean?"

Luke confirmed, "Your friend is with us, in the kingdom of heaven; he is with the apostles of Jesus."

"Wow," was our only reaction.

Luke spoke briefly. "There is little time, my friends. David must have the time to become accustomed to my intrusions."

I found my voice, asking the question, "What is the first task? You spoke about tasks and training!" I demanded, impatiently.

Luke looked at me, exasperation evident within his smile. "Martyn, you are very impatient; you must prepare for your service to us. It will be far more consuming than you can imagine. For now, you are mere pups, not yet weened."

Luke continued. "However, your first test is to travel to the temple without doors." With those words, the short visit was over. David's head lolled forward, and the eyes became unfocused. Sue reached out, catching our sleeping friend, laying him on the sofa to recover.

This time, David required a much shorter recovery period. Twenty minutes later, he began to move about, mumbling in his sleep. Worried, I questioned the movement, but Sue reassured me. "That's normal for David. He always tosses and turns in his sleep. It's like he's got ants in his pants."

When, finally, he did awake, there was a greater understanding of where he was and what had happened. David was adjusting to this unusual phenomenon quite quickly. Although his face fell when Trish explained, "You were in heaven. You were with Jesus and the disciples; it sounds wonderful." David had no recollection whatsoever of his celestial visit.

Being of the generation where constant and instant access is deemed a requirement of life, absentmindedly, I pulled my phone from my pocket, but my eyes and ears were still attentive to what Sue was saying,

"Is this dangerous for David's health?" she asked nobody in particular.

I glanced down at the screen, seeing the closed envelope denoting a waiting text message. Weird, I thought, I hadn't heard the loud buzz or felt the vibration which usually accompanied a text, but then we'd had our attention diverted by other, more important things. I flicked open my mailbox, only half listening to Sue.

GO TO THE TEMPLE WITHOUT DOORS.

My attention to the message was now complete. "Shit," I muttered, staring at the screen.

Sue's voice trailed off as she noticed my expression. Without speaking, I passed the phone over. It was a very strange thought, the possibility of Luke having a mobile phone in the spiritual world! I wondered where the message had come from. Checking the phone's log, there was no evidence of receiving a text. This was odd. My phone would record any call or text incoming or outgoing, even if a number was withheld. I can never remember receiving any message or call without it being logged. I tapped the button to reply to the text. The phone responded with, UNKNOWN NUMBER. "Hmm strange," I said. "Luke, it seems isn't on any of the recognised networks."

Trish opened her phone, hoping she would have a message from the spirit world. Instead, as she opened the phone's case, a small piece of white paper fluttered to the floor. Frowning with confusion, Trish bent to pick it up. I lost interest in my phone when I noticed Trish, transfixed by the small piece of paper.

She passed the paper over, saying, "It seems Luke wants to make sure that we get the message." The same message was written in bold capitals.

GO TO THE TEMPLE WITHOUT DOORS.

Underneath was a cross, then the one word. LOVE.

This had to be a message from the spiritual world. I wondered how great Luke's capability to interact with our world really was.

"It seems we have in our hands the first physical evidence that we are involved with the paranormal, even if we can't call the tabloids and tell them to hold the front page," Trish declared, grinning. "I think maybe we should keep them safe somewhere."

We settled down once more, discussing the task and what it could be.

"Where is the temple without doors? That's the main concern; this is our first test. We need to get it right." I declared, earnestly.

Trish made a suggestion. "The temple with no doors, could that be Stonehenge? According to the messages, we're supposed to travel there!"

"Good, that sounds about right, and we're less than one hundred miles away from Salisbury and Stonehenge. We might as well try, there's nothing to lose," Sue chipped in.

For the remainder of the week, we waited in vain, for the reappearance of Luke. It seemed that once the task was set, he'd disappeared until completion.

Finally, Friday evening arrived, and we prepared for the trip ahead.

It is always easier to plan an early rising, than the feat itself. At five on the Saturday morning the repeated ringing of my doorbell had me groaning aloud; Resignedly I reached for my dressing gown before I ambled to the front door, letting the other three in. They were all in various states of wakefulness, cursing me.

"You suggested five am. Why aren't you ready?" grumbled Sue, looking with disdain at my dressing gown.

"Get the kettle on. I'll get ready," I told them, ignoring their justifiable grievance.

While I hurriedly dressed, Trish, who was in an irritatingly happy mood for such an early hour, made tea and toast, a light breakfast before we set out.

The one compensation for lost sleep was the empty roads. This meant I was able to drive fast on the empty carriageways, within two hours we were there. Daylight had arrived by the time we pulled off the main A303, turning onto the minor road which leads down to Stonehenge. In the early morning light, we could see the monument, looking both mysterious and imperious in the pale daylight. I turned into the empty heritage site car park, parking within sight of the stones.

"What happens now?" we mused, remaining in our seats and looking at the ancient monument of Stonehenge, these days surrounded by fencing. The stones had stood there for over five thousand years, and nobody knew for sure, why they were there. Other than ourselves, not a single soul was around.

If we were expecting something to happen merely because we'd turned up, we were out of luck. Stonehenge stayed silently dominating the landscape, surrounded by the early morning mist.

Not even sure if this was the correct place, doubts began to creep in. "Maybe we're supposed to hang around until the heritage site opened for business." Sue suggested.

"I'm not going back home just because we've seen the stones. He must want us to do something." David pushed his car door open. We followed him out of the car, guessing that something hadn't yet happened, though what?

It was too early to pay the exorbitant fees to enter the visitor centre, so Trish suggested," Why don't we walk, circumnavigate the monument, get as close as the fencing will allow."

For lack of a better suggestion we quickly agreed,

With senses heightened by nerves, we set off. The morning mist, drifting across the grass at the base of the stones, added to the air of mystery. We crossed the grass towards the chain-link fence, bunching as we went. The eerie surroundings stifled any enthusiasm for chatter, until David lightened the mood and broke the moment with a cheery and well timed theatrical, "God, it's cold this morning. I forgot my long johns." With one sentence, the tension dissipated, returning us to sanity.

We followed the fence clockwise but nothing out of the ordinary happened. We simply trekked on until the full circle was completed, getting wet feet from the dew, in the process. After this we halted, wondering just what to do next.

Trish spoke, suggesting, "We've completed the visit. Let's go back to the car and find a café. David's right, it's

March. What on earth are we doing in a field at eight o'clock in the morning, freezing our nuts off."

"Two of us are. You're exempt from that particular consequence." I grinned. "But, I agree, it's freezing, time we're out of here."

Disappointed by failure, feeling cold, miserable and hugely let down that nothing had transpired from the early morning sortie, we trudged towards the car park.

David halted abruptly, returning my attention to the moment. I looked past him, following his gaze. He was staring towards the car. Something had happened to grab David's undivided attention. Inside the car, behind the screen on the dashboard, there was a white envelope. An envelope that hadn't been there when I'd locked up, half an hour earlier!

Excitement returned in a heartbeat. Cautiously, I opened the car door, reaching in slowly and grabbing the envelope before turning to my companions. "Got it," I announced triumphantly, holding it up like a trophy.

On the reverse of the envelope was a cross, depicted in gold. No addressee, just the cross.

We climbed in, shutting the doors and running the heater to escape the cold. I opened the envelope. Inside there was a single sheet of paper, folded once. Printed on the paper the message.

CONGRATULATIONS, YOU HAVE
COMPLETED TASK ONE.
TASK TWO
YOUR NEXT QUEST IS FURTHER AFIELD,
A NEXUS POINT AND A BURIAL PLACE
VISIT MICHEAL ON THE HILL.
AN ISLAND IN THE FIELDS.

There was instant jubilation and excitement. "We've done it! The first task completed; now for number two, hopefully just as easy," said David.

The car pulling into the car park made me look twice: a dark, maroon-coloured Jaguar saloon car, big and powerful. What made me look again were the tinted windows, which hid the occupants. The Jag crunched across the gravel, parking away from us on the opposite side of the car park. We watched, waiting, but nobody got out of the car.

"That's weird," I said, wondering why nobody had got out. I shrugged. "Oh well, nothing to do with us. Maybe they just want to look at the stones or are waiting for it to open. We're done here anyway, let's go!"

The suspense had made me hungry. "Remember that American diner we passed some miles down the road. Let's stop for breakfast." The thought was appealing, meeting with a chorus off 'yes's'.

"Lead on driver, I'm starving," Sue instructed.

We crunched across the gravel, turning onto the road half a mile on. I glanced at my rear-view mirror. Following at a distance was the Jag. Whoever it was hadn't stayed to visit Stonehenge. As David was seated in the front passenger seat, I surreptitiously motioned for him to look behind. He gave a barely noticeable nod, letting me know that he'd also seen the Jag, identifying its presence behind us as unusual.

By mutual understanding we remained silent, choosing not to frighten the girls without cause.

I turned left, joining the main West Country to London Road. Continually observing my rear-view mirror, I watched and waited, wondering what the other car would do. The Jaguar followed, resolutely remaining about two hundred yards behind us. Now, the early hour became a curse; the traffic on the A303 was not very heavy, easy to monitor the Jaguar tailing us and, conversely, easy for its driver to observe us.

Over the next few miles, I drove irrationally. I tried speeding up, then slowing down, but the saloon stuck steadfastly to our tail. The gap between us neither diminishing or increasing; a dogged and determined stalker; raising my heartbeat and causing a dry mouth.

Absently, I wondered if its occupants were hostile and, consequentially, whether or not it was safe to stop, but the decision was no longer mine. We had already decided. There was no option. We would stop for breakfast, hopefully at a place with a busy car park. I realised, if the Jag followed us in, it might allow us to get a look at the occupants.

I glanced once more at the rear-view mirror, jerking back for a proper view. There was no Jag. I motioned for David to check. "Nope," he confirmed.

The Jag had disappeared, probably turning off on a side road. We let out a collective sigh of relief; any real or imagined danger was over. "It seems we're conjuring up threats that aren't there. They, or it, have gone," David affirmed triumphantly, turning to reveal all to our girlfriends.

"Probably out for a morning drive and got lost, or only wanted to view the stones on their way somewhere," I conceded, our heightened imaginations had done the rest.

Sue was brilliant. On the Monday, she phoned me at work, tentatively suggesting, "Glastonbury!"

While I had been taking life very easy on the Sunday, claiming to be recovering from a bruising game of rugby, Trish, Sue and David had continued the research, coming up with this current suggestion.

"Brilliant," I yelped, realising the potential of her suggestion. "You're my hero."

I pulled the keyboard towards me, searching the net for the English heritage site. Opening the Glastonbury page, I began reading, excitement mounting. A short while in and I realised that Sue and David had had a productive Sunday.

Glastonbury Tor is a mystical place, associated with the legend of Joseph of Arimathea, the uncle of Jesus, who'd reportedly pilgrimaged there. It is reputed to be the oldest Christian shrine in the country. On the top of the hill stands a church, called St Michael. I read on, forgetting work, becoming engrossed in the Glastonbury legend. According to the website, it was possible that Joseph of Arimathea had once brought the boy Jesus on a pilgrimage. After the death of Jesus, there is speculation he returned, bringing the Holy Grail, the most sacred of all the Christian relics. Bombarded by all the conjecture and fable, I allowed my thoughts to wander off on a daydream. Was our task to find the Holy Grail? We would be forever enshrined in the history books, one up on Indiana Jones, I thought. Though it was highly unlikely that the Grail would have remained hidden for so long. And I doubted that four people who turned up and attacked the base of the Tor with shovels would be particularly appreciated.

Dismissing the daydreams, I returned to the reality of the present. According to the site, Glastonbury is as important to the Druids as the Christians. It is a nexus point for druid lay lines. Leaning backwards away from the screen, stretching my arms out, fists clenched, a barely perceptible, "yes," escaped my lips. This was it! Come the weekend, we were going to Glastonbury.

During the remainder of the week, Luke again remained elusive. We were hopeful. We waited, willing him to appear and tell us that we were right, but David remained as David.

Trish had warned me, "Cut the stupid wake-up time, just so you can play rugby, set your alarm for seven a.m." This week there was no rush. We had a lay in until 7 am.

Setting off with a holiday atmosphere in the car, we decided to enjoy our day out, taking the scenic route through the Wiltshire countryside. The sun was shining, and we were engaged on a mission from the apostle Luke, as David joked. "We're getting to see Britain's history by serving the Lord. I hope he's going to pay our entry fees, as well."

We made good time on the road. Willingly, I consented to the general demand, when Sue suggested, "We've done well, Martyn. Pull over at a café for breakfast."

After one unhealthy, but very tasty, full English, we stepped out through the door of the café into the early April sunshine.

Once it had disappeared, I hadn't given the Jaguar a thought since the previous Saturday – it'd left my mind. Suddenly, I was forced to confront my doubts once more. Parked outside the roadside restaurant chain was a gleaming dark maroon Jaguar motor car, darkened windows concealing the interior.

During the past twenty minutes, nobody had entered the restaurant. Ten minutes earlier, I'd looked out of the window into the car park; the car hadn't been there so where, and who, were the occupants?

This set my mind racing. We'd set off for a day out. Now, it seemed, we were facing a potential and unknown threat. The angle was all wrong. I couldn't look through the windscreen of the Jag without making a detour across the car park.

"What's wrong?" Trish asked, a rising note of anxiety in her tone. She'd sensed the change in atmosphere, feeling the unseen danger.

"We'll tell you once we are underway," I answered somewhat brusquely, glad that they still hadn't identified the Jaguar as a threat. "Get in the car!"

Starting the engine as they climbed in, I gunned my motor across the car park, settling down to drive normally once we were underway and out of sight.

As I told them about the Jag, I was monitoring the mirror closely. So far, the Jaguar hadn't appeared, we began to relax. Our reaction was rash. Far back, and travelling at great speed, was a dark car. As it gained ground on us, we recognised the familiar shape of the Jag moving up on us, until it was close enough to unnerve. Only then did the Jaguar throttle back, remaining too far away to get a good look at the occupants, staying a constant one hundred metres behind.

Straining to see, Trish observed, "There are four silhouettes in the car. I can't see their faces, or what sex they are, but there's definitely four of them."

"Four eh, makes it even numbers if nothing else," I commented, grimly, aware that I felt a sense of foreboding.

Deliberately I slowed, hoping to glimpse the driver and passengers through the transparent windscreen. In response, the Jaguar decreased its speed. We just couldn't see them clearly.

Even though my car was a reasonably powerful Ford Focus, a car which I was proud of, being three years old and well maintained, I knew I couldn't outperform the Jag. I told my passengers, "There's no way I can outgun the Jag. I'll feel a lot safer on the motorway. David, can you reprogramme the satnav, get a route via a motorway."

To reach the motorway would take us well away from our original route, the diversion adding considerable distance to the journey, but we relaxed a little knowing that we were heading for a well-monitored main arterial highway.

While I drove, the Jaguar remained behind me, keeping a steady distance. "It's making no move to overtake us," I said when I again tried to slow down. But when I attempted to place other cars between us, the Jag would always reappear, obviously driven by a confident and outstanding driver.

There was a time when we thought that we'd done it, that we were safe. Just before a series of long sweeping bends in the road, I managed to overtake a lorry. Then I'd taken the first available turning, before cutting back on ourselves. "That'll fox him." I grinned with conviction before rerouting for a different junction onto the motorway.

The road behind remained clear. Every few seconds for almost ten minutes, I was glaring at the mirror, but the mirror was clear. There was no sign of the Jag. Once more, we allowed ourselves the short-lived and premature indulgence of relief.

Sue suddenly yelled, "There's a dark car moving up fast." Our spirits plummeted!

"It almost feels as if they have a tracker device on my car but how did they know where to find us in the first place? More importantly, what does their appearance mean?" I asked of my co-conspirators, who had as few ideas as I did.

Continuing, the jovial holiday atmosphere of an hour earlier had disappeared entirely. Replaced by a real and palpable foreboding. Soundlessly I prayed under my breath, "Luke, appear and tell us what to do." But there was no sign of him.

Having a sudden thought, I speculated aloud. "I wonder if this is part of the test. Maybe Luke's putting us under pressure to see how we handle it."

"Could be," David responded, grasping any offered straw.

The mood lifted a tiny bit when we realised that they were maintaining a distance; we began to feel a little happier, realising there was no identifiable and actual threat, just a constantly present Jaguar motor car putting us on edge.

The Jaguar made no attempt to disguise its interest in us, but Sue complained, "Every time we try to see inside, the Jag slows down, ensuring that it is just out of effective eyesight range."

If you approach from the right direction, Glastonbury is very impressive. The green fields surrounding the Tor are flat, the steep Tor, which is a hill, stands out like an upturned ice-cream cone. On the top of the Tor, like a sentry looking down protectively over the countryside, is the tower of St Michael. I thought of the work involved, centuries earlier, building the church so high up.

"It's easy to understand how the legends of the isle of Avalon arose. With a little imagination, it would be easy to travel in time back to the court of King Arthur," Trish said, wistfully.

Even with the Jag in the background, we still had the task to complete.

"Assuming we've come to the correct destination, is there a task to complete, or do we just need to visit Michael on the hill," Trish wondered aloud.

Now we'd arrived, I began to worry about the intentions of the Jag's occupants. I didn't mention any concerns, but I guess they were having similar thoughts. "Make sure the car park, you park in is well populated with pedestrian traffic." Trish instructed.

Fortunately, Glastonbury is a very popular tourist attraction. I pulled into a busy car park close to the town centre. There were plenty of people milling about aimlessly, tourists seeking present day excitement from ancient myths.

The same thought passed through our collective minds. "Hold on, let's wait to see what they do. Stay in the car," said David. Warily we observed the Jaguar as it slowly coasted across the parking area, stopping away from us in the far corner.

On tenterhooks, we remained seated, watching and waiting. No one got out of the Jag; it remained there, sinister and foreboding!

I glanced at David. There had been no sign of Luke to enlighten us. I guessed we were going to have to act on our own initiative.

I have always been happier taking the fight forward. I reasoned that they had been openly following us so I would be direct, also. Steeling myself for the confrontation, I spoke. "I'm going over there to ask what on earth are they playing at."

When I revealed my intentions, David, Sue and Trish gasped. "No, you can't, it might be dangerous," Sue stammered, looking appalled.

However unhappy I felt with the idea, I'd concluded that it needed doing. This was the perfect opportunity. "There're lots of people around; what danger can there really be?" I comforted both my friends and myself.

"Here goes," I said, opening the car door and stepping out. I looked directly at the Jaguar. Inwardly I prayed that I appeared more relaxed than I felt. I wanted instant answers.

On jelly legs, I began walking forward, hoping my fear didn't show to Trish or, more importantly, my adversaries. Before I'd walked ten paces, the Jaguar's engine burst into life. Without speeding, the car moved purposely forward, driving away from me in a wide sweep across the tarmac, aiming towards the car park exit. I stopped, flabbergasted, scratching my head in wonderment, unsure if I felt relief or disappointment!

"Wow, not sure what I was expecting but it sure wasn't that" I told the other three, sliding back into my seat. We regained our composure, realising this time, they had indeed disappeared.

"The only thing to do is to put that Jaguar and its occupants out of mind. Let's try to enjoy our day. We do have a task to complete," Trish stated, grasping the nettle.

We joined the stream of tourists walking up the footpath to the top. After a steep climb, we reached the small church of St Michaels and were able to marvel at the wonderful views across the Somerset countryside.

In vain, we searched for any message that may have been left for us but, after examining every inch of the tower, we found nothing. Twenty fruitless minutes later we decided the chill April wind at the top of the Tor was too cold. We retreated, intent on finding a warm pub with good food.

Reaching the bottom of the Tor, anticipation grew. The previous week, we'd found the message in the car; would there be a repeat? Or would the Jaguar be in the car park, waiting? Neither! We all envisaged another envelope but this time we were disappointed. The car remained empty, lacking any communications from the heavens.

"Nothing more we can do here, may as well enjoy our day out for what it is. I've never been to Glastonbury before," Trish revealed, pulling my hand and steering me in the direction of the town centre. Swallowing disappointment, we moved on, seeking and finding an inviting pub for lunch. After which, putting Luke and Jaguar motor cars to one side, we were able to enjoy a spring day out, exploring the historic town and its abbey.

Later in the afternoon, returning to the car, I again felt a surge of anticipation approaching it but again it was empty. Doubts rose. David, mirroring my thoughts said, "I wonder if we've made a mistake and gone to totally the wrong place?"

"It is possible, but the clues seemed to fit so well, and then there's the threat from the occupants of the Jaguar. What's the significance of that?" Sue remarked.

"True, but we still haven't found anything," I said, resigned to returning home empty handed.

Driving through the outskirts of the town, I glanced towards my mirror. There it was. I remained silent, watching apprehensively. However, within a mile, Sue twisted in her seat, letting out a gasp. "They're back, bastards."

Driving towards the motorway, it stayed rooted on our tail, never attempting to come any closer, unquestionably a sinister presence behind us. I tried to understand their motives. They were seemingly just watching, biding their time. Could they be waiting for an opportunity?

When we reached the motorway, the three wide lanes of the road were almost empty. I watched fixedly as the Jaguar pulled out into the middle lane. Very gradually, at a seemingly calculated rate, it began to speed up.

"This is frightening. We don't know their intentions. If they want to run us off the road, the weight of that Jaguar is ample," I said, instantly regretting my words as Trish and Sue paled significantly.

The tense atmosphere grew as we watched the other car gradually narrow the gap. "There's nothing we can do other than to carry on and hope." Trish voiced her thoughts to a strained audience. I tried focusing my eyes on the road ahead, an impossible task. In the twilight the dark menacing shape remained there in my mirror, growing larger as the distance between us shrank.

Eventually the Jaguar began to pull level. Trish made another comment, trying to bring normality to the abnormal, but it was easy to detect the anxiety in her voice. David spoke. "Now we might see what these bastards look like."

Wanting to hide my own nerves I reached out to give Trish's hand a reassuring squeeze.

Then they were level. I glanced sideways, trying to see past the dark windows, wanting to identify these people who'd tormented us all day, but all we saw was four nondescript shapes; the twilight was too deep. They had timed it well.

The Jaguar eased off, staying level.

"Speed up. If they get in front, they'll have us trapped."

I recognised the fear in Sue's voice. I fought the impulse, controlling my own emotions. We were cornered in a completely alien situation. "Are we under attack?" David croaked, letting the fear show." My tongue was stuck to the roof of my dry mouth. I sensed my heartbeat as adrenaline pumped into my blood. Sue's words cracked my fragile resolve. Instinctively, I put my foot on the accelerator. The big car stayed level effortlessly, more menacing by the second.

"At the very least, the occupants of the Jaguar mean to intimidate." David managed to control any fear in his voice.

For over a mile, on the deserted motorway, the Jaguar stayed level, its occupants' indistinct shapes through the darkened windows. I'd given up trying to outrun them. Now we would have to wait and see what transpired.

The Jaguar began to edge closer; the gap between our cars began to narrow. "Shit, they're going to run us off the road," I shouted, gripping the wheel tighter.

I braked hoping to lose them but, anticipating my move, the Jag slowed almost at the same time, leaving us nowhere to go. Less than a foot separated us. I glanced over but it was too dark. I could only see shapes. I managed to look in my mirror, desperate to see headlights, but the road behind us was dark, devoid of other road users.

I felt sick. We were going to be forced off the road!

Suddenly, amazingly, they were gone. With a savage burst of acceleration, the dark car shot ahead, then continued motoring, dwindling into the twilight distance. We waited, but it didn't reappear. The release was massive. All our accumulated tension dissipated in just moments.

"Have they gone for good?" The desire and expectation was evident in my voice, even to me.

"I hope so," Trish laughed. "The appearance of that car has spoiled a good day out. I hope he gets a puncture on the way home."

"No chance, we might meet them again if they did," David joked.

With the burden removed we could begin to appreciate what stress we were under. The adrenaline rush forced me to pull into the next services, allowing me time to recuperate; a cup of tea was essential before completing the homeward journey.

On our eventual return we decamped to the flat. There was a general air of disappointment. If our goal wasn't Glastonbury, then there was a much needed discussion.

I aired my opinion. "I don't have a clue as to the way forward. If not Glastonbury, then where? I'll make the coffee," I said, standing up.

"I'm desperate to ask Luke about the Jaguar and what it all means?" Trish told the room as I departed towards the kitchen.

Before I'd filled the kettle, Trish shouted me sharply, "Martyn, quickly Martyn, Luke's back."

I ran through the door seeking out David, the stance of his body and that steady gleam of the eyes. Instinctively, I knew. David had left us. Luke was in residence!

Briefly, I thought of the strain to David after such a hard day, but I dismissed the thought. It felt good to be talking to Luke again. A thousand questions sprang to mind. "Luke you're back, what was the..." Before we had chance to finish the question, Luke motioned us to silence; he began talking.

"Today you were in some danger. In that car were your enemies!" I'd felt the strain of the day, part of that strain was not knowing. Now we had the stark reality; they were hostile.

Trish asked, "Luke, who are they? How do they know us?"

He replied, "They are a devil's syndicate. Your opposite numbers: they worship Satan. They are dedicated to stopping you at all costs."

This was new to us, the "at all costs," sent a shiver down my spine. From general warnings of danger and evil, suddenly it was very real, an opposition syndicate.

Luke reminded us, "During your early teaching period, you were advised that you have the option of walking away from the syndicate. This is a choice which always remains."

I retorted without a moment's thought, metaphorically puffing my chest out and putting a stake into the ground. "I'm darned if I'm going to walk away at the first provocation."

"Me too," Trish and Sue both echoed instantly.

Luke said, "We have been watching you all day. There was no real danger; they are unsure; they don't yet know how they will make their move."

Darkly, I considered the only way the other syndicate could really stop us would be to kill us, a conclusion I would keep to myself for as long as possible.

To our great relief, Luke changed the subject bringing good news. "Glastonbury Tor was the correct destination; you will receive your next task, soon." With that, his eyes glazed over, his posture changed, as David re-joined us.

The ever-practical Trish moved towards the kitchen, to finish the abandoned coffee. Just then, Trish called out again, "Martyn." An urgency in her voice made me spring from the chair, moving with alacrity. Dashing through the door, the first thing that caught my eyes, resting against one of the coffee cups, was a white envelope. Trish stood there motionless, staring at it. An envelope which hadn't been there when I'd left the kitchen. Sue quickly joined us. "What's all the commotion about?"

When I walked in and saw the envelope, I knew exactly what it was. I felt a great surge of excitement.

Trish picked it up, passing it to me. Turning the envelope over, I saw on the front a large silver cross. In my hand was another blessing from the apostle Luke; recent dangers were instantly forgotten.

TASK THREE
HARDER AND HARDER WILL
YOUR TASKS BECOME
THIS IS BY WATER, BUT THE FLEET ISN'T THERE,
WHEN THE BRENT LEAVES
YOU WILL RECEIVE A GIFT FROM THE HEAVENS.

CHAPTER THREE

By Monday morning, we'd been trying to decipher the clue for almost two days. This time the clue gave us little which we could take to the internet. The fleet, we were sure, referenced the navy, but what aspect of it? As I sat at my drawing board, staring into space, a small light flickered within, a seed of an idea which needed to germinate to see if it would bear fruit. I opened the internet to search.

Meeting up with David at lunchtime, I was eager to expound the idea with another syndicate member. "The first thought that comes to mind is a place on the Hampshire coast called Buckler's Hard. It's not far away. I remember going there on a school outing with you and Colin. We were all too immature to absorb the history, but I still remember it as a fun day out," I informed him, seeing the flash of recollection in David's eyes.

The internet had surrendered further supporting information. Buckler's Hard had been a ship building yard at the time of Nelson's navy. "This, I reckon, is why the fleet is no longer there." I claimed triumphantly. "As well as the name Buckler's Hard, it fits brilliantly with the line of the clue, *HARDER AND HARDER*. We might be getting somewhere," I concluded, certain of my own genius. "Trish is on her own in the office. This afternoon, I'll get her to search further" I told David, as we parted.

Trish phoned back during the afternoon, eager to share the results of her search. "Buckler's Hard it seems is a good bet, but I couldn't fit the reference to *Brent*, specifically, *THE BRENT*. I have tried researching the records of Nelson's navy, in particular searching for a ship called *The Brent* built at Buckler's Hard but I couldn't find anything whatsoever that even looked remotely promising," she acknowledged, the disappointment evident in her voice.

"Okay, well done and don't worry. We'll have a meeting of the syndicate this evening to discuss further; maybe we need to go there to find Brent," I said, trying to put some optimism in my voice.

Driving home through the drizzle, I decided to go for a run as soon as I reached home. Running was a great pleasure, the stresses and tension of living could be washed away by a hard and aggressive run, especially when it was raining.

I picked up post in the foyer, three letters, carrying them up to the flat, unread. Opening the door, my mind was already on a hard five miles. Moving towards my running kit, I wasn't expecting anything of real interest. So, I paid scant attention opening the first letter; that is until I glanced down at the paper in my hand. Instantly it had my full attention. Any thoughts of a run completely disappeared.

BASTARDS!

WE KNOW WHO YOU ARE.

STOP NOW,

OR FACE THE CONSIQUENCES.

"Bastards," I muttered, shocked. The chilling message was crudely written on a single sheet of paper in what I hoped was red ink. We now had contact from the enemy, the mysterious occupants of the Jaguar car, an enemy who knew where we were going, and now where I lived. The Devil's syndicate had stepped forward and nailed their colours to the mast. Our exhilarating adventure was quickly becoming sinister.

My instinctive reaction was to burn the evil note there and then, but I decided that it was best to show David and the girls. At the very least, they would be aware of the need for caution from now on.

I studied David, Trish and Sue while they read and absorbed the letter. A hint of fear, then concern passed across their faces, as they understood what they were reading. With pride, I also noticed a hardening of Trish's mouth; she pouted her lips, and I watched her brow furrow while she read. This I knew from previous experience meant she was annoyed. I'd often induced the very same disapproving glare. Trish was angry at the people who'd chosen to oppose us. "Dunno why they bothered. Just makes me all the more determined to carry on and beat them," she said casually giving the letter to Sue.

Pleased with the reaction the letter was getting, I voiced my opinion. "I have always hated threatening behaviour, and this is no exception."

"We are vulnerable though. We can't respond to this. Whoever these people are, they are faceless and unknown to us," David said, a note of caution in his voice.

"They appear to know all about us, though, and why we were here. They probably know more about the reason for our calling than we do," Trish responded.

"And it is you, David, it flows through. If you choose to walk away, then we have no option; we will respect your decision," I told him, hoping my voice didn't betray my real feelings.

"No, no, I'm going nowhere, just playing devil's advocate, so to speak – literally in this case." He smiled at his own pun.

Sue interjected. "The only realistic response that we can give is to ignore the letter and burn it; bullies need to be faced." We all agreed wholeheartedly, so I put a match to the letter, watching as the paper flared.

After the somewhat ritualistic burning of the letter, we again turned to the unsolved clue.

"If it isn't Buckler's Hard, in Hampshire, then the reality is we're stumped." Trish detailed the results of her investigations, which had proved reasonably fruitful. She told us, "Buckler's Hard was a place where part of Britain's wooden navy was built, but I found no reference to *the Brent*.

"Everything else fits – the word *harder* in the clue seemed very significant, compared to the name of Buckler's Hard. I feel sure it must be correct," I explained, desperate for my theory to be proved right.

This time we were forced to plan our travels for two weeks hence. Annoyingly the Christian calendar intervened. The forthcoming weekend was Easter. Despite the four-day holiday, Trish and Sue had previously made plans with Richard and Lynda. They were going to visit their grandparents up north, for a rare but eagerly anticipated social visit.

On the Thursday, I said goodbye to Trish. "Go with joy in your heart; we'll do Buckler's Hard next weekend," I told her, aware that my words and tone did not match.

She replied, "Sorry, nothing we can do about it." Then more firmly. "Live with it grumpy!" Smiling, she turned away from me and walked towards the door.

"Buckler's Hard is a secluded hamlet of eighteenth-century cottages on the Beaulieu estate. During the eighteenth century, the 2nd Duke of Montagu tried to build a major port there to rival Southampton and Limington. To these ends, he cleared a vast acreage of the new forest, letting the land for nominal rents. To begin with, all this planning was for nothing, until the war with France brought the need for a much larger fleet and more oak-built ships for Nelson's navy. Buckler's Hard, with its sheltered position, access to the New Forest's oak trees, gravel banks for slipways (which is the hard), was in the ideal position to benefit, and several ships of Nelson's Trafalgar fleet had been built here."

I knew this because I was listening to Trish recite from the guidebook, the warm April sunshine warming our bones. We were standing at the centre of the wide grassed street of Buckler's Hard tourist centre.

Once again, I'd given up rugby to carry out field research into the quest. We'd set out early and, once the sun had burnt off the morning mist, the day was shaping up to be one of those warm sunny springtime days which epitomises the joys of Britain in springtime. Blossom on trees, a cloudless sky, with the enticing promise of summer to come.

We'd undertaken the seventy-mile journey rather nervously, lots of sly looks through the rear window. However, thankfully, the journey remained uneventful; no ominous Jaguar appeared to dampen the mood.

Now, in the visitor centre, listening to Trish enumerate from the guidebook, thoughts of danger had receded.

The afternoon found us wandering around the heritage centre, eagerly searching for a name, or anything connected with *the Brent*. We found nothing, no sign, no Brent and no gifts from heaven. We'd walked up and down the single village street endlessly, anxiously searching. "Look carefully at each house. There must be a clue to the identity of *the Brent*," I'd instructed, but to no avail.

Eventually, by early evening, after spending what would ordinarily have been a pleasant day out, but was a day ruined by failure, we accepted defeat.

David broached the obvious. "We still have no clue as to the meaning of *when the Brent leaves*. Let's go home and regroup." As one we agreed. A dejected group, retreating.

Strolling towards the car park, hand in hand with Trish, I noticed something in my peripheral vision. Trish gripped my arm. She'd also clocked the maroon Jaguar parked away from us, on the other side of the car park! Simultaneously we stopped dead in our tracks causing David and Sue to bump into us. Promptly, I felt the need to be elsewhere.

"Let's go." Hurrying forward, I hastily unlocked the car, chivvying my passengers. "Time to scarper." All the while, our eyes were darting towards the pathway we'd just walked along.

In the comparative safety of the car, we relaxed. "Calm down, we're safe. There are plenty of other people still around and no sign of the owners of the Jag. We're in no danger just yet," David said.

I turned the key, starting the engine, turning to stare at the foreboding Jaguar.

There was still no sign of its absent occupants. This was the attractions car park, which could only mean they were still inside the heritage centre.

It was slightly unnerving to know that during the day, without our knowledge, these people may have been spying on us. How easy would it have been to attack one of our group, slide a knife into an unsuspecting back; all the while we were unprepared. I wondered; in reality, just how far would these people go, to back up their threats? The thought made me shudder.

Now, with plenty of bystanders still about, I reached forward and turned the key, silencing the engine. Maybe the day's failure had affected me, but I suddenly realised that I'd had enough of retreat and evading. "It's time to stop running, time for me to wait and watch, time to take the offensive. I want to know who these people are, these people who think they can threaten us at will. They seem to know where we live and where we are going to be. I want to observe them, to gauge my enemy and put a face to them. I want to be able to recognise them when they come," I told a stunned audience.

"You're off your rocker!"

"It's stupid."

Trish and Sue both exploded, different words but the same sentiment.

"It's utter foolishness to stay where there's risk and God knows what danger," Trish continued articulating her objections.

I have always been stubborn and headstrong. As the argument developed, I began to get annoyed. "Why, are we going to continue to take it, being threatened and not even know who our enemies are? All I'm going to do is hide and have a look at these guys; where's the harm in that?" I barked back in anger, not understanding why they thought it a bad idea.

"This isn't a game. These people want to harm us, to do us damage," Trish snapped, her own annoyance obvious.

"So, we sit back and take it, always wondering, never knowing when a knife is going to be inserted in one of our backs," I retorted, my voice dripping with sarcasm.

Trish spoke, managing to convey without the need for words that she thought she was talking to a fool. "No, but our car is here; they know we are here. How can you observe without being seen?"

"That's easy. I'm not asking to put any of you in danger; you go, I'm staying here. I'll hide in those bushes," I returned, pointing to some undergrowth and woods twenty yards from the Jag, while managing to express my exasperated tone to my three friends.

The more they tried to dissuade me, the more determined I was to stay and spy. I saw this as our opportunity to fight back.

"They seem to know all about us, but we know nothing about them." That was the core of my argument. "You saw last week; they shot off as soon as I got out of the car. I can't see how it's dangerous," I announced, feeling pleased with my logic.

"That was in broad daylight. People are leaving; this place will soon be empty," Trish replied.

My stubbornness grew. I hate to lose at anything. Trish was as inflexible as I was. Eventually, in a fit of pique I forced the car keys on David. "Take these two home. I'm not coming! I want to do this, and I'll be safer on my own! Go." After this tantrum, I demonstrated my resolve by climbing out of the car and walking away, not looking back.

In the cool of the evening, I slowed, listening to the sounds behind me as David resignedly climbed out of the passenger side. He looked warily towards the portentous Jaguar.

"Don't be stupid. Get in the car," he begged, following after my retreating back. But I am as stubborn as the best of them, even with the doubts which had now begun to niggle and creep in. Once I'd so forcefully declared my intentions, I was determined to continue, whatever the cost.

I stopped, turning back towards David. "Go," I said, moderating my earlier angry tone. "I will be safe. I am going to stay hidden in the bushes. I'm only going to monitor the Jag's owners when they return to their car. As soon as they've gone, once it's safe, I'll take a taxi to the train station and meet you at home." I argued enthusiastically, "You and the girls must drive off now. I'm far safer with only myself to worry about. I'm going to hide and simply watch. Get me a pint in at the Welly. I'll meet you there."

David continued to voice doubts. He had known me for long enough. He knew that I was being obstinate, that I could dig my heels in, so reluctantly he agreed. "OK, you win," he told me, glancing over his shoulder at the empty pathway. "Stay, but I think your mad."

Trish, I knew, would be as stubborn as myself, angry from the argument; she wouldn't attempt to prevent David driving away.

The Ford travelled slowly across the gravel car park, taking with it my bravado, which instantly began to evaporate. Inwardly I cursed myself for being so stubborn and foolish. Twilight was approaching, and with it the shadows grew longer and more ominous.

I sank back into the surrounding bushes, easing myself into a comfortable position, praying that I was invisible to any onlookers. Within minutes I started to feel the cold seeping through my lightweight jacket. I wished I'd brought my big winter coat.

Seeking the solace, I tapped my pocket, wanting the reassurance of my mobile phone with its connection to Trish and to safety. To my horror, the pocket was empty. With a cold nauseating realisation, I remembered throwing the phone into the side pocket of the driver's door before turning the key. Intractability and wilfulness had caused me to charge forward with my hare-brained scheme, no time to stop and plan. Me at my obstinate best, I thought.

Time passed. I began to feel very isolated; there was nobody around. Now, only the Jaguar remained in the car park.

Four people were making their way down the path towards the car park. I realised that the centre had closed well over an hour earlier. I'd been hidden and motionless in the bushes long enough to begin cramping.

As they walked towards me, I felt the sense of isolation, even more acutely, I felt a shiver go through me. Easing forwards, very carefully and slowly, I moved the leaves apart, hoping the poor light would hide any movement. Cautiously, I began to study the four walking towards me. Before they'd even reached the car park, I knew that these were our opposite numbers, our sworn enemies. In the lead were two men. I estimated they were in their early thirties, a little older than us. The man leading the way was a tall slim man with short dark hair and narrow mean-looking eyes, an aquiline nose. Handsome, if sharp angular features are what attracts. I noticed he was well dressed, a charcoal suit under a long dark raincoat. The one thing which stood out about this man was an earring, a large gold ring, which seemed out of place, making me think of gypsies. I studied his gaunt features carefully, ensuring that, should we meet again in different circumstances, I would recognise him again.

His friend was shorter and stockier, wearing a leather coat that tried, and failed, to hide a bulging stomach. In the gloomy twilight I couldn't make out the colour of his eyes, but a deep scar on his forehead, beneath the untidy blond hair, made the prospect of recognising him easier.

A pace behind these two, the women followed. The first was medium build, mid-five foot in height, short mousy hair; she was sporting made-up features. I studied her, trying to etch her features into my memory, all the time knowing that were I to meet her again in an unrelated situation, I wouldn't recognise her.

Not so, her companion. The second woman was elegance personified. From across the car park, I could feel the aura of haughtiness which surrounded her. tall, with long legs, she was dressed in a fox fur over a black dress. I recognised from her bearing that this elegant beauty had class, a class that didn't require the heavy make-up of her companion. She exuded sophistication, a sensual aura, which couldn't be defined by looks alone. Shiny dark hair, cascaded over the shoulders. The brilliant white smile aimed at her companions was noticeable even at that distance. However, there was something aloof and cold about this woman. Even as she smiled, I sensed this woman was cool and calculating – danger. Cruella de Vil, you live and breathe, I thought to myself.

I watched as they climbed into the Jaguar; the well-dressed gypsy holding the door open for Cruella. I released a silent breath, beginning to relax, thinking, all I need do is wait for them to leave, then I'll find a phone and call a taxi.

The Jaguar revved its engine. Turning its lights on, it began to move forwards. Something was wrong! The Jag didn't turn towards the entrance as it was supposed to do. Instead, with the engine screaming and the wheels throwing up a shower of gravel behind it, the car hurtled towards me. Screaming to a halt only feet from my hideout.

Blinded by the glare of the headlights, stunned by this new and unexpected turn of events, I fell backwards.

The car doors sprang open. Loud and angry voices pierced my reeling senses.

"There he is. He's in the bushes." The hostile and unforeseen threat galvanised me into immediate action. Twisting, I launched myself upwards and began to run, charging blindly through the bushes.

"He's in the lights!" A sharp, excited female shouted as I stormed forwards. Perversely, the words had a calming effect on me, dispersing panic from my scrambled brain, forcing me to focus on the need for rational action. I grasped the necessity of being out of the headlights. I veered to my left, flight from this unexpected threat my sole goal. Hurtling through the foliage, I stumbled on the uneven ground several times, nearly tumbling to the earth. In the gloom I took a hard knock on the arm, a tree I didn't see until too late. Yelling as the tree swiped me, twisting my body in space, I stumbled and staggered, willing myself to stay upright. I regained my footing.

I doubt I ran for thirty seconds but, to my panicked mind, it felt like hours.

Suddenly my mind registered, the only noise I could hear was myself. I slowed a little, listening hard for any noise of pursuit; there was nothing, no chasers.

Gradually easing to a stop, I crouched down, gratefully to hide in the foliage, recovering with my forehead resting on my knees. Desperately I fought to quieten my rasping breath, listening out for any unusual or unexpected sounds around me. With my breathing easing, I considered what to do next.

I'd come about five-hundred metres. I could just see the lights from the car park, which appeared totally devoid of activity. While I plotted, the lights were extinguished. They had shut for the night.

Now I'd stopped, the sweat from my exertions began to cool quickly. I quickly felt distinctly cold. Making a plan, I decided to cautiously head towards civilisation. From there I could get a taxi to Southampton where

I could call my friends or get on a train that would take me home.

Parallel to where I crouched ran the access road which carried visitors to Buckler's Hard. I knew that it would be silly to walk on the road. The enemy could well be waiting, but I could locate it, follow it at a distance, keeping parallel to the road, but hidden from sight. At least, then, I would know where I was. Apprehensively and slowly, I stood up, looking all around; gingerly, I began moving, aiming at where I thought the road was. I was thankful that, in a crisis, I usually react fittingly. I knew I needed all my wits about me.

The ground was uneven and by now so dark that in the shadows I could only make out shapes. Even with all my senses tuned, I still blundered onto the road. Mentally I'd miscalculated its location, judging the road to be at least another hundred feet further on. I'd planned to crawl the last few feet military style but suddenly the bushes fell away and I was standing on tarmac.

In the distance, coming from the direction of the visitor centre, headlights appeared, lighting up the sky in front, as well as the road only feet from me. I only just had time to fling myself flat on the verge, head buried in my arms. The car rushed past, a few feet from my head, not slowing, going far too fast for the narrow road. After it passed, I rolled over, trying to determine if it was the Jaguar, but the red taillights were already dwindling into the distance.

At least I knew it was safe to walk on the road. If there had been an ambush, then the car which had just passed would've highlighted it. As long as I vacated every time a set of headlights appeared, then I was safe. Twice in the next half hour I had to take evasive action as cars sped past, but neither car was a Jaguar. Trudging through the dark, I ruefully thought that the devil's syndicate, as well as David, Trish and Sue were all warm and comfortable, while I was getting progressively colder.

With enormous relief I recognised the welcoming lights and exterior of a pub beside the road ahead. I trooped into the bar of the Montagu Arms, no other thoughts but warmth and fodder.

On my appearance at the door, all conversation halted; every patron stopped to stare. For a single second, I wondered if I'd fallen into a trap, but looking around I didn't recognise any of the devil's syndicate. Following the direction of their frowns, I looked down; suddenly understanding dawned. I'd run through marshy land, woods and bushes, plus, on occasion, I'd had the need to throw myself onto the ground or cower in ditches. My arm was sore and I noticed dried blood on the back of my hand. I looked like a tramp, an exceedingly dirty tramp.

As soon as they decided I was non-threatening, the customers turned their attention to what had previously occupied them, though some still examined me curiously as I trudged tiredly to the bar.

The landlord, at least, deserved some form of explanation for my condition. I proclaimed the first explanation that came to mind, hoping my words would carry. "Sorry about the mess I'm in." I blamed Trish. "I had an argument with my girlfriend; she drove off without me. I got lost, tried to find a short cut across the fields; it's muddy out there, especially in the dark. I kept falling over."

This contrived excuse had the desired effect. "As long as you can pay for you drink, I'll serve you," the disinterested barman responded, turning towards a rack of glasses. Gratefully I accepted the deep mahogany pint of bitter, savouring its arrival with anticipation. Taking my first deep draught of the nutty liquid, I asked him, "Have you a phone and the number of a local taxi?"

Following a speedy and superficial clean up in the gents, I swallowed my pride, calling Trish's home number. I was hoping that she or one of the others would answer and come and collect me. Unless somebody answered, I would have to get the train home.

Fortunately, Sue was there, managing to sound both panicky and relieved at the same time. "Trish isn't here," she informed me. "She's gone with David to look for you."

Sue explained that they'd driven nearly seventy miles before David discovered my mobile in the car door.

I asked, "What time did they leave to find me?"

"We were nearly home, they dropped me off here, then turned around to go find you. When she cooled down, Trish became worried. She was upset that you'd parted on an argument, particularly with the Jag in the vicinity. Trish was scared for your safety. When we found your mobile phone, Trish begged David to turn around and begin a rescue mission. I stayed here in case you phoned our home number."

Sue's revelation had the effect of making me feel like a total shit. Here was Trish rushing back to find me, while I was blaming her for my own stupidity to a room full of strangers.

Thankfully, both Trish and David had their phones with them. I advised Sue of my whereabouts, then wrote Trish's mobile number on a scrap of paper.

"Trish, it's me. Come and pick me up. I know I've been a total idiot. You won't believe what happened, but I'm safe, the mission was successful," I said, feeling uncontrollably pleased to hear her voice.

"Martyn, we're heading back; where are you?" The relief portrayed in Trish's voice was music to my ears. Once I'd relayed my location, she promised, "We're on our way. We'll be there in half an hour." There was nothing else to do. I ordered another pint of best bitter, and a cheese sandwich, before settling down to wait.

An hour later, safely in the car and heading homeward, I was feeling like a hero returning from the front. Sadly, I recognised my choice of metaphor as appropriate, we were in a war, good versus evil, and the stakes were high.

CHAPTER FOUR

A new week, a new beginning. Time for another evaluation of the clue. After work on the Monday, I collected the clue from the strongbox that we'd purchased earlier in our training. I had dreaded to think what a casual burglar would have made of these articles, so we played safe and procured the strongbox, which was then hidden under a floorboard.

> HARDER AND HARDER WILL
> YOUR TASKS BECOME
> THIS IS BY THE WATER, BUT THE FLEET
> ISN'T THERE
> WHEN THE BRENT LEAVES
> YOU WILL RECEIVE A GIFT FROM THE HEAVENS.

What did it mean? Maybe the first line had nothing to do with the clues. Maybe it was only telling us that this was a difficult task. *By the water, but the fleet isn't there* – with *fleet* and *water*, this had to be a coastal town. The fleet couldn't be anywhere else. Already we'd spent the previous weeks poring over maps of Britain's navy towns and coastline, all to no avail. We'd even searched maps of every naval town looking for a district called Brent. There wasn't one. The internet is great as a research tool but, when you don't know what to look for, it is a tool of limited use.

Sue picked the clue up from the tabletop, looking at it again, a quizzical expression on her face. "This doesn't say anything about the sea," she declared to the room in general. "It also says the fleet isn't there, not that it has been in the past."

"Why mention the fleet if this hasn't got anything to do with the navy?" Trish asked, unsure at what Sue was trying to say.

Sue continued developing her hypothesis. "Look at the word before fleet, BUT this," she emphasised, "puts that line from the clue in a different light, *but the fleet isn't there*. This indicates a place where we would expect a fleet but there isn't any."

Trish frowned; a brief expression of appreciation manifested. "I think I get it."

David and I looked at each other, totally bemused by the conversation. Sue continued. "If there was a place called Fleet, which wasn't a significant seaport, then you would need to qualify the statement with the word BUT." Slowly recognition dawned.

"It's the best we've got so far; at least we're moving forwards again, some kind of light at the end of the tunnel. I say we run with it!" David turned to me. "Fire up the net, let's have a look; time for some research."

There seemed several good possibilities: Fleetwood in Lancashire, a coastal town. "Maybe in their fishing fleet, a boat called *Brent* is the answer. Or in Dorset, the Fleet, an inland lake separated from the sea by Chesil beach. That's where they tested the bouncing bomb," I said, looking up. "These fit." I theorised. "Also, Chesil beach is stony. It could have the same meaning as the Hard, in Buckler's Hard."

Trish, who had been reading over my shoulder said, "The town of Fleet in Hampshire also has good possibilities."

"Too far from the sea. I prefer Dorset," I countered.

Trish, who was still looking over my shoulder, pointed to the map – two small lakes called Fleet ponds, a nature reserve.

David agreed with Trish. "All three are possibilities. For the want of something better, we could visit them all, starting with the closest, and hope that *the Brent* will become evident on the day."

I had no better suggestions. We were on our way again. To the fleets we were going.

The small Hampshire town of Fleet lay about an hour's drive from us. We held very little hope of this Fleet being our destination, so we figured a very early Saturday start would allow us to return home well before noon, "giving us the rest of the weekend as free time," David reasoned.

Trish had been sensible enough to buy the ordinance survey map covering the ponds, woodlands and associated grasslands. This and Google allowed us to spend the evenings familiarising ourselves with the area and terrain, though I was a little disturbed after noting the amount of woodland in the area, as well as the distance from local roads. A perfect place for an ambush, I decided, but what choice did we have. I kept my thoughts to myself.

Five o'clock, on a bright and invigorating April morning, once more, overcoming a reluctance to rise so early, we were ready to travel. The faintest hint of sunrise in the east, the day promised to be clear and sunny.

The early rise had again given us the advantage of empty roads, as well as almost a whole weekend free, on our return.

Inside the car we were contemplative, the early rising and expectations of failure had absorbed any enthusiasm. The banal and cheery banter of the morning DJ was an unwelcome distraction to our pensive thoughts. "Shut up," I grumbled, stabbing the radio with my finger, searching for a less jovial travelling companion.

We drove through the town of Fleet just before six, witnessing the occasional early commuter on their way to work, huddled against the unseasonal morning frost. The car crunched along the long cinder track, leading to a deserted car park.

Climbing out of the car, adjusting clothing, we stretched, preparing to search for something which we mightn't recognise, even if we found it.

A man passed, walking an inquisitive and excited black Labrador. He nodded "good morning" towards our uneasy and guarded group. The two of them disappeared into the woods, leaving us alone in the clearing.

It was cold for April, still below freezing in the early morning sunlight.

"The ponds are about a mile from this car park." Trish had the map open. We knew where we were going. The only problem being we didn't know what we were looking for, or where we could find it. The absence of the opposition probably meant we were in the wrong location, again. There was nothing for it; go there, get it done, then go home.

Once kitted in warm clothing and good footwear, we were ready. "We'll walk to the lake, then follow the circular path right round," I suggested. "If nothing occurs then it's a wasted morning, nothing more." In agreement, we all set off down the path towards the lake, me leading, David bringing up the rear, the two girls in an unplanned, protective sandwich.

It may have made logistical sense to set off early in the morning but, in reality, the sun was just over the horizon.

"It's light, but it's still dark enough for the shadows in the trees to play some silly tricks on my already tense imagination," whispered Trish in a theatrical manner, guaranteed to ramp the tension another notch.

"Should we meet the devil's syndicate, then we have cleverly picked a time of the day to suit their needs, few passers-by and well away from civilisation. I wish we'd considered every single aspect of the trip," I muttered, under my breath.

With only a few false alarms caused by four overactive imaginations, we reached the lake without significant mishap. Once the sun had a chance to warm it up, the day would turn out to be a good one; the clear sky, which brought the frost, also brought the sunshine. A morning mist lay eerily over the surface of the water, making it look almost magical, though slightly Arthurian.

However magical the lake looked, there was still no message or sign from Luke. "I guess we've come to the wrong place; we're wasting our time," Sue articulated to an agreeing audience.

"Maybe we should walk around the lake, then go home," I said, wondering if I would be home in time for a decent breakfast.

The strengthening sunlight enabled us to relax. I now regarded this as simply a walk with friends.

"We'll plan the trip to the Fleet in Dorset during the week." Trish had obviously given up on this one.

The girls took the lead, following the path close to the water's edge, half-heartedly scanning around for clues, though we had no idea what Luke meant by *when the Brent leaves*. What was the Brent? One thing was clear, we were again in the wrong destination – *the Brent,* would have to wait until another day.

The ground became marshy. A small stream feeding the lake made the surrounding ground very soft. We were over halfway round the lake, well away from civilisation; apart from the man walking his dog, we had seen nobody since arriving.

Trish and Sue turned a bend in the path, me and David following. Suddenly, there was an eruption of noise. A flock of smallish dark birds took off from the water's surface, alarmed at our unexpected appearance. I thought they were geese, though smaller than I would expect. Flapping their wings, they gracefully glided across the surface of the pond, disappearing over the treetops on the far side.

My eyes caught a small movement to the side of my head. Mentally attuned, I span, instantly preparing to meet whatever challenge we were about to confront. Trish and Sue, closer to the movement, gasped in unison. I froze, ready, fists clenched, body taut.

Sue exclaimed, bending to pick up a silver envelope from the ground. "Look, where did that come from? It just appeared."

We had no idea as we'd been watching the birds fly away. According to Sue, who'd been closest, "The envelope seemed to appear in mid-air, before my eyes.

I was watching the birds but I'm sure it did." She trailed off, suddenly becoming self-conscious. We'd all caught the movement, in peripheral vision but, concentrating on the birds, we'd been looking away.

"Did it really appear in mid-air?" Trish asked, sceptically.

Sue repeated, "I can't be sure, but I think so, wouldn't be the first time." She pouted.

I glanced at the envelope, now in Sue's hand: a silver envelope with a gold cross of Christ on. It dawned on me with an elated lift of the soul. "Yes, we're finally in the right place. We've done it."

David intervened hurriedly, "And every time we are in the right place, the Jag turns up; let's open it elsewhere." Our initial joy was rapidly quelled by David's revelation. Time for a redeployment, back to humanity.

"Good thinking, let's go," the unanimous response. Our decision to redeploy was vindicated. When we reached the car park, there was the sinister maroon Jaguar, deserted but silently menacing, parked on the other side of the grassy car park. There could only be one reason why that car was there!

As we studied it, the car's engine creaked, hot metal cooling down. "Obviously, they haven't been here long. It's possible they could be close by. This time I'm not going to play the foolish hero," I told Trish. "Let's go."

I glanced across at David, seeing a flash of humour deep within the eyes as a thought occurred. I knew David's capacity for mischief when the mood arose. Without asking what he was thinking, I gave a slight shake of my head. "No," I said, letting him know that whatever he was planning wasn't a good idea.

Hastily we scrambled into the Focus, driving off without delay. Usually, the owners of the Jaguar seemed to know where we were. They seemed to anticipate our every move, even before we did. This time though, they'd made a mistake; they were late. Maybe they didn't like early mornings as much as us.

A few miles on and Sue proclaimed, with relief, "No sign of them, the road behind is empty." Soon, we were safely on the motorway, feeling secure in the knowledge we had left our enemies behind.

"Brent," exclaimed Sue, leaning forwards. "Maybe they were Brent geese. They left when we arrived. I covered wildlife with my schoolkids. Brent are the smallest of the goose family; Luke must have known we would disturb them before we even received the clue. Wow awesome," she gasped, sinking back into the upholstery.

Excitement mounting, we headed for the service station, anticipating a well-earned breakfast. But first we'd open the silver envelope, still gripped tightly in Sue's possession. Hurriedly, I eased into a parking space, turning towards Sue.

Sue, as eager as us all, tore open the envelope. We craned forwards, impatient to see the contents. She read aloud, increasingly incredulous. Luke had promised a gift from the heavens; this was totally unexpected, inconceivable, even to us.

CONGRATULATIONS, MY FRIENDS.
YOU HAVE COMPLETED YOUR FIRST THREE
TASKS WELL.
HERE IS YOUR REWARD.
GOD HAS GIVEN YOU TEN COMMANDMENTS.

THESE WILL REPLACE THE TEN
COMANDMENTS GIVEN TO MOSES.
HEED THEM WELL FOR THEY WILL
PROTECT AND GUIDE YOU
IN THE TRIAL AHEAD.

Then there was a second, folded sheet of paper, which Sue quickly opened

YOU MUST HONOUR YOU PARENTS
YOU MUST NOT STEAL
YOU MUST NOT KILL
YOU MUST NOT COMMIT ADULTERY
YOU MUST CONSIDER THE WELFARE OF OTHERS
YOU MUST NOT DESIRE THAT WHICH
BELONGS TO OTHERS
YOU MUST FORGIVE THOSE WHO SIN
AGAINST YOU
YOU MUST TRY TO LOVE THOSE WHOM
YOU DO NOT LIKE
YOU MUST FOLLOW THE TEACHING OF
YOUR GOD
YOU MUST HONOUR YOUR GOD

I flopped back into my seat, unintelligible sounds replacing words that I was unable to find. Trish, more effervescent than I, let out a yell of triumph, "Yes, yes, yes, we've done it." She twisted in her seat in an attempt to hug us all.

David and Sue simply looked as stunned as I felt. A grin slowly developed across David's face, as the implications gradually crystallised. He finally uttered,

"We're blessed, trusted by God, the first to receive commandments since Moses."

Expressly forbidden to tell another person about our communication with the heavens, I still felt an urge to run up to the people around and show them the new ten commandments, which had appeared out of thin air, before our very eyes. Fortunately for them, I resisted the temptation.

The animated and enthusiastic chatter blossoming out of success continued all the way through a hearty breakfast – bacon, eggs, sausages and beans, with plenty of tea and toast. The overcooked meat and watery eggs did little to dampen our pleasure in the afterglow of achievement. As David had pointed out, "Not only did we not have to climb a mountain to receive our commandments inscribed on heavy stone, but it is also open season on our neighbour's sheep and ox. It seems the Lord has modernised, for the twenty-first century." He grinned, biting into his toast.

We returned home before the afternoon, parting to go our own separate ways. David and Sue disappeared to London, choosing to go shopping on Oxford Street, while Trish and I made an appearance at the rugby club, where Trish supported me in the last league game of the season. My first game for over a month. After all the stress of the previous few weeks and the elation of that morning, a hard, invigorating eighty minutes of sport was exactly what was needed to rid me of any stress. Walking off the pitch, I felt drained but relaxed. "I enjoyed that," I told her, giving her a muddy hug, which she failed to appreciate.

Until the next appearance of Luke, we had an opportunity to enjoy the rest of the weekend, time to bathe in the inner warmth of the successful outcome of our quest.

A week since our successful foray to Fleet, a week of essential rest. Disappointingly, despite having congregated in my small living room on three separate occasions. Luke had failed to materialise at all.

Richard, the girls' father had gone to Sweden on a business trip, staying in Stockholm for ten days; he was overseeing the installation of the state-of-the-art electrical security system in a new modern office complex, which his company was involved in.

Lynda encouraged Trish and Sue to invite me and David to stay overnight. Lynda was used to having people around her. Now that they owned a large house, I guessed Lynda felt rather lonely rattling around an empty house when Richard was away.

The proliferation on television of quality cooking programmes having hit their mark, as always, Lynda provided us with an excellent meal. Being single, I am capable around the house, used to cooking for myself, but Lynda always made us feel so welcome. The home-made liver pate followed by lemon and honey glazed duck Moroccan style was both plentiful and fabulous. A world away from the snatched meals before the television screen I was used to. David and I were always made to feel extra special by Lynda.

"That was amazing," I said, placing the knife and fork onto the emptied plate. "However much I enjoy my independence, it's good to be spoiled once in a while;

you're a fantastic cook. You should go on one of those programmes on the telly."

"My pleasure," Lynda replied, removing the plate from before me. "Always a pleasure feeding you two; you never moan like these two do." She grinned at her daughters, only half meaning the implied criticism.

After the meal, I ventured an idea. "Lynda come to the Wellington with us. After such a great meal, it's the least we can do; we would really love your company." Lynda demurred only slightly; she enjoyed both the company and attention. I knew she didn't like the thought of spending an evening in the big empty house, on her own.

"As long as you're all sure. I wouldn't like to get in the way." After this, we spent an hour in the bar, swapping stories, buying Lynda drinks. Though I was secretly glad when she said, "I'm getting tired. I'm going to make a move for home. You guys stay."

"No way," I told her.

"Not only do we not want you to walk home alone, but I'm knackered, *Match of the Day* will do just fine," David assured her, with Trish and Sue agreeing.

Returning to the house, Trish disappeared towards the kitchen, shouting over her shoulder as she went "tea?"

Lynda politely made her excuses. "I am really tired; thank you for a lovely evening. I'll see you in the morning. Come on, Toby." Toby, the short haired Yorkshire Terrier jumped up, following Lynda as she disappeared, leaving us to make our own amusement.

Sue began yawning soon after. "I'm going too. It's been a long day." Kissing David, she followed her mother's example, vanishing up the stairs.

David and I both wanted to watch the football on television. "*Match of the day*?" I asked, turning to Trish.

"Go on then, at least I won't get a muddy hug at the end of the game."

We turned on the box, settling down to appraise the day's matches. I lay across the floor on my belly, head supported by cushions, watching two teams play out a 1-1 draw on screen. Trish joined me, cuddling up. "Budge up, make room for a little one." She rested her head on my shoulder. David was settled in the chair across the room.

This picture of contentment was exactly what I felt at that moment. The pressure and stress of the previous few weeks over; for now, we were safe. Time for relaxing with friends.

Apart from the commentator's voice, there was no sound in the darkened room, illuminated only by the flicker of the television screen. The game was absorbing as we concentrated on the large flat screen, admiring the skill and finesse of the players.

When the match finished. I glanced up, noticing that David was no longer in his chair. Bizarrely he was ten feet away from me, behind the coffee table, but there was something very odd about him! David was on his hands and knees, peering at us around the corner of the table, rather like Toby did occasionally.

Still on his hands and knees, David crawled towards me, top lip drawn back, revealing teeth in a half grimace, half sneer. I stiffened remaining still, laid on the floor, watching curiously, Trish by my side. Both of us were bemused, wondering what David was up to. Very gently David began to nuzzle my neck like a dog.

"Get off you daft bugger, not funny," I said, pushing him away and rising to my knees. I was beginning to feel a little uneasy. David had always been a bit of a practical joker, but this was strange behaviour indeed.

He rolled over, flopped onto his back, ending close to the coffee table, laying there quietly for a couple of seconds, arms raised in the air like a prostrate dog begging. A loud hiss emitted from him; it sounded almost like a wild cat preparing to pounce. Unexpectedly, David's back arched violently, his feet and shoulders remaining flat to the floor as his back rose upwards. I felt sure it must soon reach, then surpass, breaking point. The hissing grew louder, David's features contorting to a snarl. I tensed waiting for the scream of pain. I knew it must come when his back broke, but no!

Without warning he sprang upright, towering over the both of us, leaning forward to glare into our faces. I sprang from my haunches to full height. Beside me I felt Trish rise, still grasping onto my arm. I felt her fingers tighten, and I knew why.

I knew then that we were staring straight into the eyes of the devil incarnate.

"Get back, stay behind me," I hissed to Trish, conscious that something very wrong was happening.

The eyes glared back at us, glowering with malevolent evil. Subconsciously I realised time had slowed, as it so often does in moments of terror. Staring back, unwilling to flinch, I tried to memorise every detail of those evil features, features, which no longer belonged to David. His eyes, normally cornflower blue, had darkened to midnight. The pupils were invisible pinpoints in the centre of the iris. The cornea yellow and bloodshot.

The face scowling back at us was the personification of the phrase ice-cold hatred; a hatred which truly made my spine tingle and sent a shiver through my body.

This beast controlling my friend's body hated us and wanted to harm us. For the first time on this adventure, I felt the chill wind of real fear, a cold sickening feeling deep in the pit of my stomach, a terror which had to be mentally controlled before it took over and panic overwhelmed.

I heard Trish gasp in revulsion. She whispered, "Where's David?" I forced myself to pause and take stock. I had to make the effort to think logically.

We had no time to react. A hand stretched out, shrivelled up like a claw, moving too fast for me to duck out of the way. It raked its nails across my cheek. Instantly, I felt the blood begin to trickle down my skin.

I jumped backwards, almost knocking Trish over; she recovered, moving with me. I swallowed, forcing down the taste of my own bile. Conflicting thoughts raced through my mind. I had to think calmly, do the right thing, get us both out of danger. This was not mild-mannered Luke before us. Somehow, David had become possessed by pure evil, a devil within David's body that wanted us dead.

Without conscious thought or decision, I started to move forwards, intending to confront the monster. I realised I must protect both myself and Trish, who remained on my arm.

"It's OK. I'm bigger than David, and fitter. He can't hurt us. It might be best if you vacate the room," I said, addressing Trish without turning.

With the benefit of clear thinking, some of my initial and rudimentary fears were subsiding, replaced by anger at this usurper. "You've missed your chance buster; we were defenceless at your feet. You allowed us to stand up. I'm bigger and physically stronger than David, as well as fitter. Leave him now or I shall be forced to overpower you and hold David down, until we find a way of driving you from David's body, even if we have to tie him up. I'm not afraid to do it." I couldn't believe I was having an argument with the Devil.

With a swift lunge, the claws went for my throat. I was prepared for the attack, but this was still the body of my friend, I didn't want to cause any unnecessary pain. I jerked my arm up, blocking the lunge, then grabbing the extended wrists, intending to use my greater strength to overpower, then subdue, this evil devil. "Got you, now leave him, and us alone."

Within seconds it was apparent that I'd grossly miscalculated its strength. The claws twisted easily from my grip. Instantly it was my wrists which were held in a vice-like grip. The brute strength now being exerted on me, in return, was inconceivable from David's slight frame. I could feel my hands going numb as the blood drained from them.

"Your mistake," he growled into my face. I smelt a sulphurous stench coming from his mouth as he spoke, the very stench of hell.

Relentlessly the pressure was applied. I was forced downwards, towards the floor. The evil beast had strength well in excess of my own. Slowly, I felt my knees begin to buckle; I knew that I couldn't hold out much longer. I would soon be defenceless, prostrate before this determined and unremitting attack that I was unable to resist.

In adversity my mind became calm. I can remember thinking, as a last resort, I would use blind panic; then I thought of Trish. I could sense her behind me, having ignored my instruction to flee. Fortunately, she'd placed herself out of range, but had stayed as close as she could.

"Go," I whispered, through clenched teeth. "Go." I hoped that she could use the little time that I'd gained to escape.

Under the unrelenting onslaught, my last ounce of resolve was draining away; my knees touched the floor. There was little I could now do to prevent the inevitable. I wondered what he would do once I was completely helpless and defeated. This creature with no mercy in its eyes.

Astoundingly and without warning, the creature released my wrists, grabbing at its own throat. Without stopping to ponder this unbelievable redemption, I twisted out of range, as fast as my exhausted body would allow.

I glimpsed Trish, holding the door open for me, her facial expression frozen in horror. Trish, whose strength of character and love for me eclipsed her desire to run. She stood rooted to the spot, mouth hanging open, skin whiter than a ghost.

"Out of here." I grabbed Trish yanking her through the door behind me.

Once through, we both turned. The creature spasmed in great torment, writhing about on the floor like a fish out of water. It appeared to be in great agony. I gawped in amazement while rubbing life back into my sore wrists.

"Oh, Martyn, what's happening?"

"I've no idea," I told her. "I think it's the devil." We hung onto each other in the doorway, prepared for flight.

For an instant, it raised its head and emitted a torrent of foul language and abuse, aimed towards us; then the head fell back, hitting the carpet.

There was an abrupt silence as the creature (for we had by then stopped thinking of David's body), slowly stopped flapping around on the carpet, becoming still as if going into a coma, sleep, or even death.

Trish and I waited, vigilant and tense, fearing the worst. "I can just about make out a slight up and down movement of his chest; he's alive at least," Trish stated, sounding worried. We stayed put, wondering what would happen next. "I'm not going back in there, but we can't leave David either. We're stuck!" I said, gripping Trish's hand.

Unexpectedly, David sat upright, causing us both to cry out in alarm, to grip the doorframe, preparing for instant flight. However, before we moved, the gentle and calming voice of Luke filled the room, emanating from David. "Beware, Martyn, the Devil has found a way to enter David's body."

"Thanks for telling us; this I think we already know," I said, rubbing my still aching wrists.

After our ordeal, we were so grateful to hear the reassuring voice of Luke. However, I had no intention of moving any closer. We stayed put, holding onto each other's hands for comfort and reassurance.

Luke continued. "You must be able to fight him. I cannot hold him for long, remember your teaching." The head fell back, David's body slept once more.

I turned to Trish, commenting, "If Luke can't hold the devil at bay, what chance do we have? What is the teaching that we need to know? Do you remember?"

Fortunately, Trish was one step ahead of me. "Luke taught us that the Bible and the colour white are a barrier to evil, don't you remember?" She frowned. "Fortunately, we have a family, Bible. It doesn't get much use; hopefully it isn't on the bookshelf, over there." She indicated a bookshelf on the far wall, beyond David's sleeping body. "I'll look in Dad's study. I think I remember it being in there."

Trish rushed off, frantically searching her father's study while I remained, monitoring the motionless form. It was a blessing that Trish happened to be wearing a white sweatshirt, even if it did have a red sparkly love heart emblazoned on the front. Sue was safely asleep upstairs, under a white quilt. It was just a shame that I wore blue jeans and a red sweatshirt.

Finally, Trish located the Bible, handing it to me; I opened it, randomly. Cautiously I edged forward. "Have that door open and ready," I whispered, then I pushed it hurriedly onto the chest of the unconscious David.

As the open pages came into contact with his chest, the body gave a huge heave, trying to throw the book off. Valiantly, I flung myself forwards, fighting with all my strength, realising I could only hold the Bible there for seconds. With an almighty lunge I was thrown backwards across the room to land with a thump flat on my back, almost ten feet from the beast. The fall knocked the air from my lungs; I lay there winded, unable to crawl away.

Springing upright, the beast hurled the Bible at me as if it were red hot. I was groggy and vulnerable. For the second time that night I was at the mercy of the beast. I recognised the futility of trying to compete. I knew when the devil came at me, I would be incapable of resisting for long; this power that opposed us was beyond imagining.

Instead of coming for me, the devil turned towards Trish. "Martyn," she yelped.

The power of love, as a force in the battle between good and evil, was something I hadn't considered. The same mistake the devil now made. On hearing Trish scream, I knew that somewhere I must find the resources to continue my fight. Driven to ignore the pain in my body, I had to go to Trish. Desperately, I searched for and located the fallen Bible, fortunately within easy reach. I scuttled over and picked it up.

Trish, who still wouldn't turn to run, was frozen in terror as the Devil slowly advanced towards her. I witnessed as her knees buckled in panic. She hit the floor with a soft thump. Curled up in a ball, Trish started to whimper. He was close; the devil towered ominously over the petrified Trish. Her white sweatshirt didn't seem to deter him in the slightest. I knew I had to act fast.

Trish's pitiful moaning spurred me into action. Summoning every gram of remaining strength, I pushed myself upright, lurching forward. The Devil turned to meet my stumbling charge. In that moment, I realised that I could not think of David. This, as far as I was concerned, was life and death. I held the book open and forced it towards his face. "Get away, you bastard, pick on somebody your own size." Instantaneously my wrists were again gripped in a vice-like hold, but my forward momentum prevailed. I managed to keep the book open, driving it towards his startled eyes. My knees started to buckle once again. The relentless pressure exerted by those claws forced me down towards the ground. I called on all the strength given me by fear, adrenaline and prayer to lock my elbows, to keep the Bible extended towards the devil, holding it just inches from his eyes.

In an attempt to escape the open page, my adversary went into a frenzy of panic. His grip loosened as he tried to push me away, spinning us both around towards Trish. Against such frantic power I could only hold on for seconds; then I gave way, but these few seconds were enough.

I heard Trish shout, "Martyn, run." She finally managed to escape through the kitchen door.

Rather than attack me, the devil was trying to escape from the Bible. I was able to push him away, following Trish through the door to blessed safety, the door slamming behind us.

We stood in the kitchen panting, both our bodies leaning our weight on the door, just in case! Trish was gulping, her mascara smudged, tears seeping down her pale cheeks. On the other side of the door, we could hear a scratching sound on the woodwork, accompanied by the frightened whining of a wild animal. An animal that was in torment and pain. Burying her head in my arms, trying to protect her ears from that anguished sound, Trish mumbled, "Oh, Martyn, that's horrible; what do we do now?" She folded into my embrace,

"No idea, way beyond my experience," I told her, feeling the helplessness flood through me.

We both remained rooted, all our weight pushing against the door. The noises gradually dying out while we held fast.

With the room beyond the door quiet again, Trish and I looked at each other, experiencing shared relief. Only then, in the quieter moments, could we begin to consider our friend David.

"What about David. What's this doing to him?" Trish voiced the fears that I was only beginning to articulate within.

We couldn't hide forever. Soon, far too soon for my liking, driven by the compassion of Trish, we would have to open the door and find out what was happening to David. In my rush to escape, I'd dropped the Bible – now our only dubious weapon was a white towel.

With extreme caution, I inched the door open until I could put my eye to the crack. I could sense the presence of Trish close behind, so close that I could feel her breath on the back of my neck. With the white towel held out before me, like a shield, I pushed the door, widening the crack an inch. I expected confrontation at any moment, alert and prepared, every muscle tight and tensed, ready to retreat at the slightest provocation.

It could only be sixth sense but, when I looked into the room, I knew that we were safe. I knew this was David who was in a sitting position. Ever so slightly, I began to relax, opening the door a little wider. David was about ten feet away, unmoving, silently crying.

Trish pushed past, saying, "It's gone. I can feel it!" In that moment, Trish sensed the presence of David, as did I.

David had re-joined us, eyes open, but no recognition within those eyes, and very little movement of his body. I stepped forward, entering the room. As I did, David flopped backwards, hitting the carpet with a lifeless thud. Trish let out a short sharp shriek.

Suddenly, emanating from David's stomach, a ball of bright light rose. It hovered about a foot over the unmoving body of our friend. We froze, but the light didn't frighten. We were becoming attuned to the atmosphere of our surroundings. This light was not evil, instead it was hauntingly beautiful. We watched, mesmerised, completely transfixed by what we were seeing, hands reaching out to each other, touching, coming together so that we could examine this phenomenon as a shared experience. In the midst of all the evil, we were now experiencing the beauty and power of an awesome manifestation. As a great leader has an aura of power, this light imbued the room with an atmosphere of love and beauty, an encounter which we both felt the need to share in silence. An emotional understanding, which surpassed any words.

The ball became steadily more defined; there were many lights within it. The centre, a large bright clean white light, surrounded by many smaller glowing lights: these were lilac to purple in colour. The outer lights seemed to dance around the centre, sparkling with great intensity. Altogether about the size of a tennis ball, it hovered there over David's inert body, turning night into day and fear to love.

Then, without warning, the light moved, amazingly fast, flying across the room and disappearing through the opposite wall. The most beautiful thing that we had ever seen. Its loss felt like the loss of a warm and lively friend. Trish and I turned to each other, finding words unnecessary. We both knew instinctively: David's soul was now protected.

Lying on the floor, his body relaxed further, then seemed to settle into deep sleep. Fear now banished, we retrieved the fallen Bible, laying it open on David's chest, simply there as a precautionary measure.

Time passed slowly. David continued to lie peacefully. "We have to stay, to watch over him," Trish warned. After the flight or fight adrenaline rush, we were now both exhausted. It was the small hours of the morning and we craved sleep. Unfortunately, there was no way that we could justify leaving David alone, asleep on the floor. I tried to make him as comfortable as possible, placing a throw over his prostrate form. We sat with him, keeping vigil over our sleeping friend, finding the company of each other a godsend.

I wondered aloud, "Silence was our least consideration when it was all happening. Why has nobody complained about the noise or even investigated it? At one point, we were screaming and yelling blue murder, but the noise seems to have stopped at the bottom of the stairs!" Trish shrugged her shoulders, finding no answer.

Around three a.m. we heard movement, originating from Lynda's room, followed by soft footsteps descending the stairs; we looked at each other in panic, convinced that Lynda was going to demand an explanation for all the riotous noise. We listened as Lynda went straight into the kitchen; then we heard a tap running. Maintaining silence, I mouthed to Trish, "Find out what your mother's doing."

When Trish popped her head around the door, she startled her mother. "What are you doing still up? You scared me, bursting in like that."

"Sorry. Mum, Martyn and I fell asleep on the sofa."

"I'm sure you did," her mum replied, with a knowing look and a smile, seeing the smudged mascara on Trish's cheek. "Make sure you get some sleep soon." Lynda disappeared back up the stairs. Little did she realise how close she'd come to discovering the mayhem under her own roof.

As the night continued, we stayed there, uneasily watching over the lifeless David. About four am, David's body went into sudden convulsions. We must have been so taught and ready for action. Instinctively I managed to respond without plan nor thought. Sensing Trish move, hearing the door opening as she prepared my escape route, I reached David, managing to lay hands on the Bible before it was thrown from his chest. Thrusting down hard with my full weight, I forced it downwards onto his chest, just able to hold it there by applying all my strength.

The beast below went into a frenzy, eyes opened wide, yellow and bloodshot, the pupils fixed on mine, pure hatred aimed towards the very centre of my soul. My blood ran cold as I was drawn into the very centre of its loathing, but I stayed, fighting for the sake of my friend. The short battle continued for several seconds, with every ounce of my strength used to hold the Bible in place. I knew I had to maintain contact between the book and the beast. Fortunately, I had the advantage of gravity; my weight bore down unremittingly, but by the time the fight evaporated from the fiend, I felt totally drained and exhausted. His eyes slowly closed and, once again, our friend David slept. I turned towards the pale and frightened Trish, easing myself away from the now sleeping form with great care. "I don't know how long we can go on like this. What if it's still happening in the morning?"

"Well, I guess we'll have to reveal the whole story. I'm not sure how Mum and Dad will take it though, Satan in the sitting room," Trish replied, employing common sense and practicality.

Twice in the next hour we needed to react with the same instantaneous aggression, quelling the evil ferocity, which wanted, so badly, to possess David's body. We were both mentally and physically exhausted, almost intoxicated with fatigue. I could feel my eyeballs, gritty with tiredness. "I can't even begin to imagine what this is doing to David's body," I told Trish.

"We both know and trust that the Lord has his soul in full protective custody." She raised my morale, in memory of the wonder we'd seen.

Once it was fully light outside, I suggested, "Now it's daylight, it's probably safe enough for a cup of tea. I could certainly do with a drink."

Trish was unwilling to leave me on my own with the devil incarnate. "We should both go. I don't want to be on my own, and the thought of you being here on your own, if it returns, urgh," she shuddered.

Relieved at not having to pretend to be fearless, I thankfully agreed. "It's light; it should be safe to leave David for a few minutes."

In the kitchen, waiting for the kettle to boil, there came an evil hissing from the other room. We froze, eyes meeting in dread, the hairs on my back rose.

Realising the significance of the situation, Trish voiced my own feelings. "Shit, that wasn't supposed to happen!" We'd left the Bible open and face down on David's chest; now we had to prepare to meet the beast without it.

"I though the Devil would flee with daylight, but it seems he isn't a vampire, and this isn't the set of a hammer horror movie. I guess we're having to learn the hard way. The rules of this game haven't been written by Hollywood," I told Trish, trying and failing to get humour into my words.

For a split second I considered the possibility of flight. "We could get in my car and drive over to my place." Glancing around, I rejected the idea immediately. "No, I can't do it, think what damage the devil would wreak on this unsuspecting household!"

Trish agreed. "Unfortunately, we're duty bound to fight on."

I tried to do the honourable thing, telling Trish, "Go upstairs, get into bed with Sue, hide under the white quilt. Stay there until it's safe to come down. I'll stay here." But we both knew I wasn't being sincere with my willingness to confront the beast alone. I was immensely grateful for Trish's stubborn streak.

"Don't be an idiot all your life," she told me, flatly refusing to leave. By nature, I worried about her being in danger. But that was my failing, not Trish's; this was now the twenty-first century. It was so good to have her beside me, sharing and fighting the same battle.

It needed a tremendous, determined effort to even think about approaching the door. We heard a hissing snarl through the woodwork, almost as if it could smell us approaching. Trish hung onto my arm, hanging back. "Don't cramp me," I warned. "Make sure we've both got room for a rapid retreat."

For the second time that night, I opened the door about an inch, putting my eye to the crack. David's body was on all fours, facing towards the door, about four feet away. His mouth twisted into a snarl as those evil, unsettling eyes focused on mine. He launched himself at the door, and at me, teeth barred, like a wounded and cornered tiger. The door shuddered as he hit it. "Shit," I yelped, withdrawing swiftly, holding the handle tightly closed.

Trish declared, "We're now in a bit of a predicament. He's in there, unable to get at us, and we're outside, too scared to open the door – stalemate, I think. Explain that one to Mum in the morning."

"You may enter now, my friends, the beast has again been driven from the body of David!" The voice was Luke's, but we weren't yet ready to believe our ears, aware that this could be a deception by the great deceiver.

With the utmost caution, I inched the door open, Trish still welded to my free arm. A few seconds later, I let it swing open wide, intuition revealing that this was indeed Luke. We were again safe.

Luke beckoned us forwards. "Come in, sit," he said, indicating the sofa. In that moment, we identified Luke's manner as somewhat disturbed, making us both wary. I glanced towards the door, ensuring we still had our escape route.

Luke began speaking! To begin with the full meaning of his words failed to register in our exhausted minds. Once we grasped what Luke was trying to say, the impact of his words hit like a sledgehammer.

"The trauma of tonight has been too much for David's body. I'm afraid he will die tonight. His body is wasted, an empty shell. It is too dangerous and too difficult for his own spirit to re-enter the body. Satan prowls and wants possession."

At that moment, this simply spoken, bland statement was too momentous for us to even begin to conceive.

Trish let out a gasp, a meaningless, "why?" falling from her lips. I felt numb, utterly devoid of all feeling, the shock bringing with it incomprehension. We couldn't really hear, or listen, as Luke continued talking.

"God despatched his angels to protect David's spirit. Indeed, you watched as the angels removed David's spirit to safety. Now his body is just too weak to allow the spirit to re-enter. He will pass peacefully tonight." As understanding dawned, I nearly vomited.

"No!" I jerked my head, gawping in amazement at Trish. The single word she'd spoken had been in real vehemence and anger. Trish has always had a hot temper; it could easily be directed at me and was usually well deserved, but this was Luke she was shouting at. I almost expected a bolt of lightning through the ceiling, striking her down for her impertinence. Demonstrating very real anger, she continued.

"We've given our very existence to you, and you repay us by taking our friend. Sue loves David, we all do!" Trish burst into tears, sobbing loudly, unable to continue with her speech. I understood what she felt. Dimly I perceived that if there was to be any hope, then it would be our love for David.

"Please," I implored Luke to try. "We love David; he's far too young to die."

Luke explained, "There is only a very slender chance. I will have to stay in possession of the body until Satan leaves and David's body has had rest enough to allow David's human spirit to return. The death of David is essential to the devil and his syndicate. You are finished as an entity if David were to die. This evening is a deliberate ploy of the evil one. He did not like your success last weekend. He has planned his revenge carefully. But" Luke continued, "this is not a small thing I do. The evil one is more powerful than me. With the Lord's angels I will fight him and hold him back until he tires and leaves. It will be a hard battle, one that I may not win."

In the end, I believe that our love for David saved his life. While his body rested motionless on the sofa, we covered him with a blanket. Continually examining for any traces of life, I could find no signs, not even a pulse. David may well have been clinically dead. We couldn't tell.

For over two hours we waited, praying hard, not daring to leave the room.

Self-recrimination entered my mind. I had been the instigator of this. I'd driven things. Now it was out of control; it could cost the life of my friend.

Somehow, Luke managed to keep the devil at bay. I hoped our prayers were helping. What we knew for sure was that the devil was becoming frustrated. As we monitored our friend, a small china ornament flew off the shelf, just missing Trish's head. But by now exhaustion had taken its toll; we were too fatigued to feel frightened, only relief that David still had a chance.

We hung on, waiting and watching, never daring to hope. Two hours later, astonishingly and without warning, causing both of us to jump in fright, David sat bolt upright on the sofa. He was incoherent, almost zombie-like,

"What... No... where?" he slurred.

But it was David, totally bemused as Trish hugged him, tears of joy running down her cheeks. The relief at his deliverance was mighty. Our hearts sang as we helped him up the stairs and into bed, telling the confused David, "Just sleep, mate, we'll explain later."

Safe in the knowledge that the night was over. Trish and I hugged each other, almost shyly. Almost as if, having been through this ordeal together, we were learning about each other anew. Spent, we fell into bed, craving a long overdue and richly deserved sleep.

CHAPTER FIVE

Six days had passed since the night of horrors, as it came to be known. After we'd furnished them with full details, Sue and David were truly appalled. David could remember nothing at all. Even with an abridged version, Sue had been petrified by what we'd revealed, though she still stuck close to David, even spending time alone with him.

Luke, however, remained conspicuous by his absence. We'd met every evening during the week, wanting answers, but it seemed the heavenly forces had decided to leave us alone. All we could do was watch and wait, wondering what would happen next.

It being a Friday, we vacated the flat in favour of our usual spot, the hospitable lounge bar of the Welly. Although still wary, five nights of inactivity had relaxed the jittery atmosphere a little. As the evening passed, Sue edged closer and closer to David until they were happily cuddled up, any previous restraint seemingly forgotten.

"Greetings my friends!" Sue shot out of David's arms.

The calming, gentle voice of Luke did nothing to placate Sue's nerves as she moved around the table to join Trish and myself.

Luke waited to allow us to settle and prepare.

I quickly glanced around the bar, checking if Luke's appearance had drawn attention, but the rest of the clientele were absorbed in their own activities, paying our small group no attention whatsoever.

Once we were comfortable, Luke began to talk. He started by apologising. "I should have warned you about Satan, the Devil. You are his total enemies; I emphasise how important it is for Satan to stop you from completing your task. If you fail, then mankind is at the mercy of the evil one. He seeks to devour and destroy all that you do." Luke pointed at David's face, continuing. "David, who is the vehicle of communication, is the pivotal member of the syndicate. If Satan can kill David, then your work will be finished before it has begun."

I sneaked a glance at Sue; she had an expression of abhorrence. I wondered if we should impart this news to David when he joined us again.

Luke carried on speaking, "The devil's syndicate, your opposite numbers on Earth, will try to kill David, but they are humans, with human frailties. He will have a host of angelic protection in the spiritual realm." I noticed, Luke failed to say that the rest of our syndicate was protected in this way, by hosts of angels. I hoped so but I resolved to be doubly on guard when we were out or together.

Sue, whose confidence had gradually grown, asked the question which continued to consume her. "What are the chances of the beast reappearing through David?"

"You are safe for now," Luke assured us all. "The devil will try again, when he feels able to inflict damage."

Then Luke promised, "We are watching over David, but the method of communication can be hijacked." To her immense relief, Luke delivered some good news to Sue. "The beast has been bound when you are alone with

David. You are a special servant of God. The Lord has forbidden the evil one any part of David when you are alone with him."

Luke turned to me. "Martyn, you may go to the bar and buy another round of drinks for the group."

Waiting to be served, I mused how when Luke visited, he managed to keep up the alcohol intake for David's body. This would have been David's round. That, I thought wryly, is a price I have to pay for this extraordinary adventure.

Once, seated comfortably, Luke continued, with surprising news. We'd been happy in the knowledge that we were Luke's syndicate, he was our team leader. Now this was about to change. "We, the apostles of the Lord," he warned, "have our own very differing characters. I was chosen as your first teacher for my patience." With a wry smile, I recalled all the pointless and stupid questions that we'd asked, again and again, then Luke's unruffled responses. Luke really did have the patience of the saint that he was.

Luke wouldn't tell us the name of our new spiritual guide. He did, however, tell us, "Your new teacher has been chosen for his strength, but beware, his patience isn't as boundless as mine. You will still see me on occasions but my time with you will be limited!"

With this, the eyes glazed, and his body slumped slightly. David had returned.

"I wasn't expecting that," said Sue, slipping around the table to re-join David.

"It feels kind of sad in a way. Luke has been with us for nearly three months; he's definitely been a friend," Trish announced.

All the attention in the world made no difference. David remained as David for the remainder of the evening, and in fact for the next five days.

Wednesday evening found us, for the fifth consecutive evening, hanging around in my living room. We'd gathered to wait once more. That week David must have felt like a rare Siberian tiger, about to breed; every time he made any kind of move, three people leant forward expectantly!

The apostle John still managed to catch the three of us completely unaware, but then, we couldn't be expected to follow David to the toilet.

I looked up as David returned. Instantly, and without knowing why, I knew that this wasn't David or Luke. I now know why it is so easy for a parent to see the difference between identical twins. The same body for all three yet it was easy telling the different mannerisms when John or Luke paid a visit.

I tensed, observing cautiously as he walked to the chair and sat down. Trish and Sue were both staring. They'd immediately sensed that there was something different here. He sat down, then looked around the room before turning to us. Surprisingly I felt no fear, only anticipation.

I waited, not speaking or moving. We allowed our visitor to open the conversation. From the first sentence we could tell straightaway, John was a strong character. We were to learn that he didn't suffer fools gladly.

He announced to the group, "I am the apostle John, an apostle of Jesus. I have been observing you from the beginning, watching the way you conduct yourselves;

you are learning, but not quickly enough." John had some praise for Trish and me for the way we fought the beast. "You both had compassion and concern for your friend, even though you were frightened, you still fought on, protecting David. That is good."

Before I could get too conceited, John continued. "However, Martyn, by your stupidity and wilfulness, your behaviour at Buckler's Hard put yourself and, therefore, the whole syndicate at risk. This is not a game; the stakes are enormous and vital for the human race. The journey is going to be hard, unbelievably hard, but the prize for mankind is worth it."

I recognised that John was giving us a motivating speech, in the tradition of all the best generals. I felt an icy shiver down my spine. It dawned, Luke's role was to break us in gently, educate us in a situation, way beyond our comprehension. John was here to toughen us for the battles which lay ahead. I was unable to understand the bizarre enormity of our calling. Just what the task ahead would comprise of, I couldn't begin to comprehend, but after John's speech, I knew that I was willing to follow forever, whatever the cost!

Carrying out the syndicate work was an all-consuming task but the passage of time continued relentlessly. Colin was due home, on leave from his merchant ship. All four syndicate members had known him since we'd been young children: Trish and Sue lived next door to Colin and his family, before Richard's success allowed them to move to a more salubrious neighbourhood.

I'd known Colin longer than anybody. At the tender age of five, we'd sat next to each other on our first day at infant school. Despite normal and petty wranglings, we'd continued to sit together all the way through our schooling, and beyond. We were almost inseparable, until Trish and the merchant navy came along. I figured it was going to be hard to keep this gargantuan time-consuming secret from Colin. A man I had trusted all my life; however, I had no choice.

Colin Winters, twenty-four, short blond hair and a wiry frame, shorter than I at five feet eleven. Just after his eighteenth birthday, Colin had surprised us all, one day in the Wellington announcing, "I'm going to see the world. I've joined the merchant navy." This astounded me, Colin was an intelligent, quite shy character. I imagined him to be far too sensitive a person to enjoy the type of lifestyle which I believed from popular myth was common to the merchant navy. But when the urge to travel is there, then it must be sated.

"You caught me out with that one, and I reckon you'll be home within weeks, but go for it, mate," I told him, driving him to Gravesend and the Merchant Navy school. "Bring me back a beer from every port," I'd told him before we parted company.

The urge to travel must have been hereditary. He was the only family member still living in the UK. His parents left the country when he was eighteen, emigrating to Canada, which may well have been the catalyst for Colin's own decision to leave everything behind for the joy of the ocean waves. Sailing the seven seas on container ships.

Despite continually moaning about spending nine months a year away from his friends and home life, I sensed that Colin loved this life. When he was home, he had some great stories to tell, tales of reckless adventures in faraway countries.

When I had bought my flat, there was another for sale on the floor above. Colin had purchased it, using the savings he'd hoarded from his years at sea as a deposit. This arrangement was ideal for Colin. When he was away, I could keep an eye on the flat for him and when Colin was due home, I would turn on the heating and supply the flat with bread, milk, other food items and a case of John Smiths, his favourite beer, ready for his return.

The homecoming which concerned me now was only two days away. I looked forward to seeing my friend with a mixture of anticipation and concern. The whole syndicate knew Colin, this was the problem. John wouldn't be put off. I told Trish, "To accommodate John we are going to have to exclude our friend, and that's going to be difficult."

By this time, John had also become our friend; we would spend evenings talking to John, through the conduit of David. We'd found it easy to differentiate between the mannerisms and characters of Luke and John.

Although we counted John as a friend, it was difficult to take liberties. As we'd gauged during the first meeting, John was impatient to continue our instruction. We'd spoken to him about it, but John did not seem to appreciate how Colin's presence would hinder our available time.

"You're to be available to me when I'm ready to visit; everything else is for you to sort," he'd told us!

Friday, the day of Colin's return, I sat in my drawing office, anticipating that Trish and I would be expected to celebrate the start of a month's leave, in the Wellington. I knew Colin really looked forward to his first night on leave. I made my decision, ringing Trish. "This time my oldest friend comes first. I hope that John will understand. But I'm not letting Colin down his first night home, not tonight."

"I totally agree with you. John will just have to be discouraged for an evening," Trish said. "Sue, David and I knew what you were going to say, even before you thought it through. We're all intending to join you for a drink in the Wellington."

It was great to see him, sun-tanned and looking fit. We occupied our usual spot in the pub, listening to the stories of Colin's latest trip. He'd just completed three months on a grain carrier, circling the pacific, stopping at any number of exotic ports such as Bali and Japan, as well as some less salubrious stopovers.

After regaling us all with stories of adventures on land and sea, Colin lowered his voice and, almost embarrassed, he divulged, "Something weird happened during this last trip. I saw a ghost in my cabin."

Immediately I was intrigued, asking, "Go on, this sounds interesting."

Colin revealed, "Halfway through last month, I was twice woken in the middle of the night. I saw a figure dressed in white standing at the bottom of my bunk, studying me. My cabin mate saw it as well!"

I glanced nervously at David, expecting to see John staring back, but David was still with us, feigning disbelief at the possibility of ghosts or spirits.

"Maybe it was the ghost of Bluebeard, or Captain Bligh," I suggested, hoping the subject would change.

The evening turned out to be a success. We'd had a rest and the chance to relax with a friend, who knew nothing of our adventure. Sometimes it was good to put all thoughts of our own exploits out of mind.

The pub emptied so we all adjourned to Colin's flat for coffee. I had expected Colin to be tired after his long flight from Tokyo but he had arrived home mid-morning and taken the chance of an afternoon siesta. That, and the time difference, meant that at midnight, Colin was now wide awake and seeking company. Unfortunately for me, after a working week, I was ready for my bed. Trish and I made our excuses. "Sorry, mate, it's really good to see you but we're knackered, and I've got a big rugby day tomorrow, see you Sunday." We excused ourselves, leaving Colin talking with David and Sue.

The next day, a Saturday, I was on an excursion with the rugby club, an annual away friendly match in Wales, involving a 130 mile coach journey. This meant, at best, after home team hospitality, I wouldn't be returning home until very late in the evening.

Unexpectedly, due to a rush order, Trish was working that morning. She then planned to spend the day with her family. We wouldn't be able to see each other until the Sunday.

Trish left for the office, earning some extra spending money.

After finishing work, Trish went shopping in town, with a colleague. The two girls spent an enjoyable couple of hours wandering around the mall, checking out the clothes shops. Once Trish and her friend, Sarah parted, Trish planned on catching a bus home.

Today, she was in luck. She was loaded down with shopping bags, waiting at the bus stop, when Colin happened to pass in his car. Seeing Trish, he screeched to a halt, winding down the window. "Want a lift home?"

"Yes please, you're a godsend with this lot to carry." She gratefully accepted, dumping the shopping bags on the back seat.

"Fancy a coffee? There's something weird I need to discuss!"

Having no reason to rush home, Trish happily accepted his proposal. Back at his flat, Colin made them coffee before launching into his tale. "I had a very strange encounter after you left last night. David began to act very peculiarly indeed." Colin continued. "He began to talk about heaven and Earth, the meaning of life. When I looked straight into his eyes, I had the strangest sensation that I wasn't talking to David at all. I've known David almost as long as I've known Martyn. I'm telling you, Trish, I'm sure that wasn't David I was talking to!"

Trish probed. "What happened next?"

"Well, I asked Sue what was happening. I thought she would be freaked out by this, but she just advised me to wait and listen. It certainly freaked *me* out, talking to David, but not David. I can't explain it in words and now in daylight I feel an idiot. Did I imagine it all?" he said, suddenly losing the courage of his convictions.

Explaining all this to Trish embarrassed Colin. After his big speech, Colin became reticent, trying to withdraw from the conversation. "Maybe I've said too much. It was a hard trip. It might be that I need the rest more than I imagined. I don't think I drink that much, but some of those exotic drinks are potent, weird ingredients." He trailed off, looking at Trish for some kind of confirmation.

Trish began to probe further. "Did David mention a name?"

Reluctantly Colin replied. "That's the weirdest thing. David claimed to be the apostle John, the fisherman. Last night when you'd left, after a while, he stood up and pronounced that I was a member of a syndicate, that I forgive and I forget, so I am at heart a Christian as I love my fellow man! He should have witnessed that punch up in New York last year if I'm supposed to love my fellow man!" he muttered to himself.

A perplexed Colin told Trish, "He even claimed to have watched me when I was at sea. I know David was there when I said I might have seen something in my cabin one night. Funny thing is he was able to describe my cabin in detail. In the pub last night, did I talk about my cabin?" he asked, puzzled.

As soon as she was able, Trish made her excuses, leaving a puzzled Colin wondering if it was himself or David who'd suffered a breakdown during the previous three months.

Trish went straight home, asking Sue, "What happened last night. Did John appear?"

Sue confirmed it. "John did indeed appear to Colin. He explained the existence of the syndicate. I didn't confirm or deny anything at the time. I wanted the rest of the syndicate to know first. Colin was dumbfounded by what he was witnessing but too drunk to rationally accept what was happening before his eyes. It is an unbelievable tale to hear out of the blue, that one of your best friends had manifested into the apostle John."

Trish knew when we played an away game that I always enjoyed the hospitality of the home team. I never returned home until late in the evening, so she left a message on my voicemail. "Don't worry unduly, but I would appreciate a phone call as soon as you get up on Sunday morning."

However, after some wonderful hospitality from the Welsh club, I was unable to check my voicemail on my return. Instead, at eight o'clock on Sunday morning, I was awoken by the continuous ringing of the bedside phone. Despite rolling over and burying my head under a pillow, the ringing would not go away. Bleary eyed I reached out and fumbled for the receiver, knocking it to the floor in my muddle before, I finally managed to get the earpiece to my ear.

"Owwww, who is it?" I croaked, feeling the night before."

"It's me, Trish, and if your head is hurting, then I have no sympathy for your self-induced condition. John appeared to Colin on Friday night," she said, yanking me out of my lifeless state into something which approached consciousness. "Oh, and of less interest to me, did you win?" She disconnected without waiting for a reply.

I lurched out of bed and staggered to the shower, stopping to take two aspirins on the way.

Several cups of coffee and one long hot shower later, I was beginning to feel almost human.

Walking to David's, I was determined to speak with John to ask what was happening. I'd explained to John that Colin was returning. John had made no mention of Colin joining us on our adventures.

It was David who answered the door to my insistent knocking. I looked behind him, ensuring we were alone. Before exchanging any of the usual pleasantries, I demanded, "John, please appear." My friend's eyes, which were staring with bewilderment at my agitated manner and sudden appearance, glazed over instantly. I was speaking to the apostle John.

"Walk this way, my friend," he commanded, steering me down the garden path by the elbow. As soon as we were out of earshot, I demanded, "What happened on Friday; why were we not informed?"

John revealed, "We have been monitoring Colin for the past three months. We knew he would be part of the syndicate from the beginning, but" he said emphatically, "it's nothing to do with you who we chose to be in our syndicate; you are here to serve us!"

"You're right, you're the boss, still would have been nice to know. We wouldn't have had to keep secrets from Colin then."

"It was I who appeared in Colin's cabin, observing while he slept. I did not inform you of our intentions towards Colin. You are mere humans. It is probable that one of you would divulge the secret before he could be made aware of the importance of silence. Colin would then repeat this strange tale to somebody else and your secret would be out."

I realised with pleasure that we four were about to become five. There was no need to keep our secret from our friend.

John gave me a task. "Visit Colin and explain what actually took place on Friday night; you are to explain all."

Enough time had passed since I'd woken. I felt just about able to tackle breakfast. Returning home, I cooked a traditional English breakfast for two before phoning Colin, requesting he join me for food. As we ate, I told him the complete account of our experiences over the previous three months.

At the end, not surprisingly with such a bizarre account, Colin still appeared somewhat dubious, to say the least. "You're telling me that I've had the apostle John in my cabin, and I was talking to him on Friday night. You sure you haven't taken up drugs since I've been away?"

I guess it was a natural reaction to such an extraordinary and peculiar tale. However, I had the contents of our strongbox as evidence. Looking through the notes from heaven, Colin seemed unsure how to react, not surprising as I had just told him that he was part of the greatest story in the history of mankind. I'd followed this up with the news that his life was in danger because of it.

"So, I'm known personally to Jesus's apostles, Luke and John, but watch out because there is a group of devil worshippers who also want to kill me. Great, thanks, Martyn. I thought Venezuela was a dodgy run ashore. Seems the home counties is more dangerous."

"Stop moaning and embrace it," I told him tritely. "After all, your part of something massive, makes your life worth living, and you'll soon get used to the reality of John and Luke appearing through David."

Colin's initial response was obvious. "I want to meet John and Luke. I know I've met John once, or is it twice, but now I want to meet him with the benefit of understanding. Ask him some questions. It should be interesting."

"A slight problem. David and Sue have taken advantage of the late May bank holiday by going away to Kent for a few days," I informed the obviously disappointed Colin.

"Well, that's rude, just when I'm ready to believe and embrace him," he said.

I'd taken my time, comprehensively detailing our escapades to my friend, explaining how we'd started and what had happened since. Trish had taken notes and these now came in useful. Colin was able to read the transcripts of all our encounters.

Impatience is a normal human failing; there is no shame in this fact. Now he knew a little of our escapades, Colin was desperate to meet with John and Luke.

"It really is stupid timing of John, or David, whoever. I want to meet them," Colin moaned. Then he had an inspiration. "Why don't we use the calling table? There is only the two of us, but it should still be possible to make contact, after all, I've never tried it." I gazed into his eyes, full of excitement and expectation.

With only slight reluctance, I answered, "Probably not the best decision I've ever made but, OK, we'll give it a go."

Eagerly, Colin helped me clear the table and prepare the circle. I had done this so often before, the original letters safe in a drawer from the last time we'd used them. Colin seated himself on the floor facing the circle, with me opposite. Extending my finger to touch the base of the upturned glass beaker, I took the lead. "Is there anybody there?" I intoned. I repeated the question several seconds later. "Is there anybody there?" The glass remained stationary for a brief moment, then, slowly and erratically, it began to move towards the word *YES*, stopping and then returning to the centre of the circle.

Colin looked towards me, asking with a raised eyebrow, "Is this John?" He mistook my slight shake of the head as my not understanding his question. He asked again in an imperceptibly whisper, "Is this John?"

The question was aimed towards me, but our visitor responded. The glass began to move again, stopping by the NO and confirming my expectations that it wasn't John whom we'd contacted. I was worried. "I don't think we've reached one of our friends," I muttered, looking warily at Colin.

One of the lessons we'd been schooled in, was that most of the time they were watching over us. I just hoped that they were looking now.

None of my fears had occurred to Colin yet. I could sense the excitement within him as the realisation that the glass could only be moving by external forces dawned. He didn't yet appreciate there was a dangerous side to all of this.

"What is your name?" I asked, but the glass did not respond to my question. It remained stationary. I hoped that the spirit had left or, perhaps, even that the spirit was making way for John, but the glass remained motionless. I asked, "Are you still there, spirit?" It began to move, halting by the YES. Repeatedly we asked, "What is your name?" But to no avail. The glass simply stopped moving after reaching YES. It would reveal no further information.

I was now troubled and nervous by the situation. I guessed that the spirit which we'd disturbed wasn't a friendly one. The sooner we could end the experiment the better. But I decided it was best to keep these fears to myself.

Colin didn't seem to realise the danger. "Awesome, truly amazing," he kept repeating.

Remembering another lesson from our early training, I recalled Luke saying that it was very dangerous to walk away when you were in contact with a spirit. "If the glass is still possessed when contact is broken, the spirit can easily escape into the room and remain to haunt it," I said.

We were in my living room. I had no desire to release an unknown, probably antagonistic spirit, one which may wish me harm. I realised that we would have to stay until the scenario played out to a conclusion.

I then recalled the teaching, regarding the seven plains of existence. Colin had read the transcript earlier and asked questions. He would know what I was talking about once I'd started.

I asked, "Are you on plain seven of existence." The glass began to move. Luke had instructed that God alone occupied plain seven. Jesus and the apostles reside on plain six, down to mankind, who inhabited plain three. Plain two was the demonic kingdom, while plain one was the domain of the devil alone.

The glass stopped by the word NO, which wasn't unexpected. I ploughed on. "Do you reside on plain six." Immediately, the glass started to move, halting once more by the word NO. "Are you on plain five?" I asked. For a third time I received the same reply.

By now Colin had recognised anxiety in my voice. It was contagious; all his euphoria evaporated as he nervously asked me, "Is everything in existence on a plain?"

"If it exists as a conscious entity, then we've been educated that it has to be on a plain of existence; there are no exceptions!"

Our spirit denied existing on plain four, then three. There were two plains remaining – one didn't bear thinking about.

Repeatedly, I reminded Colin, "It's too dangerous. Don't walk away or break contact." By then, I was extremely worried by what we'd started.

"Are you on plain two?" I asked, fearing the affirmative. NO was the instant reply. Colin and I made eye contact, knowing that only one plain remained and the identity of plain one's occupant. There was little choice, I had to ask, "Are you on plain one?" The glass moved towards the two words. I swallowed, dry mouthed, watching the glass's progress across the table. NO. My eyes opened wider in surprise. I very nearly broke contact with the glass.

"That's a turn up for the book," said Colin.

The glass beaker glided back to the centre of the table. Before I could think of another question, if I could in such strange circumstances, the glass slowly began to circle. I couldn't gauge just what was happening, but I was alert enough to warn Colin. "This is worrying;

don't break contact, whatever you do!" The glass followed the inside of our circle of letters, now travelling with swift and purposeful movement. We were forced to stand up, simply to maintain our contact, as the glass sped up. I glanced up from the glass, looking towards my friend. Colin's eyes betrayed his anxiety.

"Not fun anymore," he said grimly, through gritted teeth.

Neither of us knew what was happening. "I'm sure it's evil; we have a problem. This is getting out of control," I warned him, concentrating on the beaker.

The beaker was moving faster than I ever thought possible; like a runaway roundabout, thundering through its relentless circle. I had problems keeping up with the speed. By now, my arm was beginning to hurt with the constant strain of maintaining contact.

Subconsciously my thoughts were for my home and the dangers caused by releasing an evil spirit into the flat. "It's impossible to remove a spirit, unless the spirit wants to go. Please don't let it loose into the flat. I've got to live here," I grunted, sweat forming on my brow.

"Let's try to slow the glass," I directed, in desperation.

By placing my left hand on my forearm and exerting pressure, I found it was possible to get a lot of downward force onto the base of the glass. Colin saw my actions and copied me, trying frantically to slow the glass. Between us we were exerting a lot of downward pressure onto the upturned base of that glass.

We were both well-built guys in our prime, but this made no difference whatsoever – the beaker maintained its pace. We were now in a situation, totally out of control.

Movement caused me to look to my left. I saw a book fly from the shelf, travelling several feet through the air to land on the floor; then another, and another, until the whole shelf emptied itself, one by one. A small china dog, a gift from Trish, leapt off the shelf, shattering two feet away from me. We jumped in fright, beginning to panic; we couldn't slow the glass.

Colin reached behind him with one arm, stretching to reach the window.

"What are you doing?" I asked, desperately hoping he had a plan.

He quickly explained, "We can't release the evil spirit into your home but if we can trap it in the glass, then we just might be able to dispose of it through an open window. I grasped Colin's intentions. A desperate plan and likely to fail, but it might be our only chance.

"I can't think of anything better," I told him.

Searching for something that we could place under the glass, I picked on an envelope, just within reach. Stretching, I managed to slide the envelope closer, within easy reach. This would have to be done in one swift movement. The window was open, ready. All I had to do was insert the envelope between the glass and the table. Then, I had to pick up the glass, with the envelope in place, hopefully preventing the malevolent spirit from escaping, before throwing the lot out of the window. I didn't care if this spirit wanted to haunt the gardens below the flat, but I certainly didn't want it to haunt my home.

"On the count of three," I warned, mentally preparing for action. I counted down. On the three, I dropped the envelope on the table, in front of the moving glass. The glass continued its movement, sliding over the edge, catching on the address box. Envelope and glass beaker continued onwards, coupled. Working with a swiftness borne of fear, we dragged the glass towards the edge of the table. Hastily I slid my free hand under the envelope, all the while retaining contact with the base of the glass.

"Gotcha," I yelled. Now we had it trapped. In my hands was a malevolent spirit, which, I hoped, was unable to escape.

As I pushed myself away from the table, twisting towards the window, I felt a searing pain of heat in my hands. My immediate reaction should have been to fling the glass away from myself, but this would have been disastrous. With the smell of burning flesh in my nostrils, I dived for the open window, throwing the glass as hard as I could.

With huge relief, we heard the tinkle of breaking glass in the gardens below.

"Now's the time for a witty one liner, something like hasta la vista, baby, but I'm all out of them," Colin said, peering out the window into the darkness.

When he next appeared, John was livid. After David returned from Kent, we waited two more days, Colin no longer as eager to seek spiritual insight. When he finally did appear, we were assembled in Colin's flat, the four of us schooling Colin on the teachings we'd been given.

John immediately turned towards the two ladies. "Please leave us and go home. I wish to speak to Martyn and Colin alone."

John's persona was one which made people obey him easily; his body language was such that Trish and Sue quickly jumped up without asking a single question, departing with a "See ya," firing a tiny smile of encouragement in our direction, before closing the door behind them.

We'd told them the complete version of our experiment. It was obvious why John wanted to talk with us on our own – we were in big trouble.

"You fools! Colin, you have some defence. But there is none for you, Martyn. You've been taught the dangers of meddling, yet you still persisted in putting yourself in danger," he barked, not allowing us any time to respond. "Do you realise, do you have the slightest inkling of the danger you were putting yourselves in?" John sighed loudly in exasperation.

There was no defence I could offer against this anger. I knew he was right. One of the important early lessons we'd been taught, with emphasis, was the danger of messing around on the calling table. I should have known better!

Colin glanced in my direction out of the corner of his eye, then grinned. An unwise move. John saw the grin and began to fume at Colin. "Do you really think this is a funny matter. Do you not realise that Satan himself covets your death? It was the Devil who you inadvertently contacted. Satan wants to occupy your home and frighten you off. If he had become loose in your flat, you would never sleep again. He can't touch David, but you are fair game. So, what do you do? You open the door for him and make it easy!" John concluded.

Colin and I stood there, like miscreant schoolboys chastised by the headmaster. This created a problem; I knew we were in the wrong; I had known how dangerous our experiment had been. But unfortunately, I was standing beside Colin. We'd been here before, being castigated in the headmaster's office. We couldn't help it, our eyes kept meeting, then a grin would inevitably begin.

My thoughts wandered back to those schooldays and the admonishments we'd received for schoolboy pranks. I knew that very soon we would collapse in helpless schoolboy laughter. We'd earned each other many hours of classroom detentions in situations like this. I tried turning my eyes away from Colin, focusing on a point over John's shoulder, but it was no good, the twinkle in my friend's eye kept drawing me.

John became even more irate with us, his anger both real and valid. Finally, he demanded in exasperation, "Do you really want to confront the devil?" Only one answer to this, a loud, "NO," but we were still smirking. We couldn't stop. Eventually John lost patience, announcing, "You can learn the hard way who it is you face." David's body flopped back, lifeless into his chair.

This turn of events was alarming. "Oops, I think we went too far," I whispered. The situation was no longer amusing. We sat down slowly, all the while examining the inert frame of David from across the room.

The eyes opened and a familiar repulsive hiss filled the room. Instantly, I knew what John meant by "the hard way". Lucifer looked at me, loathing in the eyes, spittle beginning to dribble from the corner of his mouth. He spoke with a harsh gravelly deep voice, which seemingly emitted from the back of his throat.

"Martyn, we meet again." I didn't feel the need to reply to this, allowing him to continue. "I am following your every move!" I knew this, but this didn't make the message any less disturbing.

The Devil stood up, moving towards me, talking as he came.

"Give it up. It's your only chance." He stood over me as I cowered in the chair. I smelled the same sulphurous odour as before. "Boy, you could do with some Colgate." I hoped I sounded braver than I felt. I could see Colin out of the corner of my eye, mesmerised, like a rabbit caught in the headlights.

My resolve failed. I reacted without thought. I wasn't going to remain there at his non-existent mercy. I shot my hands out, violently pushing Satan away from me as hard as I could, at the same time, shouting, "I'm getting out of here." My words had the same effect as a fox in a hen house. I'd moved first but Colin exploded out of his chair as if someone had dropped a cobra in his lap. He preceded me through the door of the room, then through the door of the flat. We pulled up short on the landing. The prince of darkness hadn't followed but we could still hear him. From the room came an indescribably horrific laughter, a deep resounding sound, which hung menacingly in the air.

I looked at Colin who said, "What do we do next?" We were trapped on the stairs outside Colin's flat.

"You may come in friends." Thankfully John had returned. Sheepishly, with heads bowed, and ever cautious, we entered the lounge. John justified his actions. "I wanted you to see the force of evil which opposes us and all that we stand for. The Devil and his demons," he advised, "are only part of this evil empire. You are aware of the devil's syndicates, whose job is to directly oppose your works and endeavours."

"Until now," John said, "they have only followed to intimidate but they will become bolder in their approach."

The lesson had finally been absorbed; there was no longer amusement when Colin and I glanced at one another. Things were only just beginning.

CHAPTER SIX

Beyond the evenings and weekends spent with John and Luke, we each had normal lives to live. Trish had been invited for a girls' night out with the girls from the office. Alongside Trish, there were three other girls. The four planned to celebrate a forthcoming birthday with a trip to "Supertramp's", the most popular of our local nightclubs.

I was pleased. An evening with Colin, and hopefully David, away from the business of the syndicate was just the thing I needed. "A few ice-cold Stella's whilst we while away the evening, talking sport and general rubbish – just the tonic." I told Trish.

Friday arrived. I'd promised to drive Trish and her friends to "Supertramp's".

After bolting my evening meal in front of the television, I drove over to collect her. When Trish goes out, she always makes a big effort. Tonight, was no different. Complementing her slight figure and dark hair, she wore a slinky emerald-green silk trouser suit, chosen to amplify the sparkle in her warm green eyes. Around her slim neck she wore a thin gold necklace, one I'd bought her the year before, for her birthday. The sheer simplicity of the necklace amplified the impact her beauty made on my humble senses. Her delicate perfume caressing my nostrils.

I conveyed to Trish the simple truth. "You look absolutely stunning. If it's possible, I've just fallen in love, all over again." I raised my eyes heavenward, secretly thanking the Lord that such a beautiful woman as Trish, bestowed with such an impulsive, vivacious nature, had found me attractive enough to want to know me. I half smiled as I thought, drolly, her major failing was probably poor taste in men.

Four twenty-something females, primed and prepared for a night's clubbing, were loud, laughing and boisterous.

"Martyn, do my tits look big in this?" said with a cheeky thrust of the chest. I kept my eyes on the road; it was all in jest. I only had eyes for Trish. I accepted I was going to be the butt of many jokes during the two-mile journey from Trish's house. I didn't mind in the least. They were out to have a good time. "Have a great night. Try to behave, at least a little." I wished them well as they disgorged from the car in the town centre.

Returning home, I walked straight past the front door of my flat up to Colin's. That night we'd arranged a drink in the Wellington. With David and Sue having been warned, they were making the best of the short reprieve, a meal for two. It was decided, Colin and I were having a lad's night out.

The two of us were soon joined by some of the friends we'd neglected over the previous months. We relaxed, enjoying a pleasant evening, swapping jokes and stories, generally unwinding with a couple of pints. One of the regulars, our friend Mike, did comment, "You seem to be exclusive these days, ignore us most of the time. What have we done?" But the landlord Ken saved me.

"He's in love. Even I would prefer to spend my time looking at Trish than your ugly mug."

By midnight, though restricting the beer intake to only three pints, I had thoroughly enjoyed myself. Letting our hair down and occasionally living a normal life helped to relieve the worries of our other-worldly existence.

Across town, the four girls were also having a wonderful time. Before reaching the nightclub, they'd settled in one of the town centre pubs enjoying a few drinks. Unlike the Wellington, they'd chosen a modern-styled, disco-themed pub, one frequented by the town's younger generation, all looking for excitement and stimulation. The music was loud, the décor, one of chrome, glass and mirrors. The girls leaned forwards, raising their glasses and shouting into the din. "Happy birthday, Lyndsay," repeating the exercise several times, while trying out various cocktails on the way. By the time they left the pub, Trish and her colleagues, Lyndsay, Sarah and Alison, were all slightly liberated, laughing loudly during the forty metres to Supertramp's.

They were in luck, the four of them managing to obtain a table for themselves in an area locally known as *the mezzanine*. A section of seating close to the dance floor which was raised several feet. The mezzanine was just far enough away from the sound system so that they could have a conversation, without having to shout at the top of their voices.

Lyndsay, Sarah and Alison were all young, and single. Influenced by mother nature and alcohol, they quickly began noticing and appraising the male club goers.

"Cor, look at the bum on him," Alison yelled, pointing, causing a young man to blush deep beetroot.

The club started to fill up. The four girls were soon being asked onto the dance floor. Trish was happy to join in when dancing with friends around handbags, but she rejected all advances from would-be male suitors.

Sarah, in particular, was enjoying a great night out. The weekend was here, and it was rare that she made it to a nightclub; she was letting her hair down. Sarah had hardly left the dance floor, since arriving at the club. One particular partner of Sarah's was slightly different from the run-of-the-mill, regular male club goer in Supertramp's. Usually, the young men in the town's nightclubs were freshly scrubbed lads from the factories and offices of the small town, slightly self-conscious and dressed to impress in their Sunday best. Sarah now found herself dancing with a tall, slim dark-haired man. Her dance partner was immaculately dressed in a dark charcoal suit, which must have been made to measure. The image was completed with a black cashmere polo neck under the suit jacket and discrete gold jewellery. Slightly older than the average guy in Supertramp's, Sarah guessed that he was in his thirties.

On Friday nights all the club goers dressed to please, but there was something about the confidence and poise of this stranger, causing him to stand out from those around him. His presence was almost arrogant, a man who was utterly confident in himself and his own capabilities.

Sarah laughed as he leaned forward and spoke to her, lightly gripping her elbow as he did so. The pair remained together for the next track, then a third, until Sarah's partner again leant forward, bringing his mouth close to her ear, suggesting something. His words were agreeable.

She nodded assent, turning away from the dancers, leading her new friend by the hand towards her three companions seated at the table.

Over the sound of the music, Sarah introduced the gentleman. "Girls, this is Jerome Brendon-Smythe." Jerome smiled confidently at the three girls, gazing directly into each of their eyes, before bending and kissing each on the hand.

"My evening is now perfect; may I buy each of you lovely ladies a drink to make my night complete?" While Jerome was away at the bar, Sarah excitedly updated the others with what she had learnt about him. "He told me that he is the owner and director of a kitchen equipment company. It's obvious from the cut of his suit and the subtle gold jewellery, Jerome has both money and taste." Sarah was excited that she'd managed to entice a guy such as this, amongst all the self-conscious town boys.

On returning, Jerome effortlessly and gracefully complimented each of the girls as he presented her with a drink. "You are a jewel to delight any eye," he told Trish, as he passed a vodka and tonic over the tabletop. Jerome squeezed into the space between Trish and Sarah, his conversation flowing easily as he enchanted all four with his charm and sophistication. In such fascinating company, the girls were captivated. The evening passed enjoyably. Jerome effortlessly managed to involve all four in the conversation, freely distributing compliments to all around.

Trish thought that Sarah looked slightly miffed now that Jerome was being shared equally with her friends, but he was such easy and pleasant company. Sarah found she was unable to resent him for not giving her his undivided attention.

The club was due to close at two in the morning. The last half hour has always been devoted to slow dancing, enabling couples to get to know each other intimately. The DJ announced, "We're winding it up, guys and dolls. It's time for the first slow one of the night. All you lovers out there, grab your partner and ease in close."

Jerome immediately turned to Sarah, politely but expectantly, inviting, with a grin. "Shall we get close?" Laughing with pleasure, she gladly took his hand as he led her towards the crowded dance floor.

Sarah expected to stay enclosed in Jerome's arms until the slow tracks finished but Jerome had other ideas. After the first dance, to Sarah's dismay, he led her back to the table, before asking Lyndsay. "I've been entertained by the four of you; would you like to dance?" After a moment's hesitation, and a quick glance at her sulky friend, Lyndsay accepted, joining Jerome on the darkened dance floor, merging with the other slowly gyrating couples. When they returned to the table, Jerome turned to Alison, again asking, "Alison would you do me the honour of joining me on the dancefloor?" The couple enjoyed a pleasurable few minutes together before returning.

Cutting through the music, the DJ announced to the throng, "This is the penultimate dance; only one more slow number after this." Jerome turned to Trish, asking with a warm smile, "Surely the beautiful Trish can spare a few minutes to give me the pleasure of her company and a dance?" Trish gave Sarah a glance, reflecting for several moments before deciding; it was only a dance. It would have been churlish to refuse such pleasant company. She returned the smile. "Of course, it's a delight." Taking her proffered hand, Jerome led her towards the assembled crowd.

After we left the pub, I willingly accepted Colin's invitation. "Fancy a coffee? No work in the morning." We continued the conversation for a couple of hours, drinking several cups of coffee. By half one in the morning, the working week was catching up with me. I felt tired, beginning to think about retreating homewards, and bed. Trish would be taking a taxi home with her three friends and, although Saturday meant I could enjoy a lie in, I didn't want to waste all morning in bed.

As I was taking my leave from the flat, Colin's mobile rang. I waited while he answered, wondering who would be calling him at this hour, Colin listened to the caller, a look of concern appearing briefly across his face. I indicated I was leaving, mouthing, "see you tomorrow," whilst waving cheerio, but Colin held his hand up, signifying that I should wait. He replaced the phone in his pocket before turning towards me to divulge his concern.

"That was Sue; she's just had a visitation from John! He said Trish is in danger from a member of the devil's syndicate!"

My blood froze. This was very disconcerting news indeed. "What's happening? What did John say?" I demanded details. But Colin could only repeat what he had been told. "John told Sue that Trish is in some kind of danger at the nightclub; that is all I know. After that, David returned. Sue doesn't know what the danger consists off. She's as confused and frightened as you are. Probably more so if I know Sue."

Immediately I called Trish's mobile number, but she must have turned it off, or the music was too loud to hear. "Come on, answer you silly woman," I muttered, pacing up and down. I tried several more times, but there was no answer.

I had to decide what action to take, quickly. The club was just over a mile from my town centre flat. I considered jumping in the car and driving straight over but I rejected the idea immediately. Although I hadn't drunk a lot that evening, it was a risk I couldn't take. As a runner, I could cover a mile in just over six minutes – this would probably be faster than driving.

Ordering Colin to follow at his own pace, I hurtled down the three flights of stairs, bursting through the doors onto the darkened street. Adrenaline gave me extra speed as I ran through the deserted town centre. The simple, methodical act of running let me to think and plan ahead. Deliberately, I allowed my pace to slow, realising that it would be unwise to arrive out of breath and unready for action. Praying, I hoped that my rugby playing colleague, Jamie Boulder, would be acting as doorman that night, a job he did occasionally.

The bright lights off the club door came into view. I slowed to a walk, eagerly looking around for Jamie. I couldn't see him among the doormen, but I did recognise one of the other doormen, a friend of Jamie. I asked him if Jamie was on duty. Disappointingly he reported, "Sorry, mate, Jamie's not on until tomorrow night." The despair was short-lived. I asked, as Jamie's mate, if I could go inside and collect my girlfriend.

The doorman agreed before turning away towards another club goer.

Trish allowed Jerome to lead her through the milling crowds and onto the edge of the dance floor, joining with the mass of entwined dancers. Once on the darkened floor, he pulled her into his arms, beginning to sway to the music. Warily, Trish tried to maintain a slight distance between herself and Jerome. "Not too close. I'm spoken for," but Jerome had other ideas. Covered by the surrounding darkness, Jerome placed his hand on Trish's bum cheeks, roughly pulling her towards him. Trish reacted instinctively, attempting to pull away. "Hang on there, you're acting way too forward!" but Jerome easily held her against him. He thrust his hips and groin forward, attempting to force body contact, rubbing his body against hers.

With one arm locked around her waist, Jerome used his other hand to drag Trish's head forward, bringing it close to his own. He leant forwards, beginning to nuzzle her neck and ears. Trish who, until now, had only resisted half-heartedly decided enough was enough. "Stop!" she commanded, trying to pull away in earnest. "Stop it now! This is not right. Let me go!" Jerome held her there with ease, his slobbering tongue trying to probe for her ear. He whispered, "Gods harlot, you're going to be screwed by a real man!"

Gradually understanding dawned at the implication of this statement. All of a sudden Trish experienced real fear at her predicament, increasing her struggles within his captive arms.

Jerome removed the hand which held Trish's waist, smothering her mouth with his own to stifle her scream. Savagely, he forced his free hand inside her trouser suit. Buttons gave way as the flimsy material tore. His free arm around her neck had her in a crushing hold. Jerome's other hand advanced relentlessly towards Trish's breasts. Roughly he squeezed her nipples between two fingers, brutally digging his nails into her flesh. Trish was being smothered by Jerome's face and mouth, unable to scream, her arms trapped by his. Fellow dancers, unaware that they were anything but an overly amorous couple.

Inside she felt sick and frightened as she fought against her invader. Jerome turned his attention elsewhere, thrusting his hand further down her body, inside the waistband of her panties, gripping pubic hair with cruel disregard, his fingers searching for her sex. Finally, Trish managed to jerk her head away from Jerome's smothering embrace. "No," she screamed at the top of her voice.

I pushed my way determinedly through the crowds, all making their way to the exit. I desperately searched for any sign of Trish in the darkened room. Scanning around, I noticed Alison, Lyndsay and Sarah talking at their table, but no Trish. Before I could reach the three girls to enquire after her, I heard a scream on the dance floor. I had no doubt to the originator of the scream – it had to be Trish. I was now running, pushing people out of the way in my desire to reach my beautiful lady. Just then, the lights came on, bathing the club in a harsh white light, illuminating the shabby interior of this popular club. I barged past the last dancer and my eyes fell on Trish as she broke away from an elegantly attired gent. She had tears streaming from her eyes, ruining her mascara. Focusing on the scene before me, I noticed the torn and dishevelled state of her clothing. I lost my temper! Stepping forward, I hit the man on the jaw, as hard as I could.

The two bouncers arrived at that very moment, pushing through the crowds to investigate the screams; they sprang forward, grabbing my arms, pinning them by my side. The two restrained my anger for several seconds, in a vice-like grip, until they noticed that I was no longer struggling. Warily they relaxed, cautiously releasing me from their hold, prepared to spring forward and restrain me if I made the slightest movement towards my crumpled victim.

Jerome, who had promptly collapsed in a heap at my feet, staggered up from the floor, still dazed and groggy from the punch. Vaguely, I noticed that we were in the centre of a ring of spectators. Then it dawned on me, I recognised this man; I had last seen him during a day out to Buckler's Hard. He had been getting into the Jaguar.

The manager of the club arrived, pushing his way through the milling crowds of gawping spectators, eager to discover the reason for this noisy disturbance.

"What's all this? What's all the fuss about? The manager, a short middle-aged greasy type of man, balding, and sweating in the heat of the club, looked on with disdain at Trish and Jerome. Trish, who still sobbed wretchedly, forced her way past the bouncers to attach herself to my side.

"What's the explanation for this?" the manager demanded, pointing at Jerome.

Trish sobbed loudly. "He groped me. He tried to rape me," she announced, still shaking with fear, pointing at Jerome. Jerome, who had by now recomposed himself, angrily denied it.

"I didn't do any such thing; she forced herself on me." His countenance turned puce as he professed outrage at such a statement. Trish remained silent at this false accusation, simply pointing at the ripped and open jumpsuit. The evidence was there for all to see. A ripple of consternation passed through the crowd.

Lyndsay and Alison arrived on the scene, bursting through the wall of bystanders with Sarah in tow. Turning towards the manager, they indignantly denied everything. "Trish wouldn't do such a thing. She's in love with Martyn." Clucking like mother hens, they made a beeline for Trish.

The club's manager turned to his bouncers, asking, "Did you witness anything?"

Unfortunately, the bouncers had only heard Trish's screaming over the sound of the music; they'd gone to investigate. "We arrived on the dance floor just in time to see him landing the punch on his jaw," one of them replied, indicating Jerome. "She definitely looks like she's been in the wars," he said, pointing at Trish.

It was obvious from the state of Trish's bedraggled and torn clothing that she was probably telling the truth. Another murmur of discontent rose from the assembled onlookers. I picked up several individual comments, all aimed at Jerome, but it was still his word against hers. There were no witnesses, not even me. The club's manager could do nothing, not unless Trish wanted to make the complaint official.

The manager turned towards Trish who was being consoled by the comforting presence of Lyndsay, Sarah and Alison. "Do you want to take this any further?" His manner made it clear, he was more interested in the reputation of his club.

I glanced at Jerome who stood there rubbing his jaw, feigning indifference as his fate was decided. Spotting my glance, Jerome mouthed the word, "death." He allowed a slight smirk to form on his lips. I stared back defiantly, glaring at this arrogant, haughty man. For several seconds I looked deep into those dark evil eyes, accepting the challenge, revealing my contempt for him, before finally turning away, focusing my attention on the manager.

The manager in question was earnestly imploring, "Look, you can take it further, but there's no proof; the police will simply drop the case."

Trish knew that she had to accept there was little that could be done. She sniffed, wiping her eyes with my hanky. "Make him go away," she said, pointing at Jerome. "I just want Martyn to take me home."

Probably fearing the consequences of his actions being divulged in an open court, Jerome contemptuously advised the manager, "I guess I don't want to press charges against him. He's not very strong; he hardly touched me." I smiled back, relishing the punch which was now causing a ripe purplish swelling on his jaw. Once again, we locked eye contact for four or five seconds. Jerome sneered back at me disdainfully, the corner of those thin lips twisting as we appraised each other critically. We both knew this wasn't the end, this was just the beginning.

CHAPTER SEVEN

Early the next morning, I awoke still angry. I looked down tenderly at the sleeping Trish, who'd come home with me the previous evening. Trish, so independent and self-secure, but twice during the night she'd cried out, thrashing about in her sleep. I had turned to her, holding her close until the night terrors subsided.

After we'd left the club, Trish and I met an agitated Colin, being frustrated by the bouncers on the door. Once I'd had a quiet word, the doormen, who knew of my association with Jamie, willingly agreed to prevent Jerome from leaving, giving us a chance to get Trish into a taxi and away from the town centre. Jamie's friend noticed the state Trish was in. He glowered towards the lit doorway of the club.

"It will be a pleasure," he informed us, seemingly relishing the chance to prevent Jerome leaving.

This was all very well but I knew that if Jerome was in the club, then his villainous friends wouldn't be far away. I was thankful to get the four girls, Colin and myself into the MPV taxi. On our way home the taxi dropped Trish's three very subdued and anxious colleagues off, before returning us to the flat.

Once safely home, we'd phoned a, by then, frantic Sue and David, letting them know what had just happened. "It's okay, I've got her. She's had a bad time but I'm with her. I'll protect her with my life," I told them dramatically, before finishing the call. Turning towards a tearful and dishevelled Trish, it was obvious that she needed my comforting presence far more than any theatrical promises.

Trish stirred as I sat up in the bed, twisting my body and plonking my feet on the floor. I waited and watched, seeing her eyes open, uncomprehending at first as she slowly regained consciousness. I saw the relief flash in her eyes as she recognised me gazing down at her.

Relief followed by consternation, then recollection, as the previous evening's events flooded her thoughts. "Oh, Martyn, thank goodness it's you." I reached out, holding her tightly as the fear slowly departed.

While showering, I noted that my knuckles were bruised and sore from connecting with Jerome's jaw. It felt slightly painful to clench the fist, but I grinned, realising it was a price worth paying. Fortunate it was the closed season, I would , never have been able to play rugby that day, although there was no way I would leave Trish's side, anyway.

Sue arrived first thing, eager to bolster her younger sibling and keen to learn the full detail of Trish's ordeal. We stayed indoors, seeking the comfort of familiar surroundings as well as each other's company.

The anger remained with me, simmering throughout the day. As time passed, Trish regained a little of her vitality and spirit. She was difficult to suppress for long, but she was happy to stay indoors and recover; she wasn't going to leave the flat just yet.

Trish spent a lot of her day talking on the phone, reassuring Lyndsay, Alison and particularly Sarah. "I'm okay, Martyn's with me. I don't blame you for bringing him to the table; you weren't to know he was evil. He seemed so normal." Trish glanced over to me, knowing her use of the word evil had been deliberate.

While Trish talked, I was busy arranging for Sue, David and Colin to visit that evening. It was frustrating to me. There seemed no practical outlet for the anger, which was beginning to simmer slowly. I wanted to take the battle to Jerome and his friends but there was no way of finding out where they lived.

Instead, I chose to direct my wrath at the nearest available target, John, for allowing Trish to be endangered in such a crude way, while refusing to reveal what we were called to do or be. I was determined to speak with John as soon as possible. I wanted a confrontation to demand a full explanation.

With Sue demonstrating maternal concern for her younger sister and surrounded by a wave of compassion, Trish began to relax further, allowing us glimpses of her normal, energetic and vivacious self.

David and Colin arrived early evening, showing slight annoyance that I was so brusque and insistent. "You only have to ask normally. There is no need to tell me I have no choice, I'm quite happy to be here," David told me reproachfully. Mentally, I reined myself in, reminding myself that David wasn't John. David was as concerned as the rest of us at Trish's ordeal.

John permitted David to receive a mug of coffee before making his appearance. I'd been scrutinising David closely, instantly recognising the tell-tale glazing within the eyes, and the slight shift in body posture. This time I was in no mood for pleasantries. Angry and fearful, I was going to demand answers. "John, please explain why Trish had to be placed in so much danger without warning. Where is our protection? Why weren't we fully warned of the opposition at the very start?" And, importantly for me, "Why have we been placed in increasing danger four times, without knowing the real reason for our existence as a syndicate?" Trish, Sue and Colin looked on, content to allow me to express my frustrations. John said very little, sitting there quietly as I gave utter to my vexation. John gave me the freedom to rant, releasing emotions based on fear.

At last, I slowed to a stop, gradually calming down having had the chance to express my irritation. I'd recognised before starting that I'd directed my anger and disappointment at the wrong target. "I'm sorry, John. I know it's not you, but you are the only target available."

For the first time that evening, John spoke, responding to my tirade. "You are perfectly right, my friends. I should have given you a more specific warning of the dangers you face."

This admission took some of the wind from my sails; I'd expected John to respond assertively. I'd almost planned for this, as a way to release my pent-up frustration. I was temporarily lost for words, exasperated at being hurtled from a safe mundane everyday existence into this dangerous, precarious roller coaster of an adventure.

I stood before the contrite apostle, hands planted on hips. In my irritation, I hadn't even noticed that I'd risen to my feet.

Within seconds the anger evaporated. I suddenly realised I was looking foolish and immature, angry with John for no reason.

John, though, wasn't annoyed at my outburst. Instead, he deflected it, apologising to Trish for her terrible experience. "Please forgive us. When it became clear the evil syndicate was planning a foray into your town, we should have warned you."

What became evident to all gathered in my humble, suburban lounge was that John really meant these words.

Finally, John relaxed a little, revealing more information about the battle between good and evil. "I will have to have permission to disclose the reason for your existence as a syndicate. I will ask the Lord."

He explained, "You are the first syndicate on Earth to have a direct method of contact with myself and the other apostles. I have told you previously that there are other syndicates in existence, but you are the only ones with this form of communication. The opposition from the devil's syndicate is expected, but we underestimated the ferocity and speed of the attack. I was unprepared for the response, which has been instantly forthcoming. Once you were formed into a syndicate, we expected them to take their time, to build up to this level of attack."

John turned to Trish. "Rather than yourself and Sue here being frightened going about your everyday life, if you so desire, I will end your syndicate and erase your memories. You will all return to a quiet and safe existence."

Any residual annoyance was extinguished with John freely admitting that he, an apostle of Jesus Christ could make a mistake. This left me feeling oafish and bad-tempered.

Once again, I felt fired up, ready to do the Lord's good works, whatever they were?

My companions, who'd sat passively observing the exchange from the couch, also seemed inspired. I studied Trish, expecting, but dreading, to observe fear or even horror at the thought of continuing. She managed a weak smile before rising to her feet and hugging me. "We can't give in to evil, because then, evil will win."

"Good, that is what I expected you to say, but you have to choose." John showed evident relief that Trish stayed committed but there was the question of protection for us all. "We are opposed by the most evil force in the universe; we need protection," we told him.

Ominously, John warned, "These evil interventions and attacks won't go away. They will only get increasingly intrusive and persistent." But he promised, "Protection is imminent; you are monitored night and day. If any of the devil's syndicate comes close, then you will have the full protection of a host of angels. Things will get worse, but you will be getting physical protection, very soon. I will seek permission from the father to explain the reason for your existence."

After this disclosure, John left. David returned, eager to know exactly what had been revealed in his absence. We passed on the teachings and advice to an already anxious David. "Well, there is some good news but, also, we are all in a lot of danger which will only get worse." Not surprisingly, after these depressing revelations, the unanimous decision was for a quiet Saturday night in front of the television.

The following day we had no other plans, but it was becoming a ritual, Lynda and Richard invited David and myself to their home for Sunday lunch. David and I were happy to encourage this fledgling tradition; there is nothing better than a good meal with friends, and Lynda was proving to be an excellent hostess.

For once she waived the traditional Sunday lunch, opting for a lighter option of Merlot and honey-glazed lamb, salad and a couscous enthused with peppers and raisins. She loved to experiment in the kitchen, so David and I happily found ourselves willing guinea pigs. To Lynda's obvious delight, we applauded it. "Again, a triumph for your culinary skills. Excellent, just the right amount of spice and flavour, cooked to perfection!" I enthused, kissing my fingers in simulated appreciation.

"One of your most successful yet, and that's directed at the best chef I've met," David charmed, drawing a quick blush of pleasure in response.

After such a large lunch, I was looking forward to sitting down with Richard and David, allowing the meal to digest, watching the afternoon's sport on television, hopefully with a glass of wine or cup of tea.

Sadly, to my consternation, Trish had other ideas. "No way, Mr Holloway. On your feet, we're going out." Dragging me up from the comfort of the sofa, she insisted, "You're coming with me. Toby needs a walk, so you're not blobbing there doing nothing all afternoon – move it lard arse!"

"I see you've regained some of your va-va-voom," I muttered, lurching to my feet, mentally preparing for a walk across the fields and down to the river, which meandered gently through the meadow behind their estate.

For June, the day was bracing, colder than the average temperature for that time of year. Low grey clouds scudded across the depressing windswept sky. Pulling my jacket tight, I briefly envied David and Richard, back in the warmth, sustained by an endless supply of tea, biscuits and home-made cakes, that were always within reach.

Grudgingly, I conceded. There was no reason to complain. The riverside walk was indeed enjoyable, as long as I wrapped up against the brisk wind. With Trish by my side, I decided, what could be better?

We walked along the riverbank, hand in hand, greeting similar couples and lone walkers as we passed with a smile and an "afternoon." Toby was delighted with his afternoon excursion, contentedly running ahead to investigate any strange smell he could find, stopping to cock his leg and scent his territory, before burrowing under the bushes in futile attempts to capture the wild meadow residents.

Trish linked her arm with mine, leaning in towards me, choosing to rest her head contentedly on my shoulder! "You okay?" I asked, giving her a brief hug of support, recalling her recent ordeal.

"You know, Martyn, sometimes life just feels so perfect, the future all rosy and bright; then I think about our secret life and what happened to me on Friday. Sometimes I get a cold shiver up my spine, as if someone's walked over my grave."

I hugged her again, anxious to relieve her fear. "You shouldn't worry," I answered. "Remember what John said last night, how we are protected and how there are other syndicates to protect us, all supported by hordes of angels. We've got more protection than the queen," I declared dubiously.

"I know," she said. "It's just the enormity of what's happening. I wasn't expecting this when we started playing on the board for the first time."

I sensed that now she'd had time to reflect and think, Friday's ordeal may have taken more of a toll than she cared to mention. I questioned then, was it time to think again? In reflection, would Trish choose to walk away.

"You heard what John said. If you have had further thoughts and want to pull out, I will support you all the way. We can tell John to forget it, ask him to erase our memories if that is what you want." I said, hoping for the sake of Trish's peace of mind that my ardent desire to continue didn't show too much.

"No bonehead," she said, squeezing my arm. Stopping for a moment to turn and gaze deep into my eyes, she gave me a warm smile of encouragement. "I meant what I said. We walk away, then evil wins. We were chosen for a reason. It's just sometimes, until we know that reason, then" – she hesitated a moment – "well sometimes, something like Friday makes it a bit daunting; his clammy hands left me feeling so dirty and grimy, but it's a price that has to be paid." Trish shuddered and grimaced, recollecting her experience.

I stopped walking again, pulling her towards me for a proper hug. "Don't worry. They'll have to come through me first, before they can touch a hair on your head," I whispered, holding her as tightly as I could. All the while, wondering to myself if I had the ability to keep this promise.

After three enjoyable hours along the river, we arrived home at six in the evening. A contented but exhausted Toby flopped down into his bed beside Lynda's chair.

Rosy-cheeked from the bracing wind, we were more than ready for the buffet tea which Lynda prepared every Sunday, just in case the massive lunchtime meal didn't quite satiate our appetites.

I delight in that type of carefree day – good company, good conversation and no worse worries than work the following day. Having built up quite an appetite from our riverside trek, we were again ready to tuck into another one of Lynda's delicious spreads. An informal relaxed meal was laid out, buffet style, on the kitchen island, eaten from plates resting on our knees. On Sunday evening it was always help yourself, as and when required.

Piling my plate high, I again complimented a delighted Lynda. "I don't know how you do it; your meals are the highlight of my weekend, and today I've had the pleasure of knowing I've worked up an appetite this afternoon."

I smiled benevolently towards my lazy friend David, conveniently forgetting Trish's input, feeling self-satisfied and superior for having successfully resisted the temptation to collapse into a chair and do nothing but gawk at sport, all afternoon.

The lazy June afternoon turned gently into evening as we helped ourselves to generous plates of cold meats and salad.

The meal completed, the four of us shared the clearing up and washing of dishes. Giving us, the younger generation, some unaccompanied and quality time together. Richard and Lynda took the opportunity to disappear, settling in the lounge for a Sunday evening's viewing. Once the final pot was in the dishwasher, Trish, David and I remained in the kitchen, content with our own company.

Recognising that we were heading for a "boring political debate" as she called them, Sue jumped down from her stool. "You carry on. I'm going to join the fogies in the lounge, to watch *Antiques Roadshow*."

Lynda's kitchen was a large bright room, very white and modern; the high-gloss handle-free cupboards, contrasting the slate-grey granite worktops and island. With a cream tiled floor, the only splash of bright colour came from cheerful watercolour originals of fruits or flowers, which Lynda loved to exhibit on her clean white walls.

I seated myself on a stool, facing Trish and David across the island; they'd both chosen to sit on the opposite side, possibly a reflection of the adversarial nature of British politics. The conversation had indeed become heated in its nature. Politics and current affairs, discussed and debated with the passion and conviction of youth.

In a subconsciously agreed decision, our conversation refused to include John and our secret life. We were all secretly trying to avoid talking about it for a while, respecting Trish and her need to fully come to terms with the ordeal. I was determined not to allow the conversation to drift towards the unworldly. It seemed that Trish and David were on the same wavelength as we avoided any talk of the spiritual world.

Most probably, John would have respected Trish's, and our wishes to be left alone for the evening, but the unwelcome guest who did appear certainly didn't have any respect for Trish, or concerns over her fears.

I was busy making a forceful point to Trish about a government minister. "The man's a buffoon; he hasn't got the intelligence to run a pub, let alone a government department." Without warning, David arched his back and hissed violently, his eyes rolling back into his head. Trish left the stool in a millisecond, scuttling around the island to grab hold of my hand. Pulling her arm, I made a prompt retreat towards the door. Halting our flight at the back door, we prepared for an instant withdrawal to the garden. We both turned fearfully, seeking to establish the situation generated by this latest development.

Quickly realising there was no pursuit and also no danger, as yet, to the unsuspecting family in the next room, Trish and I let out a collective sigh of relief. "Don't say it's going to happen again," Trish groaned, squeezing my hand.

David was looking at us quizzically, seated on his stool as if nothing had happened. He appeared perturbed. In David's words, "You instantly materialised at the other side of the room, by the door, without appearing to move."

Keeping distance and the island between us, I asked him, "Did you feel anything strange in the past few seconds?"

Because of our instantaneous transmogrification, David was aware that he'd probably had a visitation. "Obviously something's happened! You don't just suddenly appear on the other side of the room, but I felt nothing whatsoever," he claimed.

Warily we slowly edged forwards, Trish choosing to perch by my side, the kitchen island as a barrier between herself and David.

Gradually the conversation resumed its previous theme. Twenty minutes later, David, again, violently arched his back and hissed loudly. This time we were both in a safer position; there was no immediate need to run. Instead, we stayed where we were, protected by the kitchen island. Trish grabbed hold of my arm, voicing the same concern that had just occurred to me. "This noise is going to bring one of my parents to investigate any moment!" I had gloomy visions of Lynda entering, unsuspectingly into hell incarnate, simply by walking into her own kitchen.

"There's nothing we can do about it," I told Trish. "Hopefully it won't come to that."

On this occasion, as David's body relaxed from the spasms, the beast remained; he had gained domain. Instantly, he began spitting vile abuse towards Trish and myself. In particular, Trish was vilified, the encounter with Jerome being the thrust of the attack. To her open-mouthed horror, Trish was called all kinds. "You are a whore, a degenerate slut who opens her legs for anybody. Jerome is going to take you at his leisure. He will force Martyn to watch." Trish stood there inactive, facing down the abuse without a word. I could feel her holding onto my arm as if it were the last lifebelt on the Titanic, her fingernails digging deep into my forearm.

Deep within, I understood. This abuse was aimed as much at myself as Trish. I was afraid to look away from the beast, scared of his actions were I to be distracted. I tightened my grip on Trish's hand, squeezing it, trying to communicate the knowledge that I was with her, by her side. Instinctively, Trish understood; this was a challenge for us both. She returned my squeeze, remaining impassive, whispering, "Hold on to it; don't let him win." She continued listening to the torrent of abuse with a dead-pan expression fixed on her face.

Knowing that this verbal assault was for my benefit was one thing, but I could still feel the red mist rising. Trish was right, I was fighting my own internal battle to remain unresponsive. Again, I felt Trish squeeze my hand, conveying the awareness that we were in this together. That I was doing the right thing not reacting. "Hold on, Martyn, you're winning, we both are." At last, running out of insults, the beast slumped on the stool, silent for the moment.

The words came from David's lips. Having regained control of David's frame, John spoke. We recognised John, his voice and body language, but we still remained out of reach, protected by the kitchen island between us.

John spoke softly, almost apologetically. "The devil has slipped through our defences. After the actions of his disciple, the evil one knows that Trish is demoralised and undecided. The devil wants to capitalise on this. He is hoping you will be overwhelmed, forcing you to turn away from us, and the syndicate."

"I can only hold the beast off for a certain amount of time; I am already under great strain. The beast is fighting desperately to regain possession and control of David's body.

"Move closer, grasp both of David's hands in yours. You must be prepared to oppose Lucifer when he arrives."

Gingerly, I edged forward, Trish glued to my shoulder. I grabbed his hands, gripping as tightly as I could, remembering how weak I'd seemed the last time. Staring deep into John's eyes, I received last minute instructions. Repeatedly John emphasised, "Your only weapon is love."

What happened to white, I thought, looking around at the kitchen walls.

"He has become too strong in ownership. The devil hates love, the pure unsullied love of friendship between David and you is an anathema to Satan. He hates something that he can't control or debase into a sordid imitation. If he feels the love directed towards David, then he won't remain." John warned, "You have to keep stressing your love for David. You have to seek deep within and believe, then you will drive the devil from David's body; your love has to be from the heart.

"Good luck, your task is a difficult one, but we are with you," John promised, as I watched the eyes lose focus.

It was terrifying, but there was no choice. I could not let David down. I felt Trish's hand give my shoulder one final squeeze. "I'm with you, Martyn. I love you and I don't need to fake that one." Feeling like a condemned martyr, I waited.

Over my shoulder, I suggested to Trish, "Go and watch *Antiques Roadshow*." But to my immense relief, she flatly refused, insisting, "Sorry, not my type of telly, and you're a sexist pig for even thinking of getting me out of the way. If you are going to get splattered, then I want to watch." She managed to find humour, even at this darkest time.

"Okay," I replied, "but hang back, remain out of reach of a possible lunge; remember the damage he did to my face. I'm here in the lead because of my greater strength; there is no sense in both of us getting hurt, just to prove a point."

Trish nodded in agreement. "That's fine, I have no worries about letting you get a beating instead of me, doesn't mean I'm going to run away though."

I had few doubts about Trish's opinion of my outdated, chivalrous attitudes.

John appeared briefly, speaking softly. "Be strong and be ready, Martyn. I am with you." I could still hear the strain in his voice as he struggled to hold the beast.

Finally, John's spiritual strength gave way; the body arched backwards away from me, nearly ripping the wrists from my grasp. Again, he emitted that horrible unearthly hiss through clenched teeth. The head shot back towards me, snarling as he rose.

There were no thoughts in my head other than beating this devil. Up close, I could smell the foul breath, the repellent sulphurous combination of rotting flesh and sewage; worse than we'd noticed during the night of terrors. This time, I thought grimly as I hung on, the devil has a better toehold within David's being. "And still no toothpaste, dog breath," I gasped.

Determinedly, I struggled to retain my grip on his wrists, feeling the strength of my opposition.

The eyes bored into my soul, showing no relation to David, for whom I fought. Yellow and bloodshot, the irises almost black. Scornful eyes, glaring back at me, full of pure undiluted hatred. It is said that the eyes are the doorway to the soul. Fighting to sustain a hold of the wrists, I continued to stare unceasingly, straight into the eyes of hell, incessantly repeating the message out loud, again and again. "Leave our friend. Go, we love him, we want him back."

I was straining with all my might to hold him. The vastly superior strength opposing me, slowly began to win control in the battle. I could only sink downwards, forced onto my knees, like a boxer on the ropes. I was fighting as hard as I could, trying to remain in contention in this encounter with such evil power. White spots began forming in my vision as I fought to retain consciousness.

From behind me, merging into the noise of the incomprehensible and continual outpouring of filth directed at me, through David's mouth, as if I was listening through a wall, I could just hear Trish urging my defeated mind, "Martyn, I love you. I love David. Hang in there; I love you. Win for me, win for us."

Through the fog of battle, I had lost the truth; my weapon wasn't strength, but love. I could faintly hear it in Trish, through the agony of defeat, Trish reciting our battle cry.

"Leave David alone. We love him." My exhausted mind dimly comprehended, it was this love that my opponent was afraid off, not the words I was reciting, but the love behind it. My tired muscles ached, burning with the lactic acid of concentrated activity.

Despairingly I tried to tighten my grip on his wrists, slowly repeating the incantation. "We love him." My lips, only inches from that putrid, fetid breath.

Without warning, the body I held went limp. I almost fell as resistance suddenly ceased. I nearly succumbed to my natural reaction, to catch the body when it slumped towards the floor. But, by now, my brain was working at lightning speed. Instinctively, I calculated this might be a trap. Instead, I lowered him gently to the floor, before cautiously releasing my vice-like clasp from his wrists, stepping backwards with care. I gave a silent prayer, hoping that it wasn't a mistake to release him.

With the arrival of the relative peace, our first and automatic concerns were for Trish's parents and Sue.

They were only feet away, protected from mayhem by a thin internal door, yet they hadn't moved throughout. Nobody came to investigate, even though the noise we'd been making must have resembled bedlam. I glanced towards Trish. "Do you think it's gone?" she asked.

David's eyes fluttered open and once again we found ourselves speaking to John. "Satan," he cautioned, "is not yet defeated; he has retreated to gather his strength."

The thought of continuing the battle sickened me. My muscles ached, a steady dull pain. I could feel the sweat cooling on my skin. As I recovered, now John was warning, "It will soon be time to go again."

I glanced at Trish, seeing the dismay in her eyes, but she managed a weak, half smile of support. "I trust in you, Martyn; you're doing fine, we both are." Stretching her hand out towards me, she willed encouragement, boosting me with her words of reassurance. "We have to continue this fight for the sake of David.

I grimaced. "Half time it is then, a tough game, but we're winning. Focus, it's time for the second half."

Kneeling cautiously, I took up my position and grabbed the wrists, all the while listening intently to John's instruction, "Be strong in love!"

His eyes opened and again I looked into the malevolent, satanically possessed eyes from close quarters. Where kindly and compassionate John had been seconds earlier, now I could only see hatred and loathing glowering back, causing my very soul to shudder.

The lips curled, exposing clenched teeth. He emitted a hissing snarl from deep within the throat. A snarl which caused my heart to skip a beat. The prostrate form below me heaved and wrenched as he fought to free himself of my determined restraint. My position crouched, kneeling over the body, gave me a slight advantage. I used my weight to bear down. This, I knew from experience, would only restrain him for a few precious seconds. The unnatural, unearthly force opposing me was just too powerful to defeat physically.

My breath came in short sharp gasps. I hung on grimly for dear life. But this time, I was mentally prepared: love was the key. I didn't hesitate to bring our only weapon into immediate use.

"Give us back David! We love him." Again and again, I chanted the words in Satan's face, as we wrestled on Richard's kitchen floor, barely hearing Trish as she echoed my words, from behind the kitchen's island, directed against the beast,.

"Leave him, we love David."

Afterwards I could smile, guessing what a sight we would have made had Richard or Lynda entered the kitchen. Fortunately, they stayed in the next room, watching television.

I continued, almost spitting the word, "Love," at his face, as I tried to counteract the torrent of obscenities still being directed towards me. I gagged from that foul malodorous breath, as he twisted to avoid the love poured out towards David.

The body beneath again went limp, flopping backwards, landing with a thud. David's head rattled the flooring. His body suddenly motionless. I remained where I was, still clasping his wrists in my tired hands. Examining David for several seconds, I didn't dare move. Eventually, slowly, I released my grip, resting on my hands and knees. My taut muscles gradually relaxed before I could stand up.

For several minutes David's body remained motionless, totally unresponsive to my gentle kick. Then momentarily he stiffened, before succumbing to a huge convulsion. I felt Trish flinch and I shuddered in trepidation. The eyes opened, staring directly into mine.

For a third time, in just over an hour we confronted an evil, which had to be overcome, for the sake of our friend. We'd been caught out; we were unprepared. I didn't have a hold of David's wrists because we'd moved away; we'd been expecting John to return, allowing us to prepare.

I was physically drained, irritated by the constant invasions into our quiet Sunday evening. Without thought, I harnessed anger to love as a weapon: anger for the ones I loved. I was fed up with the liberties taken towards my friend by this prince of darkness.

I leant over the horizontal form and angrily harangued Satan to his face. I was angry for the usurping of our friend's body whom I kept telling, "We love". I was so angry that the words used weren't contrived to be used as a weapon: they flowed naturally. I meant every word I uttered.

"Get out, David is loved. He belongs to those who love him, not for your evil purpose," I declared, snarling at him, in moral anger and indignation.

Amazingly, this was effective. The devil didn't stay to fight. Almost immediately after entering, he accepted defeat in this minor encounter, retreating from the body, which again slumped unconscious.

John returned immediately, blessing us when he told us. "The devil has given up the fight for tonight. He has withdrawn in the face of righteous love to lick his wounds. But be careful and watchful, he will plan and come again."

We have won this small skirmish, I thought, but winning the war would be a whole lot harder.

Through my weariness, I felt the relief and joy of victory being overcome by exhaustion. Unsteadily returning her hugs, I needed the support of Trish to hold me upright as my legs suddenly turned to jelly. After all, I reflected, all we could do was fight each battle as and when it arrived.

John didn't stay for long. "You are now safe; you must allow David the time to recover. The family in the next room have been subdued by angels all evening."

Turning to Trish I smiled. "Thus, explaining their failure to investigate the racket we made."

With Trish helping me to lift David from the floor, we seated him on a chair, his head lolling forward towards the island, resting on his folded arms as he slept.

The clock revealed we had been engaged in conflict for most of the evening. Trish filled the kettle. "I'll make a drink. On a Sunday evening, Mum would usually have made a drink by now."

Trish disappeared into the lounge, asking the family if they wanted a cup of tea. Richard, Lynda and Sue were contentedly engrossed by a historical drama, seemingly blissfully unaware of the age-old drama of good and evil that had been taking place, literally feet away.

As we prepared the drinks, David slowly began to stir, waking with a sudden start which nearly made me faint, but it was David, who appeared very groggy, confused, disorientated and repeatedly asking, "Where am I, not again."

We made him a drink, trying to explain to his befuddled mind, in very broad terms, what had just happened. The words entered his ears but understanding remained elusive.

Finally, David was conscious enough to give the impression of being fully alert, even if the truth was a little different. Appreciatively, I took my hot drink from Trish, anticipating the soothing effect of the hot tea, before following Trish through to the family lounge, gratefully sinking into the comfy sofa.

Once settled, I tried to take my first sip of the drink, but as I raised the cup, I noticed my hands had started to shake. Try as I might I could not control the shaking as the shock of our ordeal began to take hold. To my dismay, the drink spilt over the edge of the cup, sprinkling the carpet; the shaking grew more violent and uncontrollable. I looked guiltily at the other occupants of the room, noticing Lynda staring back. I tried a half-hearted grin.

"Sorry, Trish tired me out, all that walking this afternoon, that and lack of food," I joked, but I could read Lynda's puzzled expression – she didn't believe me! Fortunately, Lynda was too polite to dig deeper, instead, leaving her seat to fetch a cloth from the kitchen.

It took several minutes before I was able to put the cup to my lips and take a sip of the tea.

David also encouraged suspicion through his demeanour. Slumping into the corner of the sofa, he remained as if in a trance, head lolling on the shoulder of the blissfully unaware Sue. Several times he missed comments directed at him. Finally, I decided enough was enough. "Time to leave I think, work in the morning."

CHAPTER EIGHT

After returning from work the next day, I was unable to even sit down before there was a hammering on my door. I found an agitated Colin standing there. Following me into the flat he explained, "I met up with David for a lunchtime burger. John showed up briefly, unannounced. He said that the syndicate must gather around the calling table this evening. We are going to be given an announcement of great importance."

Excitement rose at the thought of some new supernatural revelation. Could this be our calling, our *raison d être*? But my excitement tempered as I told Colin of the events of the previous evening. Even afterwards, the recounting of the tale sending a shiver down my spine.

"I wonder why John needs to use the calling table and not appear himself," I wondered aloud.

Colin rationalised it. "Maybe the necessity for David's body to recover after last night's battle.

"But he's already appeared once today, to you!" I replied, in puzzlement. "Sorry, John and the spiritual world are way beyond me."

Colin had no answers to my questions.

Whatever our concerns, by seven that evening we were all present and expectant, fingers firmly on the upturned glass. Trish spoke, calling on the apostle John to appear. Given previous experience with the table, I was extremely thankful when John was prompt in replying. Even before Trish finished speaking, the glass began to move across the tabletop, unwaveringly towards the YES. Trish continued, asking, "Do you have a message for us?" Again, the glass propelled itself towards YES, continuing, spelling out the message which sent a shiver of delight through me. The news we'd been waiting for, "*The Father has consented. You are to learn of your destiny, and duty.*"

Elated, I grinned at Trish, my excitement mirrored by her delighted smile; her face and eyes glowed with exhilaration. "Maybe all the horror and trouble might now be worth it. Now we will know what is worth fighting for," I said.

While Trish recorded the message in her neat and meticulous handwriting, spelling out one letter at a time, the glass continued with almost mechanical precision. "You have a task to complete. At the completion of this task, you will receive your reward, the reason for your existence."

I studied the glass, my excitement growing. Another task, at the end of which, the answer to our most fundamental question was going to be revealed.

Our eyes remained mesmerised by the glass beaker. It began to spell its message. Each time the glass stopped by a letter, we recited it out loud. Trish scribbled furiously, recording each letter with growing bemusement. We were totally unable to make any sense of the nonsensical string of letters she was writing down. EZESP NLAFE ZWEZD PPESP ELMWP ESLEF DCZFY O.

"It's a code," I announced needlessly. "We've received our mission in code."

The glass halted at the centre of the circle, waiting several seconds, then continuing. Spelling out its message in plain English, a one-line communiqué, "*No contact until solved.*"

I exhaled, releasing the breath I was holding, simultaneously allowing my aching arm to drop to my side.

I was eager to inspect this new message, desperate to try and make sense of the coded letters or words. "Let's have a look; hand it over," I said, holding out a hand.

Trish, as eager as the rest of us, had far more patience and common sense in such situations. "No chance, wait just five minutes, blockhead. We're going to do this properly." She snatched up the code, insisting firmly, "Martyn, make the coffee. I'll copy this out, so we all have our own duplicate."

I wandered to the kitchen to fill the kettle.

Paper in hand, I stared clueless at the coded letters before us.

A short-lived high. We'd believed we were going to discover the reason behind our syndicate existence. In an anti-climactic revelation, we were left none the wiser, and exceedingly baffled.

Sue spoke. "Don't worry. John wouldn't give us an assignment that we ultimately weren't equipped for."

"True," Colin agreed. "It all depends on the complexity of the code as to how long we have to struggle before we break through. We'll get there. It's just a matter of when."

David said. "Britain needed her greatest brains to crack the German enigma code during the last war. Super intelligent we're not, though I doubt if John encrypted his message in an enigma machine."

Later, in bed, I dropped off to sleep, images of groups of meaningless letters floating through my mind.

Morning failed to bring insight, just work and more perplexity. I stared at my drawing board, unable to concentrate on the job!

While I was pretending to work, Colin had roused himself early, the occurrence a rarity when on leave. Initially Colin surfed the net, occupying himself by reading the story of Alan Turing, Bill Tutte, Tommy Flowers and the other heroes of Bletchley Park. Becoming fully immersed in the story, he even went into town to purchase a book on the code-breaking marvels and the methodology they had used to break the German messages.

I'd viewed many a documentary on the history channels. It was a story that I found fascinating. Likewise, Colin was totally absorbed, devoting several hours of his day quietly reading in the corner of the Wellington, a half-forgotten pint on the table, beside him.

It had been a captivating read; hours passed without Colin stirring.

I turned up fresh from work. "Find anything new?" I asked, plonking myself down on a seat. Taking a sip of a fresh pint, Colin explained what he'd gleaned from the research.

"This stuff is fascinating. They really were super intelligent. If ours is just a tenth as difficult as theirs, we are in trouble! Surely John wouldn't do that to us. Imagine, six years down the line and no further forwards." Colin concluded with a grimace.

Eager to progress, we abandoned the Wellington in favour of home, and an opportunity to experiment with the rudiments that he had picked up about simple code breaking.

Using the card from a cereal box, we cut a simple circle and wrote the letters of the alphabet, evenly spaced on the circle. Then we fashioned a smaller circle, lettered with the same spacing as the outer circle. We now had a very basic, crude coding machine.

Silently, I prayed that our friends above had taken into account that we were pure novices, with a tiny sliver of the brain power of Turing and his chums.

Looking at the original letter groups, we counted the frequency of the letters that appeared most. We found seven E's and five P's. The basics showed that the commonest letters in the English language were E and A. As long as each letter remained the same in code form, this would give us a clue. Obviously, E wouldn't represent E, so we lined E up against the A of the inner circle and began to translate the message as it was written. AUAMV. We stopped, evidently this wasn't correct; time to try again.

Checking the message, I counted. The letters P, L and Z appeared a number of times. If this was right, then these could be the vowels; that is, if this were the simplest code where each letter was only coded the once. I stopped, taking a sip of tea, looking again, long and hard at the meaningless jumble of letters in groups of five. EZESP NLAFE ZWEZED PPESP ELMWP ESLET DCZFY O.

Impulsively Colin jerked forwards, pointing to the message.

"Don't you see it?" he asked, in an excited tone. "The PP in the middle. Our code has to be very much simpler than the ones the Germans used in their enigma; this double P should represent a letter repeat; the enigma never repeated letters, it wasn't able to." He continued. "The most common repeat letters are E or O, which means at the very basic level this might work. As long as John hasn't gone for something really difficult." He leaned forward, eagerness expressed by his movements. Colin moved the cardboard dial around in the circle, until the inner E was opposite the letter P. Then he began to decode as I wrote, TOTHE CAPIT ALTOS EETHE TABLE THATI SROUN D.

"You genius!" I grabbed his arm in excitement. Joy, we'd broken the code at our first attempt. "The simplest code imaginable and it only takes us to the position where we've begun our previous tasks."

"Maybe John doesn't rate our brain power," Colin concluded.

"Well, we were never going to be Alan Turing but it still feels like a massive achievement; you've certainly earned your oats today," I told him. "Or in this case, fish and chips!"

To the capital to see the table that is round. We would go.

Celebrating Colin's achievement with fish and chips, we wasted no time summoning the others, eager to proclaim our genius. Even Trish was suitably impressed, only slightly miffed that we'd failed to wait for her or the rest of the team.

We binned the greasy papers and cold chips to gather as a group, pooling our brainpower in an effort to decipher this new riddle.

"The capital is obviously London, and I'm sure the reference to the table that is round refers in some way to King Arthur's round table, or something to do with the Arthurian legends," Trish surmised.

"Maybe it's in a museum," suggested Sue. Though none of us had any idea where.

"Another day on the internet," David suggested to Colin.

A quick internet search that evening returned a motley collection of furniture manufacturers, men's groups and restaurants, when *London* and *Round table*, were inputted into the search engine.

Colin would have to do the research while we worked.

"Not the leave you were suspecting, I guess. Still, as you're here you can do all the work, so early to bed for you," I counselled, with a grin and no sympathy. "You'll need to be up and at the laptop, by six!" Smiling, Colin responded, advising me what I could do with my early start.

As soon as I could safely leave work, I hurried home, eager to discover the outcome of the investigation. Colin met me at his door, an excited infectious grin spread across his face. "Amazing, I woke up early, well before nine anyway, so I did manage to spend most of the morning researching the net. "It's exciting," he said. "London's cathedrals, museums and tourist guides returned a blank, no meaningful reference to a round table anywhere." I guessed from the ever-present smile, that Colin had at least had some measure of success. Allowing him his moment of glory, I remained composed but expectant, as he teased the story out for maximum benefit.

"So, after a fruitless morning's research, no mention of King Arthur's legends or any reference to the round table in London's guides, I changed tack. I switched my investigation towards the Arthurian legends. That is when I had my first breakthrough. Did you know in Arthurian times, the ancient capital of England was the city of Winchester, in the south? And," Colin triumphantly announced, "the Great Hall, which was once part of Winchester castle, houses a round table, reputed by some to have been Arthur's round table of legend, even if the table has been carbon dated to several centuries later. Though it doesn't have to be Arthur's," he concluded, with an infectious smile. "The task doesn't require Arthur's table, just a round table; the fact that it is a later date is insignificant for our purpose."

I caught the grin. "This has to be it! No wonder you've had a smile, like the cat who nabbed all the cream."

Finishing with time to spare, Colin had explored the net for tourist attractions in the ancient capital city, including the opening times of the Great Hall, containing the round table. It was all settled. On Saturday we were going to Winchester. We even had the luxury of knowing that, with no contact until it was over, we had a few days of relaxation: no interruptions from our friends.

Again, we planned on hitting the road by seven, eager to miss the summer holiday traffic and be on our way, traffic all heading for the West Country holiday destinations. The night had been clear and cold, leaving, the screen misting over as our breath warmed the glass.

We were in reasonably high spirits for such an early hour, but then, we knew we were heading towards a revelation which could be world shattering for our lives. The five of us had piled into the car, eager and excited to discover where this adventure was leading.

Once underway Sue dampened the jovial mood, warning cautiously, "Every time we set out on a task, we meet the opposition in their sinister Jag. Does anybody really think today's going to be any different?"

"Probably not, but then what choice do we have," David countered, resignation evident.

The first hour of our journey passed uneventfully as we settled down into relaxed watchfulness. The car sped along busy roads, filled with travellers and lorries, all heading towards the beaches and countryside of the south-west.

"Let's stop for breakfast, before completing the journey," I suggested to an ever-willing audience. "After all, it is almost a tradition."

Bacon, eggs, sausage, tea and toast digesting, I gently eased the car back into the flow of busy Saturday morning, city centre traffic, completing the journey without mishap. As we pulled into the pay and display car park, just a short walk from the ancient thirteenth century castle and hall, we were all beginning to relax into the day, enjoying the anticipation and absence of opposition.

For a summer Saturday there were fewer tourists than expected. I guess because it was still too early in the morning for them to be out in number. Paying the entrance fee, we joined the sparse crowds already there, meandering through the halls and gardens, all eager to learn of the Arthurian legends and the mythology of the fabled round table.

"The round table was actually made for king Edward I, who, it seemed, was an Arthurian enthusiast." I told a disinterested Trish.

We read the claim that Winchester was believed to be Camelot, centre of Arthurian legend, so who knows the purpose of the table!

There was plenty of time for us to wander around, gazing about, absorbing the feel and the history of the place. The great hall was wonderful, vast and moving, with its sense of medieval history; the twelve-foot circular wooden table hung on the far wall as we entered, looking straight at it, down the length of the aisle, archways supported by gothic carved marble columns.

As a group, we moved cautiously, edging forwards towards the table expectantly. Each of us was on tenterhooks, eager to know if this was indeed our holy grail, but unsure, not knowing what to expect.

The groups of tourists and visitors milling all around, with guidebooks in hand, made it extremely unlikely that John would materialise something from mid-air. But who knew John's capabilities? Trish gripped my arm. I could feel her excitement transmitted through shared touch. "It's got to be here somewhere," she whispered.

At the entrance, Sue had insisted, "Purchase the official guidebook; it'll save time and effort in the long run." Now she read aloud as we stood listening, gazing up at the giant table hanging on the far wall. I noticed the great hall was suddenly deserted. Only the five of us remained, waiting for something to happen, anything to demonstrate we had solved the riddle. Nothing changed.

"We can't stay here all day." David turned away. David, whom we'd been monitoring for any signs of a visitation, was the first to become bored with the pointless waiting, suggesting, "Let's return to the car, the reward might be waiting for us there like it was at Stonehenge."

We agreed willingly but, when we arrived we were to be disappointed. The car was as empty as we had left it two hours earlier.

In desperation, we adjourned to a nearby café, sustenance and a pow-wow. Another chance to read the message again. We examined the words carefully, hoping to find some clue we'd missed. The precise message read *to the capital to see the table that is round.*

"This is what we've done, at least if our deciphering of the message is correct, which, I'm sure it must be," Trish claimed.

Finally, we reached a decision. "Look, as we are in Winchester, there's nothing more we can do. Let's make the most of the day now it's turned sunny and warmed up! I vote we explore the rest of the castle and cathedral, then visit the shopping centre, I hear it's quite good here." Sue proposed, quickly supported by her sister.

After which, we enjoyed a few short hours in the busy city centre, joining in with the bustling throng of afternoon shoppers, a sunny afternoon of window shopping and rampant consumerism.

Returning to the car, we climbed in, legs aching from all the walking, tired out after a busy day, almost contented. I had nearly, but not quite, forgotten about our earlier failure and disappointment.

"At least we've had no trouble from the opposition," I ventured, reversing out of the space.

"Probably sat in some pub with a long cool drink even as we speak, lucky bastards," Colin retorted, in mock envy.

I drove out of the car park, easing into the jam of the one-way system, which would take us through the city centre, then back onto the motorway and home. Nonchalantly, I glanced towards my rear-view mirror, then froze. "Shit, I spoke too soon." Behind us, in the mirror, was the Jaguar. I recognised, seated at the wheel, the nefarious features of Jerome, sneering back, as he became aware that I'd recognised him.

I experienced a feeling of despondency welling up.

We were edging forwards slowly, a queue of traffic, within the busy city centre one-way system. Hundreds of shoppers making their way home.

"It's too crowded; there's no easy escape," Trish muttered, almost to herself.

"Think of the crowds as our friend for now," I suggested. "At least they can't do anything... yet," I hypothesised.

Sue interjected. "They have already proven their willingness to bring the fight to us. John's warning that they will only get increasingly persistent and more intrusive keeps jumping to mind."

Continuing to focus on the rear-view mirror, I could see Jerome and his three comrades laughing and joking, repeatedly eyeballing, or pointing at us, making unheard observations to each other. I wondered aloud, "Just what they're planning in such a busy area, I've no idea, but I really don't want to find out."

"Ignore it. They are out to intimidate and frighten," Colin suggested.

"Probably, but they are getting more and more intrusive as I know from experience," Trish told him. "I really don't want them following us to a place where there are no witnesses."

I felt helplessness, trapped in a car, unable to drive away, only feet away from hundreds of shoppers totally oblivious of our situation and any danger we were in.

The packed traffic crept forward, extremely slowly. Jerome edged the Jaguar to within inches of my Ford, aiming to intimidate and menace.

My gaze darted rapidly backwards and forwards, monitoring the rear-view mirror, observing our evil counterparts as they laughed and gloated, knowing the fear they induced by their very presence and proximity.

David glanced behind, sneaking a quick look through the rear-view window, this causing Jerome to laugh and wave. Beside Jerome sat the dark-haired ice queen, whom I recognised from Bucklers Hard, Cruella de Vil. Jerome spoke, turning his head to include the two occupants in the back, again indicating our car. They all laughed, sharing a private joke!

We were approaching a set of traffic lights. I calculated rapidly, disappointed that we couldn't use the light sequence to evade our pursuers. It seemed there was no escape, even if we could flee the heavy traffic, which would be worse, there would be no outrunning the fast and powerful Jaguar, not in my humble Ford Focus.

Waiting for the lights to change, I watched the blank expressions on the myriad of hurrying shoppers, completely unaware of this, the most ancient of spiritual conflicts, fought amongst their midst, as they made their way through the familiar and mundane city streets, towards their safe and comfortable homes.

Fortune may have deserted us, but faith gave me strength. I'd noticed the somewhat unfamiliar sight of a pair of policemen walking towards us on foot patrol.

I briefly considered, then immediately rejected, the idea of throwing ourselves at the policemen's mercy, revealing the truth behind our association with Jerome. But this seemed a sure-fire way of seeing a psychiatrist's couch in the very near future. A simple denial by Jerome would see to that.

But the thought had given me the germ of an idea. Checking the progress of the policemen and realising that they were absorbed in their own conversation, I calculated that I had time to act. "Just go with me," I said, slipping the car into reverse gear. Jerking my foot away from the brake pedal caused the Focus to lurched backwards. I hit the Jag with a sharp thump on the bumper. I had gauged it just right, hard enough to cause some damage, but not enough to draw the attention of the approaching police officers.

If Jerome had thought the situation through, or, if he was intent on any treacherous plans towards us, he should have stayed in his car. But a very human concern for his motor car transpired. He immediately jumped out to inspect the damage. Playing the game and praying that the hordes of angels weren't on tea break, I told the others, "Stay put, and go with whatever I say." I leapt from the car, glancing towards the approaching policemen, praying that they would arrive on the scene promptly.

Deliberately raising my voice, ensuring I had the attention of the coppers, I begged loudly, "Leave us alone; what have we done to you?" By then, the policemen were only twenty feet away, coming forward with purposeful strides.

Before Jerome had a chance to open his mouth, I continued my onslaught, turning to the policemen who had arrived at my side. I complained stringently and convincingly. "His car hit me when I braked instinctively for a cat back in that car park," I asserted vociferously. "When I got out to swap documents" – I jabbed my finger in the direction of Jerome – "he threatened us, and he's now following us. I think he's intent on causing us harm in a fit of road rage."

I knew then, acting could have been a career choice; even I was astounded at the level of intensity and fear I managed to convey, or maybe I was just terrified.

Although duty bound to be impartial and now listening to Jerome's spluttered explanation, I could tell from the policemen's expression that they were fooled into believing the road rage scenario. Especially as, when asked by the second policeman, my four passengers, who'd listened through the open windows, quickly supported my protestations. "That's right. He's been following us for ten minutes," Sue declared, managing to get a note of indignation and fear into her voice.

My accusation was made all the more believable when one of the police officers asked us both to open our car boots. To their bewilderment the policemen found a range of heavy-duty tools, hammers and a baseball bat in the boot of the Jag. Frighteningly these may have been intended for us.

The primary officer asked us both, "Do you want to take it further?" After making a big show of inspecting my damage, surprisingly much less than expected, and pleasingly less than the Jag, I said, "I'm not after compensation. Just keep him here till we can get away." I pleaded.

The policeman turned to Jerome, asking, "Do you want to take the matter to the insurers?" I was sure he wouldn't want to give us their address and I was right.

We got our wish. We gave our details to the officer, out of earshot of Jerome, then we were allowed to make our getaway, while Jerome stayed behind to explain the contents of his boot.

We drove home from Winchester in relative silence, agitated by the recent confrontation. Choosing to take an alternative route, we hoped they wouldn't follow us again. Once in the relative safety of the open road, I accepted that Jerome had probably only been planning on playing mind games designed to frighten us. "A city centre is no place for confrontation," I agreed, "but then there had been the car boot full of nasty hammers and pickaxes."

Although we remained jumpy, fortunately, during the journey, there were no further signs of the Jag. Feeling exhausted but relieved, I pulled into the Wellington's car park.

Safe, we were on home turf. Tossing the keys to Trish, I made the decision to enjoy the luxury of a couple of drinks, then a taxi home. "I need to relax after today. Lead me to the bar," I joked, as I pushed through the door of the pub.

The five of us plonked ourselves around a table in the corner of the bar, the warmth and familiarity of our home surroundings doing wonders for stress relief. "I can almost feel the physical release of the stored tension," I said, as I sipped the first pint.

Now we were on home territory, we had a chance to puzzle over the task.

"Have we failed?" asked Colin. "I felt sure that *the Capital* and *the round table* were correct, but we've seen no sign of John or Luke at all during the day."

"Only time will tell," Sue told him. "But John did say there would be no contact until it was completed."

"There were always angels present, my friends." Four heads twisted in the direction of David whose soul no longer occupied his body. John had materialised and was now talking with us. He explained his initial statement. "The human race is constantly, and at all times, under surveillance, protected by the angelic forces in the unseen spiritual battle." Warrior angels is how John described them. "As a group, you are especially blessed with your own angelic warriors." Somehow in this strange game we'd found ourselves in, it was comforting to know that our backs were guarded.

We settled expectantly, waiting for our *raison d être*, eager to discover our purpose in life.

"Well, my friends, I did promise." Unexpectedly, there appeared in John's hand an envelope. One second it wasn't there, the next it had materialised from nowhere, clasped in his hand.

I glanced around but the other customers hadn't noticed! The spiritual world was a mystery. We'd been involved in this deadly game for less than four months and it was still difficult for me to comprehend, the existence of a whole world occupying the spiritual realm, a realm which we couldn't see, but it was there, and would occasionally interact with our own world, unseen by the majority of this planet's occupants. The patrons continued their conversations, blissfully unaware, ignoring us.

David returned to us, staring down at the envelope with amazement. "What the... Where did this come from? Though I can guess," he finished somewhat lamely.

I was pleased. "At least they've decided to bless David, allowing him to share this moment with the rest of us," I told an agreeing audience.

The envelope in his hand was cream in colour, almost parchment-like, thick, bulky to touch, full of promise. It looked like something that could be brought in any high-class stationer, but then I reflected, what exactly did I expect an envelope from the spiritual world to look like?

"Well open it then; don't just look at it," an impatient Trish chivvied David in mock exasperation

We watched expectantly as David opened the envelope; he'd missed much excitement, through his very unique position. It felt right for David to lead the way as we found out what it was all about.

From the envelope, he drew a single sheet of paper, similar cream-coloured paper to the envelope. The sheet was covered in neatly written blue ink. Simultaneously we craned forward, eager to know our fate.

"Well," he muttered. "We desired revelation and we've got it." David placed the paper flat on the table for us to read!

Well done, our friends, you are living at the end of time;
the time of complete revelation is almost upon mankind.
The battle intensifies; time is coming to an end; the first
horse of the apocalypse has left the heavens.
The six of you were chosen before birth;
you shall join the battle.

The earth and the heavens are being shaken.
And shall be shaken again.
Into this fallen world will be born another son. A son to
rise up and shine his light into the world. He will draw
the people to him; the son will be the subject to intense
battle and conflict, in your realm, and ours.
The heavens and the earth will be ripped asunder, as
time draws ever closer to the end.
You my friends have been chosen to walk this earth as
his apostles; you shall pave the way for the new messiah
to be born.

CHAPTER NINE

A revelation guaranteed to stun, we who lived in the modern, fast-moving, pleasure-seeking, possession-centred, celebrity-worshipping, twenty-first century world. A world centred on the individual. We, as a group, were having to learn first-hand, some of the ancient mysteries of a spiritual world. A world which we didn't have time for; the complexities of which I couldn't begin to comprehend. We'd learnt some of the truths of the battle, between good and evil, a battle which apparently had been fought since before time began. I couldn't even begin to grasp the meaning of this wild adventure that we had been plunged into without warning. All we could do was hang on, like driving a runaway train, and hope for the best.

Before this, I had proudly considered myself a practical man, resourceful, able to cope in all situations, but to be honest, I felt hugely out of my depth by our current situation.

As the reality of the revelation grew over time, I was immensely glad of the presence of Trish. Her unquestioning excitement, and wholehearted acceptance of the spiritual, supported me as I slowly came to terms with what had been revealed.

"Nothing important then, only the end of the world!" said Colin.

"Try going into work or to training and announcing that to friends!" I said.

"Impossible, so I won't," David grinned.

Instead, we did the only thing we could do in this circumstance. We kept quiet, got on with the daily grind, and continued to meet with John, and occasionally Luke, during evenings and weekends.

Colin stood staring at a mysterious brown-haired girl expectantly. Under his observation, the girl lifted her hand, making an unconscious adjustment to her hair, looking downward in a nervous gesture, before looking up and meeting his eyes. She smiled, a slightly amused smile of co-conspirators, thrown together by the twists of fate. Making a swift decision, she picked up her suitcase, moving with a purposeful stride towards the waiting Colin. No words were exchanged but, without understanding, I just knew that she was French.

I woke in an instant, eyes open wide, staring into the dark; the dream had been vivid and real, not frightening, but very real. Almost as if I had been there observing. I believed that I was being shown something. Although what Colin meeting a French girl in a train station could mean, I could only guess at.

Lying there in my bed in the middle of the night, bewilderingly, I became aware of an all-invasive aroma. The smell of fresh apples! By itself a pleasant bouquet, but in my bedroom, in the middle of the night? This was bizarre and out of context, to say the least. I rolled over in the sweaty sheets, searching out the neon blue-green light of the bedside alarm clock. It was three twenty-five. A whole three hours and thirty-five minutes before I needed to be awake, to face the day.

The apple smell slowly began to fade. I sniffed again, making sure the smell wasn't my imagination. The aroma had been powerful, but as invasive as it was, I hadn't felt threatened. Still, even though it was an unexplainable anomaly in my modern flat, the apple fragrance did not require any immediate action. I rolled over, muttering the word "bizarre" into the empty room, before attempting to make the most of my three and a half hours by recapturing sleep. I finally dozed off, wondering why I'd had such a vivid dream about Colin. It made no sense!

The merchant navy is such, that not every trip is on the same ship. On joining the navy, Colin had trained as a cook, not that we saw much of his cooking skills when he was at home. As a cook, once his leave period was over, Colin would sign on at what he called the Pool. The first ship requiring a cook would go to the pool for the list of available men.

Following a three-month trip, Colin had paid off his last ship a month previously. His funded leave was now coming to an end, so, one sunny day, while we worked, Colin jumped in his car and drove to Southampton, registering his availability. He was in luck: a Fyffe's fruit boat had only just conveyed its need for a second cook. It was sailing in three days' time. The trip was only for a month, but it was work. It also meant that Colin had a paid trip to South America and the Caribbean to look forward to. He signed the form and took the job. Later in the pub, Colin told me, "Two days of freedom, then I'm packing my suitcase once more. I'm getting fed up with never being at home when I want to be. Look at all that I've missed this last time away."

"You're mad. People pay thousands to see some of the places you go to. You only have to look at the number of cruises advertised to know that," I counselled.

"Well, if they want to get up at six am and cook their own breakfast, that's fine by me."

"But you're not cooking for passengers; you told me there would only be about thirty crew this time. Surely you can handle that?"

"Yeah, guess so, cruise liners are the worst, always a hard trip." he said, taking a swig from his glass.

Colin was a dichotomy. When he spoke of the job during the voyages, or when it was time to go back to sea, he claimed to hate the job intensely, and being away from home for most of the year. But invariably, he went back time after time. Knowing my friend well, from what I could work out, I suspected he actually loved it.

Like the rest of the population, his was only a job; admittedly a job that took him all over the world, allowing him to visit places most people would only dream of, but still it was a job with attendant hardships, accompanied by long periods away from home. I guess it is the human way to moan about one's lot, no matter what that is!

The evening before the departure, it was a somewhat grumpy Colin, who turned up in the bar of the Wellington Arms. A last night of freedom before the trip. Sue, Trish, David and I were all present to wish Colin bon voyage. "We'll miss you, but not if you don't buy a round, the bar's that-a-way," Trish told him, as she thrust an empty glass into his hand.

The cold beer and warm atmosphere began to do the trick. He started to drop the grumpy geezer facade and enjoy himself. "Think of all that sunshine, and me with afternoons to kip on deck." He grinned, raising a pint to the group.

Surrounded by friends, encouraged by those close to him, Colin was now almost enthused by the prospect. "Tomorrow I'm off to the Caribbean, while the rest of you will be working away in cool damp England, nothing but the grey skies and drizzle of an English summer to look forward to." Colin grinned at the prospect of tropical sunshine, reminding us that the summer was shaping up to be a cool one.

"Let's hope you don't get sunk by a hurricane," I retorted.

Happy that our friend was now taking a positive outlook on life, Trish and I left, conscious that work was beckoning the next day. Soon after, David and Sue left Colin happily propping up the bar, romanticising to the bubbly barmaid, Tina. "I'm on an island-hopping trip to the Caribbean and Venezuela," he told her. "I'll bring you a present back."

"As long as it's not a bottle of beer or a bunch of bananas." She laughed, responsive in his company. "Is there any chance of another one of these, after you shut up shop?" he pleaded, looking at the empty pint glass.

The next morning, while I worked away in my quiet office, Colin awoke, feeling like a noisy and argumentative family of woodpeckers had set up home inside his head. He woke in strange surroundings, gradually remembering that, when the Wellington had closed, Tina had allowed him to walk her home. She'd invited him into her flat for a coffee. Not that it had done him any good. Even if Tina was prepared to allow him to stay, the beer had done its work. Colin fell asleep on the sofa! Ruefully, Tina covered the sleeping form with a blanket, before going to bed, on her own.

Realisation, coupled with embarrassment, slowly filtered into Colin's befuddled brain, as he remembered where he was and what had happened. Fortunately for Colin, Tina was laid back enough to take him in her stride.

"I'm not exactly used to men falling asleep on me before they've laid a finger on me," she joked. "But you're forgiven, this time, as long as you bring me something nice back."

When on leave, with the amount of time that Colin spent in the Wellington, they had become good friends; nothing further had developed between them, until then. Now she might be feeling regret, or maybe even relief, but the opportunity had passed. At least for now.

Colin gave the excuse of his impending departure, leaving for his flat and final packing, before departing in the early afternoon, driving to join the ship at Southampton international maritime docks.

Colin lugged his suitcase and a carryall down to his VW Golf, saloon, mentally reminding himself that the car needed a good clean and tidy out on his return. He'd arranged with a Navy pal to leave the car in Southampton, parked on his friend's driveway. A regular arrangement. This made the house looked lived in when his friend Mark was at sea, and it gave Colin somewhere to park the car while he was away from Southampton, a win-win. This particular day, Colin's friend Mark was home on leave so there would be a chance for a catch-up. Colin would join the ship the next morning, for a two o'clock sailing, at high tide, on Southampton water.

A couple of Nurofen, a long hot shower and breakfast had finally banished the woodpeckers from his head. The circumstances of his night with Tina, already becoming an amusing tale of misfortune ready to amuse his new shipmates with.

Colin slid into the driver's seat, settling down for the trip.

Southampton was only one of the several ports from which Colin sailed, but it was by far the most frequent. With the number of ferries and liners which used the port, and living only sixty miles away, it would usually be Southampton where Colin was headed when he set off to sea.

Twisting the dial and finding an 80s rock station, Colin ramped up the sound, easing forwards to peer through the rain, which was falling from the low hanging, overcast, gun-metal sky.

"Glad to be leaving it behind. They weren't joking when they said it was going to be unseasonable," he muttered.

That late June afternoon the weather was atrocious, dank and miserable. The drizzle made the day feel like autumn had come early. It felt as if the twilight had somehow settled across the UK mainland during late morning, a time when, if you had nowhere else to go, it was best to be inside, watching the rain through a window.

The day caused Colin to strain his eyes through the windscreen. Peering through the enveloping drizzle, he was already dreaming longingly of the sunshine which would be his in a few days. First a catch-up with his mate Mark, then a month-long return trip to a warmer climate. Observing the English weather, he felt sheepish as he thought about his previous grumpy self. "Not so bad after all, could be worse," he told himself.

Despite the weather, the route was a familiar one. Colin had travelled it many times before, so it was several minutes before he noticed the Range Rover closing the gap in his rear-view mirror. The car was far too close, causing him to reflect on the Jaguar with which we'd, had the run in.

Colin was unconcerned. There was no reason to be unduly worried; this wasn't a Jag. This was a bad driver in appalling conditions. He eased his foot down slightly, edging the throttle open, hoping to extend the distance between himself and the Range Rover behind. Glancing across at the rear-view mirror, he was suddenly alarmed that the tailing car had also increased its speed. The distance between them remained steady, as if an invisible rod joined the two cars.

Colin wasn't one to panic unduly but neither is he the strongest character I know. This was unexpected and worrying, and he was alone. All of a sudden, any fears he'd felt about scary Jaguar motor cars from hell were no longer abstract things, surreal experiences to be shared, then joked about over a drink afterwards. Now he was isolated, on his own in a vulnerable situation; this made his predicament very frightening indeed.

Colin remembered our lucky escape in Winchester, how I'd outwitted them. "That's it. I'm their revenge. I'm the scapegoat," he told the empty car.

Logic, borne by despair, filtered into his panicked mind. This must be just a coincidence; the car wasn't the Jag. Although he could see several occupants through the misty rain, they might not have anything to do with the previous encounter or the devil's syndicate. Hoping anxiously that this was a family in a hurry, late for their ferry crossing, he slowed dramatically, giving the Range Rover plenty of room to pass him on the straight sections of the A road. This, it transpired, was a forlorn hope. The Range Rover remained rooted to his bumper, as if tied there.

The road sign indicated the dual carriageway one mile hence. Slowing further as the dual carriageway approached, Colin's feeble hopes were raised marginally. His attention flicked continually back and forth, far more concerned with the car behind than the road ahead, but it still registered that the road was widening. There was now no longer any conceivable reason for the Range Rover to stay behind him. "That is, unless the intentions of the driver and its occupants are malevolent. I guess I'll know for sure in about twenty seconds."

His breath escaped him in a dejected gasp of resignation; the Range Rover maintained its proximity to his rear bumper. Feeble expectations deflated like a burst balloon; his pursuer was preserving a gap of ten feet between the two cars.

So far, from the tales we'd recounted, the Jaguar had only threatened, causing fear without physical contact. Colin knew this himself from our confrontation in

Winchester. He kept going relentlessly, hoping that something would occur, or the danger would pass. "They isolated Trish and look what happened there. Jerome wasn't for holding back then," Colin mumbled, searching the mirror, trying to identify his pursuers.

Colin realised he was on quite an isolated section of road. He'd deliberately chosen the rural, scenic route, over the fast motorway, but this was still England: busy towns and villages, or service areas with petrol stations are never that far away. Mentally, Colin forced himself to suppress the rising panic. "Plan carefully, keep a clear head and concentrate, don't stop," he ordered himself, speaking out loud to emphasise his words. "A town will appear soon enough."

As if realising that opportunity had to be taken, or perhaps even as a pre-planned event, the Range Rover increased its speed, closing the narrow gap between the two cars. Colin, whose eyes were rapidly alternating between the road ahead and the car behind, only had a second to realise that the cars were going to touch. His foot instinctively reached for the accelerator, pushing down, seeking acceleration and speed, but too late. He felt the slightest jolt as the cars came together, the bumper of the Range Rover scraping Colin's rear wing. The rear of the VW fishtailed, sliding across the wet, greasy road, before gripping the road surface once again.

Colin knew he was a competent driver, but this was way beyond his experience. His heart felt like a beating drum within his chest, threatening to rip out through his ribs at any moment. Now he knew their intentions were hostile; they were active; they wanted to force him off the road!

His desperate hands gripped the steering wheel, as tightly as a winning lottery ticket on a windy day. He recognised grimly this section of road had been chosen well. Two miles further on, he knew he would be safe. The road passed through the village of Huntly Corsham, full of shoppers and passers-by; he could stop for a coffee with a hundred witnesses, but, until then, there was only open road and heathland between him and safety.

The two cars grated as they came together once more. The Range Rover just touched his rear bumper, then, scraping his wheel arch, they parted again. Apparently, the other driver appeared to be building up courage, seeking the final killing stroke. Colin glanced down briefly, seeking the speedometer, recognising that he was doing over sixty mph, enough, by far, to kill him, should he lose control on the greasy surface.

The Range Rover held back a touch before edging across the dual carriageway towards the central barrier. Where were the other cars on the road? Colin wondered. He realised, although he had seen the occasional car flash past in the other direction, very little seemed to be going his way.

The Range Rover edged forward again, its nose and knee-high bumper alongside Colin's rear wing, the 4x4 overlapping the Golf by about a third. For a third time there was a coming together with a screech of tearing metal. The front bumper of the Range Rover edged in slightly towards the rear of Colin's VW. He inched his wheel towards the other car, fighting to oppose the force exerted on his own. This time he couldn't hold on! His grip tightened on the wheel, but it was not enough. Colin fought all the way as the rear of his own car slid sideways across the wet road surface. He sensed the Range Rover retreat from the confrontation. With the rear drifting, the nose was pointing at the central crash barrier. It rushed forward to deliver the VW a glancing blow on its offside wing. Before his relief at remaining on the road had time to register, the car careered back across the wet carriageway, hurtling towards the verge: a verge which fell away sharply, beyond the tarmacked surface.

Just like the soldiers' stories, at the moment of greatest stress, all things slowed.

Within view, he clearly saw on the bonnet of his car, something he later claimed was an angel. This was no cherub-like figure with wings, the story book versions of angels, but a huge laughing figure. At least ten-foot-high, lying horizontally in a casual pose across his bonnet. Long blond hair flowing out behind him.

Colin didn't know if, in the spiritual realm, an angel's hair could be blowing in the wind, but, at that moment, he didn't care. He was in the protective arms of the angels. The angelic figure turned to regard him, a warrior protecting his charge. Colin only had the time to return the stare for a millisecond, gazing into the calm confident laughing eyes of his protector. Then the vision faded.

Time slowed to a standstill; the verge, with its dreadful drop loomed into vision. As the plunging car shot over the edge, a total calmness descended over Colin. It was a twenty-foot verge, dropping towards the gardens which flanked the road. Colin felt a lurch as the car took off. With a sickening thud, the car hit the verge once, before crashing forwards. Inside the car, Colin's mind had completely disassociated itself from his situation. As he sailed through the damp, rain-soaked air, he later recalled casually wondering how Jerome and his cronies had known where he would be.

A vicious thump shook his body when the car landed once more. He shot forward, only to be arrested by the air bag erupting in his face, the seat belt stopping his forwards momentum. The car came to a sudden halt as time returned to normal.

For several seconds Colin remained seated and motionless, before slowly leaning around the flapping airbag to turn the racing motor off. Very shakily, he opened the door, carefully climbing from the car.

Peripheral movement caught his attention, causing him to stop and look back towards the road. Had the Range Rover stopped? Were they going to come down and complete the job? On the verge above, he glimpsed the sideview of a Jaguar. Colin couldn't make out the occupants; the drizzle was too heavy, but he knew it was the dark Jag, the one he'd seen before. Of the Range Rover there was no sign.

As this sight penetrated Colin's dazed mind, the Jag revved its engine, driving off, leaving Colin confused and bewildered, standing alone besides his crashed car. It had gone from a routine journey to near destruction in moments. Who's going to believe my tales of rogue Range Rovers and laughing angels, he thought.

"Are you OK, mate?" Colin turned to see a guy, about fiftyish, coming towards him.

Still dazed, it took several seconds to register where he was and what his situation was. Finally, he grasped it. This was the homeowner, the owner of the garden on the edge of Huntly Corsham where his car now resided.

"I've called the police; they're on their way." Indicating the car, the man said, "Are you OK? Do you want a cup of tea? What actually happened?"

"Yeah, thanks, mate, tea would be good, shock and all that. I skidded and came of the road. An idiot in a Range Rover driving too close."

"Not surprising, some of these 4x4 drivers shouldn't be let loose with a tricycle," the homeowner agreed, nodding.

Out of the rain, the hot tea felt good. Colin sat on the man's sofa, who'd now introduced himself as Ron. Colin was beginning to think coherently again.

After he'd inspected the scene, he understood how lucky he had actually been. The car had smashed down the verge, hitting a small tree in the Ron's garden. Inches cither side of the VW's wings were much bigger trees, trees which would have caused a huge amount of damage and at the speed he'd been travelling, wrecked the car. As it was, he had uprooted a small tree, which then halted any further forward momentum. The car was hanging precariously over a garden pond. A preliminary and superficial first inspection of the vehicle indicated that, for such a significant crash, the damage appeared to be extremely light.

The police arrived, taking control and asking for a routine sample of his breath. Colin agonised a moment, his thoughts returning to the previous evening. Fortunately, the breathalyser indicated that Colin was well within the safe limits for driving.

Once they'd established that he was safe to be driving and where he was going, the police rapidly began to lose interest. For his part Colin felt it was prudent not to lay too much emphasis on the Range Rover and its fundamental contribution towards the cause of the accident. "The Range Rover was driving far too closely, particularly for the conditions. It was right on my bumper. I kept looking in the mirror. I couldn't help it. It caused me to lose momentary concentration."

The policeman asked, "Did you get a number for this Range Rover?"

"No, he was too close, and I wasn't expecting it. I was just driving to work. I wasn't expecting anything like this," Colin told him.

"Do you think the driver of this Range Rover was acting deliberately? Did he mean to cause the accident?"

Colin realised discretion was the safer course of action. "I don't think so; maybe he was in a hurry. There is only one bit of dual carriageway on this road; it's possible that he misjudged his overtaking in the conditions."

That and wet roads were officially recorded as the cause of the accident.

The policeman concluded, "I guess we'll never know, sir, without the Range Rover Though we see a lot of accidents when fast drivers meet greasy road surfaces in summer rain. The good news is you're uninjured."

Remarkably, the damage to Colin's VW Golf seemed minor, even if the car was overhanging a garden pond. When he tried it, the engine burst into life, first time.

The police were good enough to give Colin a lift to the local garage after Colin had given Ron, the homeowner, his insurance details, promising he'd pay for the damage and thanking him for the tea.

Safely delivered to a garage in Huntly Corsham, Colin was able to arrange for the recovery of his car. He asked for it to be delivered to Mark's driveway in Southampton. A taxi was called, and a shaken Colin finally completed the last few miles to his destination.

Mark was duly shocked by Colin's descriptive narrative, but apart from being slightly subdued, there were no obvious injuries for Colin to show off. Mark happily promised to arrange for any repairs to the VW before Colin's return. With the VW sorted, Mark said, "Come on, mate, no good sitting moping, time to relax and enjoy and your evening. We don't get together enough these days."

Colin wasn't due to join the ship until the morning. "Great an Indian meal and a catch-up, sounds just right."

Later that same evening, from the privacy of his room, Colin called me, and related the details of his eventful day. "Frightening, mate, they definitely desired doing me harm; it might have been a revenge attack after our trip to Winchester."

"Food for thought," I replied, "and definitely very worrying; they've upped the stakes a notch." Despite the late hour, I listened attentively, for over sixty minutes, as Colin explained the true facts of his crash – facts that he had been unable and unwilling to reveal to Mark, or the police.

The next evening the four of us gathered in the flat. We needed to consider the latest violation perpetrated against our syndicate.

"Colin's been attacked, and it seems they were out to cause him real injury."

I took my time, describing to the group exactly what Colin had conveyed to me the night before. Their expressions noticeably paled during the retelling of Colin's traumatic and disturbing experience.

"Firstly, Trish at Supertramp's, now Colin. Both isolated, then attacked." We need to consider our every move." David expressed his concern.

"I couldn't agree more but we do have the problem that we have no idea when they are going to strike," I responded. "After all, Colin was on the way to work; we all have to do that, every day."

"Any one of us could be isolated, driving to work in the morning!" Sue agreed, looking vexed.

Cold realisation concerning the dangers involved were beginning to dawn, causing a figurative, but collective shudder to pass through the group.

"Greetings, my friends." I had been looking towards Trish, so I hadn't witnessed the tell-tale shudder, or the distinctive flicker of his eyeballs, revealing that David had left and, once again, John had borrowed our friend's body.

"Colin is safe. He joined the ship this afternoon," John disclosed, quickly adding, "but yesterday, he was in great danger from your counterparts." We remained subdued, listening carefully to what he had to say, knowing that, somehow, the stakes had been raised, that we were in a tight spot.

The danger levels were rising, with no expectations of things becoming easier anytime soon.

As a group, we were becoming more alarmed.

It was difficult, in the comfort and safety of my modern living room, but we had to accept that we were in mortal danger. John informed us, "Your warrior angels were with Colin yesterday; he was protected."

I recalled Colin's claim. "At the very moment of greatest danger, as I took off from the verge, I saw for a moment what I think was an angel lying on the bonnet of my car. This brought me complete peace of mind. I knew I wasn't going to die."

John's assurance was comforting but it still required faith. The awareness penetrated; we were the prey in this particular fox hunt.

John explained. "As has already been explained to you, we cannot interfere in the choices of humans, which is why we cannot prevent these things from happening. Mankind has been created with the freedom to choose. You know you have the freedom to walk away from myself and the Lord, and subsequently your enemies. This means that your enemies equally have the choice to pursue you!"

John expanded, telling us, "You live in a world which is always observed by our spiritual world. The Devil knows you and is watching you."

John explained again what we already knew. "Satan has raised a syndicate of his own disciples. They are dedicated to stopping you, or even killing you. They have an expressed aim to prevent the Lord's will on Earth. There is always a reaction by Satan to what the Lord is doing. Your world is a battle between the forces of good and evil; there are many millions of people who have chosen evil and don't always realise they had done so, they were blinded by the spiritual darkness. However, your enemies are not blind. They have willingly chosen to serve their master, Satan," he said, a touch of sadness in his voice.

"How do they know where we're going to be?" I demanded, curious to understand.

"The Lord has his angels but there are also demons who roam the earth. Your antagonists, the Devil's syndicate, don't always know where you are, but his demonic angels are always watching. The evil master has contact with his disciples but only through the calling table. He directs them to your journey and destinations. Though, not every journey has been rudely interrupted. The Devil and his demonic angels can't read your thoughts. Therefore, you are in greater danger from longer standing plans, especially if you are on your own. Their tactic is to isolate and destroy."

He continued, saying, "Colin has had a very lucky escape; he was protected by your guardian angels. Your enemies, the devil's syndicate, have been Satan's disciples for a long time. They are fully prepared to cause you injury or even death, should the opportunity arise."

It was clear, we would have to carefully consider our laid-back lifestyle, danger could be lurking anywhere.

I glanced around the room, studying the other three. Trish was biting her bottom lip, a nervous, or angry reaction, which I had seen before. Sue leaned forwards, asking the question that was occupying her. "What about David? How much danger is he in?"

"Physically, as much as the rest of you from your evil counterparts, though I think they will refrain for a while, unless their master orders them. They are seeking to weaken you for now. However, David is the chosen conduit of our communication. The spiritual purpose to which David's body is being utilised is tremendously draining to his physical body. As you know, this alone could be too much for the body, or soul of David. His body may simply give up," John confirmed, alarmingly.

He revealed, "If it were myself and Luke, things wouldn't be so bad, but the constant attempts of Satan and his evil demons to hijack this form of communication, means that a constant battle is being fought in our realm: the prize, the possession of the body and spirit of David. As you know, this battle could be fatal."

Sue turned whiter still. My heart went out to her.

John forewarned, "Physical attacks aren't your only danger. There is a spiritual world which badly wants to stop you in your tracks. You will also be attacked by this spiritual realm. Do not be afraid by these attacks! Although you have to contend with the sensory perception of this type of spiritual attack, the physical danger is minor. Our spiritual world inhabits a different plain to your own. Other than the fear that these attacks generate, minor object manipulation is the physical limit of any otherworldly assault."

John concluded, stating, "Tonight, be aware, there is activity in the spiritual realm! Also, your enemy, Jerome's syndicate is close by. We do not know, as yet, what their plans are."

David's head flopped onto his chest. Sue caught and cushioned his body as it lolled sideways. John had left as quickly as he'd arrived. Gone, leaving David asleep on the sofa.

Leading the way through the outer door of the flats, towards the open air, I immediately recognised that something felt wrong. Behind I sensed Trish stiffen. Her hand reached forward and grabbed a handful of my jacket. John's earlier warning had put us all on edge, prompting me to offer to chaperone the others. I was keen to know Trish and Sue were safely in their own home.

I sensed that there was something amiss in the immediate locality of the flat. Possibly the stillness of the night had put me on edge. In the modern world, where there is always a background noise, the absence of sound is instantly noticeable as unusual.

Normally I would barely register background noise! But its lack now sent shivers down my spine. Walking towards the car park of the flats, at ten thirty in the evening, I would have expected ambient noise. I sensed the unease within the others. Trish's hand on my jacket managed to convey her disquiet.

Making a conscious effort to take control, I swallowed my nervousness.

"There is nothing to worry about," I announced, as firmly as I could manage. Thankfully, I managed to sound far more cheerful than I felt. As a group we moved forwards cautiously, bunched together for mutual, perceived protection. Eyes focused on the darkness, nervously darting back and forwards, searching for the threat within the lifeless night. Not even a breeze stirred the silence, no wind to rustle the leaves in the trees.

"Come on, it's only auto suggestion. Remember what John told us. Nothing can harm us!" I said, making a renewed effort to quell the nerves and move freely. I reached out for Trish's hand, determinedly setting out across the car park, focused on my car in the shadows, almost dragging Trish in my wake.

From my peripheral vision, emerging from the trees at the other side of the poorly lit parking area, we caught the movement. Being so tense and expectant I reacted far faster than I would ever do normally. Dragging Trish downwards, we sprawled on the ground in a heap. There was a rushing in the air, movement over our heads. As we lay there flattened on the ground, I felt the violent turbulence all around. Peering cautiously from the tarmac, and twisting towards the retreating sound, it dawned. An owl had soundlessly swooped down on us from out of the trees.

Trish, who'd screamed when the owl dived, sat upright, watching the bird disappear into the darkness.

I looked over my shoulder. David and Sue were also spread eagled on the tarmac, reacting to the unprecedented intrusion.

"It's okay, it was just an owl," David said, somewhat pointlessly.

"Do owls often attack people?" I voiced the question in wonderment.

"Maybe it thought you were a rat," David's voice came out of the darkness.

Sitting up, I realised that the trees and car park were as motionless and quiet as when we'd first exited the communal entrance. Warily we looked around us, straining our eyes, seeking threats from within the darkened foliage.

Wondering if this was another, new type of attack, I pondered out loud. "If Jerome or his evil masters really could control nature, or the animals within it, I'm glad we live in Britain. At least the most dangerous thing in the wild is a fox or, possibly, with a great stretch of the imagination, a rampaging wild boar."

Trish twisted, mock exasperation in her words. "Only you, Martyn, would say something like that, at a time like this!"

The lack of movement and sound, coupled with the oppressive atmosphere, was still unnerving. Moving as one, we rose, rising gingerly from the tarmac, in the centre of the darkened car park, rubbing the grit from skin and clothes.

From a single tree in our direct line of vision, we all caught the movement. Not a slight and wispy movement, but a violent shaking of the leaves, a single tree, rocking as if it were in a typhoon. We jumped. I tried to work out if that was where the owl had disappeared, but in the confusion of the unexpected noise and mayhem, I couldn't tell.

Into this unnatural scene a loud screech ripped the night apart. Automatically we dived back down onto the cold dark tarmac. But apart from the piercing scream filling our ears and senses, nothing materialised from the night.

"What was that?" Sue gasped, from just behind me.

"I've no idea. It may have been a normal nocturnal bird, or even an animal in the bushes, but it's something I've never heard before" At least not in the context which had just taken us to the level of terror we were currently experiencing.

Now, more than ever, I realised we needed to take control of the situation and get out of there. Surveying all directions, searching for threats, I tentatively raised myself up, before helping Trish to her feet.

David rose, turning to me as he did, motioning towards the safety of the car. "Time to go, I think," he said. The car looked inviting, holding the promise of sanctuary, a mere five metres away. Hastily we crossed the remainder of the parking area, jumping into the car as if our lives depended on it.

"Safe!" I clicked the button, activating central locking.

Whatever danger there was outside could still be there, but inside the car we felt safe, as if putting a barrier between us and whatever was out there was the answer.

Actually, we had no idea what had happened or whether it was a threat. Now secure, Trish asked, "It was so still out there. Could it have been John's warning and our imaginations that caused us to react? Why are we cowering in a car at ten thirty in the evening? It doesn't make sense! Are we really under attack?"

In answer, directly in front of my face, there was a swift and unheralded movement. I instinctively ducked, gasping involuntarily, as the huge, outstretched wings of an owl appeared from the night. The bird seemed to be aiming directly at the windscreen, and myself. At the very last second, it lifted effortlessly over the car roof. Twisting in the seat, I watched as it disappeared into the darkness.

"Shit, that was close! But it answers the question," I declared, turning the key, thankfully hearing the engine roar into life.

What the extent of the evil capabilities were, we didn't know, but we now knew for certain, somehow, we had been attacked by evil forces again.

"Let's get out of here. You can drop me off at home. I'll collect the car in the morning," David announced.

Originally, Trish had planned on returning to the flat with me, but Sue begged, "Trish please don't leave me on my own tonight. I don't think I'll sleep a wink." After hearing John's warnings, followed immediately by this car park attack, Sue was clearly uneasy, wanting the comfort of her sister close to her.

"Right, I'll drop David off, then you girls. David, you'll have to walk to work tomorrow; harsh, but the exercise will do you good," I told him.

I considered asking to stay with Trish and Sue, or even cadging a bed at David's, but in the safety of the car, I was beginning to castigate myself for my earlier fear. Sounding somewhat pompous, I resolutely announced, "I'm coming back to the flat. I don't intend to kowtow to Satan, or Jerome and his friends. You heard John, the spiritual can't hurt me! I'll run the gauntlet of any creatures out there. I want the comfort of my own home. I want to sleep in my own bed!"

This announcement of renewed courage was contagious. David followed my lead, declaring, "You're right. I'll come with you to drop Trish and Sue home, then I'm going to collect my car and drive myself home. If we fold this early then we may as well give up altogether; after all, there is tomorrow and the next night. When do you stop?"

The short journey to Lynda and Richard's passed uneventfully. I drew strength and extra resolution from the power of Trish's hugs and kisses. Reluctantly, I watched her close the front door, leaving David and me standing on the doorstep.

"Time to confront the night," he said.

I drove the short distance apprehensively but without incident. On arrival, there was nothing to alarm us. The night air remained still, but minor movements through the leaves and small sounds from the undergrowth had returned the locality to normal. However, I still parked as close to David's car as possible, saying, "Wait until I've disappeared through the main entrance before driving away."

Within moments I was in the safety of my own flat, turning on all the lights as I went, whilst wondering what had just happened.

Trish and Sue turned towards each other as the door closed behind them. Sue dipped her head slightly, shyly asking for the first time in years, "Sleep in my room tonight?"

After the stresses and frights of the evening, Trish needed no second invitation. " Yes please, I don't think I'll sleep at all if I'm left on my own."

In the space of a few weeks, Trish and Sue had been plunged into an increasingly terrifying world, a world within which they could neither relax nor comprehend. An unseen, ruthless enemy stalked from the shadows, becoming increasingly more intrusive. When every waking moment had the possibility of turning into a nightmare, life required constant vigilance. There were times when we all needed the comfort of another person, close by.

Sue's bedroom was a large room at the back of the house away from the family living area, large enough to fit a king-size bed with no difficulty. Once Sue turned the light out, they were both glad of the familiar warmth and proximity of a sibling in the darkness. Settling into the big comfy bed, they each had the events of the evening running through their minds, and Colin's the day before.

Sue heard it first, a slight noise in the night. With heightened awareness, Sue awoke instantly. Listening for a moment, then rudely elbowing her sister in the ribs, she reached out to stifle Trish's startled protest. "What the fl…"

"Shush," Sue implored, as consciousness returned to her sleep bemused sister. "There was a noise downstairs," she whispered, fearfully.

"You're imagining things," Trish snapped, but Sue felt the tightening of her sister's muscles, as they held each other in the darkness. Both fell silent as they strained to listen for unnatural noises within the house. Then, just faintly, they both heard it, a slight creaking on the stairs, a noise where none should have been! Trish and Sue froze. adrenaline made their hearts to race.

Desperately, Trish tried to remember if her dad was at home or away on business. Richard not being there was a regular occurrence, so much so that there were times when the girls didn't know his whereabouts, but that was the price of success. It had been late when they arrived home, the house silent and in darkness. Even so, this was no indication. Richard and Lynda invariably went up to bed early. Vaguely, Trish recalled him telling her mother of a mid-week trip to Munich over Sunday's breakfast.

"Dad's not here; he's in Germany, and Toby's in with Mum," Trish murmured at her sister, feeling helpless.

Sue groaned under her breath, realising their vulnerability in this new, threatening situation. She felt nauseous as she considered the relentless nature of the pursuit. "I wish they would just leave us alone, just a little recovery time before the next attack, please," she protested.

"Seems not," Trish whispered back.

There it was again, just the slightest noise, a creak of a stair. Higher up now, close to the top, nearly on the landing. Trish's bedroom and the spare room were to the right of the stairs; Sue's was the only bedroom on the left. Richard and Lynda had the master bedroom opposite the stairway, separating their two daughters.

Alarmed, both girls hung tightly to each other, desperately wondering how to react to this new threat.

"Too late to wake Mum now. I'm not going out on the landing to Mum's room, no way!" Trish muttered.

"Might be just a normal burglar," murmured Sue, softly. In the dark, Trish wondered how they had come so far, so quickly, where they were hoping for a cat burglar to be robbing their house in the middle of the night.

They heard the creaking sound again, only this time the sound had changed slightly, fainter, more muffled. With some relief, Trish sensed, although the noise had reached the landing, it was heading away from their room.

Both sisters held their breath, waiting. There it was again, magnified by the night-time silence. Trish thought she heard the sound of a doorknob being cautiously tested. The sound originated from the other end of the landing, her own bedroom. Thankfully, not where Trish was that night. They both waited, holding onto each other tightly, transfixed, hearts thundering, ears straining to hear the next sound through the velvet darkness.

"Where is your phone?" Sue muttered.

Trish reached out, carefully feeling around on the bedside table, searching for the phone she'd placed there several hours earlier.

All of a sudden, they heard the creaking noise again; this time it was much closer on the landing, directly outside the door. Trish and Sue froze, a thousand different fears and scenarios swamping their fertile imaginations.

Sue's bedroom was in intense gloom. Fear clouding their judgement, they'd failed to consider turning the light on. The only illumination was given by the streetlights, beyond the fields, creating unfamiliar shadows.

Trish could sense the malicious presence on the other side of the door, hidden from view by two inches of wood. Both girls stared, fixated by the doorknob which rattled delicately, an unseen hand testing it in the darkness. They gazed in terror as the knob began to move, just slightly. Even in the dim light, there was no doubt that the doorknob was beginning to turn. Beyond the unlocked door stood their unseen nemesis. One who had come to wreak untold havoc on the already fraught sisters.

"Ahhhhhhhhhhh." Sue opened her mouth and screamed at the top of her lungs, eyes wide with fear. The sound of the scream was so unexpected that it caused Trish to drop the mobile phone, which she held forgotten, in her hands. She frantically groped about the bed, feverishly seeking the phone, their means of summoning assistance.

The bedroom door remained firmly closed, the doorknob unmoving. From down the landing they heard Lynda's bedroom light click on. Finally, Trish reached over, snapping her own bedside light switch, flooding the room with welcoming light.

Lynda burst through the door, bringing a degree of common sense and ordinariness to the situation. "What is the matter?" Lynda demanded promptly, showing obvious concern for her two daughters.

There was no reason to try and hide the intrusion.

"We heard somebody on the landing; the doorknob moved," Sue said.

"There is nobody here now!" Lynda announced, throwing the door open wide.

Both girls leant sideways, looking beyond their mother, needing to convince themselves that they were again alone and safe.

To prove her point, Lynda went from room to room on the landing, turning on all the lights as she explored. Trish and Sue joined their mother with only slight reluctance, staying close to Lynda for comfort.

"Look at Toby." Trish pointed at the dog which was showing great agitation as he ran around excitedly, sniffing at the strange smells on the carpet.

Lynda put through a 999 call to the police, conscious that if there was still an intruder hidden, they were three women alone in the house. Sticking close together for protection, they hurriedly explored downstairs and then the immediate vicinity of the garden under the glare of the security lighting.

There were no signs of any intruder, but, although they had found it closed and locked, the back door did have signs of damage: indentations in the wood and the lock had been eased by a metal tool.

She could tell the policeman wasn't interested. It was not that they weren't believed, the entry point was obvious; however, with the current lack of manpower and no evidence of any theft, the two young constables, who, indeed, arrived promptly in response to Lynda's emergency call, were now eager to be on their way, keen to fight greater crimes.

"Thank you for your time and patience. I'm sorry that it wasn't more exciting for you." With that slight touch of sarcasm, Lynda escorted them to the front door, knowing that a report would be written, but nothing else would result from this late-night disturbance.

Four o'clock in the morning, the mid-summer dawn was just beginning to promise from the east. Trish and Sue were able to return to the king-sized bed, more than ever thankful for each other's company.

Sleep eventually returned. Trish managed a whole hour before the insistence of the alarm stole her respite, forcing her to confront another day.

"Glad you were there." She thanked her sister, before slipping through the door and into her own room, needing a shower before work.

Trish's room was always chaotic, the clutter and confusion mirrored her own exuberant and energetic personality, opposed to the organised, tidiness of her sister.

Daylight had brought confidence and pragmatism, replacing the fears of the previous night. Trish glanced at her bed, unmade for a couple of days. Lynda was far too busy with her own activities to mollycoddle her daughters. Trish reached for the quilt, intending to adjust the bedding so she wouldn't have to climb into the tangled heap later. She stopped, frozen, the quilt sliding to the floor ignored. During a cursory inspection the night before, Trish had noticed no difference in the customary disorder of her bedroom. Now in the daylight, resting on the sheet, having been hidden by the quilt, was a noose. Trish fought her reaction, arresting the scream, dead in her throat. Instinctively, she understood that it would serve no purpose to alert her sister or mother. But here was the evidence; they had been stalked, for a purpose that she could easily guess at.

Instead of the police, Trish reached for her mobile phone, calling me for comfort and consultation.

"Martyn, they're getting closer and bolder; they've been here." I listened in silence, while Trish described the terrors which they had experienced during the night, followed by her gruesome discovery.

It seemed to me that the darkness was indeed pushing in closer and closer, from all directions. Colin had been in danger, now Trish and Sue. Trish for the second time.

There would surely be the type of person who had a natural predilection to live their life surrounded with a macabre sense of danger, but that certainly wasn't us.

Privately, I resolved, we would need to meet with John very soon. Something needed to happen; there was too much danger. I knew they had reacted, prematurely, and unexpectedly, but our enemies seemed able to appear at will, intruding into our lives and threatening our lifestyle with impunity.

CHAPTER TEN

There was no waiting around expectantly! John appeared as soon as we gathered at the flat. The previous forty-eight hours had taken its toll on us all. The others agreed with me, "We now need something more constructive from John. They are coming too close. If he's asking us to continue, we need, as a minimum, greater protection."

I'd spent my morning considering Trish and Sue's traumatic ordeal of the early hours, wondering what more could be done to deter these constant attacks. I was hoping that John had a plan, because we had none.

Fortunately, when we'd met for lunch, Trish revealed that Richard had been horrified by the intrusion in his absence. Lynda was no nonsense; she'd convinced him that, despite the lack of damage or loss of property, he needed to protect his three most valuable treasures. Calming his wife's fears, and to put his own mind at rest, Richard immediately called his design team. "I want you to develop, then install at my home, the best alarm system that you can conceive off," he instructed.

Great news for myself, as well as Sue and Trish. But I was also aware, we didn't know how persistent or dogged our enemy was. At least in the physical worldly realm, this was the best we could do. Just a shame we couldn't all have one fitted, I thought, wondering about the security of my own flat.

Up until then, despite the frights and occasional disturbing confrontations, I still regarded this as a game, an adventure to become excited about in my private moments. Slowly, I was realising that this enterprise was real. It was not a film on the telly to be viewed dispassionately. This was something which was actually happening. We were involved with something that was dangerous, very dangerous indeed.

"You are angry and frightened!" I noticed that John was speaking to us all, not just me. I knew from talking with her that Trish felt as much anger at the violation of her parents' home, as her fear to the intentions of the intruders. Possibly, I guessed, anger was the only realistic, emotive choice of response.

Sue also declared, "I'm equally as angry as Trish at this blatant intimidation. We have to have protection if he wants us to carry on."

Now he was here, Trish and Sue remained quiet, leaving it to me! I turned to John.

"Colin was nearly killed! Trish and Sue have had their home violated, somewhere where they have a right to feel safe! What are you going to do about it?" I asked, with resentment.

"I agree," John responded. "I have told you; we were taken by surprise at the speed and ferocity of Satan's response. More so by its tenacity," he said, making no effort to offer excuses.

"I thought that the Lord knew everything?" Trish interrupted, rounding on John. "I thought that the Lord knew what the future holds! How come you didn't know this was going to happen?" Trish asked sarcastically, suspicion evident in her voice.

John was able to field the question, allaying Trish's doubts effortlessly.

"Indeed, he does" John advised calmly. "However, even Jesus is not privy to all the Lord's knowledge. Jesus said on Earth that he did not have the information of the Father. This is true for us all. If all events were known, then the battle would be very different."

This was no comfort whatsoever. I was very uneasy and distressed by our situation.

"Unfortunately, they are now coming for us in our homes, not only when we venture out on a quest. It is only a matter of time," I moaned.

But John was not finished. "We did give you warnings! Only last night you were warned, they won't go away." Patiently, he reminded, "There are still warrior angels guarding you, at all times; no actual physical harm has happened yet to any of your group. When it became dangerous, Colin was protected."

He became firmer in his tone. "You have all been repeatedly warned that the dangers are great; you can choose to walk away whenever you want."

"True," I responded, "but we're in unknown danger. We, or at least I, want to be able to hit back when attacked, to deflect, rather than suffer the attack!"

John sighed, muttering to himself, "Turn the other cheek and love thy enemies." But he was ready for my request. "I have known all along, at times, you will require external human-sourced, physical protection," John continued. "Remember Luke's teachings in the early days of your training; there are other syndicates in Britain. These syndicates have been selected for one purpose, your protection. There is a group of four people: two men, two women. This syndicate doesn't live far away from you." But, at that point, John refused to reveal where this was.

John continued, revealing the exciting news. "You are to be given coded activation words. When you feel threatened, these words will trigger a protective reaction within the heavenly realm." He was clear in his assertion. "You are watched at all times from our spiritual realm. These code words are more for your peace of mind than any actual weapon for the battle which you find yourself in."

Even as John dismissed the dangers, it came as a great relief to us all, knowing we only had to shout out to instantly summon help.

John gave us three words. "Angelikinus, as it sounds, this will summon the angels to your side," he said. "It is a battle in the heavenly realm between Michael's angels and the evil demons." It felt good to be able to call up the cavalry with a single shouted plea. Angelikinus, we were told, translated as "angels come".

He then gave us the second word to activate immediate protection. "Corriendo, this will call upon your human syndicate counterparts, who have been preparing for some years to be your earthly protection!" Once more we pushed for their actual whereabouts, or anything we could find out, but John remained coy. "You won't meet them or know anything about them until the time is ripe. It is enough for you to know that they are out there, ready to give their lives for you." Corriendo, we were taught, meant "come running".

It felt good to have something positive to focus on, something to fight back with, but, I thought, if they were observing that closely, "Help!" would have been just as sufficient in all cases.

"Your third shout out is Abba." This, even I knew, was from the Bible. John said, "It means *Father* and calls on the Father's protection. In your case, the protection will arrive in the form of myself, as long as you have David with you." Drily I wondered if David was permitted to call out and initiate spiritual ejection from his own body.

We had three different and very unusual words to remember but I imagine that none of us would have the slightest worry whatsoever about forgetting them, any time soon.

These simple three words were a relief for us all. John continued to stress the total scrutiny of our activities by Michael's angels. Now that we had a proactive means of calling on protection and fighting back, we began to relax, just a little.

John had been with us over an hour, fulfilling his mission to placate us and put our minds at rest. Although David's body would be under greater stress the longer John remained, he hadn't finished for the evening.

"Your training is not yet nearing completion," he instructed. "You are now ready for your next task; you will receive instructions within the next few days!"

John left, returning a bewildered and questioning David, who appeared as relieved as the rest of us by the knowledge that we could call up the rapid intervention forces from our own side.

ON THE HILL CATHERINE STILL WATCHES.
THE MONKS CHURCH TOWN
YOU WERE NEARLY RIGHT BEFORE
IF YOU SWAN OFF, YOU WILL BE REWARDED.

David passed the envelope and paper around the group. Four nights after John's promise, it had appeared overnight, on the dashboard of David's locked car. Regrettably, we were all a little too blasé about this kind of minor miracle, as we considered it.

Another quest. Although the prospect excited us, work got in the way. We couldn't congregate until late in the evening, too late for any but the most cursory assessment and general discussion. We decided that we would each carry out our own research before reporting back to the group!

The next day at work, by sneaking peeks at the internet, sandwiched between half-hearted spells of the day job, I tried to decipher clues from the wording of the puzzle. We were *"nearly right before?"* I wondered, was this the reference to our trip to Buckler's Hard? That time we had been wrong, nowhere near right. But Buckler's Hard just didn't seem to fit the clues in any way at all.

Who was Catherine? Was she a normal person? And what did she still watch? I spent a fruitless morning searching.

I hoped that my friends would be more productive and more imaginative than I was proving to be.

It took six days for us to break through. Sue, who didn't have access to the internet at her school, diligently spent her evenings researching with David.

At my instigation, we'd decided to work in pairs, deliberately not meeting up as a group until we felt we were getting somewhere. "This," I'd pointed out, "will prevent preconceptions and the suppositions of others, clouding original thought." However, I have to admit that Trish and I enjoyed our time together, more as a respite from recent activities than an assignment to push forward with.

On the seventh evening, Trish cheerfully announced. "Sue and David think they've worked out the puzzle. They will be arriving shortly to dazzle you with their brilliant intellect."

To my immense annoyance, despite being in the know, Trish kept quiet, delighting in my ignorance, refusing to steal her sister's glory by spilling the beans. "As you've done virtually no research all week, you're just going to have to wait," she told me with a smug grin.

"ABBOTSBURY, on the Dorset coast," the pair announced, triumphantly.

Sue explained, "I remember learning a little bit about the Abbotsbury swannery at school. I thought the instruction to *"Swan off"* was weird, particularly from John, because we know he has a reason for everything."

Instead of searching for place names, as Trish and I had been doing, Sue had typed one word into Google, *"Swans."* Buried several pages into the list of results was the website for the famous Abbotsbury swannery.

Grinning happily, Sue passed me a page printed from the official website. "Read this," she said. The page contained a potted history of the village of Abbotsbury, as well as the swannery itself.

Eagerly I read on, scanning the words, pleased that we were moving forwards and identifying a target. A brief read through was enough to suggest it might be, and probably was, our destination.

Abbotsbury had had a monastery up until the dissolution by Henry VIII. The swannery was on the Fleet. Sue was quick to remind me, "You suggested the Fleet as a possible destination for the earlier quest, when we searched for a non-existent fleet."

I turned back to the printed webpage and read on. The tower on the hill at Abbotsbury was called St Catherine, which had been left standing by the crown forces of Henry to serve as a landmark for sailors.

"Maybe she still watches out for sailors!" I grinned, looking towards Sue and David; things were looking very good indeed. I continued, learning that the site of the Abbotsbury monastery had been chosen about the time of the Roman withdrawal from Britain, when, according to the website, the priest, named *Beltfuls*, had visitations from St Peter.

We wondered what form these visitations had taken. "I wonder if we're mirroring those visitations across the centuries?" said Trish.

Abbotsbury, it seemed, fitted all the clues; we were off on another weekend jaunt.

Unfortunately, despite being eager to travel, we had almost a full week in which to plan our trip. Sue and David had unveiled the solution on a Sunday evening. We knew it would be safer to go to Dorset on the spur of the moment, but there was little we could do; work commitments intervened. "There is no choice; we have to plan and travel next Saturday," Trish said, the regret evident in her voice.

Realisation dawned. "Following recent events, there's every chance of another intervention into our day. They are getting bolder and bolder," said David.

"Yep, but there's little we can do. At least now we have the trigger words, that's something," I replied, hopefully.

On the day, Trish agreed to drive her Nissan. David had offered, but he'd been dissuaded on the grounds that John might be called upon. A mute acceptance that we could be setting off into danger. Also, it is fair to say, Trish was probably a better driver than me, and certainly better than David.

It felt good to be sitting next to Trish as she drove her Micra towards the Dorset coast. The windows wide open, we were enjoying the rare feeling of sunshine on our arms and faces. All of us had chosen to dress for the forecast: warm and sunny weather. We sported sunglasses and bright casual shirts or summer dresses. Despite constant vigilance, there was nothing to concern us on the drive through Dorset, concluding with our visit to Abbotsbury; everything went without a hitch. The day was made even more enjoyable by the gloriously warm and sunny weather.

The village of Abbotsbury is the type of rural ideal expected by tourists in the British countryside, Portland stone cottages under lots of thatched roofs.

Encouraged by the warm weather, the village and its tourist centres were full of visitors, all expectant, eager to experience a picturesque, rustic, ideal.

Joining the rest of the tourists, we climbed the hill, looking with awe at the magnificent views from St Catherine's church. Gazing along the magnificent

Jurassic coast over the stretch of water, which is the fleet, the swans could be seen as small white shapes, moving across the surface.

We explored the monastery and all there was to see, waiting expectantly for John, who didn't show. Finally, by the late afternoon, we settled for a small tearoom on the main street, opting for a Dorset cream tea.

Sipping my tea from a dainty little cup, I was content. "I'm certain we've come to the right place," I told my friends. "The original puzzle didn't seem to specify anywhere particular, just the village. We've fully explored that, including the swannery and tower. I feel sure we only need to wait patiently for John to appear." Three pairs of eyes turned to look at David, but it was David who smiled back; John remained elusive.

There are two possible routes home from Abbotsbury: the coastal road would take us to Weymouth, then on to Southampton and a motorway nearly all the way. Or, if we cut across the Dorset countryside, we could meet the main road near Yeovil, enjoying a more relaxed, slower paced journey. "This sunshine is too magnificent to waste; we don't want to spend the evening on a soulless motorway. Let's go cross country, with a pub dinner halfway home," said David, as he climbed into the car.

At David's suggestion, Trish pulled into the car park of *The Bell Inn*, a travellers' inn on the London to West Country road. "I stopped here previously. As I recall, this place possesses a reasonable menu, which was also good value," I told them.

The cream tea had been our only food since breakfast, so sustenance was definitely required. Scrambling from the car we were full of anticipation. "Something really filling is just what's needed; lead the way," Trish grinned.

"The finest wining and dining this side of Stonehenge." I smiled as I held the door open for Sue, Trish and David, waiting as they entered the pub. I suspected at least three of us would also be anticipating a visit from John, even if David wasn't keen.

The food was every bit as good as I'd portrayed, all four of us tucking into our meals with much appreciation. Finishing my ribs and wings combo with side salad, I contentedly scanned the sweet menu, waiting for the others to complete their main courses.

Four puddings later, we retired for coffee, into the pub's garden, watching the sunset with delight as the sun disappeared over the horizon, bathing the sky in a warm reddish glow. With still no sign of John, it was time to resume the journey.

The lack of threat throughout the day resulted in complacency. We failed to notice the dark-coloured car following us out of the car park of the public house. Apart from isolated pockets of streetlights, as we passed through small villages, the road was now in darkness. On a Saturday evening, there was very little traffic about at that time.

Trish noticed them first but failed to realise the significance of the approaching headlights in her rear-view mirror, closing rapidly to within feet of us.

Angrily Trish snapped, "He's driving like an idiot, right up my tail."

The three of us turned, gawking through the rear window, slowly realising the probable and stark implication of the intimidating headlights. "Slow down, tap your brakes," I suggested, hoping there was a normal explanation for this tailgating, praying this was an inconsiderate driver, who needed reminding that he was driving too close.

No response, our pursuer's headlights remained on full beam, just feet from our bumper. I reached up, twisting the mirror from her direct sight, addressing Trish, "You won't be able to help it. Looking in the mirror will be involuntary. Try to concentrate on the road ahead. His headlights will only blind you, as well as being dangerous. We'll let you know what he's doing."

The headlights remained close to our bumper. I looked back, staring intently through the rear window. They began to creep perceptibly closer. Because of the height of the lights above the road's surface, I realised our pursuer was a 4x4, or some other raised vehicle. Briefly, I thought of Colin and his unequal battle with a Range Rover, two weeks earlier.

Trish was an excellent driver, but the size and power of a 4x4 would be no contest against her Japanese compact.

With a grinding sound, accompanied by a jolt, our pursuer finally touched. Owing to the discrepancy in height, the chaser missed Trish's bumper, instead, making contact with the rear wing of the Nissan. "Shit, that was close." Trish gripped hard, steadying the wheel and controlling her car; we surged ahead as they fell back slightly.

Straining to see beyond the dazzling glare, I watched our pursuers edge forwards. "Here he comes again, hang on." I recognised the name Range Rover on its bonnet, in white lettering. Again, the two cars touched. Underneath me, I felt the rear wheels begin to slide sideways. Then Trish fought and once more regained control, holding the car steady, knuckles white, hands fastened onto the wheel.

"They're getting more persistent," she said, staring ahead grimly.

"You're doing brilliant, Trish. Remember, concentrate on the road in front of you," I reminded her. "We'll watch behind, warn you when he is coming."

The road was a single carriageway, seemingly devoid of other traffic. Unconsciously Trish had stamped on the accelerator, searching for as much speed as possible from the little Nissan.

"Slow down," Sue yelled at her sister, through the confusion. "You can't outrun them; the slower we're going, the better chance we have, if you come off the road."

Despairingly, I hoped their objective was only to force us off the road, then drive on as they had with Colin. But I also knew, with each incursion into our lives, the opposition had increased the stakes. Sue's advice made sense. We would be the losers in a high-speed crash. Against all her instincts, Trish braked hard, forcing the car to slow.

The unexpected worked, at least to begin with. Instantly the Range Rover fell back, putting a little distance between our brake lights and his car. This reprieve lasted seconds. Once more our powerful pursuer crept forwards, seeking to close the distance between us. For a third time, we heard the excruciating sound of metal against metal. The two cars touched again. Trish, her arms rigid and locked, gripped the steering wheel, fighting the car beneath her, instinctively bringing it back under her control as it fought against her.

"You're doing wonderfully; hang on in there." I squeezed her arm in encouragement.

"Abba," Sue shouted, realising that we had the protection on whom we could call at will.

David's back arched. He let out an anguished hissing, lips curling back in a snarl, exposing the teeth. He growled, a low hostile sound. I saw the eyes glowering at us, dark pinholes of hatred in yellow corneas. I had been here before. The route of communication had been hijacked. Suddenly, we were in far deeper trouble, attacked from the outside, trapped within the confines of our car with the devil incarnate himself.

"That worked well then," Trish said, glancing over her shoulder.

"Abba," I shouted again, panicking. Out of the corner of my eye, I could see Sue, horrified, trying to put as much distance as possible between David's body and herself.

"Trish," I yelled, "have you got a bible with you?" Desperately, I was trying to calculate a responsive strategy to this latest terrifying invasion.

"In the glove compartment," she replied, eyes only inches from the windscreen, straining to drive the car while bedlam reined all around her.

The second shriek of "Abba" was more effective. David's form twitched, then slumped backwards, collapsing across the seat. Inertia replacing demonic snarling.

John's voice spoke out calmly, "The evil one has intervened."

"You don't say," I replied, not caring if I sounded flippant.

"This time, you need to prevent these intrusions with the good book," he ordered. "I'm ahead of you there," I told him. I had already pulled Trish's new pocket bible from her glove compartment. Turning towards the now slumped David, I held the open Bible out to a cowering Sue. She was in the best position to apply the book to David's oblivious frame, which was now lifeless in the corner of the seat. As John vacated his temporary habitat, Sue edged forwards, nervously holding the Bible out in front of her, until she could reach out, placing the open Bible on David's chest. David's body gave a small shudder, seeming to relax slightly.

"Hold the book there. Your life might depend on it!" I instructed, turning my attention towards the dangers presented by the relentless enemy outside.

Again, there came a crunching jolt; we were once more nudged from behind. I felt the car jerk sideways, sliding across the black tarmac. Trish was brilliant; she fought the small car with consummate skill and determination, righting the skid, controlling the slide. "I don't know how much longer I can keep this up," she gasped in a whisper, sweat beginning to form on her forehead.

"You're doing fine, brilliantly, hang on in there."

We drove onwards, hurtling across the dark countryside of southern England, our evil enemy's intent on forcing us off the road.

What atrocities they were planning were yet unknown. There were short moments of reprieve when they were forced to fall back because of the appearance of other road users, or small well-lit villages.

Briefly, I considered our options, asking Trish to stop at a service station, then confronting our enemies.

Trish thought, before responding. "It won't work. If they do want the confrontation, David is still asleep, if it is David in his body at this present moment. He will certainly be of no use in any confrontation, at least, not until he regains full consciousness. Until then, it's only you, me and Sue. I don't fancy those odds. Remember Colin reporting the Jaguar appearing after the Range Rover. I bet that's not far away."

As she drove the car, I noticed Trish constantly mumbling under her breath. I leaned closer, listening carefully. "Angelikinus, Corriendo," Trish repeated over and over, just audibly. A cry for help in this desperate situation. At least one of us remembered at the time of need, even if nothing seemed to be happening. Dourly, I noticed the lack of "Abba" in her appeal.

Motorway 1 mile, the sign flashed past giving Trish and me the seed of an idea at the same moment.

"Martyn" – Trish turned to me declaring – "I'm going to speed up, as fast as it is safe to do so. At the very last moment, I'm going to take the slip road onto the A road. Hopefully, leaving our pursuers to continue onto the motorway. It's a long shot but it's all I can think of."

We knew the area; hopefully the Range Rover would be unable to follow us at the very last second, allowing an escape.

"Half a mile to go," I whispered, as a second sign shot past. I gripped the door handle. Trish's judgement was fantastic. As we sped up to eighty miles per hour, I yelled out, "It's too late." At the speed we were doing, I thought we were going to miss the turning, but Trish judged it to perfection, wrenching the steering wheel hard to the left. The small Nissan shot sideways, bouncing across the chevrons. Trish fought the juddering wheel, desperately struggling to maintain control across the gritty surface. Unexpectedly there was a smack and a vicious jolt; one wheel mounted a kerb. I was thrown in my seat, my head thumping into the roof lining. Then the seat belt arrested my momentum; we were over. Trish applied enough brake to regain control of the car. All eyes looked behind, searching for the following Range Rover, but there was no sign!

The car was awash with relief as we joined the carriageway.

"You've done it, magnificent." Thanks to Trish's calmness under pressure, we'd escaped from danger yet again. Trish slowed, pulling over to regain her calm.

Now safe, we backtracked before joining the motorway, knowing we were several miles behind our rivals.

Stirring and trying to stretch out, David groaned, showing distinct signs of waking. He began pushing at the open Bible, which Sue had diligently held against his chest, even when we were being thrown around like proverbial rag dolls. I turned to find out what was happening.

"Where am I?" I immediately knew this was David returning to consciousness, but we weren't going to take any chances. Sue remaining poised, attentive, hovering the Bible over David's groggy form until he was fully awake. Then we were reassured that David had returned to the living.

"Where's he going?"

I glanced towards Trish, wondering what was concerning her, thinking, what now?

Trish's gaze was concentrating hard on her rear-view mirror, checking what was happening on the road behind. I turned, searching. Peering through the window, I shaded my eyes from the glare of headlights, which were far too close!

"Surely not again!" I muttered.

I thought I could vaguely discern the shape of the car behind the lights. "It looks distinctly like a Jaguar driving very close on our tail. Way to close to be anything but a deliberate act of intimidation." I told Trish, despair bringing a lump to my throat. "When will this ever end, this constant persecution and terrorisation?" She gritted her teeth in concentration. Once more determined to evade pursuit.

Lit by our headlights, a sign for the town of Basingstoke appeared, the turn-off half a mile away. Praying second time lucky, Trish repeated the subterfuge, which had worked so well, moments earlier. This time she left it even later, holding on until I knew it was too late. With a tortured squeal of brakes and a vicious twist of the steering wheel we were off. For an instant I thought we were going to turn over. I felt the off-side wheels begin to lift. Then we were upright, off the motorway, gunning down the slip road, aiming to lose ourselves in the town of Basingstoke.

The Jaguar's occupants must have been in phone contact with those in the Range Rover. The driver of the Jaguar anticipated the tactic. As soon as Trish twitched the wheel to go left, the Jaguar followed, as if attached by rope. The better roadholding of the Jaguar was more suited to the sudden change of direction. The ploy was expected, easily forestalled. We hurtled down the slip road, the Jaguar only inches behind, glued to our bumper, pitiless and intimidating.

We made hurried plans. "Our best hope is to find the town centre and dump the car. Hopefully, with lots of Saturday evening revellers thronging around, we might be able to get away," I said, twisting in my seat to share my thoughts with David and Sue in the back.

Trish voiced her opinion. "Might as well. It's the best idea we've got at the moment, but I don't know Basingstoke particularly well. Look for a sign – I don't know where I'm driving."

Gradually, in response to the road condition, Trish began slowing. We pushed onwards, tracking along unknown roads and streets. In the confusion, we'd missed the signs for the town centre.

The Jaguar remained behind us, not closing the gap, for now content to terrorise. Without their close-quartered intimidation, the atmosphere of agitation within our car subsided.

However, the headlights in our rear-view mirror remained a constant.

Trish spoke. "There seems little urgency in the chase now; they're not pushing in like the other car; they're just following!"

"I can't guess their intentions, but they have their prey in their sights. They're stalking us. We can't hope to outrun them, not on these streets." I glanced over my shoulder.

With David awake, in the guise of David, we filled in the blanks. To his relief, David had missed most of the ordeal. Now with David awakened, and cognizant to the dangers, we considered the possibility of stopping and confronting our pursuers.

Studying the road behind, David suddenly said, "That's another car behind the Jaguar. I think it's a Range Rover!"

If this was the same car we'd evaded earlier, then it was the worst possible news. We were certainly outnumbered and cornered.

The appearance of the Jag supported growing evidence that these guys weren't there simply to threaten and intimidate. The persistence of these repeated attacks was gradually bringing us close to desperation.

There was nothing Trish could do to prevent it happening on a long straight stretch of road; the driver of the Jaguar took his opportunity, charging passed us. As it overtook, I tried counting the number of occupants in the car, but in the darkness this proved impossible.

Pulling across and in front of us, the Jaguar slowed dramatically, causing Trish to do the same. It was obvious we had skilfully been out manoeuvred. Now we were caught like rats in a trap.

Hopelessness rekindled resistance. Trish declared, "We're not giving up yet, but I have no idea where we are!" I looked glumly through the window. We were in an unlit suburb on the edge of town, but where was a mystery?

In a single swift movement, Trish yanked the steering wheel to the right, almost hitting an oncoming car, yelling as she did so. "We're outa here." She'd taking the first opportunity which presented. I was enormously thankful that Trish was no capitulating wallflower.

Fortunately, Trish was an achiever, capable and willing to take the battle forwards under her own initiative.

"No sign of them," I shouted, excitement rising. For several seconds, we thought the ploy had worked. The Jaguar had passed the turning, and briefly the Range Rover disappeared from sight. We ploughed onwards, rushing through the unknown streets of what seemed to be a suburban housing estate.

"They're back!" The dread encapsulated by David's voice was self-evident in the two simple words, as he announced the return of the Range Rover on our tail.

"This is never ending." Trish was driving to her utmost ability, twisting and turning, frantically trying to lose them, throwing the small car carelessly round corners and through the empty residential streets, all to no avail.

Abruptly, the Jaguar appeared in our headlights, heading towards us, steadfast and unmoving. We were trapped between the two cars with nowhere to go.

Partially hidden in the dim street lighting, an unlit opening appeared on our right, an escape route. A short driveway leading towards a darkened school building. "Over there!" I shouted, jabbing my finger in the direction of the dimly lit entrance, hoping that Trish would understand in time.

With the benefit of hindsight, this was a wrong move. The area was in darkness, away from the residential homes and street lighting. There was minimal chance of this being a throughway, but hindsight is something that few can benefit from.

Instantly understanding, without slowing Trish wrenched the Nissan sideways, arrowing for the entry to the school. We followed the tree-lined drive for only fifty yards. To our horror, we realised that this was a dead end. The drive stopped at the locked school gates. Apart from the car headlights, the area was in darkness.

"We are going to have to run for it" I shouted, adrenaline and fear dictating my reactions. Trish stomped on the brakes as we piled out of the car, desperately searching for an escape route. Horrified, we realised there was nowhere to run. The school fence, enclosing the turning circle on three sides, was too high to climb. We were totally trapped and compromised. The only exit was the route which we'd driven in on. The Jaguar and Range Rover now drove towards Trish's car at a leisurely pace, exuding purposeful menace as they came.

Jerome climbed out of the Jaguar first. As he did so, with detached curiosity, I noticed that his gypsy style earring, absent on the night of the Supertramp's' incident, had now reappeared. He looked more a gypsy than ever. Joining him, Mr Scarface, Jerome's blond accomplice I recognised from Buckler's Hard, clambered from the passenger side. They were immediately joined by the instantly recognisable, sharp-featured, Cruella de Vil and her friend, Miss Mousy Average.

To our dismay, crushing any thoughts I'd been harbouring of a full-on, equal numbered, confrontation. From the Range Rover three new sinister looking characters emerged. One woman flanked by two men. All three newcomers appeared roughly the same age as Jerome and his cronies, about ten years older than us. All looked very much more confident in this situation than we currently felt They took up station just behind Jerome and Scarface, who stood side by side, in the vanguard of this offensive formation.

"We meet again, Martyn," Jerome said, sneering. He addressed me directly while very slowly sidling forwards, vengeance was revealed by the tone of his voice. "Only this time, there are no bouncers or bright lights to protect you." I glowered back at him defiantly, in silence, not trusting my voice to reply. I locked my legs against the feeling of weakness, which had spontaneously engulfed them. I was determined not to let this arrogant adversary achieve any advantage during this preliminary verbal skirmish.

Behind me David pushed forward, coming alongside, trying to screen Trish and Sue.

"Don't expect this is going to turn out alright in the end," Jerome continued, enjoying the drama of conquest. He spoke without rancour. "There is no way out; we had hoped to kill you, or at least some of you, in a car crash. Easier for the authorities to accept. But it doesn't matter, your deaths will simply be the consequences of a bizarre and inexplicable suicide pact. Your bodies found in the woods some way from here." He announced this emotionlessly, as if he was announcing dinner was ready. "We have people in place who will ensure the correct conclusions to any investigation the authorities care to mount."

Somewhere, deep inside, I wondered how these people had become involved with what they were doing. Was it really a choice? Did they possess the necessary callousness and ruthlessness to actually murder us in cold blood? It seemed we were going to find out very soon.

The butterflies within my chest suddenly intensified. Jerome and Scarface continued moving slowly forwards with menacing purpose, their companions eagerly crowding in behind, watching on with ghoulish delight, relishing our plight, which now seemed hopeless.

My blood froze. In the harsh, unforgiving light of the Jaguar's headlights, I recognised something which I hadn't noticed before. Jerome and Scarface both held something cradled in their outstretched hands. We heard an audible double click and the switch blades appeared, blades pointing towards David and myself. They adopted an unmistakable attack posture. I fought to control my body; my stomach had turned to jelly at the sight of those wicked blades.

"What the...?" Jerome twisted in astonishment, fresh headlights suddenly appearing behind him. Entering the school driveway, rapidly covering the distance between us a car approached at speed, scattering Jerome's colleagues as it advanced. Brakes screeched as the car halted alongside Jerome, raising a veil of dust. Even before the car stopped, the passenger door was flung open hard, hitting Jerome, knocking him to the ground. Instantly, there were four protectors, two men, two women, creating a human shield between ourselves and Jerome's crew. The obvious leader of this new group ignored us, instead turning towards the prostrate and flapping Jerome.

"Numbers are more even now, care to continue?" he said.

Jerome would have had difficulty starting a fight from the ground, but Scarface still seemed intent on causing mischief. Unwilling to give up the prey, he advanced, thrusting the knife forwards in a jerky motion. "Look who it is," he sneered, aiming the blade aggressively towards our protectors.

A loud crack preceded Scarface's scream by a millisecond.

The leader of our protectors, in a single swift motion, had produced a short wooden club. This had crashed down on Scarface's wrist with startling and pitiless vehemence. We heard the metallic clang of the knife hitting concrete. Scarface stood, features grimaced in pain, his right wrist gripped protectively in his left hand. It was difficult to be sure in the gloom of the headlights, but I felt certain that blondie was now harbouring a broken wrist.

This wasn't enough for Cruella de Vil. "Get up and kill him," she snarled at the sheepishly rising Jerome.

Whatever else he was, Jerome was obviously a realist. Instead, supporting Scarface by his good arm, Jerome manhandled him, not too gently, towards the Jaguar.

"Shut up," he growled at her, ignoring her demands. "Get in the car."

It was over! Raising a curtain of dust and gravel with the wheelspins, they were gone in seconds.

In the blink of an eye, we had been transported from desperation to salvation.

"I'm Paul," the leader said, turning towards us. As he spoke, I noted the faint aroma of apples hanging in the air.

Half an hour later we were pulling into the car park of an all-night service area, safe and sound. After introducing himself as Paul, the leader of our rescuers hadn't waited for further introductions. Brusquely he ordered, "Get into your car and follow me to safer territory; they might be back." Shocked and dazed by the pace of events, we meekly obeyed. Without thought or comment, we dutifully followed Paul's vehicle northwards, through the Hampshire countryside, until we linked up with the main road heading north. Fortunately, we'd met our protective syndicate: Paul's group were the good guys.

Once settled in the brightly lit, Formica rich restaurant, we began to relax a little. Now safe, introductions could be made. Paul, the obvious leader, once again introduced himself. "I'm Paul Harrison." I appraised him while he spoke. Paul was clearly older than us. I'd guessed in his mid-thirties, short wiry black hair with just the hint of grey at the temples. Eyes, also grey, and almost disconcerting, the intensity of his gaze. He was obviously sizing us up. Paul looked very fit, an air of total confidence in himself and his ability to deal with those around him. There was nothing hesitant about the way he was now taking charge of our meeting. "This is Sandra," he said, indicating the woman beside him.

Sandra had strawberry blond hair, slightly lighter than Sue's, and blue eyes. I judged her age as similar to Paul's. Just a hint of wrinkles, the newly forming crows' feet around the eyes. Slight rosy cheeks gave an impression of healthy outdoor living.

Taking control, Sandra continued with a smile and a twinkle, raising her left hand to silence Paul's attempts.

"I'm his wife," she interjected, leaning forward to shake hands with us all individually. Then Sandra completely flummoxed us by announcing, "We were instructed to find you and protect you."

Stunning news! Trish had used the trigger word, Corriendo, in hope rather than expectation. Now, it seemed, it had worked!

Forestalling any questions for now, Sandra hastily continued. "This is Kate," she said, introducing the red-headed woman sitting on her other side. Kate had a very serious look about her. Possibly the black plastic glass frames, copper-coloured hair tied up in a ponytail, and accompanying granny cardigan, was designed to achieve the impression she desired.

Sandra proudly informed us, "Katie's the intelligent member of our group." Katie blushed ever so slightly as Sandra continued. "Katie is a post-grad doctorate at the University of Oxford, in their physical science faculty, researching, stuff way beyond the understanding of the rest of us."

However serious Katie was in her day job, she had a welcoming, self-effacing smile, simply saying "hi" as she held out a hand to each of us in turn. Katie's husband, Robert Bolt, or "Bolty", as he instructed us to call him, sat by his wife's side. Introduced by Katie, Bolty was a thick-set man, maybe five feet ten, brown hair, just beginning to recede. His muscles were starting to run to seed at the onset of middle age. As Bolty spoke, I noticed a slight Scottish twang in his words.

"You're not from around here!" Trish stated the obvious, shaking Bolty by the hand. Robert replied shyly, "No, I'm originally from Motherwell. I stayed down south after leaving the Royal Engineers. There was nothing to go back for up there, so I took a job in a local garage near where I was stationed."

Introductions completed, both groups began the flood of questions that such a mind-blowing introduction created. It was soon obvious that Paul and Sandra were the chatty members of the group. Katie and Bolty seemed happy to sit back, allowing the conversation to wash around them, chipping in occasionally when they felt it was required.

Trish immediately launched in with the question which we all wanted answered. "How did you know where to come, and when?" We leant forward expectantly, collectively waiting for the response.

Paul answered, "Strange really," he said recalling. "Katie got a text this morning telling her to gather the syndicate together and contact through the calling table. Once we did, the message was to go to *Winklebury school* in Basingstoke, this evening, to arrive at 9.48 precisely. We did, as you know we found you!"

"So, you use the calling table?" I asked.

"Yes, we've used the calling table for about three years now," he informed us. "The text was the first time that the disciples have used another method to contact us."

"Ah, so you don't have the apostles Luke or John physically manifest through one of you?" I asked casually, savouring the effect I knew my words would have on the other group. The statement did indeed elicit the anticipated response, amazed denials and open mouths all round. Katie stopped, a fork full of chips frozen between the plate and her mouth.

Glancing sideways, I noticed David shrinking backwards into his chair. He was listening uneasily as the conversation developed, knowing that, very soon, he would be the centre of attention.

Trish, Sue and I, briefly outlined a sequential summation of our recent past, starting with the original experiments that Sunday evening. At the correct moment during the narrative, seven pairs of eyes twisted to stare at a reticent and uncomfortable David, all wondering if this was the prompt for John to appear, but David remained as David, head bowed, sipping tea diffidently. Once they'd expressed fulsome astonishment at our adventures, I asked them, "How did you manage to become involved in such an astonishing adventure?"

Sandra answered, revealing, "We first met Luke almost three years ago, after a night in the pub. We went home and experimented with the calling table; initially, like you, just for a laugh, a way to pass the time. Slowly, we were drawn in deeper by the spirit of the apostle Luke. He identified himself when we asked the question, does Jesus really exist? Over time, things slowly escalated until we met the opposition, the devil's syndicate, last year. Only then, with the ferocity of the opposition, did we realise the seriousness of our involvement. However," Sandra explained, glancing towards David, "up until today, the calling table was the only form of communication between ourselves and Luke."

"How much do you know about the evil syndicate?" Sue asked, realising that the conversation would falter if we continued to focus on manifestations through a self-conscious David.

Paul took up the tale. "Prior to last year, our time in contact on the calling table was infrequent and sporadic, only when the mood took us really. Then out of the blue, like you, we received a threatening letter through the post. That weekend, the evil syndicate appeared, confronting me and the group. That's when we realised how serious this all was."

"What did they do?" we asked eagerly, displaying our ghoulish enthusiasm.

Sandra detailed the sequence of events.

"Well, Paul and I were preparing for a Saturday evening out. He checked the outbuildings on our family farm and discovered a fire, just starting to take hold." Sandra told us. "Originally, we hadn't associated the fire with the bizarre letter we'd received through the post earlier in the week. Crudely penned on a single sheet of paper, written in red ink, stating GOD = DEATH."

Paul chipped in. "I simply dismissed the letter as a crank and threw it away without another thought. At the time, our visits to the calling table were so irregular and rare that the connection between us talking to Luke and the letter simply didn't occur. Anyway, the fire brigade spent several hours dousing and controlling the blaze; we lost the barn. When we returned to the farmhouse, we found it, written in animal blood on the walls of our bedroom, STOP OR DIE."

Sandra declared to her engrossed audience, "I guess the evil syndicate sneaked into the farmhouse while we were attending the fire. Only then did we begin to think that we were targeted victims, although we still failed to make the connection to Luke's visitations. Why would we?"

Paul took over the narrative from his wife. "The next day, a Sunday, we phoned Bolty and Katie, asking them to drive over to the farmhouse, the scene of the attack. It was a mess, the barn burnt out and the blood on the walls. We had to sleep in the spare room but we still couldn't work out why we were targets. No conclusions were drawn; it was perplexing, so the four of us decided to adjourn to a local pub to continue our discussion over Sunday lunch."

Sandra was eager to complete the tale. "During the journey, a dark maroon Jaguar appeared on our tail, driving much too close for comfort." She indicated Bolty. "Our driver dismissed the Jag as a Sunday idiot until they sped into the bend of a tight corner on a narrow rural road. The Jaguar recklessly forced Robert to swerve to avoid a collision. Even so, Robert still skidded, ending up resting on the very edge of a ditch. When we came to rest, sitting in an unstable car, recovering from shock, we realised that the Jag had stopped further down the road. Nobody got out at first. Then they did but, strangely, they didn't come over to see if we were all right, like you would expect from a normal person. They were just standing there, looking at us, all four of them."

Paul admitted, "I was the first to recover. I've always had a hot temper the anger rose, boiled over. On impulse, I sprang from the car, wanting to confront the irresponsible driver of the Jaguar. So, I sprinted the twenty metres between us to be met by two men with knives and knuckledusters. That was Jerome and Maurice"

"What happened then?" we asked, enthralled.

"I stopped short, recognising this was far more than a careless road traffic incident. Before I had time to think and plan, Jerome stepped forwards and spoke. 'Stop what you're doing. You use the calling table again and it will be more than a barn that gets burnt.' With that warning, Jerome's sidekick stepped forward, ramming his fist, complete with knuckleduster, hard into my stomach." Paul looked up, embarrassed, as if we would think less of him, in the role of protector, for being caught out like that!

"It was the totally unexpected and ruthless nature of the attack, along with the force of the impact, which left me winded and bruised, on my knees in the middle of the lane. Before I had chance to recover and respond, they were gone," Paul told us ruefully.

"Never mind, you were certainly up for it tonight," I told him.

Katie spoke. "The whole confrontation, from Paul leaving the car to Robert arriving at his side, lasted no more than ten to twelve seconds. By the time Robert arrived to help Paul up, we were watching the Jaguar speed down the lane, as if chased by the hounds of hell. Robert then helped Paul back to our car.

"What happened next?" Trish asked. "You obviously haven't stopped."

"No, I don't like to be intimidated," Paul informed us. "We continued to use the calling table. Luke gave us the names of the evil syndicate and we researched them. With Luke's help, we now know a lot about them."

This little gem of information filled me with delight.

Jerome Brendon-Smythe was the leader of the group, for Jerome was indeed his real name. Surprisingly, his elegant companion Cruella, who had urged Jerome to kill us only hours earlier, was Jerome's sister Rosalind, not, as I had imagined, his wife or partner. With names like Jerome and Rosalind, I wasn't expecting them to hail from a rough council estate, and I was right.

Sandra explained, "The evil group, led by Jerome, live in the village of Tufton Gray, a village, a few miles from

Basingstoke. They aren't titled, but they do come from a family with land and money, as well as owning the local hotel. Hence, they can afford posh cars such as Jaguars and Range Rovers."

Paul continued. "Jerome's sidekick, Scarface, is called Maurice White, and his partner is Anne Giddes. Maurice and Anne live together in the village. Maurice works as a chargehand for Jerome on the farm.

"I hope he has insurance," I joked, recollecting Paul's harsh treatment of Maurice earlier in the evening. "I'm sure you broke his wrist."

"Would you rather we had left you there for Maurice to knife you?" Paul asked, somewhat drily. "I owed him one anyway."

"No, glad you were able to ignore the death threats and be there for us tonight; you did a great job." I smiled, not wanting to antagonise our protecting guardians.

Once again, Paul astounded us, detailing how he and Bolty had gained knowledge of the everyday workings of Jerome's syndicate. They'd reconnoitred the village, including Jerome and Rosalind's manor house.

"Didn't they catch you?" I asked, remembering my experiences at Buckler's Hard.

"No, though they definitely knew we were there." Paul grinned, before boasting of his army training. "We are trained in that type of thing. It's something you don't forget. I guess that is why we were chosen as your protectors."

Although this counterpart syndicate hadn't been sent all over the country seeking clues to riddles, after encountering Jerome and the evil Maurice, they had visited the calling table much more frequently. Luke and

John had been quite forthcoming with information about the satanic opposition.

Paul explained, "The evil syndicate use the calling table, just like us, and sometimes you. The manifestations through David are indeed unique to your group." Again, he flicked a glance towards David. "We'd been warned about planning in advance. Robert and my reconnaissance had some scares, but Satan and his demons hadn't time to warn Jerome sufficiently early enough for a reception to be prepared for us; we did it on the spur of the moment."

"Still," I reflected, "it must have taken quite a bit of courage to undertake such a mission."

"It's not the safest place to go, so don't go charging off to Tufton Gray yourselves on the way home," Sandra warned. "It seems the place is a little coven of Jerome's evil acolytes. We were warned through the calling table; almost half the village has some knowledge of, or a willing connection to, Jerome, Rosalind and their syndicate."

"Wow," said David with a nervous laugh. "Wait until the local TV news hears about that."

Katie changed the subject, leaning forwards. "We were advised, almost a year ago, that we were together for a purpose. A momentous event for mankind is about to take place. We were told that our task is to act as protectors to the chosen ones." Somewhat smugly, I realised, this was obviously us.

Katie revealed, "We have been informed there is to be a historic event, but we have no idea what it is. They told us so long ago that the information had almost lost its relevance to our everyday life, until now!" she said, staring at us each in turn!

Trish immediately chose to reveal all to our astounded audience. "We are here to become apostles for a new modern-day messiah who is going to be born soon, into our world, to draw all to him."

Personally, I was unsure if it was wise to reveal so much, so soon, but I figured, if he disapproved, John had the option of appearing. I also reasoned that we owed Paul, and the other three, our very lives. It would have been churlish for me to intervene at that moment.

Their total surprise at the disclosure of a new messiah, for our time was complete. Appropriate superlatives were difficult to conjure, set against the enormity of the revelation. They listened to Trish, open-mouthed and in awe.

With the collective sharing of discovery and disclosure, time had simply whizzed past. I looked at my wristwatch, realising that it was nearly two in the morning. Gazing around, I saw we were the last in an empty restaurant. Stifling a yawn, I realised it had been a long day. It seemed a lifetime ago that I had crawled out of bed, impatiently preparing for the three-hour drive to Abbotsbury. Surreptitiously, I examined Trish, who had done all the driving, hence suffering the majority of the stress caused by Jerome's gang of cut-throats. I recognised the fatigue in her eyes as she leaned back in her seat, trying to remain interested and attentive to the conversation around her.

"It's getting late; we'd better go." I made a move, the others followed. Turning to Paul, I asked, "What happens next?" deferring the decision of further contact between us to my older colleague.

Sandra interjected before her husband had the chance to speak. "Well, I guess, unless expressly forbidden, it would be good to know you all better." Turning to Paul, she announced firmly, "They can come over to the farm for lunch next Sunday."

This was fine with us, and Paul. "Great," Trish responded, "now we've got your number, I'll call in the week to make the arrangements."

Finally, we were driving home in a buoyant mood. Apart from the obvious terror, the day had turned out to be amazing. Hopefully, we'd completed our mission, and despite the fraught journey, we'd met another syndicate in the process. Our protective guardians. We'd also learnt their identities and lots of useful information about the enemy. In the quiet contemplative car, I smiled to myself, imagining the possibilities. If required, we could now go on the offensive, take the battle to the enemy!

On the Sunday I slept late, not surfacing from the depths of my pit until almost ten am. There was no hurry. I planned a long, lazy shower, followed by a leisurely brunch. Then I would call Trish to make plans. Shuffling to the bathroom, still yawning, I sought nothing further than a lazy day of nothingness.

The jet of warm water hit me in the face, refreshing in its intensity. With eyes closed against the jet, I groped for the shower gel, working up a fierce lather. Soaping away happily, not a care in the world. Tunelessly singing the words of "Killer Queen", I completely failed to do justice to the Freddie Mercury classic. Looking down, I languidly examined the water effluent, as it created a soapy vortex at the trap.

It was then that I noticed the mark on my left hip. Ah, I thought, rubbing at it with a soapy palm: dirt or maybe a bruise. I pondered, trying to remember if I'd had any accidents lately. The mark remained untouched, stubbornly refusing to be washed away following my soapy administrations. I looked harder, staring at my hip, wondering where I'd received this strange small bruise. My hands slowed their soaping motion as I tried to concentrate and take a closer look.

On one's own body, the hip is a difficult place to scrutinise but, peering closer, I realised this was no dirt or bruise. It looked like a tattoo! In mild panic, I pushed the shower door open. Standing in the middle of the bathroom, the water draining off me. I reached for my small shaving mirror. It was indeed a thumbnail sized tattoo that had apparently appeared on my hip during the previous twenty-four hours. I'd showered the previous morning and, although in a hurry, I was fairly certain I hadn't seen a tattoo.

With the help of two mirrors, and lots of twisting, I managed to inspect the tattoo properly. It was a circle with an eye inside the circle. The tattoo was in black ink, no bigger than fifteen millimetres across. By passing my fingertips over the tattoo, it revealed, although the skin was slightly raised, there was no pain. It seemed that, somehow, I'd gained a tattoo overnight, without any of the pain associated with new tattoos.

Trish answered her mobile on the third ring. In answer to my weird question about her state of dress, she replied, with bewilderment, "Both myself and Sue are in our dressing gowns at the breakfast table! No, neither of us have showered yet. Why?"

I revealed my discovery.

"Wait there, I'll check!" Trish said, immediately taking the phone with her to the bathroom. "Yes, it's there. I've got one too!" she informed me, breathlessly, after an intimate inspection of her hip.

Listening to Trish's description, her tattoo appeared to be different to mine. "I've got a small circle with the star of David positioned at its centre! I'll call you back when Sue's checked herself."

After speaking to Trish, I picked up the phone to call David.

By the time we met in the flat, it had been established, overnight, we had all acquired a small tattoo on the hip. We'd also established, these tattoos were all different. I had the eye, Trish had a Star of David, Sue received a small right-handed spiral and David a circle with a cross which quartered the circle. It was obvious where the tattoos came from, but what was the meaning?

"Greetings, my friends" John arrived with unusual alacrity. There had been no waiting around once we'd gathered.

"You have discovered our gift to you!"

We'd known where they'd come from. "But what do they mean?" I asked.

John explained, "You have all been given a mark of my Lord. Just like the Jewish circumcision is a symbol of ownership, then you have each been given a unique tattoo, to identify your roles as individuals within the syndicate." He revealed to me, "Martyn, your eye signifies that you are the watchman, watching over the group, just as the Lord and his angels watch over you all."

Great, I thought sardonically and somewhat ungratefully, the burden of responsibility is increased.

John counselled, "Trish has the star of David to signify that she was chosen because she is loved so much. Sue's spiral denotes the spiritual aspect of your group." John promised Sue, "You are the most spiritual receptive among you all."

"Finally, David has the circle with a cross, cutting it into equal quarters. This represents the centre of the syndicate. It is David who it all flows through. Without David you couldn't carry on!"

I asked, "Will Colin receive his mark, wherever he is in the world?"

He replied, "Colin hasn't yet received his marking; you have earnt yours. Colin will receive his gift of ownership once he earns the right to own such a marking."

Fortunately, the tattoos were small and discreet. I quickly got used to it being there, thanking the Lord he hadn't chosen to circumcise me as I slept.

The next Sunday we piled into the car for the mercifully uneventful, two-hour drive to Oxfordshire. Our aim, to become further acquainted with Paul, Sandra, Bolty and Katie.

During the first meeting, Paul and Sandra told us they were a childless couple in their mid-thirties. They lived alone on a dairy farm that they ran as a business. The farm, near the Oxfordshire village of Watling, was inherited unexpectedly by Sandra, after her Father collapsed and died of a heart attack at the early age of sixty.

Paul had told us the previous week, "At the time, I'd just left the army. I was seeking a new direction in life. It wasn't great on Sandra, or her dad, I guess, but for us the timing was perfect." The couple dropped all other projects to painfully learn the disciplines of dairy farming.

"Mainly through trial and error; we've made some horrendous cock-ups on the way, but we think we've turned a corner. We're hoping to make a success of the enterprise now," he'd told us.

I drove the Ford through the gate into the farmyard, just in time to observe Paul and a farm hand, urging the last of the cattle from the sheds, across the yard towards the open farmland.

"Just finished milking," he explained, clattering across the yard, a broad grin across his face, hand held out. "Sandra's inside. Go on in. I'll be there in a few minutes, once these beasts are safely in the fields."

Sandra was indeed in the kitchen, in the act of putting the kettle on, having heard our arrival. Sunday was a day of rest on the farm, though Paul quickly educated us to the seven-day working week required in farming. "There is still milking to be done, cattle to monitor," he said earnestly, biting into a scone.

Following our recent, terrifying encounters, the day turned out to be a welcome and congenial respite. Sandra and Paul were perfect hosts. When Robert and Katie joined us, it became obvious that the newcomers were totally relaxed, in familiar surroundings, and we were made to feel part of a happy family.

While Sandra cooked, Bolty revealed the story of himself and Katie. They had been married for almost three and a half years. He had been a mechanic in the REME, stationed just down the road on the Andover base. "The home of Army Flying," he announced proudly.

"Approaching my date of discharge," Robert disclosed," I didn't want to return to Motherwell. After a ten-year absence, I had the feeling, there would be nothing there for me. Too much water under the bridge. Anyway, my parents are dead, nothing to go back to!"

Instead, Robert followed up on an advert, securing a job in a garage, in the well-known town of Henley. "I left the army and rented a small cosy flat in the nearby village of Watling. It's cheaper there," he told us.

Starting out in his new life, Bolty noticed Katie, a fellow resident, who lived a studious and solitary life in one of the other flats. "I pursued her, but she was a bit shy. Every time I asked if she wanted company, she'd find some excuse. I was beginning to think she thought I was out of her league!" He glanced at his wife and grinned. Bolty chased the reticent Katie for several months. "Until one cold morning, a faulty starter motor in her little Fiat 500 gave me the opportunity to spring to the rescue," he said, looking proudly towards her.

"Finally, I made my mind up. I let him cook me a meal." She smiled. "A year later, we got married in the local church."

"How did you meet Paul and Sandra?" Sue asked the obvious question.

"Simple really," Katie replied. "Soon after we married, we ventured out to a local young farmers' social evening, making an effort to integrate ourselves into village life."

I grinned inwardly, a no-nonsense engineer from Motherwell, Bolty, to me, didn't seem the type to be a young farmer. But then, Katie, a Doctor of Physics at Oxford University, was talking to the apostles John and Luke though the calling table, so what did I know!

Katie continued. "Sandra and I formed a good friendship via the young farmers. Sandra's really good with newcomers; she's really friendly, a mother hen!"

Once they'd fathomed that Robert and Paul both had military backgrounds, introductions were made, and friendships forged. "The guys get on great," Katie told us, a touch of pride in their menfolk!

All this had been several years previously, most Friday or Saturday nights the couples met up to socialise and relax. Following one boozy session, someone suggested an experiment on the Ouija board, as Bolty put it, "The rest is history."

"Dinner's up. Get yourselves in here." Sandra summoned us to the kitchen, serving a massive traditional farmhouse Sunday roast lamb, with Yorkshire puddings and plenty of vegetables, all topped with a rich meaty gravy.

Despite an average ten-year age difference between ourselves and our hosts, they were so welcoming, it didn't take long before we were fully relaxed in such easy company. We tucked in with relish, enjoying the banter.

Over the lamb, Paul and Bolty regaled us with further details of their investigative reconnaissance on Jerome and Tufton Gray. One tedious Saturday afternoon, four months earlier, Paul and Robert had both decided that the lair of the enemy should be investigated. "We wanted at least a framework of a plan for a retaliatory response, should it be required at any future date," Bolty told us, conspiratorially.

Paul picked up the story. "We didn't wait to ask Luke or John on the calling table; we kind of knew the answer! Instead, we told Sandra and Katie we were going for a cross-country test drive in Rob's classic MG, and we would be gone for several hours." They'd donned old army camouflage jackets and jumped into the MG BGT, shooting down the A34 and cutting across country towards the village of Tufton Gray.

"The only pub in the village is the Green Man; it's a hotel pub. What we didn't realise, at the time, is that it is owned by Jerome. Fortunately, Jerome employs a manager. He hardly ever frequents the place himself. Though I guess, the staff, or at least the manager, is one of his!" There was no need for Paul to explain further; we knew what he meant by, *one of his.*

"When we entered the lounge bar, everything became silent. We fell under some severe close scrutiny; the locals watched as we walked to the bar and ordered."

I think the retelling was embellished for dramatic effect but, still, the thought of a British village in modern times being dark and sinister, felt like a script of a horror movie. The two of them stayed in the bar for over an hour, eating a meal, surrounded by low murmurs and accusatory glances. They joked, "I guess they don't do much passing trade. Eating the food, we felt like extras in *The League of Gentlemen.*"

The two managed to leave the Green Man without being accosted by the suspicious locals, but Bolty admitted. "We then made a mistake. We knew exactly where Jerome and Rosalind lived because we'd scouted it several times, on Google maps. The manor house was only a few minutes' walk from the pub. We're fit so we decided to leave the MG in the pub's car park,"

"As we carried out our scouting mission," Paul told us, "I believe somebody in the pub noted the MG in the car park when we left the pub. It's not the type of village for walkers. They most likely informed Jerome, there were strangers in the vicinity!"

Bolty stated confidently, "We were well trained in the army; we both reached the rank of sergeant, him in the parachute regiment, and me in REME. We know we're good at concealment, so it seemed like a good idea to go in on foot. We just forgot to conceal the car."

After walking from the pub, they hastily left the road for the cover of the bushes. Paul and Robert trekked undetected through the trees and undergrowth of a small wood where they reached the walls of the manor house estate.

Paul attested, "The tree-line concealment was excellent. We were able to shin up a handy oak tree and view the house from a distance of approximately fifty metres, totally concealed amongst the branches. I had a pair of old army field glasses, so we began to monitor the comings and goings."

"We spent over an hour observing the manor house. We even saw Jerome and Rosalind, apparently discussing something, or arguing, in one of their drawing rooms. Though we didn't see Maurice or Anne; maybe they were working on the farm, but, in addition to Jerome and Rosalind, there appeared to be two or three others moving around the property. Possibly staff," Paul suggested.

Remaining hidden Paul and Bolty observed the activities while identifying likely routes of entry, as well as positions for possible hidden cameras or alarms.

"Through the glasses, Bolty noted Jerome taking a phone call. Instantly, Jerome turned, staring towards the window, as if looking for something."

"I instinctively shied away, seeking deeper cover within the leaves, even though I knew we were well hidden and couldn't be seen at that distance," he added.

"With great care, Jerome replaced the receiver before turning towards Rosalind; she was sitting on the sofa, reading a book. When he spoke, she looked up sharply, glancing towards the window, speaking urgently to her brother."

Robert said, "Then they both left the room quickly, as if intent on action."

Paul and Robert remained hidden in the tree, wondering what it was they'd just witnessed. A door at the side of the manor house burst open with a loud crash. They heard the deep menacing barking of the dogs.

"Then we saw two ferocious looking Dobermans appear around the side of the house. I bricked it, even though the dogs remained under the control of Jerome held in check by short metal leashes."

The chilling howling of the baying dogs intensified as they caught the scent. Jerome bent, speaking to the two animals, before releasing them for the prey.

"The dogs instantly bounded across the lawn, howling and barking, saliva-coated fangs visible in their widespread jaws. They were aiming directly for us," Bolty recalled, with a grimace.

"We were safe, in a tree, outside the grounds of the estate, but still, it was time for us to vacate," Paul told us.

Not caring if they were seen or not, they shinned down the tree in seconds, as if chased by Failinis himself, the mythical devil-dog of folklore. On the other side of the wall, they could hear the blood-chilling howling of the cheated dogs. They sprinted through the shrubs and trees, heading to the village centre and the safety of their car.

Paul acknowledged, "We weren't followed on our retreat, but once we'd reached the village, it certainly felt like it had become more active. We left Tufton Gray immediately, noticing villagers coming from their houses to stare as we passed in the car."

With a rueful grin, Robert reported, "John and Luke weren't impressed by our actions; we got a right telling off." Something I recalled rather sheepishly, following my activities with Colin and the calling table.

It was only then that John began to fully inform Paul and the others of the dangers in Tufton Gray, including Jerome's relationship with the Green Man. Instinctively I glanced across the table to David; he returned the glance. It felt good to know here were two allies, prepared to venture out once in a while, prepared to steal the initiative away from the enemy.

Silence descended; Paul and Robert stopped talking, waiting for our reaction.

"This is a battle you will only win by stealth and cunning, not necessarily direct action." Although we'd been attentive to David, wondering if John or Luke would choose to make an appearance, John managed to appear unexpectedly. The four newcomers stopped eating, glancing towards us for confirmation.

Being forewarned of this method of communication, they swiftly sensed it wasn't David who they were talking to. Gently, Sue informed them, "Yes, you're talking to the apostle John, of Galilee."

John had permitted the meal and conversations to finish before commandeering David's body. We were conscious, this was the first time that Paul's syndicate had spoken directly to the spirit of John so, for the most part, we were happy to remain quiet as John passed on instructions to Paul's team regarding their duties of protection!

He warned again, "There are dangers involved in unauthorised visits to Tufton Gray. You have seen the lengths they are prepared to go. You have a purpose in life. This does not include indulging in battles with the Devil's syndicate. You have to be single minded, not side-tracked, distracted by diversionary tactics. This is the strategy of the evil one."

To the delight of Paul, Sandra, Bolty and Katie, though possibly not David, John remained for the rest of the afternoon, imparting teaching and wisdom to all. Listening quietly, I wondered, when he occupied David's form, could he experience the delights that we experienced in our daily lives, such as food and wine. Certainly, I thought, Luke or John didn't allow David to go without when they graced us with their presence.

Finally, John warned, "Socialising as different syndicates is good, but it shouldn't become too regular. The dangers of you all being in one space are high." After this, David returned, expressing his acute displeasure at having missed a second helping of Sandra's delicious apple cheesecake.

"Never mind," I told him, without pity. "Think of your waistline."

The time for the evening milking arrived, presenting us with the perfect cue to thank our hosts for a delightful and, fortunately, stress-free day. We took our leave before, thankfully, an uneventful journey home.

CHAPTER ELEVEN

Colin came home again; his voyage had only involved two round trips, a Fiffes fruit carrier between Portsmouth and Barbados then Venezuela. Can't be bad I thought, thirty-six days at sea, then he gets a month off, but maybe my assumptions about Colin's easy life at sea were off the mark. On the very first day of leave, Colin announced, "I've had enough of being away all the time. I've signed up for a short foundation course at the tech, computer programming for beginners."

Maybe my friend was indeed becoming tired of globetrotting around the planet, wanting to settle down instead.

Whatever his reasonings, the course started the very next evening, giving Colin a full day to indulge in shopping for the latest in ultra-thin, fast processing, laptops.

After his first night on leave, I didn't meet Colin for several days. With no sign of John, Trish and I were managing to spend some time together, allowing ourselves the luxury of being a normal loving couple. Twice I'd knocked on Colin's door in expectation, but he was otherwise occupied; there was no answer.

Come Friday evening, I was relaxing in front of the telly a portion of fish and chips, bought as a rare treat, resting on my knees. Colin rang the doorbell. Beside him, smiling nervously, stood a woman in a loose, emerald green summer frock. Around our own age, a full six inches shorter than him, Yvette had long dark hair swept back in a ponytail. Brown twinkling eyes and a skinny figure completed the picture. "Martyn, this is Yvette, Yvette Sanchez." He ushered her through the door.

Yvette hailed from France. Explaining her surname, she said, "My father was in the Spanish diplomatic service. He was posted to Paris, where he met my mother."

Colin watched on, pinching a chip from my plate as we asked each other exploratory questions.

In good, but accented English, Yvette explained, "We met at college. Colin accidently deleted my homework while trying to show off his newfound computer skills."

Thankfully, Yvette forgave him with a laugh, producing a memory stick from her pocket, proving that she had far more foresight and common sense than Colin.

He smiled happily, explaining, "During the tea break, our conversation flowed naturally, like we'd known each other all our lives!"

Yvette was also a traveller. Driven by her father's career, she'd spent her youth in Spain, France then Denmark, before leaving home in her early twenties. She had come to Britain to improve her English. Now, Yvette was employed by a local builder's merchants. She, like Colin, was also determined to improve her computing skills, entertaining eventual desires of a career in computing.

I was delighted for my friend, as we hastily made plans for the evening. I called Trish, learning that she was agreeable to meeting later for drinks and introductions. Although delighted, I experienced some disquiet about Colin's relationship. We were full steam ahead with the syndicate. Now it seemed a lot of Colin's free time would naturally revolve around Yvette. I planned to speak with John as soon as possible.

"Colin is smitten!" Trish whispered later that evening when they'd both gone to the bar.

"It is easy to see why," I replied. Yvette turned out to have a wonderful, effervescent, persona, a permanent smile, captivating all around her. Underneath the light-hearted manner, I could discern a fundamental strength at the heart of her make-up. A strength which helped her survive the travelling, borne out of a nomadic childhood and constantly changing schools.

She spoke French, Spanish and excellent English, all delivered with a charming continental accent. I chuckled, looking forward to Colin learning French, to be able to converse in her native language.

The evening turned out to be a great success, both Trish and I instantly taking to Yvette, truly, thrilled for our friend.

Later I reflected, "It's about time he had a partner in life; maybe now he really will settle down, give up the sea."

"I totally agree. If he's as happy as us, then he'll be very lucky indeed," she answered, giving me a quick hug.

Next morning, I drove to David's, planning on revealing Colin's good news. Also, I was hoping that John would appear and enlighten me to the significance of this unanticipated change in Colin's circumstances. It had been only a few weeks earlier when I'd reacted in the same way to Colin's introduction to the syndicate. Maybe I was becoming insecure! Surely John and

Luke should be able to manage a simple human relationship? I thought.

"We'll go into town for a coffee," a harassed looking David informed me, firmly shutting the door on the yelling and squabbling of his younger siblings. "It's okay, Janet's home," he said, letting me know his sixteen-year-old sister would be there for the younger ones.

Seated with an extremely expensive, piping hot, flat-white, I recounted the events of the previous evening, telling David of Colin's new-found love, all the while examining David's eyes, wanting spiritual intervention.

"You seem somewhat anxious." It was Luke who'd appeared within seconds of my completing the tale. Vainly, I fought to find adequate words, words which would convey my worries, without proving myself selfish. After all, it was true, I really did wish all the best to my friend.

"Can you remember your trip to the capital and the round table?" Luke asked, staring beyond my eyes, deep into my soul.

I thought back to the day, chiefly recalling the confrontation on the drive out of Winchester. "Yes" I replied, "Why?"

"Remember the prophecy you received," he continued. Slowly the realisation dawned, with the jogging of my memory. *Six*! The prophecy said that there would be a new messiah, but it had also said six members of our syndicate. "Is Yvette the sixth member?" I blurted out, relief portrayed by my voice.

"Yes," Luke announced, seemingly a little exasperated by my bafflement. "You received a prophetic dream, don't you remember?" Vaguely, I recalled the dream, nearly two months earlier, Colin meeting a girl.

"Where are the trains?" I joked, remembering the dream had Colin in a train station. Not realising my jest, Luke told me factually, "The train station symbolises an arrival. Yourself and Colin have the job of instructing and educating Yvette into the syndicate; we have prepared her, but you will reveal the role of the syndicate to her."

Great, I thought, poor Colin, first week of a relationship and he has to casually drop this into the conversation.

"By the way, my friend's body is occasionally inhabited by the apostles of Jesus, and they want you to be part of this! Tell her that, you won't see her for dust," I predicted, sceptically. "What a way to end a relationship!"

"You do us a disservice," Luke responded evenly. "Like you, Yvette has been chosen from before birth, prepared for this very time. Do you not think that we know each of your soulmates, that we couldn't bring you together? The rest is simply up to Colin and Yvette."

Luke revealed, "For the previous three years, Yvette has been prepared for her part in your undertaking. Myself, then John, have appeared to her, as visions in the night. Yvette has been given a word of knowledge by a spiritual medium; the medium promised her, she is chosen, that the Lord was watching her. This filled Yvette with pleasure and pride."

He continued. "Recently, Yvette has also been given a revelation, the aroma of apples. Several times she's noticed, she was wrapped in the fragrance, with no possible explanation. When you tell Yvette about the syndicate and her calling, the scent of apples will be evident, far stronger than anything she's previously experienced. Yvette will realise this is the calling she's been waiting for."

I shrugged my shoulders. "Oh well, I guess you know what you're doing."

David returned, to his disconsolation, while away, his coffee had cooled. I brought him another before explaining all that Luke had revealed. It was time for us to seek out Colin, let him know the good news.

Colin took it all in his stride, saying, "As a singleton, I've been wondering about my role in the syndicate."

Now Yvette was to join, he was over the moon. Colin confessed, "Even though it's early days with Yvette, in my heart I really feel right with her!"

I knew that Colin could give his heart easily, but it seemed that love really was on his horizon. Being told that she was his soulmate delighted him.

The three of us agreed, Yvette should be told about the syndicate and then be asked to join, though it would be another matter to convince Yvette that we weren't barmy. We had to plan, then choose our moment well, before educating a hopefully willing Yvette, to her part in this spiritual voyage.

Turning to David, Colin announced, forcefully, "Forget you being there at the start, once she learns of our method of communication with the spiritual realm, you will be too great a distraction. I'll do this my own way."

Colin confided, "Some of our conversations have involved the existence of a spiritual world and her strong belief in it. She shared with me the prophecy that she received and a strange vision that awoke her one night. She said she thought there was someone in her room, watching her. I tried to laugh it off!" Confidently, he said,

"She will be accepting, I'm sure. It is just how we start the conversation that's the difficult bit."

It was his relationship, Colin decided. "The best way to handle it is for me to broach the subject over dinner this evening, in the restaurant. The meal is planned anyway, the table already booked. If more detailed explanations are required, or supporting evidence, then, after the meal, we'll visit Martyn and his strongbox, with all the evidence you've kept, the tasks and gifts from the spiritual realm and suchlike."

So much for the notion of a romantic meal for young lovers, I thought, but it was a good idea.

Having informed Trish of our plan, she insisted, "She'll need me for moral support. At the beginning of a relationship, it would be unfair to subject the poor girl to a bizarre story of spirits and fiends, then isolate her in a flat with two guys she's known for less than a week. She'll need a female presence." I agreed with her wholeheartedly, not daring to mention the names of Myra Hindley or Rose West to the obviously considerate Trish!

In the event, Yvette's induction went well. Even before seeing the evidence in the strongbox, she was remarkably accepting of Colin's strange spiritual narrative. Maybe a distant catholic upbringing and Sunday school helped. As far as I could see, any doubts were swamped by excitement. She'd believed the prophecy from the medium was genuine; here was the proof. Yvette grasped the concept with open arms. She squeezed Colin's hand in delight, elatedly looking at the messages and missals contained in our strongbox. All the while, against a backdrop of the distinct and aromatic odour of apples.

To Colin's disappointment, all plans for a romantic evening disappeared out of the window. For Yvette, this was far more exciting. The wine bottle came out as we settled down, revealing our recent past to the enthralled Frenchwoman. In many cases the details were a revelation to Colin as well. It was easy to forget how much time he'd spent away at sea.

Not all of our story, however, was easy listening. She paled noticeable, grabbing his arm in consternation, as Colin retold the story of his fraught road trip to Southampton.

The wine ran out as we finally tired, the gathering breaking up at three in the morning. Accompanied by promises of meeting John and Luke, as well as David himself on the morrow, Trish and I took our leave from a happy couple, departing with me uttering repeated threats about the appalling dangers of indiscretions!

Walking down the stairs, Trish squeezed my arm in delight. "It looks like we are now six." She smiled happily.

Yvette's enthusiasm was boundless. She arrived at the door by eight thirty the next morning, dragging a reluctant and sleepy Colin in her wake. After such a late night, this was way before I would normally surface. We let her down gently. "David might not want to be disturbed at such an early hour on his free Saturday. I think we'd be best having breakfast and then finding out if David is awake," I told her.

Placing the sausages under the grill, I wondered why I was doing the cooking while a gastronomic expert sat on the sofa, holding hands and playing footsie with Yvette. Stuff it! I thought, it must be a change for Colin to be served a meal occasionally. One day, I fantasised, I would demand the return favour and persuade Colin to prepare Trish and myself a banquet of the highest order. Daydreaming off filet mignon, served at a candlelit table for two, I dished out, to my three guests, the easier, but much loved offering, a full English breakfast.

Eager to please his fledgling love, Colin had already called, inviting an acquiescent David, to join us for breakfast. Feigning resignation, I added two sausages and three rashers of bacon to the grill pan.

That Saturday, David must have been hungry, or maybe the younger children were being particularly noisy, because he arrived swiftly, walking the two miles between us in twenty minutes.

Colin made the introductions. "Yvette this is David." She took his hand in greeting, eyeballing him as if he were a volcano about to erupt. But Yvette was disappointed. Introductions done, David joined us at the table. "Great, thanks, Martyn. I'm looking forward to this, haven't had a decent breakfast in a long while," he announced, attacking a sausage with gusto. "That's the problem with two weight-conscious women in the house," he informed us contentedly, halfway through a mouthful of fried bread. "It's healthy breakfasts, all the way!"

Luke considerately allowed David to finish his meal before usurping his body to make an appearance.

"Shalom, my friend, Yvette, we have observed you for some time." Yvette stiffened. Quickly she glanced over at Colin, asking the unspoken question. Colin nodded, waiting for Luke or Yvette to speak.

"Are you one of the apostles?" she finally asked, as Luke remained quiet. Of course, I realised, not knowing him, Yvette wouldn't be able to easily distinguish the perceptible change in David as a heavenly visitor came calling. I knew, as did Trish and Colin, that Yvette was talking to Luke. To a newcomer, such as Yvette, she would have no way of knowing if she was talking to Luke, John or David himself!

"It's Luke," Colin whispered, in his haste to please, before Luke had time to respond.

"It is indeed," Luke said. "You have been educated into the reality of the syndicate and the purpose of your life. We were listening as you received instruction. Is there anything you would like to ask us?"

Usually, unless prepared, when confronted with such a question nothing pertinent springs to mind. Yvette was no exception. After several seconds, she managed to mumble, "Do you know what is going to happen, what the future is?"

The rest of us knew the answer but we listened as Luke explained, "Only the Lord God himself knows the future. Myself, John and the other spirits are present in the spiritual world and can observe, but it is the Father alone who chooses when to reveal what is destined to come."

After this, conversation became more general. Seemingly bemused by the speed of events, Yvette ran out of questions very quickly, but we knew that John and Luke were frequent visitors. As with the rest of us, Yvette would think of and ask her questions as she grew more confident in the company of ourselves and the apostles.

For now, for Yvette, as with us at the beginning, it was an embryonic, surreal and exciting adventure. I realised, at least Trish and myself had a strong and stable relationship at the time it all began. Poor Colin and Yvette would have to build their relationship on the fragile foundations of a spiritual roller coaster. Maybe, relationships forged in times of danger could be strengthened in the face of adversity. I pondered on this, realising that Trish and I had indeed grown closer through this wave-tossed ride of delight and despair.

John arrived after Luke, welcoming Yvette into our numbers. We spent the morning in a relaxed atmosphere, as friends, drinking tea and coffee, while learning in a laid-back environment. Yvette freely accepting of the presence of John in our midst.

Before he left, John thrilled us, suggesting, "You may plan a trip to the farm at Watling again. It is good that you know and trust your protectors. It will also be good that they may meet Yvette and Colin."

Once David returned, we took advantage of an almost syndicate-free weekend. Colin and Yvette left to cultivate their friendship over lunch. Trish and I opting for a mooch around the local shopping mall.

Sandra and Sue were becoming firm friends. They seemed to bond well. A rapport had grown, coupling Sandra's ability to chat alongside Sue's capacity to be an interested and attentive listener. We'd taken John's warning seriously. It had been almost a month since our visit to the farm; though Sue and Sandra had chatted on the phone at least once a week, talking about matters way beyond their syndicates, passing on gossip, news and all that was happening in their respective lives. Even without knowing them, Sandra was delighted for Colin and Yvette. She spoke over her shoulder, passing the news on to Paul. "Hey, Colin's met a girl. They're now six. John predicted it in one of the prophecies!" Sue offered up John's suggestion that we again visit the farm.

"This time," Sue insisted, "the four of you will be our guests for Sunday lunch. That's, if there is a suitable establishment in Watling which can come within a mile of your cooking."

Sandra demurred, only briefly, glad of the chance of a meal without having to cook it herself. She recommended the Thatched Cottage, a pub in the village. She said, "It's a good lunch there; the Sunday carvery is excellent, and comprehensive, they have five different meats and all the veg you want. People come from miles around for the carvery. Why don't we meet at the farm for coffee and introductions, then go on to the pub?"

Setting out in convoy, we took two cars on the Sunday. The ponderous grey and threatening skies, bringing unseasonably low temperatures, didn't affect the cheerful, expectant mood, which embraced us all. With Colin and myself as designated drivers, we agreed on four in the Focus, allowing time for Colin to be alone with Yvette. We felt free, there'd been no sightings of Jerome and his gang for several weeks.

"Hopefully Maurice's arm will keep them on the side-lines for a period. Or even put them off for good," David suggested, rather optimistically.

As usual, we left home early, planning on a stop for the now customary breakfast. As the carnival atmosphere jokes flowed around the breakfast table, a delighted Yvette made derisive observations regarding the heart conditions of the British and their full fat options, while nibbling demurely at her croissant and sipping a black coffee.

By the time we were back on the road, the clouds had begun to unload their contents, the rain pouring down from the overcast, leaden sky, raindrops drumming on the car roof as I drove. In time, the rain lessened to that dull persistent English drizzle, which we knew so well, obliterating the view of rich green countryside that we should have been enjoying on an August Sunday.

We'd timed our arrival for mid-morning, allowing Paul and Sandra time to finish the milking and to carry out whatever other tasks were required that Sunday morning. Just before we arrived, a small patch of blue broke through the clouds, the drizzle having eventually petered out.

Colin followed me into the muddy, deserted farmyard, mud spraying up from the car tyres, coating both cars. He braked sharply, spraying my Focus with brown water from the puddle he'd stopped in.

"Glad to see you made it, horrible day!" Paul strode from the farmhouse, arm outstretched; they'd obviously been waiting on our arrival. Sandra's strident voice floated through the open door, following her husband across the farmyard.

"I'll put the kettle on. You must be parched and famished!" she called.

Warily, I eyed my colleagues, silently imploring them to remain quiet about the breakfast we'd feasted on only ninety minutes earlier. Maybe there was something in what Yvette was suggesting about the appetites of the British.

Colin and Yvette were dutifully brought forward and introduced to all, Bolty and Katie having arrived already.

Sue immediately fell into conversation with Sandra, who was preparing tea and scones on the supposition that we might collapse from hunger while waiting for our lunch.

Very little had happened to both groups during the previous weeks. We kidded Paul, "You should break a wrist more often. It'll give us a quieter life." Colin and Yvette retold the account of their meeting, then Yvette's introduction into the syndicate. Yvette's alluring French accent delighted the room.

We relaxed, falling into general conversation, grouping by gender. Us guys discovered mutual interests in sport and cars, the ladies happy to leave us talking while they found something of greater interest to discuss.

Sandra had phoned ahead, booking the table at the Thatched Cottage public house for early afternoon. I calculated there were ten of us eating, quite a syndicate family gathering. Hopefully far too many for Jerome to bother with.

While we'd been in the farmhouse, the wind had got up, becoming quite blustery, blowing away the grey clouds. The sun was making a determined effort to break through, further patches of blue appearing in the sky, separated by fluffy cumulous clouds scudding across the landscape, chased onwards by the brisk, blowy breeze.

Five in each car! As the designated drivers for the day, Colin and I would drive so the rest could enjoy a glass of something with their lunch. Paul directed Colin from the passenger seat of Colin's VW, while I followed.

The Thatched Cottage, a large but quaint, whitewashed pub, was on the main street at the centre of the village. I followed Colin's car into the pub's half-empty, gravelled car park, noting the puddles from the recent rains.

Holding the rear door open, while waiting for Sandra, Sue and Trish to exit, I glanced idly at the car which followed us into the car park. With a jolt, I recognised the dark maroon Jaguar. I noticed the small dent on the front bumper, a dent I'd put there myself, several weeks earlier. Turning to warn Paul and David, I noted they'd also identified the significance of the Jaguar. We stayed still, waiting, unsure of what to do or how to react, frozen as a group by our cars.

In that instant, the Jaguar accelerated, hurtling forwards, aiming for the space next to me – a space currently filled by Sandra and Sue, who remained unaware, deep in conversation.

At the last moment, Sandra heard the rushing motor, coinciding with the dual warnings from Paul and myself. Catching the movement out of the corner of her eye, swift thinking, calmness under duress, and selfless action, epitomised Sandra's reaction. She lunged forward, shoving the unsuspecting Sue hard. Sue let out a short, sharp bellow, as Paul grabbed her from behind, steadying her flight, preventing her from falling flat on her back, and landing in the puddle. Sandra followed through the direction of her lunge, scrabbling out of the way of the Jaguar. With a squeal of brakes and a shower of gravel, the Jaguar screeched to a halt, its front fender close enough to flick the hem of Sandra's blue cotton skirt.

"I'm alright!" Sandra aimed her shout at Paul. I recognised he was about to react in a hostile and probably violent manner.

"Wait!" Sandra warned again, "see what happens!" Jerome threw the driver's door open, missing Paul and Sue by millimetres.

"What a lovely day for Sunday lunch," he announced to the world in general, stepping from the car, ignoring Paul's glowering stare. "Thought we'd have a drive out in the country," Jerome continued, his supercilious, disdainful arrogance was designed to antagonise. A now composed Sandra placed a restraining hand on her husband's arm, whispering, "Wait, your time will come!"

I noticed then that the Jaguar had been followed into the car park by a black Range Rover; they were obviously out in force. But what were their intentions? There were ten of us, and we were on Paul and Sandra's home territory!

I had no idea what Jerome's plans were but, recalling previous encounters, I doubted he wanted a full-scale confrontation, with witnesses. It wasn't his style. I concluded they were out to provoke and intimidate, to cause a scene! I joined forces with Paul and Sandra, pushing past David and Yvette in my hurry.

"Leave it," I warned urgently. "I don't know what his plans are, but he isn't looking to instigate a full-on war, unless you start it. He wants to provoke you into reacting, don't bite," I warned.

Sandra smiled, a glance thanking me for hauling her husband back from a foolhardy and risky confrontation.

"Save it," I advised. "Don't be the first to react; don't give him the satisfaction." Our words penetrated. Paul muttered something to himself, then abruptly turned his back on Jerome and his comrades.

Without looking backwards, Paul strode off up the path leading to the pub's restaurant, barging past a middle-aged couple who were standing at the centre of the pathway, open mouthed and perplexed. As a group we stood meekly, motionless for several seconds, studying Paul's back as he stormed off. Then the tension suddenly ebbed away. As a pack, the nine of us followed, seeking the welcoming haven of the pub, and lunch.

Before entering, I glanced back. Jerome, Maurice and Rosalind stood there unconcernedly, quietly conversing, grinning at the strife they'd created. Jerome waved at me, a small dismissive flick of the wrist. I was somewhat pleased to see a white plaster cast, prominent on Maurice's wrist.

Once in the pub, we congregated in the bar area, ordering drinks, waiting to be seated. By now, Paul was beginning to relax a little. I sidled across and clapped him on the shoulder. "Well done, mate, it isn't worth it. Not here anyway." But we were all conscious that the carefree mood of earlier had disintegrated.

"Close call, I really wanted to flatten the imperious turd," he grimaced.

"Yeah, I know what you mean, but not here, mate, too many witnesses. They aren't going away; the time will come, of that, I'm sure."

Seated on a long oak kitchen table, pints of cold beer or glasses of wine before us, we held a hurried conference. Jerome, or any of his henchmen, hadn't yet followed us into the restaurant area. David peeked from behind the curtains, noting the two vehicles still in the car park, but there was no sign of Jerome, or his henchmen.

There was little to be done. It was obvious that they were out to antagonise, to mess with our minds.

Sandra spoke, voicing everybody's thoughts, "There are too many off us; they daren't risk starting a full-scale confrontation here in the pub. There is little risk, as long as we remain observant and restrained." She flicked a glance at her husband.

At least until our journey home, I thought, but then why advertise their presence if they planned to disrupt our homeward journey?

The threat posed by the presence of Jerome and his henchmen began to recede. They could no longer be seen, I hoped they'd had their fun and gone home.

I found myself seated on one side of the table, Trish on my right, Katie on the left. Opposite us, Bolty and Yvette were deep in conversation about her native France and its culture of wine and fine food.

"Tell me about your physics research at the university," I asked, turning towards Katie. "How does it reconcile with this experience and what's happening to us?" Katie paused, thinking carefully about her answer, before launching into an explanation.

"Why does it need to reconcile?" she asked. "Where is the conflict?"

"Well," I pushed on, "in this modern twenty-first century world, how do you delve into the known and unknown laws of physics during the day and yet do what you do with the syndicate and the Lord in your free time. Doesn't it cause you a conflict?" I asked.

"Why should it?" Katie responded, just a flush of annoyance touching her cheeks. "I see no conflict whatsoever!"

"Doesn't science have difficulty with the existence of God?" I questioned her, eager to push home my point. Katie sighed, displaying just a little exasperation. She stopped to eat a garlic mushroom from her plate, before continuing.

"You're as bad as some of the scientists I have to deal with. Research science is no more than seeking evidence. In fact, the origin of the word science is from the Latin Scientia scholar, meaning knowledge, to learn and share that knowledge. That is all that it is. Seeking understanding of the physical nature of the universe. How God does it. In fact, the earliest base of the scientific community was the Catholic church," she informed me, in a speech that was so polished, it must have been delivered many times before.

"Belief in an omnipotent Lord, outside or within that universe is not a conflict!" she stated emphatically.

"Do you tell your colleagues you're a Christian?" I questioned, genuinely interested in how she resolved the outward dichotomy of science and faith. "How do they react?"

Popping another breaded mushroom into her mouth, she chewed slowly, then continued. "Most of my close colleagues at the university are wonderful," she said. "Of course we discuss and theologise, during conversations and breaks, but they completely accept my point of view and my logic; in fact, it was my close colleague, Graham, who gave me this analogy. No matter how much we can determine and understand the complexity of the workings and the mechanics of man's body, we can't, as a species, begin to understand thought, feelings and an individual's emotional response."

"Love," she instructed, "can be researched down to electronic impulses in the brain and responses to hormone release, but who can really explain love?" she asked. "What could explain the emotional attraction between you and Trish, which results in hormone release at the appearance of Trish, yet not for other women." She jabbed her fork in the direction of Trish. "What could scientifically explain your falling in love? It's like a beautiful painting. We can explain the chemical composition of the paint, and the brushstrokes used, but we can't explain its beauty, or what was going through the mind of the artist when he painted it!"

"There's no answer to that," I responded, glancing towards my beautiful lady, who was deep in conversation with Paul. We both stopped, waiting as the waitress served our main courses.

"How much have you told your scientific colleagues about your communication with the spiritual world?" I asked impulsively, worried about the syndicate's secret.

"Don't worry," Katie assured me, a slight smirk of amusement playing across her features. "I was brought up in Bristol, in the suburb of Yate. As far as they're concerned, my belief is the product of a lower middle-class Sunday school upbringing. My parents, despite them both being science teachers, thought it important that I had at least the basic religious education."

"Don't you get the urge to tell your colleagues what you've seen?" I asked. "The urge to proclaim from the roof that you have been talking to John the apostle?"

"No, not very often," she replied. "Only when discussing religion with some of the more entrenched unbelievers in the scientific community, do I encounter resistance." Katie revealed. "This is more common when visiting conferences or seminars. "The scientific world is full of arrogant, condescending, egotists, unable to listen to other opinions. But then, so is the church and the religious world in general. That is why I don't go to church! I've concluded that arrogance, the inability to accept other viewpoints, is a condition of mankind, rather than one of the factions within it."

"What about you?" she asked, fixing me with a direct stare. "Don't you ever get the urge to shout it from the rooftops? What is your background?"

I pondered my answer, chewing slowly on my roast beef as I reflected. "Before this happened," I said, regretfully, "I hadn't given it much thought at all. Life was too busy, too certain. I certainly haven't been to Sunday school or church; neither has Trish to my knowledge."

"So how do you feel now?" she enquired looking at me expectantly, waiting patiently, while I deliberated upon a response.

"Hmmm," I managed finally. "As I've just said, before this all happened, life was too demanding to think about God. Now, what can I say, it is terrifying, exhilarating, awesome and bewildering all in one go!" I answered, trying to sound moderately flippant. "I had a modest yet promising life lying before me. We all did. This has come out of left field, out of the blue; sometimes it is just too momentous for my brain to understand. Of course, I want to stand on the rooftops and proclaim to the world, but then there are other times I just want to run and hide. At times, it is too big for me," I concluded truthfully.

Katie looked at me openly, her eyes searching mine. Instinctively she seemed to understand the depth of confusion and bewilderment which I was trying to express. Gently she placed her hand on my arm. "Your future is even better now; but just imagine how David's feeling about all this." She laughed.

"Hi, Paul." Instantly we stopped talking, looking up to see Jerome walking towards us, his expression an evil leer. Close behind, Jerome was flanked by his lieutenants, Maurice, Rosalind and Anne. Of the occupants of the Range Rover, there was no sign, but I guess they were close. Jerome held his right arm, raised up in the air, his hand level with his ear, something red and yellow clutched in the palm.

"You might want these to help keep the barns warm," he mocked. "Don't worry, we have plenty." Jerome flicked his hand, a sneer of hostility distorting his features briefly. I watched as the brightly coloured Swan Vesta box landed with a rattle in front of Paul. Paul made to rise, once more beginning to take the bait. The restraining hand of his wife held sway, persuading him to halt.

From the corner of my eye, I caught the flash. Katie sat there confidently, her camera phone raised to her eye, aimed towards Jerome and his devotees.

"Thank you," she said, in a clear and self-assured voice. "Nice wide angle. I was able to get all four of you and the box of matches in frame. And if you're under any illusions, don't be," she announced. "I have already photographed your number plates. So much as an overactive firefly in our vicinity, and the police will have these photos within seconds. We can place you here with matches, and the landlady is watching," she concluded. "Explain that!"

Without a word, Jerome turned on his heels, stalking out of the pub, Rosalind, Anne and Maurice in his wake. Quickly recovering his composure, Bolty called after the retreating Maurice, mocking him, "Don't bother waving goodbye, Maurice. Oh I forgot, you can't."

David looked through the nets as the two cars drove out of the pub car park, turning right onto the road leading south. They'd had one aim that day, to antagonise and provoke. Ardently I hoped that we had seen the last of Jerome and his minions for the day.

Some while later, Colin myself and David held a hasty consultation with Paul and Bolty. We concluded that it would be safer for us to leave for home directly from the pub. Paul suggested we use the major dual carriageways and motorways on our journey home. We hoped to avoid the more dangerous, quieter roads, we'd used that morning.

Paul promised, "I'll keep my mobile close, just in case you run into opposition; worst case, you stay in the car, turn around and we meet you, but I think they have gone for the day. Good ol' Katie scared them off; they weren't expecting that. She might be quiet, but she's got a backbone of steel. Keeping all those students in check I guess." He grinned at her, appreciatively.

We gathered for goodbyes, handshakes and hugs all round, all of us wondering where this strange adventure was taking us.

To our relief, the journey home turned out to be as uneventful as we'd hoped. We remained ever anxious and watchful throughout the journey. It seemed Jerome, Maurice and co. had had enough for one day. There was no sign of them.

CHAPTER TWELVE

At her desk, Katie leaned back in her chair, arching backwards, yawning. She looked with disappointment at the screen before her. The computer simulation hadn't gone as well as hoped; the search for the Hawkins particle would continue! They had wanted to give some useful data to the experimental research station at Cerne in France but now it was back to the drawing board! Something not uncommon in her line of work.

"We'd better have another look at that system," she instructed her colleague Graham. "Perhaps the error is in the fourth sector of the regency programme."

"Seems the obvious place to start," Graham replied. "But first I'm going for lunch. After this abject failure, I think I deserve a large strawberry milkshake and at least two big Macs before I'm ready to start again. You coming?" he asked, grabbing his Denham jacket from the coat hook.

"No, you go ahead," she replied. "After this fiasco, I just want to sit quietly in solitude, to plan our next move."

Graham left, leaving Katie on her own, sitting in silence, deep in meditation. These setbacks happened sometimes. Soon the light would shine once more.

Turning her mind to other things, she reflected on the meal they'd enjoyed at the Thatched Cottage, just four days previously, and the escalation in activity.

She wondered, just what was happening to her ordered and compartmentalised life! Where was it all going to end?

The stringent, harsh vibration of the university issue mobile phone interrupted her introspection, catapulting her mind into the moment. Reaching out towards the phone on the desk, wanting to silence the noisy incursion, Katie noted *caller number unknown*. She hoped it wasn't Cerne wanting results from the test.

"Professor Bolt." The female voice sounded panicky and stressed.

"Who is this?" Katie demanded, the panic in the caller's voice tearing Katie away from her idle reverie.

"It's Linda Goldsworthy, professor, your second year applied physics student. I've been raped," she howled!

Katie gasped in horror, sitting upright; all other thoughts vanished.

The department ran an unofficial mentoring and pastoring programme for the students. Some of the students who passed through the college were extremely bright, some of the cleverest young minds in their field. Yet Katie found intelligence didn't always equate to common sense. Sometimes, fresh out of sixth form, they needed help and support to manage everyday life. The department liked to cosset their students, so there was always a phone number and mentor to call; this went above and beyond the support provided by the university. Usually it meant minor issues, money, relationships, or one of the many other requirements of everyday adult life; today it was much more serious than that.

"Tell me what's happened," Katie insisted, trying to get a grip on the situation.

"He came back... coffee... forced... ripped... hurt... threat." Through the sobbing tears of shock and pain, Katie understood perhaps one word in every three.

"Wait," she commanded, reaching for a pencil. "Tell me where you are, Linda. Have you called the police?" Through her sobbing, Linda gasped out an address on the London Road, a flat in part of the city, which was off campus. Sniffing, she told Katie, "I've called them, the police are on their way! Please come, professor. I'm on my own. I don't know what to do!" she wailed in anguish.

Hastily, Katie grabbed her belongings from the table, taking the pad with Linda's address scrawled on it.

Once in the car, driving through the city, Katie reflected, wondering why Linda had chosen to call her first, straight after calling the police. Surely, she had friends or relatives available, someone to come running!

Linda Goldsworthy was indeed a talented student. Originally from Hampshire she was, Katie reflected, definitely high on the brainpower spectrum, but low in the ability to cope with everyday life. Briefly, Katie considered pulling over, calling the university authorities and letting them know what had arisen and where she was going, but she decided against it; traffic was too dense to be able to re-join the flow easily. Best, she thought, get there and discover exactly what's happened. Then she, Katie, would be best placed to contact the university authorities, to organise whatever support was needed for Linda.

Katie was lucky; she found a parking space in the zone, just outside the building. She walked up the path, absently noting the lack of highly visible police cars.

Pushing through the main door of the building, she concluded, they must be detectives in plain clothes, arriving in unmarked cars. It must be to do with the university's profile.

She ran up the stairs, covering the threadbare red carpet with as much haste as she could muster. She slowed the final few steps, approaching Linda's door, beginning to muster thoughts as to how she would handle the situation. Katie rang the doorbell, hearing the distant sound of a bell ringing deep within. She heard a shuffling sound on the other side of the door, heading towards her.

"Linda, it's Professor Bolt," Katie called out, wanting to reassure her young charge.

The Georgian six-panelled door, with its faded and flaking green paint, opened just an inch. "Linda, it's me. Are the police with you?" Katie eyed the terrified, distressed girl through the crack, before hearing the clattering sound of the safety chain being drawn back. The door opened further. Linda was revealed in full, hair dishevelled, eyes puffy and red, swollen from crying. Her cardigan hung lopsided, a button missing, the rip evident on its pocket.

"Linda!" Katie's instinctive maternal, protective mechanism drew the involuntary exclamation from her lips. She pushed the door fully open, moving forwards, arms outstretched, wanting to hold the stricken girl in her caring arms.

"It was horrible," Linda gulped, fighting to hold back the tears.

The door behind her slammed loudly, causing Katie to jump in surprise.

"Hello, Katie, hope you have a photo of this." Katie spun around in alarm, noticing for the first time, there were others in the room. Jerome smirked in victory, Rosalind and Maurice joining them from the bathroom.

"The police are on their way; she's called them," Katie blustered, pointing at Linda, bewilderment manifesting.

"Why would Linda call the police? I haven't ordered her to," Jerome scoffed, in reply. Linda fully disengaged herself from Katie, crossing the room to stand beside Jerome.

"Sorry, professor," she whispered. "I like you, I really do, but he's the one who has control of me. He tells me what to do. I couldn't disobey my master; he paid for me to come here," she said, pointing at Jerome.

"Linda!" cried Katie, tears forming as she realised the betrayal.

Katie tried to fight back, grasping at straws. "You won't get away with it! I told Graham Duffy where I was going," she advised Jerome.

"I doubt it," Jerome replied. "We observed him going for lunch, climbing into his car. Linda here was good enough to remove the receiver in the faculty front office. You couldn't have received or made any calls on that phone, that just leaves your mobiles," he concluded, leaning forward and ripping her handbag from her shoulder.

"No," he said, inspecting both her university phone and her personal mobile. "No calls in the last hour, other than Linda here."

Katie felt her knees folding. She sank down onto the nearby bed. "What are you going to do with me? I know nothing," she whispered, weakly.

Rosalind pushed forward; an expression of triumph etched onto her features. "Don't worry," she sneered, with growing menace, thrusting her face close to Katie's. "We don't need to know anything; we know it all. You are merely a warning to the rest of your interfering chums. Stop now, or they'll get what you're going to get. You're supposed to protect them with your life, so giving up your life to warn them off really can't be that hard!"

A frightened cornered animal fights with a desperate ferocity, caused by terror. Katie didn't think; she drew back her head, butting Rosalind with as much force as she could muster, on the bridge of the nose. With a crunching thud Rosalind's nose split, bright-red blood shooting across the bed in a sudden spray. Katie's heal stretched out, scraping the inside of Maurice's shin, drawing a yell and an obscenity. Nimbly he hopped backwards on one leg, swearing, "Bitch, control her." Katie opened her mouth to scream for all she was worth, but before the sound was formed, a strong hand clamped itself across her mouth, leaving the sound dead in her throat. In desperation, she tried to bite the hand which silenced her. She then tried to repeat the shin scrape, but Jerome was ready. His legs and shins were well back, out of reach of Katie's searching foot.

She felt a blow on the side of her head; in the chaos, she was unable to identify from whence it came!

"Quick, give her the injection," she heard Jerome say, directing the words over his shoulder at Anne, who Katie hadn't even noticed. She jerked her leg, fighting frantically, trying to pull away from an unseen needle, feeling the invisible clammy hands grasping for her flesh, then a deep stabbing pain in her thigh. The struggle slowly left her, as her world faded into darkness.

"Martyn!" Trish phoned, sounding anxious, "Sue's just had a call from John, on David's phone. He sounded worried, said there was something happening with Paul and the Oxfordshire lot."

"What did he say?" I said, becoming instantly attentive. Trish was hazy on details. David was away for the week, attending a company training course in Cardiff. Trish repeated, "Sue's had a call from David's mobile number. She recognised immediately it was John speaking! He spoke briefly, telling her that there is grave danger, Oxford. Then the phone went dead."

Thinking hastily, I suggested, "Trish, you and Sue come over here. It would be best for communication if we are all in one location."

While waiting, I climbed the stairs, advising Colin and Yvette of the situation. They were in his kitchen, preparing a meal together, surrounded by pots, pans and tantalising aromas. I guessed, unless it was urgent, we might not have the pleasure of Colin and Yvette's company that evening.

I returned to the flat and phoned the farm to ask if there was a problem. Paul himself answered, listening with curiosity to my garbled second-hand account.

"No, I don't think there's a problem!" he advised, "but I haven't spoken to Robert or Katie today. Darling, have you spoken to Katie or Robert recently?" He called out to his wife, holding his hand over the receiver to protect my ears.

"No, why, what's the problem?" Sandra asked, looking up from the magazine in which she was immersed.

"I've got Martyn here; says they've had some kind of warning from John about us or Oxford. Sounds a bit confused though!" he told her. He turned his attention back to me. "I'll check with Robert and Katie before calling you right back," he promised.

I placed the phone on the coffee table, a modicum of relief seeping into my senses.

The doorbell rang. Trish had pressed the bell in passing, announcing their arrival, then let herself and Sue into the flat. We shared a brief group hug, Trish and Sue concerned and confused in equal measures.

Putting the kettle on, I attempted to put them at ease, describing the call I'd just made to Watling. "It doesn't sound like there's a problem. Paul seems at ease. From what he's just told me, there isn't an issue."

"Ah, but that is only him and Sandra," Sue retorted. "He hasn't spoken to Bolty or Katie yet!" My phone shrilled, halting the conversation instantaneously. We all spun, glaring at the phone as if it were the cause of our anxiety. As I activated the call, I noted Paul's number displayed on the screen.

"I don't think there is anything to worry about," Paul informed me, his words more confident than his tone. "Bolty's home; he's waiting for Katie. Though this isn't unusual. She often works late if there is an experiment on the boil."

Paul added, "Katie hasn't yet called Robert to let him know she's going to be late; that's unusual, but not yet worrying. I hope everything is okay. I've just put the wind up Bolty." Paul promised to call back as soon as they knew her whereabouts.

I terminated the call, turning towards Trish and Sue, summoning up a cheerfulness I didn't feel. "It's unusual for John to let us down! I guess we have to wait!" I recalled the evening of the Supertramp's incident. Why did David have to be away on a training course this very week? I thought, somewhat unfairly.

We sat in the lounge for two hours making desultory conversation, minds elsewhere. Sue tried to call David, hoping to make contact with John, but calls remained unanswered.

Finally, at nine in the evening, Sue's phone chimed, making us all start. It was Sandra, seeking greater detail and clarification of our earlier warning.

She told us, "Katie still hasn't returned home and, apparently, she hasn't signed out from the university. Most of the faculty have gone home for the evening, so if she doesn't turn up tonight, we will have to wait until the morning before making further inquiries. Robert's been advised that nobody's seen her since earlier today."

There wasn't much more we could tell them. Sue repeated the warning that I'd conveyed earlier in the evening. The stark message was, "there is grave danger, Oxford" not "in Oxford," just, "grave danger, Oxford." What this actually meant, we were clueless.

Sue apprised Sandra, "David's away; we're unable to contact John. We haven't even spoken to David himself; he's training and in meetings all week."

"How's Bolty?" asked Sue, changing tack, compassion her first consideration.

"So far, he's okay," Sandra replied. "It has only been a few hours. He tried to call the police, but they don't seem interested yet. The police informed him that it is quite common for adults to disappear overnight without warning, sometimes for days on end. Even if it's unusual behaviour for the individual concerned! It isn't rare for somebody to disappear like this, so they are not going to do anything immediately."

"Is that all they said?" Sue asked in astonishment. "Aren't the police going to do anything at all?

"Oh, they weren't unsympathetic," Sandra divulged. "She's a female, so she's still vulnerable, even if she is thirty-four and very intelligent. If Katie doesn't turn up by tomorrow morning, when she's due at the university, then Bolty's been promised the maximum force and resource which Oxfordshire constabulary can bring to bear."

"And how do you and feel?" Sue asked Sandra.

"I can't deny my concern. I know Katie can be a little dipsy; her head is usually full of electrons and things, but we saw the accuracy of John's interventions at Basingstoke, just a few weeks ago. I'd be a fool to be uncaring. I'm worried about what might be unfolding, as well as Bolty; we both are."

With promises of immediate phone calls should anything transpire, Sandra finished the call, freeing up the line in case Katie wanted to call.

I didn't tell Colin anything more that night, deciding, instead, to allow new love a chance to blossom freely, without a worry about which they could do nothing. There would be plenty of time to speak to Colin in the morning.

In the early stages of waking from the chemically induced coma, Katie came around slowly, her mind full of cotton wool and bells. The sharp cutting pain at her wrists and ankles caused consciousness to flood, unwanted, into her brain. Through the chemical fog, realisation began to register. She tried in vain to move her tightly bound limbs.

"The bitch is waking up!" She heard Anne's voice, as if through a tunnel. Katie hastily chose to delay the horror for a few moments more, keeping her eyes firmly closed. But a vicious slap hit her cheek, unexpectedly, causing Katie to scream, denying her the tiny luxury of a few more seconds of oblivion.

"Open your eyes, you bitch." Katie felt the spittle on her cheek. Anne's scream was aimed just inches away from her face. She opened her eyes just in time to see Anne's open hand slicing through the air, targeting a second slap on Katie's exposed cheek. Katie tried to pull her head backwards, desperate to avoid the swinging hand, but to no avail. She was securely bound, tied to a chair which had been fixed firmly to the floor at the centre of a room. Anne's hand landed with a loud smack once more, causing a yelp of pain. The bound prisoner bit her lip, fighting the tears.

Katie's cheek stung horribly from the blows. She saw the snarling visage of Anne, inches away, gloating with conquest and anticipation. Behind Anne, several feet away, leaning against the wall, Rosalind observed quietly as the performance unfolded.

With some satisfaction, through her daze, Katie noticed Rosalind was sporting a swollen and bruised nose. Katie said nothing, watching, waiting warily for the next blow to fall.

Rosalind pushed away from the wall, the corner of her mouth twisting upwards in a curious half smile. Understanding the impact of anticipation, she took her time walking across the room, moving with a leisurely, calculated pace. Rosalind passed right by Katie, before stopping just beyond her helpless victim. She turned and, with a single movement, Rosalind reached out, grabbing Katie's hair between her fingers, grasping hard, yanking her head backwards with a sharp, vicious jerk. Rosalind's hand remained there, holding the hair bunched; she bent forwards slowly, whispering for effect.

"Welcome to Hell." Her voice carried pure naked vindictiveness. "You belong to me now, and there is nothing that I want from you except your suffering, followed by a horrible death. Give up hope," she declared dispassionately. "There is no rescue, just long pain and slow torment. By the time we finish, death will be your most heartfelt desire."

With those words, Katie felt complete abandonment in her wretched situation. How had it come to this? It had all seemed such a big adventure!

Jerome poked his head around the door. "Ahh, she's awake, good," he said, coming through the opening. "It is so much more fun when they're conscious, especially with a pretty girl like you," he informed Katie, with a happy grin. Katie felt panic rising like a tide, the hopelessness of her position fully dawning. She fought back the bile, trying to clear her mind, trying to think clearly through the fear.

"You'll never get away with it; the police will be here within hours. I have the photos." Katie tried hard, but failed, to put the merest echo of confidence into her words.

"On the contrary," Jerome warned her, chillingly, "we fully expect to get away with it. We have before! Anne here wore a wig and your clothes to drive your car here from Oxford. Every camera on route will have an image of you driving your car during the afternoon, and there are no cameras on roads within ten miles of here," he announced smugly." Jerome continued, informing the horrified Katie, "Your car and clothes have been used to create the impression of a living Katie, active during the whole afternoon. And, as for the photos, don't forget we have your phones. Linda Goldsworthy will tell the police that you did indeed go around to her flat, that you took a phone call from an unnamed man you called darling! And that you left her tutorial immediately after, telling him that you would be there as soon as possible. In several days, your car will be found many miles from here, burnt out, useless to the police forensics team!"

Rosalind leant over, slipping a hand inside the cheap cotton jumpsuit they'd dressed Katie in. Firmly grasping a nipple, then digging her fingernails into soft pliant flesh, she twisted viciously. "And if they ever find it, your body will be miles from here, buried and mutilated beyond recognition!"

Katie vomited, before fainting in horror!

That night, I hardly slept, lying there staring at the ceiling in the darkness of my room. My imagination was working overtime. I jumped at every last little creak and groan throughout the building. I couldn't begin to imagine how Robert was feeling.

When I called before breakfast, Sandra revealed, "Still no news. We have sat with Bolty since we spoke to you; his overactive mind is in overdrive. We literally sat and watched the phone all night, willing it to ring, but nothing. he must have tried calling her hundreds of times, but to no avail, his calls go straight to voicemail!" Sandra promised to phone later in the morning if they heard anything new. "You sure you haven't heard from John or Luke?" she asked, a touch of desperation in her voice.

John chose to contact me mid-morning. As I was relaxing with a cup of tea away from the CAD system, my phone buzzed. Realising it might be important, the sound of the ringtone drew an instant reaction. Almost spilling the tea, I grabbed the phone and checked the screen, noting David's number. For privacy, I walked away from the communal area before activating the call.

"Greetings, Martyn." I recognised John's voice instantly. He sounded a little worried. But before I could ask, John continued.

"Tufton Gray, she is in Tufton Gray!" With that, the phone went dead. Slowly I removed the phone from my ear, looking with curiosity at the blank screen.

Paul answered on the first buzz; farm duties apart, he must have been waiting by the phone, willing it to ring. "Yeah, what's happening." His voice portrayed anxiousness. I gave the message I'd just received from John!

"So, nothing about how she is, just that she's in Tufton Gray?"

"Yes, he sounded a little worried, but he didn't give any more details," I told him.

"What news at your end?" I asked, hoping somewhere there was good news.

"Katie never turned up for work this morning," he revealed, "but at least the police are taking it seriously now. They're making enquiries and even setting up an incident room. It's the nature of her work."

Quickly we made plans. As soon as I could get away from work that afternoon, Colin and I would drive up. Trish, Sue and Yvette would come if they could get away.

I phoned Colin from my desk, dragging him away from a boring routine of daytime television. Grimly, I informed a sombre Colin about the confirmed mysterious disappearance, and John's warnings. We quickly made plans to journey up to Oxfordshire as soon as we could, though we had no idea what we would do once we got to the farm.

As soon as I explained my predicament, my boss, Stephen Price, generously allowed me to leave early. I had to be carefully vague, not wanting to raise doubts or conflicts which could later lead to difficult questions. However, my concern for my friend, whose wife was missing, was obviously evident. Stephen readily agreed.

"Just GO!" he said, pointing towards the door.

Colin picked me up in his Golf, Trish and Sue already seated on the back seat. He'd managed to contact Yvette and Sue. Unfortunately, Yvette was unable to leave the builder's merchants early that day. "She's worried that she hasn't worked there long enough to expect time off for somebody she has only met once," Colin revealed.

His car covered the miles swiftly, the Golf showing little effect from its previous encounter with the Range Rover.

Installed in the farm's kitchen, Bolty sat forlornly at the table, a cold, half-finished mug off coffee forgotten on the table before him. He stood to greet us. Trish entering the room first, walked straight up to Bolty, hugging him, holding him tight, her actions replacing any words we could ever hope to conjure. Tight lipped, I grimaced towards Paul, reflecting the solemnity of the occasion, before shaking Bolty by the hand, gripping him tightly in a quick hug.

Ever capable in a crisis, Sandra and Sue busied themselves providing tea, coffee and snacks, while chipping into the conversation around the table. There wasn't, however, anything new that we could bring to the conversation, other than what I'd detailed to Paul earlier that morning.

After Paul had disclosed John's words to his friend, Bolty's immediate impulse had been to jump in his car, drive down to Tufton Gray to seek Katie's whereabouts, taking a sledgehammer with him! Fortunately, the police turned up at that moment, asking questions about Katie's general activities and movements the previous day. Sandra's and Paul's common sense prevailed, forcing Bolty to remain and wait for our arrival.

Colin suddenly interjected. "Now that we're here, it's not a bad idea to go and knock on the door with a sledgehammer!" The room went silent; we studied Colin with incredulity.

"Explain," I managed to say. "Are you suggesting we attack the house of strangers with a sledgehammer?"

"Yes, it's obvious," Colin stated, warming to his theme. "They won't be expecting a rapid response from us. If they do have Katie down there, then the police won't find her, and you can guarantee Jerome and his bunch won't have kidnapped her to swap cake recipes." I halted, first looking towards Paul, then Trish. There was sense in what Colin was saying. It still felt like an anathema, attacking the home of Jerome, where we would have difficulty proving any kind of link; however, it was probably Katie's only hope!

"You might be right," I said, thinking furiously. "But Bolty has to remain behind; the police are bound to be here again soon, asking more questions. The girls must stay too," I continued. "It's too dangerous."

"Now wait a minute!" Trish interjected vociferously, not giving me chance to finish my words. "You find Katie, who knows what kind of state she's going to be in? If Bolty's not there, she'll need a woman to look after her and comfort her." I accepted the logic of what Trish said, even if I baulked at the thought of taking her into danger.

Bolty protested furiously, claiming loudly, "She's my wife. I must be there!"

Sandra then took charge, hugging him, holding him tightly and rocking gently. "You can't go, Robert." She grabbed his hand for emphasis. "Martyn's right. The police are bound to want the answer to more questions; think how it'll look if you disappear and" – Sandra hesitated slightly, before continuing – "if the worst happens, how are you going to explain your disappearance?"

The three women moved in on him, working on the logic of the argument to a clearly reluctant Bolty. His army training encouraged the need for direct action, the requirement of taking the fight to the enemy. Now the case for direct action was being made, a chance to save his wife, poor Bolty was to be excluded.

Mentally, I took my hat off to him; his was an extreme sacrifice. Reluctantly he agreed. "Okay, I'll stay behind with Sandra and Sue."

We made rapid plans, inventing a journey for Paul should the police ask questions of his absence when we were gone.

The farm had a plentiful supply of tools so we loaded the boot of the Golf with two sledgehammers, a crowbar, several axe handles and anything that might come in handy, as well as a baseball bat, which I decided not to quiz Paul on. After all, I thought, when called upon, they had been prepared and ready for action in Basingstoke.

"Trick is, not to be stopped and searched by the police," Colin joked. "It'd take a lot of explaining to the local constabulary."

"It's okay. Just drive well under the speed limit and we won't have a problem." It was hard to tell if Paul was joking or being serious.

Once prepared for war, there were no other plans to make. It wouldn't be until we got there and reconnoitred that we could formulate further strategies!

With false jocularity, and assurances to Bolty, we set of in the Golf, Paul and Colin seated at the front, me and Trish behind. Rush hour was almost over, but the traffic south was still heavy. We drove in silence, only an occasional observation made, while we contemplated whatever awaited us.

"Turn off your phones," I demanded unexpectedly of my friends. "I trust John. I believe Katie is there, if he says so, but I don't want a situation where he demands we turn back, you know how angry he gets when we act without asking." I couldn't choose between disobeying

John, or facing Bolty, having turned around without trying!"

I had been rueing David's absence but, amazingly, it might be a blessing, permitting us to take the initiative by ourselves. Four hands reached for pockets, searching for phones and the off buttons, anxious to kill any attempt at restraint, before inception.

Heavy traffic slowed the journey before Colin pulled up in a lay-by, half a mile short of the village of Tufton Gray. By then, sunset had arrived in the west, red wispy clouds bathed in a soft tangerine sky, full of promise for weather to come. Swiftly the sky faded to the navy-blue darkness of late dusk.

Naturally, we turned towards Paul, expecting his army training, married to a sergeant's experience of leadership, to kick in.

"You any idea of where we are, in relation to the house?" I asked, conscious that Paul was the only one who had knowledge of the village and local terrain.

"I've a pretty good idea where we are. I've spent ages memorising the terrain and layout of the land. Online maps are a godsend," he informed us. "This time, we'll reverse the car under those trees there." He indicated a copse of trees, which, conveniently for us, had a small track leading towards it. I opened the gate, directing Colin as he reversed the car the forty metres up the track until it almost completely disappeared from view, under the tree canopy.

"That'll do," Paul announced, standing back to check its concealment. Unless looking for it, the Golf was well hidden, blending fully with the shadows of night and the shapes of the tree cover.

Cautiously we prepared for action, opening the boot, distributing the various tools and weapons to individual preference. Fortunately, with the addition of camouflage jackets provided by Paul and Bolty, our clothing blended completely against the background.

"Mud up your faces and hands," Paul ordered, crouching on the grass and rubbing dirt into his forehead. We copied him, inspecting each other for effectiveness. We looked the part, dark and menacing, almost invisible against the backdrop of a night sky.

"I'm sure the manor house is over in that direction," Paul announced, indicating a route directly across the wheat fields. "Follow me, and keep as quiet as possible," he instructed, turning away.

We set off after him, moving forwards in single file. During the journey down, I'd tried to persuade Trish that this was too dangerous a mission for her, that she should stay in the car and wait for our return. But this had been a pointless exercise! Trish took her place, third in line, sandwiched between me and Colin.

Keeping low, we crossed two wheat fields until we reached the edge of a wood.

"These woods go right up to the walls of the estate grounds," Paul whispered, crouching down against a tree. "Stay low and, above all, make no noise whatsoever; there is just a chance they have hidden mikes," he warned.

Carefully and slowly, we moved into the trees, taking extreme caution not to make a sound. Though, amid the darkness, I heard an occasional creak, or crack, standing out against the normal nocturnal sounds, as one of us would accidently disturb unseen foliage.

"Quiet," Paul hissed in exasperation at our amateur attempts. Halfway across the woods we startled a fox, out for a night-time foray. The fox leapt away from our detachment, crashing through the foliage and undergrowth with what seemed to be a night shattering crescendo of noise. Out in front, Paul dropped into the vegetation, motioning behind for us to do likewise. We fell, remaining motionless, hidden in the bushes for several minutes, expecting a light to appear ahead of us at any moment, waiting for somebody to come and investigate. Eventually, Paul whispered down the line, "Nothing moving, let's go, pass it on!"

Again, we crawled forward gingerly, taking even more caution, careful not to make a sound.

Paul halted. Out of the darkness loomed the foot of the estate wall, almost invisible until the last second. I bumped into Paul's rear, only noticing the wall at the last moment.

It must have taken almost an hour to transverse the woods and reach the walls of the grounds, but we had no idea what precautions and surveillance the evil ones had taken to protect their property, and evil secrets.

"Stay still and keep down," he commanded, motioning for us to remain concealed. His irritation at our efforts was still evident by his tone. In the dark, I edged forwards, looking up at the wall.

"I guess we need to carry out some surveillance?" I queried our next move, turning to Paul for leadership.

"We'll follow the perimeter wall until we find a vantage point," he instructed me, moving away on his haunches. The three of us followed tentatively, making even more effort to move silently in enemy territory.

As we moved forwards, it was obvious that great care had been taken by Jerome and his devilish chums to clear the perimeter ground. Very little cover was available for us to hide in. I wondered about the existence of hidden cameras, but Paul suggested that they were unlikely outside the walls, as animal movement would trigger the sensors too often.

For almost forty minutes we crawled on our hands and knees, concealed in the thick darkness at the base of the ten-foot wall.

"Wait!" Paul stopped, motioning for us to halt. "Ahead, eleven o'clock," he muttered in my direction. Eyes straining into the darkness, I could just make out the trunk of a tree, about twenty feet beyond Paul.

"This is the one, I think. This is the oak," he murmured sotto-voiced, inaudible to any ears other than mine.

On knees and elbows, we edged forwards. When we eventually reached the base of the oak tree, Paul withdrew a pair of binoculars from beneath his jacket. Indicating to me that I should boost him into the lower branches of the tree, he whispered, "Stay there, I will be back soon."

Within ten feet, Paul had disappeared. I strained to see what I thought to be the shape of his torso through the branches. Unless I knew he was there, I wouldn't have been able to see him, even if I was looking. Carefully, I checked my watch in the darkness. The luminous hands showed it was 12.37. Concealed amongst the gloom, at the bottom of the wall, the three of us settled down to wait on Paul.

After twenty minutes, Paul returned, appearing without warning out of the branches above, gently dropping to the ground and landing on his haunches besides me.

"Seems all quiet," he informed us. "There are three lights on in the house, all of them on the ground floor. It's obvious that someone is still awake, but I couldn't see any signs of movement."

"Any sign of the dogs you warned us about," I asked uneasily.

"No, no sign nor sound," he replied. "Hopefully, they are in kennels, only released when required."

"Let's hope that's not every night" whispered Colin, pushing forward to join the conversation.

"What's the plan?" I asked, deferring to Paul's greater experience.

"I think we can enter the grounds from the tree," he informed us, pointing up at the tree in the dark. "Notice how that big branch crosses the wall. We will knot the rope to make a climbable escape route, then simply go in fast and open the door with the persuader there," he said, indicating the three-foot-long sledgehammer which Colin had lumped across the fields. "Then we'll quickly check every room before they know what's hit them. I will hold anybody we find in one place; you check the rooms," he instructed, talking to Colin and myself. "Trish, you stay with me once we're inside the house, let Martyn and Colin carry out their assessment."

"Ludicrous," I snapped, only just remembering to stay quiet in my irritation. "The plan has more holes than a Gruyere cheese. What about the dogs? We have to wait and evaluate, establish if they're out or not. And what if we meet opposition inside the house; we need a better plan, and a better escape route." I declared, feeling exasperated. "What are we going to do if it all goes tits-up? Get back to the car and hope Colin manages to escape with the car keys," I stated, sarcasm colouring my words.

"We haven't got time for a better plan," Paul advised me brusquely, quickly becoming agitated. "Katie is in there; she needs us. There was no sign of the dogs when I was watching!" He dismissed my concerns curtly, with a contemptuous shrug.

"We're wasting time; shall we get started?" he said, turning towards the tree.

Angrily I hissed, air escaping through clenched teeth as I fought to remain calm and maintain my cool through my annoyance. "Bull in a china shop," I muttered, just loudly enough for Paul to hear. Paul paused, turning back towards my angry display.

"Look, I don't know what your problem is. We have to go in there sooner or later. I have simply come up with a plan for rapid infiltration, then withdrawal. And, frankly, I don't see any reason to discuss it further. This is not the time for petty squabbling; we have more important things to do," he snapped, again turning towards the tree, indicating that Colin should give him a boost up.

"Let's just hope that Katie's up to rope climbing at speed," I said. Paul halted, tensing momentarily, before the realisation registered. I wasn't a squaddie who could be shouted at for insubordination.

"Martyn, shut up and move," Trish hissed, letting me know I was being an arse. In reality my outburst was fuelled by nerves. I had no alternative. There was little option but to execute Paul's plan.

Choosing to ignore me, Paul disappeared up into the tree. We sensed him unravelling the rope from around his chest. The rope dropped from the dark mass of the tree, snaking down on the other side of the wall. Paul's head appeared, briefly.

"Colin first before Trish, then Martyn," he announced, before he disappeared back into the darkness. I moved forwards, ready to boost Colin,

"Sledgehammers and baseball bats," Colin joked, as he prepared to mount the tree. "It's a bit like a night out in Venezuela." I smiled, realising the humour covered Colin's nerves. This was a long way from anything we'd ever experienced before.

Trish followed Colin up and over the wall, ignoring my last-minute pleadings for her to remain outside the grounds. Lastly, I shimmied up the trunk, reaching up over my head for the lower branches, gripping the branch first, then the rope. Taking extreme caution to keep sound and movement to a minimum, I gently lowered myself onto the grass, joining the others.

We waited a while, cowering deep in the shadows, observing the silent house before us. Now only two lights burned, both on the ground floor, next to each other, possibly one large room.

"We've been here, on this side of the wall, for ten minutes," Paul asserted in a whisper. "So far still no sign of the Dobermans!" It was hard to tell in the darkness if he was being sarcastic or simply informative, but I felt no need to reply.

Creeping stealthily on our haunches, we made our way forward, aiming diagonally across the immaculate lawn towards an unseen side door, which Paul informed us definitely existed. His assessment was that the door was adjacent to the living room, where he and Robert had observed Jerome and Rosalind previously. The room where the light now burned!

At a twenty metre distance from the house, we halted, making final plans for the assault. I was given the sledgehammer and ordered to attack the door with all force. As soon as it gave way, Paul would be through, aiming immediately for the room which was occupied. Trish was to follow him, only after Colin and I had entered!

"I will suppress any initial response," Paul declared, raising the baseball bat he cradled in his hands. I chose not to ask any further questions about his methodology. This wasn't a school outing: Katie was depending on us.

"Five minutes maximum," he said. "Any longer will give them time to regroup!"

Colin and I were given our instructions; we were to fan out but stay together, check each room in the house quickly. I would retain the sledgehammer, just in case we found a locked door during our search.

I checked behind me, feeling for the short axe handle which I'd secreted in my belt, when we set out. I was prepared in case we met opposition.

"One more thing," Paul advised. "Once we are in, make as much noise as possible; shock and disorientation are everything."

We edged forward on our arms and elbows. Five metres from the perimeter of the lawn, a security light burst into light, brightly illuminating the four of us. We froze! There was nothing we could do, unable to hide or avoid the light. Our route to the door had forced us to pass the motion sensors. Lit up like an oil rig in the ocean, we remained stock still, waiting for the shout of discovery, or the howl of dogs – seconds passed.

Realising that, in the circumstances, lack of motion was no longer a concealment from inquisitive eyes, Paul dashed forward, flattening himself against the red brick wall of the house. I followed, then Trish and Colin. We stayed there as the seconds mounted, hardly daring to breath.

"Looks like we got away with it," Paul mouthed to me, letting out a long slow breath. He eased around the corner of the house, taking up position on the other side of the door, close to the illuminated rooms. Quickly, Colin, Trish and I joined him, the seriousness of our activities at last breeding ruthless efficiency.

In the gloom I studied the door, a modern well-made wooden door, but it didn't seem like it had any extra security features. I examined the lock, deciding where to smash the door with the sledgehammer.

"On the count of three," warned Paul, "and, remember, in and out within five minutes! One, Two..." I could feel my heart pounding, an adrenaline fuelled thumping. I was sure it could be heard half a mile away in the village. "Three!" I sprang forward, sledgehammer arching through the air, crashing into the door with a shuddering thunderclap. I raised the hammer again, swinging it in a frenzy, eager to complete my task in as short a time as possible. On the third swing the door burst open, smashing into the wall of the passageway beyond, revealing a charging Jerome launched into action by this staggering maelstrom of noise.

Paul sprang past me, yelling as he attacked Jerome before he had a chance to react, slamming him back through the open door into the brightly lit room from which he'd emerged.

Colin and I were well versed for the task in hand; we ran forwards, ignoring anything that was happening with Jerome and Paul, that was Paul's problem!

We raced towards the end of the passageway, loudly yelling, "Katie!" as we ran. Reaching the stairs, we sprinted up them three at a time. We'd planned to start on the first floor, the furthest point from entry, working our way back towards the exit and safety.

I barged the nearest door open, shouting, "Katie," as I entered. An empty room greeted my swift torchlit sweep of the interior.

"No," Colin shouted, withdrawing from the room next to it.

Slamming my foot forward hard, I erupted through the next door; again my torchlight revealed a blank. On the upper floor of the house, we flung open door after door, revealing nothing but unoccupied bedrooms and bathrooms.

"Not upstairs," I shouted at Colin, more for the need to say something rather than a desire to impart what was clearly unnecessary information.

Deep within I relished the adrenaline buzz. I couldn't do this every day, but I understood why people did this type of thing. Colin grinned back at me, caught up in his own adrenaline frenzy.

We jumped down the stairs, four at a time now, swinging violently to our right, aiming for the kitchen situated at the far end of the passage. The kitchen was deserted, used plates and cutlery lying in and around the sink. A half-eaten chicken salad was on the work surface.

It was obvious, any staff they had were daytime staff, not live-in.

We turned around, heading back the way we'd come. Glancing at my watch, I saw that, so far, we'd been there less than two minutes.

Colin indicated to a door by the stairs; it was recessed back, almost hidden under the stairs, obviously an entrance to a cellar room. First, we swiftly checked the dining room, drawing rooms, then the utility room beside the kitchen, drawing a blank in each. Paul and Trish had the rest of the house. We moved forward cautiously, preparing to investigate the cellar. Our best bet!

I don't know what I was expecting from the cellar of a small country manor house. The door had no sign of a lock, so I placed the sledgehammer to one side, waiting as Colin kicked the door open viciously. "Go," he shouted, holding back to give me room. I sprang through the door, expecting the gothic horror scene of my imagination. Stairs on the other side of the door took me by surprise. I had to fling my hand out and grab the rail to stop myself plunging into darkness. Colin following closely behind. Speedily he assessed the situation, reaching out and flicking the light switch by the open door.

"Guess they'll know we're here by now – no need for a torch," he joked, grinning at me, hanging on to the railing for grim death. "Best to light the way, eh, stop you falling over and making a tit of yourself!"

I regained my balance, still nearly falling in my haste to descend the stairs. At the bottom, what greeted us, to my surprise, was a modern fully equipped gym. Of course, it would be, I thought, telling myself, you've been watching too many movies.

Despite the normality of what we witnessed, a gymnasium cellar, the sight before us still rendered us frozen in horror. Amongst the gleaming chrome keep-fit equipment, positioned at the centre of the floor, stood an old heavy wooden chair, looking out of place amongst the modern chrome and bright fluorescent lighting. The arms of the chair and its front legs sported frayed and cut ropes.

The chair was secured to a nearby bench press. The reason for this didn't require any imagination. Gathering our wits, we dashed forward as one, wildly looking for any sign of Katie, desperately searching in case she lay among the equipment. It was a futile task; the gym was empty!

Solemnly, Colin dipped his head, indicating the arms of the chair. With sickening revulsion, I saw the four scratches on each arm of the chair, fingernail marks, deep grooves in the hard wood. The person who made those scratches had obviously been in abject terror, or unimaginable agony, or possibly both.

I beat Colin to it, striding into the lounge where Paul and Trish now held Jerome and Rosalind at gunpoint.

Ignoring my compatriots, I walked straight up to Jerome, spitting the word, "bastard." I hit him hard on the chin. This time he was prepared, his body swaying backwards, taking much of the force out of the punch. Still, it must have hurt, but he remained standing, staggering, but upright. He grabbed his chin, rubbing it with his right hand.

"You keep doing that!" he snarled at me. "So unimaginative, so unprofessional for a supposed Christian!" I was pleased to see blood on his lips.

I remained there, rooted to the spot, not daring to speak through my anger.

Abruptly, I noticed the revolver held outstretched in Paul's hand; this was unexpected. He hadn't said a word about this before we went in. I looked closer, the revolver, dark and ugly, seemingly ominous in its power. The gun looked old, probably a leftover souvenir from the last war, a family heirloom handed down from one generation to the next. But however old it may have been, the weapon was still lethal. Even from where I stood, I could see the glint of brass bullets in the chamber. Paul held the gun, rock solid, its black barrel covering Jerome and a strangely subdued, but calm, Rosalind. She sat quietly and unobtrusively on the couch, calmly watching the act as it played out. Outwardly, she appeared unconcerned, as if viewing a play. I noted the bruising to Rosalind's nose and eyes.

"Where is she? You bastard!" Paul growled the words at Jerome as he moved forwards. Jerome also appeared strangely unperturbed by his situation.

"You'll never find out, unless I will it!" Jerome responded, glaring back at him. "She could be dead already if I wished. Or maybe we tortured her, then let her go, left to die in the woods, cold and alone. That is, if I knew who you were talking about." I recognised the chilling contemptuous and disdainful tone as he dismissed Paul; I swear I was about to witness a murder, that I saw Paul's finger tighten on the trigger.

The front door burst open with an explosive thump. We jerked backwards. Loud voices and shouting followed, heading in our direction.

"Time you weren't here," yelled Rosalind, with a provocative jeer. She jumped up from her couch. "Cavalries arrived!"

Paul reacted instantly and violently, shoving Jerome hard in the chest. Jerome flew backwards, arms flailing, windmilling, grasping at thin air before his feet became entangled with a rug and he crashed down, overturning an occasional lamp on the way.

"Go," yelled Paul, unnecessarily; we'd already burst into action.

Trish was first through the shattered door, pushed roughly by me. Colin followed me and a step behind him, Paul. Not waiting around, I grabbed Trish by the wrist, sprinting and dragging her with me. "Run," I shouted, desperate for the safety of the wall and the darkness beyond.

A loud sharp crack just behind us ripped the night air apart. I slowed slightly, registering no footsteps close behind. Taking a risk and turning, I saw Paul, arm outstretched, gun aimed at Jerome and Maurice, who'd pulled up sharply as the shot buried itself in the wall by their head. Framed by the door structure, they held tight. Threatened by death, or disfigurement, they'd stopped.

"What's the matter?" mocked Paul. "You afraid of joining your master, in hell." This was the opportunity we required. We ran across the lawn, faster than we'd ever ran before. I grabbed Trish's waist, lifting her upwards onto the rope. She gripped the rope tightly, using my body as a ladder to gain a handhold on the top of the wall. Colin didn't hang around; within seconds he joined Trish on the wall, reaching down to haul me up. We turned, seated on the pinnacle, looking back across the floodlit lawn. Paul pounded towards us, chased by the two snarling, yelping Dobermans.

"Come on Paul," we yelled, screaming encouragement at our comrade, steaming across the lawn as fast as his legs would carry him. Colin and I reached down towards him, stretching as far as we could reach. The dogs were rapidly gaining. Colin looked on in despair, realising, as I had, there would only be one chance of escape.

Paul leapt upwards, inches in front of the baying hounds, arms stretched towards us, desperately seeking the comfort of our grip. I felt his vice-like hold grab my forearm, wrenching me forward with a jolt. Luckily, Paul's actions had given Colin and me time to prepare. We'd sat astride the top of the wall, able to take the jerk as it came. Leaning down, each taking an arm in our hands, we hauled Paul up the wall.

A Doberman launched itself in the air, clamping onto Paul's trouser leg. With Doberman attached, its teeth clenched, its jaws locked onto the leg of Paul's camouflage trousers, we heaved him struggling upwards. The dog refused to release him, fastened to the trouser like a limpet. The other dog was going wild in an attempt to reach us, barking and snarling in an enraged frenzy.

I had no way of knowing if the dog had sunk its fangs into Paul's leg, as well as the trousers, but he managed to hang on to us for all his life was worth as we inched him upwards. Finally, with a howl, the dog loosened its jaw from the material, falling backwards, knocking its pal over in a flurry of limbs and fur.

With rasping breaths, eyes bulging, sweat pouring from the exertion, Paul briefly squeezed our arms. "Thanks, not as fit as I used to be," he said, before twisting and jumping off the wall in a single motion. Close call, I thought, following Paul down onto the floor of the woods.

On the other side of the wall, we could hear the dogs in a paroxysm of fury, as their quarry escaped.

"Come on!" Paul urged. "I doubt they'll give up now."

I paused, listening hard for sounds in the darkness.

Lights appeared around a hundred and fifty metres away, roughly where we'd passed the locked gates earlier. The lights were accompanied by voices, mostly male, yelling and shouting to each other, clearly in a state of agitation and excitement. Evidently Paul was right. This time they weren't willing to give up the pursuit once we'd reached the walls.

"Let's go," I said, identifying Trish from the size of her silhouetted outline in the gloom. I grabbed her arm as we turned, pausing to listen to the baying of the dogs through the night air. Dogs which I perceived were now outside the wall. Dogs which were baying angrily, trying to get at their denied prey.

"Run," I urged, tugging Trish's wrist hard as we set off. Thrashing blindly through the undergrowth, the foliage slapped at our legs and bodies; grasping vegetation reached out, impeding our progress. In the darkness and blind panic, I became aware we had lost contact with Paul and Colin. Now we were on our own, Trish and I, floundering through the woods, pushing through the murky shadows.

The dogs were gaining. I could hear barking and snarling accompanied by bellowing male voices. The dogs must be on chains, I thought, else they would have had us by now.

"Come on, faster," I implored the sobbing Trish. We plundered headlong through the inkiness. I tripped over an unseen root, flying forwards, arm out, dragging Trish down with me. Panicked, I bounded upright in a single motion, arms pumping, legs churning; we thrashed forwards, forcing ourselves onwards! I sensed the ground beneath us rising quite steeply. I hadn't noticed a descent on the way in. We'd become lost and disorientated in the midnight woods.

They were inexorably gaining. The dogs howled, only metres separating them from us as they dragged their handler forward towards their prey! Us.

"They're close, only yards ahead. Don't let them get away!" An unknown male voice shouted, his words slicing through the night, joyously capturing the excitement of the chase.

Trish sobbed louder, her lungs burning, gasping for oxygen, unable to quicken her pace, or even maintain the flight.

"Slow down," I urged. "Save your breath for the confrontation to come." I twisted, eyes searching towards the pursuit, instinctively feeling behind me for the reassurance of the thick wooden axe handle. Mercifully it was still nestling in the waistband of my trousers.

It was a blessing; we were exhausted, unable to speed up. Ahead of us, through the dappled moonlight, at the very limit of my vision, I could just make out what I thought was a cliff edge. The ground seemed to fall away. Stumbling, I slowed further, my eyes searching the ground ahead, seeking confirmation of what it was that lay beyond. Behind us, the sound of barking dogs grew in intensity. We could hear them, very close now, crashing through the vegetation.

The moon had risen, giving just enough light to see what was ahead, I could dimly make out a rocky cliff edge, followed by a void. Deep impenetrable blackness, as the land fell into the void. Pulling up sharply, I grabbed the trunk of a small tree, tugging at Trish's arm. She halted, grabbing my tree, preventing herself from staggering over the cliff in the dark. We knew then, the game was up – we were trapped. Things had gone horribly wrong; now we were about to pay the price!

"Angelikinus," I whispered, in resigned desperation. "Angelikinus."

The dogs were upon us, their howling reaching a new pitch of intensity. I sensed the handler release them for the final takedown.

"Go boys, go" he bellowed joyously into the night. The ear-shattering barking filled our minds. This was followed by an indefinable rush of movement through the shadowy bushes. Instinctively, I flung my arm up for protection, at the last second detecting the springing dog, launching towards me. The snarling Doberman's jaw clamped down ferociously on my wrist, bringing instant and terrible pain. Dimly, in my subconscious mind, I heard Trish scream out, somewhere to my right.

The full force of the dog's jaw remained there, clamped, ripping and shaking at my arm. Trying to bring me down. Miraculously, I remembered that I had the axe handle, still clenched tightly in my other fist. This needed to be finished promptly! I had no idea what was happening to Trish, the dogs' owners were only feet away from joining the fight.

Despite its launching attack, and its size, I'd managed to stay upright. I could feel the dog's fetid breath on my hand and arm as I struggled with the raging animal. Ignoring its efforts, I raised my free hand high above my head, whipping the axe handle down as hard as I could. I missed the Doberman's skull, hitting it with a glancing blow across the shoulder; fur cushioned the blow. The dog didn't seem to notice; it continued ripping at my sleeve, crushing my arm between those razor fangs.

Repeating the blow, mercifully, I heard a dull crack, as hard unresisting wood met fragile canine skull bone. Instantly, the dog went limp, falling away from me, its teeth releasing my arm. I pushed the dog away, not caring if I had killed it.

Spinning towards her, I registered Trish standing on her own, unharmed by the very edge of the precipice. Of the second dog there was no sign.

"Go," I shouted, "Go." I could see no point in us both staying. Maybe Trish could use the few seconds that I had bought to escape.

Within, the red mist had risen fully; the fight with the dog had taken only seconds. I spun back, just in time to see Maurice White clear the bushes and step into view. Following close behind, Maurice was supported by two menacing henchmen, heavies whom I had never seen before. It was scant comfort to recognise the shape of the plaster cast, still protecting Maurice's broken wrist. Of Jerome, Rosalind and Anne there was no sign. I presumed they were hunting my friends, somewhere in the darkness. Here, I was pumped, ready for the fight.

On clearing the bushes, Maurice forgot to pause or assess the situation. Recognising me was a red rag to a bull. He charged forwards, straight into the attack.

"Come on then," I roared, axe handle poised and ready. In the moonlight I caught the dull glint of a knife cradled in his outstretched left hand. Recklessly, Maurice lunged forwards, seeking to catch me unawares by launching a left-handed knife thrust in the dark!

God bless the game of rugby! Many a time on the field of play I'd seen a tackle coming at the last moment, avoiding it with a delicate sidestep. I didn't even have time to think, at the very last instant, I jumped to one side. It was all over in seconds. In the darkness, an exhilarated Maurice hadn't seen the cliff edge. He should have known it was there, after all, it was where he lived, but in his eagerness to get at me, to cause me pain, with his concealed knife, Maurice didn't stop to think. He simply charged forward in the dark. Fooled by my sidestep, he charged over the precipice. Even then, he may have averted disaster. Sensing his mistake, at the very last second, he grabbed in panic at a sapling, which was struggling to survive and grow in the rocky soil. In slow motion, Maurice desperately tried to arrest his charge, but he'd seized it with his right hand, the hand in plaster! With a shriek of pain, he was gone, disappearing into the abyss, falling from view into the void below. We heard sounds of crashing, rocks falling below us, followed by one short sharp scream, cut off in an instant. Then silence, apart from the animal warning calls, drifting on the night.

I turned, waiting for his henchmen to close and make their move. They halted, unsure of what to do, lacking the direction of their leader.

"Come on then," I growled at them, deciding to take advantage while I was seemingly in ascendancy. "I'm ready," I growled, knowing they were still mentally reeling from their loss and confusion. The closest henchman hesitated, taking a step backwards. His friend glanced sideways. Realising his companion was retreating, he followed suit. I cradled the axe handle, slapping it into my palm, displaying its menace to my already nervous adversaries. "Come on then," I repeated, stepping towards them. In the moonlight they drifted backwards, intimidated by my ominous sabre-rattling.

Abruptly, they disengaged from the encounter, fading from view, disappearing back into the trees.

Turning towards where I'd last seen Trish, I found her still there, watching! Of the other dog there was no sign.

Exhausted, I had to bend forwards, supporting my quaking knees with my hands, trying to stay standing, releasing the accumulated tension in long shuddering breaths. Indicating the cliff edge, I gasped, "Where is he? Can you hear anything below?" Trish couldn't speak. In the awfulness of the situation, she was lost for words, blankly shaking her head. She stepped towards me, arms wide, enfolding me in a silent embrace.

We remained there, wordlessly entwined for over a minute, luxuriating in the warmth of the other, thankful to be alive and for now, safe. Half-heartedly, I tried to disengage, aware that danger still lurked in the darkness, knowing that Jerome and Rosalind were still at large, maybe somewhere close by, in the woods.

"It was a miracle," she murmured, staring up into my eyes. "The dog, the fox... the attack... it was a miracle."

"What happened?" I asked, finally disengaging from Trish's arms, stepping back, holding her by the shoulders.

"It was a miracle," Trish repeated in awe, explaining, "The Doberman burst through the bushes and launched at me. Out of nowhere, a snarling fox appeared. The Doberman was in mid-air when the fox sprang towards it, crashing into its ribs. In an instant, the Doberman shifted its attention to the fox. Inside a second, they were fighting in a frenzy, rolling over and over, seeking to rip out each other's throats."

"What happened next?" I asked, astonished by the extraordinary account.

"They disappeared over the edge of the cliff," said Trish, pointing into the darkness.

"That fox gave its life to save me," she whispered, in wonder.

"Maybe it was just protecting its lair; it's possible it could have survived, but you never know," I concluded, recalling the trigger word, Angelikinus.

Deciding to leave Maurice for his friends to recover, we felt our way along the edge of the cliff until the ground became firmer. The cliff disappeared at an angle. Ever cautious we moved on, keeping low and quiet. Stopping often to attune ourselves to the sounds of the woods, we heard nothing but natural nocturnal noises of the night.

Then, without warning, we escaped from the claustrophobic confines of the woods, stepping from the perimeter of trees onto a dark ribbon of tarmacked road.

We'd emerged on the other side of the village, again needing to infiltrate enemy territory to reach the safety of the car. Warily we kept to the verge, creeping carefully through the unstirring village, with its silent and intimidating houses. Then, at last, we passed the final cottage. We were able to leave the daunting environs of the brooding settlement behind!

Glancing at my watch, I saw that it was 3.35. We trudged on, impatient for the warmth and security of the car.

I began to relax, fancying we were on familiar territory. "If I'm not mistaken, I think we're there," I breathed. Bathed in moonlight, I could make out the copse of trees where we'd hidden the car, five terror-filled hours earlier.

The sky above us erupted in a blaze of light. Without thought, we both dived sideways onto the verge, thankfully finding a shallow grassy ditch, offering concealment from prying eyes. The light moved swiftly downwards towards the ground, cutting through the sky like a rushing tide. I grasped then, the sky was lit up by the headlights of a car coming through the village at speed, then rising the brow of the road behind us. I twisted my neck; the headlights grew as the car sped towards us. At the last second, we ducked, hiding our heads and faces from the glare in the earthy grass. The car rushed past without slowing. Popping my head up, I told Trish, "I think it's the Jag, but at that speed and distance, I can't be sure. One thing I can be sure of is I'm fed up with ending up in the dirt every time they drive past."

We completed the final few metres in stealth. The Golf, in darkness, quietly waited for our return. I moved forwards and touched the bonnet, checking for warmth.

An unexpected movement on my periphery caused me to violently twist towards it, my arms rising instantly, ready to hit out at this new and unknown foe. Colin halted in his stride, just visible at the edge of the clearing, Paul appearing behind him. "It's us, you're safe." They moved towards us, relief and pleasure reflected by their expressions. They approached grinning.

"You took your time getting here; boy are we glad to see you," Colin beamed gleefully, grabbing us both in a bear hug.

Paul clasped my hand, holding it tightly in both of his. "Good to see you. We thought you'd had it." He smiled wryly.

"Better if we make ourselves scarce," I suggested. "I think the opposition has just been down this road."

"I know, we saw it," Paul said. "And this is the only road, so we have a choice, turn left through the village, or turn right into a possible roadblock!"

"Turn right," we instructed Colin. "But go slowly, and keep your eyes peeled."

Stress receded as heartbeats returned to normal. In the comparative safety of the car, Paul and Colin began sharing their experiences.

"When you shouted *go,* all kinds of chaos erupted," Colin told us cheerfully. He'd plunged desperately through the dense woods, blindly charging on until his flight was arrested. "A thorny bramble bush grabbed me in the dark. I was all tangled up. I was forced to stop and think. The bush was in a hollow, so I was hidden. I waited, listening to the chase, recognising from the diminishing sound of barking that the dogs had picked another victim." Colin was happily luxuriating in his easy escape.

"Unfortunately, the victims they chose to chase were us." I explained, before letting him continue.

"The rest was a doddle," he revealed. "I had huddled down in the dip, hidden below the bush. Several times feet came close, crashing and blundering about in the darkness, torch beams flicking around like fireflies in and out of the trees and bushes, but I was hidden; they didn't even come close." He laughed.

"Of course," he said, looking over his shoulder towards us, "if they'd brought the dogs back for the search, then I'd have been in the shit but, fortunately, they didn't. Gradually they slowed down, searched elsewhere, then they went away," he concluded smugly.

"Dogs couldn't come back; they're dead," Trish announced, before launching into a summary of our exploits!

Without warning, the adrenaline leaving my system caught up with me. Thankfully, I wasn't driving. I would never have been able to continue. I felt unbelievably nauseas. "Pull over," I demanded, dry retching. Colin required no second invitation; promptly he drove the car onto the verge, mercifully allowing me to lean from the door, vomiting copiously onto the grass.

Trish completed the telling of our tale as I gratefully sank into the corner of the upholstery, shaking and shivering, the sweat pouring from me. The enormity of our adventure and its consequences sank in.

Dully, as I listened to Trish, I accepted the reality: beyond the exhilaration of escape, Katie was still out there somewhere, possibly alone and frightened, maybe dead!

Jerome hadn't denied that they'd had her. Our discovery in the cellar evidenced this. We would have to admit to Bolty that Katie was still missing; we had failed in our mission.

I dozed into blessed oblivion, vaguely listening to Trish's retelling of Maurice, hurtling into darkness. I slept fitfully for the remainder of the journey, a throbbing arm my constant companion.

Fortunately, we escaped the area with no further encounters. No sightings of sinister Jaguars. Sleeping, I missed the telling of Paul's exploits. In the dark, Paul had managed to outrun two chasers and had burst from the wood into a moonlit field. Skirting the field, staying low, he'd kept his head below the level of the crops until he was sure that the chasers had given up and returned to base. Paul was the luckiest of us all, managing to reach the car first. He'd then endured an uncomfortable two hours, imagining all kinds of fates for the rest of us. He remained hidden behind a hedge, working out how he was going to make it home, until Colin appeared from the darkness, his hands and face streaked, mud clinging to clothes which were ripped and bloodstained from the brambles.

We arrived safely back at the farm. Sue and Sandra were apoplectic with anxiety. We'd failed to turn on our mobiles again. "Where have you been? What on earth happened? Why didn't you call us?" Sandra's words expressed annoyance, but the relief was there for all to see. The three of them had been waiting on tenterhooks for nearly ten hours.

Bolty received the news stoically, crestfallen, but expressing grateful thanks that we'd tried, aware that we had risked a lot. Paul led him aside by the elbow, gently informing his friend of our grim discovery in the cellar of the manor house. Venting his forlorn hope, Bolty tried to persuade us to go to the police, saying, "We need to tell them what we know."

"We can't, mate," Paul advised, probably thinking of the revolver which I hadn't seen since the manor house.

"How would we describe our association with these guys?" he said, indicating the four of us. "Let alone, our knowledge of Jerome and his ilk. We got the impression from Jerome, it's too late!" Paul warned Bolty, his voice breaking with emotion.

We looked on in sorrow as cold clinical realisation struck the quiet Scotsman. This exciting and thrilling adventure had turned disastrously sour for Bolty. It had cost him the life of his wife!

CHAPTER THIRTEEN

It was a blessing that the next day was a Saturday. We left the farm just after six in the morning, driving towards the dawn, the morning sunlight streaming through the car windows, failing to lift the mood as Katie's fate sunk in.

Sue left a voicemail message for David, who would be clueless about our trip to Tufton Gray and subsequent activities.

John was furious, that we'd acted without permission. I'd answered the door to David and found myself confronted by John's tight-lipped anger. Trish was in the flat, pottering and lazing around, generally recovering from the previous night's ordeal.

"Wait there!" John commanded in a clipped tone, which broached no dissent. He pointed at the couch and we both sat meekly, nervously anticipating John's wrath. He picked up my phone, without looking at the screen, inputting a number; all the while his eyes remaining fixedly focused on Trish and myself.

As soon as Colin answered, John informed him brusquely, "You are required in Martyn's flat, immediately!" John terminated the call, not allowing Colin any chance to reply. We remained on the couch, sitting quietly, waiting. I glanced across at Trish, trying to lift her spirits with a tiny smile.

When I'd turned my phone on, there'd been no message and no missed calls from David's number. We'd returned home, falling into bed; mercifully, sleep was quick to overcome us both. Despite the trauma of Katie, I'd been dog-tired, we slept until early afternoon, waking to the afternoon sunshine.

"Come in, sit," John said curtly, indicating the couch where Trish and I waited tamely. Colin meekly did as he was ordered.

Without preamble, in an emotionless statement of fact, John announced, "Katie is dead. Fortunately for you, she was dead long before you left the farm in Watling. We were merciful to her," he declared. "Katie died of a heart attack, induced by shock, before Rosalind and Anne managed to fully inflict their intended and very evil desires!"

The clinical matter-of-factness of John's manner, coupled with the grim monotone with which the news was delivered, was far more worrying than any roof lifting accusatory shouting, which we were expecting. I sensed this was way beyond our earlier misdemeanour with the calling table.

Whatever John wanted from us, I couldn't respond. The icy realisation, caused by John's statement drained all emotional response from the three of us. John's monologue became background noise. The confirmation, "*Katie's dead.*" Slowly penetrated.

Through the fog of despair, John's voice gradually became clearer again. "Mankind are arrogant fools," he stated, forgetting that he had once walked the earth as a man. "A possible outcome of your unwise, reckless and unauthorised incursion could have been your deaths, your subsequent eradication as a syndicate. Did you not think? Mankind are arrogant fools," he repeated, almost to himself. "Fortunately for you, the only outcome was the death of Maurice White, a disciple of Satan, and his two dogs."

"What," I exclaimed, suddenly becoming fully focused, jolting upright, my mouth opening in shock.

When I'd made myself think about the chase the previous night, and our confrontation I managed to convince myself that Maurice would be lying in a room somewhere, hurting and angry. People didn't really die in real life, that was for films and books, or someone on the news. Now there was Katie, then Maurice, in three short minutes.

"Where does that leave me?" I questioned him, terrified of the idea that I was guilty of manslaughter, or even murder.

"Do not worry," John replied solemnly. "It is not a result we desire in any way! That is because it will most certainly prompt an unforeseen response, one that is both undesirable and alarming. However, don't fret. At this present moment, Mr Jerome Brendon-Smythe does not wish a full police investigation across his property and lands. It will be reported to the authorities and accepted as an accident."

John reiterated, "You are free to leave the syndicate at any time of your choosing." Then he sent a shiver through us all. "The Lord can take this decision from you. Last night was both foolish and deliberate. My Lord does not suffer disobedience; he can turn his back on you at any time." John ignored our stricken expressions, saying, "You may never see myself or Luke again."

Ominously, he declared, "We will consider this possibility; remember, many are called, few are chosen." With that gut-wrenching bombshell, David returned, wondering why he'd spontaneously appeared in my flat. The last thing he remembered was watching television at home.

I phoned Paul on the Sunday morning, wanting an update to the police investigation. Paul revealed, "Due to the sensitive nature of her research work, the police have now made it a full missing person's investigation. There are officers all over the village, and on her university campus. The police have found CCTV pictures of Katie driving her car south, with an unknown man in the passenger seat. I've been inundated by questions from them, wanting to know about my absence on Friday night; you'll probably get a visit from your local police in the near future, just to corroborate my alibi. The visit shouldn't be too daunting. I've been alibied by several shop owners and their CCTV systems on the afternoon of Katie's disappearance. They just want to make sure."

I didn't like lying, but there seemed little choice; it presented too many opportunities for confusion and, hence, a more thorough investigation into aspects of our life, which I wished to remain closed to the authorities. Miserably, I wondered what damage Jerome would do within the investigation, given the slightest opportunity.

"Sure thing," I reassured him. "No worries, you stayed at mine."

I told him of John's visit on the Saturday and what it meant for Bolty, who hadn't yet completely given up hope. I left the decision with Paul and Sandra as to whether to remove that hope completely or leave Bolty in tortured suspension. The tiniest crumb of comfort for Bolty, was that he had two good friends to comfort him.

That evening, two detectives did indeed pay me a visit, armed with professional suspicion and curiosity.

I didn't perform well in their company, saying the right things, but with a certain level of guilt, which they seemed to pick up on. I hoped they'd identify my stuttering responses as simple nerves at the presence of police detectives. The two detectives painstakingly dissected our friendship with Paul and Sandra.

"How well do you know Paul and Sandra; they are a bit out of your area."

"I know, Trish and I met them last spring, on a weekend away to Dorset." An explanation which brought a snort of derision from one of the detectives.

"And that was enough to forge a lifelong friendship, was it, sir?"

"No," I replied, "But we haven't got a lifelong friendship, just an occasional thing. They are a nice couple. We get on well."

"And you'd vouch for Paul, would you, sir. He was with you last night?" He glanced across at me as he spoke.

"Yes, well I'll vouch that he stayed here overnight. He was going somewhere, to look at a bull, or maybe meet an army friend, I'm not really sure," I told him, stuttering in my confusion.

"How well did you know the missing woman, Katie Bolt?" he asked, suddenly changing course.

"Not well at all. I mean, we all had lunch last weekend but that is all; previous to that I'd only met her the once."

"How did she seem to you when you met her at the weekend. Did you talk to her at all? he asked, leaning forwards.

"Yes, we had a conversation about theology and also her work," I told him. "I'm not too sure; it was just one of those throw-away conversations you have with somebody you don't know that well."

His friend joined the conversation. "Thursday afternoon, you say you were at work all afternoon, is this true, sir?"

I was on stronger ground here. "Yes, of course it is!" I said, indignantly. "Ask my boss. There will be an electronic record of my key swipes to confirm it."

"We will do, you can be sure of that!" he said, snapping his notebook shut.

At last, the detectives left with barely concealed threats, promising further visits and greater in-depth questioning, should it be required. It was obvious that I hadn't performed well.

Monday evening, watching *Points South,* I viewed it with fascination. The disappearance of Katie was the main news item. The reporter, from her outside broadcast pitch on the pavement opposite Katie's laboratory, informed the viewing public, with professional garnishment, of the rising scientific star in the sub-atomic particle world. She explained how Katie had been involved in research, which was critical to that being carried out at the Cerne institute in France. Our local news anchor enlightened the public how Katie had last been seen visiting a female student for a tutorial. Then Katie had, unexpectedly, taken an alarming phone call, after which she'd driven off in a hurry. The broadcast cut to a grainy shot of Katie in her bright red Nissan, driving south on the main road, a male passenger by her side. "Anybody with any information is urged to come forward immediately. Police are extremely anxious to talk to this man and eliminate him from their enquiries," the practised blond journalist concluded, impressing the camera with the grim smile she kept especially for such tragic occasions.

Somehow, being so close to such a big news item wasn't very thrilling at all. My only sensation was a deep emptiness at the loss of such a beautiful, rational and intelligent woman! My overwhelming compassion was for Bolty, in the depths of his despair.

I reached for the coffee cup by my side, then spluttered the hot drink across the carpet, as the face of Maurice White appeared on my screen.

"In other news, a local man was killed early on Saturday morning when he was thrown by his horse, which pulled up on the edge of a quarry. The man, Mr Maurice White of Tufton Gray, near Basingstoke, fell over sixty feet to land at the base of the cliff in the old disused Tufton sandstone quarry, breaking his neck and skull in the fall."

The presenter continued. "It is reported that the horse bolted when disturbing a fox, and, in a sad twist of fate, Mr White's dog followed him over the edge of the quarry, also dying in the fall. Police are treating the incident as an accident!" the presenter reported, looking up and shuffling his papers, seeming to stare accusingly, directly into my eyes!

While *Points South* moved on to the happier news of the Guildford half marathon, I sat there, utterly dazed by what I'd just seen, my coffee forgotten. Idly I wondered what had happened to the second dog. This was becoming too big. What would happen next!

It failed to lift my spirits, the fact that my colleagues knew that I was loosely connected to the disappearance of the pretty young and brilliant physicist they'd seen on telly. They examined me closely, asking endless questions about the missing girl and her life. Questions which I couldn't answer. I stated curtly, "I'd only just met her. I barely knew her at all." A fresh ripple did circulate through the office, when it wasn't denied. "Yes, I have been questioned by the police in connection with the matter. They left happy." The office excitement quickly died when they finally grasped that I was still there among them. They didn't have a murderer in their midst!

Being the brief focus of office attention failed to make the days go any faster. I spent the majority of my nights lying awake in bed, questioning, asking myself, what if...?

Trish came around most evenings, sometimes with Sue and David, but our time together became desultory. There was still no sign of John. I couldn't get his words out of my head. Was it all over? The kidnapping of Katie, the subsequent death of Maurice, then John's disappearance. Just when we needed support the most, he wasn't there!

We only saw Colin and Yvette the once; they'd chosen to put the events of the weekend behind them, spending their free time together and alone. Colin's leave was drawing to an end. I guessed the thought of going back to sea, leaving Yvette behind, was playing on his mind.

Paul phoned on Saturday evening. "They've found Katie's car," he informed me, in a flat voice, revealing no emotion. He went on to share how a young couple in Kent had visited a notorious rendezvous for lovers on the Friday evening. Deep in the woods, they'd realised that the burnt-out car, which had appeared during the previous week, was the newer model of Nissan's Micra. A car too young to be a burnt-out wreck, unless it was there for a nefarious reason.

On the Saturday, the conscientious woman reported the car to the police. They investigated, checking their missing car database, instantly realising they had a significant and important find on their hands.

"Katie?" I asked bluntly.

"No," Paul replied. "No sign, but they're looking. They've promised Bolty that they've cordoned of the woods; they're going to search it inch by inch."

He disclosed, "Bolty's told me a considerable amount of suspicion has fallen on the girl, Linda Goldsworthy. Apparently, the phone company has produced records of activity on Katie's phone. There are doubts about the calls she received, at least the timings. There was no call when Linda claimed to have witnessed one. The girl, Linda, has been questioned by the police for the past twenty-four hours, any more than that I don't know."

Katie and her car again made the headlines on Monday's *Points South*. The viewers were informed the police had carried out a detailed and thorough fingertip search of Border Woods in Kent, the location of the car's discovery. They reported, "No trace of the missing scientist has yet been unearthed. The car is too badly burnt-out to reveal any clues for the police forensic team," the reporter concluded, handing back to the studio from a windswept field in Kent.

As a group, we began to perk up slowly. When we met up, we waited patiently, hoping for the reappearance of John or Luke. We were always disappointed!

Three days after the *Points South* broadcast, the same two detectives visited me once more. This time I had Trish by my side. As soon as they were seated, they launched in with the questions, not giving me a moment to compose myself.

"Your relationship with the missing scientist, did you enjoy her company?"

"I think I told you last time, I've had a conversation with her, maybe two. I wouldn't call that a relationship," I replied. "Would you?"

I'm not the person linked with the disappearance of one of Britain's top scientists," he told me tersely. "Did you get on well with her husband, Robert, as well as Paul and Sandra?" he asked.

"Yeah, I liked them all, felt relaxed in their company; we didn't know them well, but they seemed okay. We liked what we saw, I think," I said, turning to Trish, who nodded in agreement, giving my arm a quick squeeze.

"And you claim you never met Katie Bolt alone, away from her husband Robert!" he stated, waiting for my confirmation before continuing.

They changed direction, hoping to catch me unawares. "When you met up for lunch at the Thatched Cottage public house, there seemed to be a slight altercation with another member of the public in the restaurant area. Can you tell us about that?" The question flummoxed me. I wasn't expecting that. I had no idea how much information they had.

"Just one of the regulars, I think," I told him. "I'm not sure what it was about; he spoke to Paul and I didn't catch what he was saying. I was over the other side of the table. I got the feeling they didn't like each other." Inwardly I felt pleased by my quick response, but the questioning had left me wary.

"And Katie, what did she say? We have CCTV film of Katie speaking to the person."

I adlibbed. "I don't know. I only caught half of the conversation. I think she said, I'm watching you. I'm not sure if she was being serious or joking with a village friend. I didn't pay much attention."

"And this person she spoke to, can you describe him?" It began to dawn, the CCTV they did have was obviously unclear. It obviously hadn't revealed Jerome to the inquisitive eyes of the investigation team. I was unsure if this was a good or bad thing.

Trish interjected before I could gather my wits. "He was quite tall with dark hair. There is nothing else I can remember; the exchange only took seconds," she said, leaning in towards the conversation.

"Yes, some sort of suit on, but all I can say is it was dark," I told him.

They were obviously at the end of their prepared questions. We were alibied, so it seemed we were off the hook. The detectives went away, seemingly satisfied with our answers, parting with a polite, "Thank you, sir, we'll be in touch if we need to ask you any more questions."

Paul or Sandra took to phoning me or Sue every two or three days, keeping us fully informed on the lacklustre and slow progress of the investigation.

Paul told me, "Linda Goldsworthy has been released without charge. The timings of the calls received by Katie's phone, evidenced by the phone company records, didn't match the times that Linda claimed calls were received. However, this isn't a lot to go on. Traces of blood found on the carpet in Linda's rooms are unidentified. But it wasn't Katie's. DNA matching eliminated Katie. Linda claims it came from a lover, a one-night stand, whose name she can't remember. But that's not a crime."

He also told me, on another occasion, "Linda was also able to furnish the police with a solid alibi for the period after she claimed Katie left her, a time when the police believe Katie was driving southwards; the police had little option. They've released her," he said, the regret obvious.

Two days after Linda was released, Sandra spent a further hour updating Sue on the investigation. Sue supplied us with an update. "Apparently, the police are still desperate to identify the unknown mysterious man in the passenger seat. They've eliminated all of Katie's friends and colleagues, including us I'm glad to note," she said with an inscrutable glance at each of us in turn. "Suspicion briefly fell on the university and her male colleagues, but no evidence has been found, so the police have been forced to drop that line for now. It is now thought, by the police, there is a slight possibility that the mysterious man may have been a distant colleague from Cerne Physical Science Institute, a man whom Katie may have met on a visit to France, but no names have been presented as possibilities. Her phone records failed to identify any unusual or regular callers during the previous months. So, unless they were communicating by pay phone, that kind of eliminates that line of investigation.

"The one unidentified caller in the past month called from a pay-as-you-go mobile, on the day of her disappearance. They even identified the point of purchase for the phone, a supermarket in London, but CCTV couldn't identify the purchaser." Sue flopped back into her chair in resignation, her body language screaming frustration.

"And all the while Jerome and Rosalind walk around as if nothing has happened, and we can do bugger all about it," Trish snarled in disgust.

"Calm down, I agree with you, but if we told the police what we know, mayhem would hit our lives, and for what reason? You heard what John said. We've just got to carry on and survive, trust that they'll get theirs when the time is right," I told her, inwardly feeling the same revulsion that Trish had articulated.

Sandra had also told Sue about the anxiety all this was causing. She spoke of Robert. "He's withdrawing into himself." The quietly spoken, no nonsense, self-effacing Scotsman was grieving by retreating inwards, refusing to entertain or seek out friends and relatives. "When we invite him over to the farm, he flatly refuses, choosing to remain in their empty flat. Just him, alone with a bottle and his memories."

Two weeks passed with no news of Katie. There was still no visit from John or Luke to distract us, or even provide succour at that time of trouble. I became increasingly reflective to the meaning of it all, unfairly feeling resentment towards John and Luke for allowing it to happen, then running away from the aftermath.

I even picked up the Bible, which John had declared was written by man, only containing the essence of God, not his heart. Whatever the truth, the words from the books of John and Luke meant absolutely nothing to me, remaining as a jumbled collection of words on the page. The verses danced before my unseeing eyes, making no impression at all. It was clear, I was in a malaise. My questioning mind sought, and failed, to find answers. Desperately, I wanted to make sense of it all.

On the Friday we finished work at lunchtime. Steve occasionally gave us this bonus as a thank you for a productive week; maybe when he fancied an afternoon himself. Whatever the reason, the day itself was warm and sunny, a pleasure to be free from the confines of the workplace. We were free to seek solace in the sunshine, or even in the "Hearts of Oak", the pub which some of my colleagues immediately planned on visiting, begining the weekend with a sociable cold beer. To their surprise, I politely declined the offer, earning in return protests of, "You're no fun lately, not now that Trish has got you under her thumb!"

I smiled in response. "Have a good one. I just have things I need to get done, and Trish is still working! Enjoy the weekend; see you on Monday." I watched them pass through the door into the bar, before making my way into the town centre.

Inextricably, I found myself passing through the gate and entering the grounds of St Mary's, the Norman church at the centre of town, a church which had been there as long as the town itself.

That afternoon, the churchyard was a peaceful place, bathed in dappled sunshine. I wandered around looking at the old headstones, reading the inscriptions, wondering with idle curiosity about the people who were buried there, people who had lived in our town before us. I speculated as to what their lives were like, their worries and successes, their hopes and failures. What was their relationship with this church?

Eating a ham sandwich and drinking a Ribena, which I had bought on my way through the shopping mall, I sat on a nearby bench, lifting my countenance towards the sun, allowing its rays to warm me.

Finishing the sandwich, I closed my eyes to the sun's brightness, feeling the warmth seep deep into my torso. I yawned. Gradually I was falling asleep, the recent sleepless nights finally catching up with me.

"You look comfortable," said a voice. Instinctively, I flinched, opening my eyes. I saw a middle-aged, round-faced, bearded man with brown hair and a receding hairline. His Harris tweed jacket had seen better days. It covered a middle-aged paunch. A black jumper, topped by a pristine dog collar, announced his vocation to the world. He was staring down at me through full moon glasses. His expression revealed mild apprehension.

"Hi," he said, sitting down beside me. "I'm William Dean, vicar here," he declared, indicating the church behind him. "People call me Bill, or Billy. If you don't mind me saying, your expression looks slightly troubled. Is there anything I can do to help?" he asked, staring at me intently. I stared back, noticing the concern reflected somewhere deep in his eyes.

I pondered, deliberating, wondering how to answer his question. There was something about the man that made me feel I could open up to him: someone with whom I could share my concerns and confusion with, but what to say? How to start on such a difficult narrative. Eventually, I decided to go ahead, to confide in this vicar, this man of God. In my heart, I was hoping desperately that this encounter was ordained, that it would lead to peace in my soul. "Do you believe in God?" I asked bluntly, staring him straight in the eyes, wanting to know what was at the very centre of his faith!

"It's my job to believe in God," he responded finally, following a loaded pause.

"No, do you really believe in God, believe that there is a spiritual world surrounding us, that God created all this," I retorted, waving my arm aimlessly around me. Once started, I was determined to persist with the questioning. I was determined to understand the truth, as he saw it.

Billy, the vicar, waited, pondering his answer carefully. Eventually he asked, "Can I offer you a cup of tea? After all, with the weighty nature of your question, it might take some answering."

Meekly, I followed Billy through the church and into the vestry, trailing him down the aisle. As I walked, I studied the swirling dust, dancing in the sunlight. Looking up and around, I couldn't help but realise the beauty and pageantry created by the ancient stained-glass windows. In some cases, windows which were nearly half a millennium old.

"Take a seat," he directed me kindly, indicating a small table and two chairs in the corner of the room. He himself moved towards the kettle, and teabags, stored on the drainer by the sink.

"Sorry, we can't provide digestives; congregation's too small," he said, placing a mug of tea on the table before me. Billy sat down on the opposite side of the table, tea in hand, facing me, waiting for me to take a sip of the hot drink before repeating my question out loud. "Do I really believe in God, believe in a spiritual world which surrounds us, a spiritual world which God created."

He considered his answer carefully. "You know, I've never had to examine and evaluate my belief that deeply. I've always had God. My father was a vicar. I grew up believing in God."

"What about Satan? Do you believe in the devil?" I asked, pushing again.

"God is God," he responded flatly, totally ignoring the question I'd just posed.

"But do you believe in ghosts or spirits?" I asked, pushing on. "If a spirit were to appear to you tonight, would you believe in it?"

"You're asking me to believe in ghosts!" he said, a warning note of caution revealed by his tone.

"What's the difference?" I responded. "Your Bible talks about the holy ghost and Satan. Would you dismiss him if he turned up?" I enquired, genuinely interested in his point of view.

"Ghosts," he said, "do not exist."

"But your Bible says they do," I blurted out, surprised at being scorned so hastily.

"No, ghosts and spirits are figments of the imagination," he stated, tapping the tabletop with an open palm, seeking to emphasise the strength of his unbelief.

I stopped momentarily, deciding to give myself a few moments for reflection, hoping to restart the conversation on a more positive note. So far, I was dismayed by the direction the conversation had taken.

Starting again, I asked, "Tell me about your beliefs. What, or who, is God to you?"

"God is just God," he countered, almost angrily. His reaction took me by surprise. "He's my job; he made the world!"

"So, God is your boss!" I said, eyeballing him across the table.

"Yes, I suppose so. I haven't really thought about it," he retorted, after a moment's reflection.

"Do you have a relationship with God? Your boss," I asked, sounding slightly flippant, through exasperation.

"Don't be ridiculous. Of course I don't have a relationship with God," he exploded, again thumping his fist on the table for emphasis.

This blunt, spiritual talk wasn't leading where I wanted, or expected. The man of God, it turned out, wasn't spiritual at all. He, it would seem, was a mere automate, unable to philosophise or seek answers for himself. Probably, I reasoned, trapped amongst the ceremony and pageantry of organised religion.

I decided to change tack once again. "Can I tell you of my experiences, the events which brought me here this afternoon?" I asked, deliberately seeking to soften my voice and avoid a confrontation. Billy thought for a second, seemingly weighing up my words, possibly deciding what was the professional response to my questioning.

"Go ahead," he declared. I saw he was visibly trying to relax his posture, allowing me to report my experience without challenge. I drew a deep breath, sipping my tea and settling myself on the chair, before attempting to articulate to Billy the basic events without too many of the grim details. Particularly, the recent details. I had no idea if the Anglican church was under the same constraints as the Catholic church, regarding confessions to ministers. But I had no desire to be investigated for my involvement in Maurice White's death.

I explained, "It started when we experimented with the Ouija board, but things have become gradually uncontrollable and definitely more frightening over time, spiritual occurrences continue to happen in our lives." I explained our encounters with Luke, then John, that we had a personal relationship with these apostles. That we also had horrific encounters with the devil and his disciples. I told him that it was all becoming extremely bewildering and very confusing.

After twenty minutes of a continuous monologue, I finished the tale, placing an empty cup on the table before me, looking across towards vicar Billy. I waited expectantly for his response. In his countenance I recognised the glazed, faraway stare. Vicar Billy could hear the words, but they weren't registering within. The man of God didn't want to know.

"Well," he shifted uncomfortably in his seat, suddenly realising that I had finished. "That is quite a story," he said, standing up. Refusing to make eye contact, he moved towards the door, hoping that I would get the message, the meeting was over. "Just goes to show, you can never be too careful. Best to steer clear of the Ouija board," he warned, placing a fatherly hand on my shoulder, while gently propelling me through the door. "There's a reason the government made it illegal back in the Victorian times," he said, closing the vestry door firmly on my retreating back.

I stopped, standing motionless in the churchyard for several minutes before eventually finding the strength to move on. Checking my watch, I noted the afternoon was almost over. Trish would finish work within half an hour.

Once I'd announced myself to the receptionist, she smiled. "Go in, sit in the reception area; she won't be long. I'll let her know you're here."

Trish joined me shortly afterwards, grateful to have another working week under her belt. Together we adjourned to a local pub, where, over a pint, I explained my unfruitful consultation with the vicar of St Mary's.

"Never mind," Trish philosophised, squeezing my hand in sympathy. "It was obviously not meant to be; just forget about it. It is a weird tale, even for a vicar." We drained two further pints before making a night of it, devouring a Tex-Mex, then visiting three further pubs, followed by a taxi home at midnight.

John returned the very next evening, catching us by surprise. During the previous weeks, we'd gathered together in expectation so often, without a sign of John. Beginning to lose hope, we were totally unprepared. Nursing drinks, all six of us were seated in an alcove of the Wellington.

"Hello, my friends." His gaze settled on each of us in turn, after which he directed his words towards myself. "Martyn, you are troubled, you seek answers!" There was no denying it, he knew my every move.

"Yes," I replied. I carried on, needlessly revealing what he already knew. "Recent events have disturbed me, disturbed us all," I said, indicating the group. "When this began, we didn't really expect people to die."

"You have the option to leave," he countered quickly, in a matter-of-fact tone, seemingly unconcerned with the anguish we were enduring.

"You always say that! You know I don't want to leave," I assured him. "It is just overwhelming at times."

"I know," he said, suddenly exhibiting greater compassion. Intentionally and slowly, he eyed all five of us, keeping eye contact with each of us for several seconds. "We do understand. That is why we have not visited you in a while, so you could have the chance to recover from the battle."

"There is so much we needed to ask you," Sue insisted. "What happened to Katie? Where is her body?" she demanded.

"We cannot tell you where her body is," John said gently, again holding eye contact.

"Why not?" Sue demanded, pouting.

John explained the wisdom. "It would be impossible for yourselves, even Robert, to know where the body is. If you did and you informed the police, then you would be the prime suspects. Also, if they were to ask you any direct questions, it would be impossible for one of you to convincingly deny that you didn't know where she lay. He reported, I can't reveal exactly what has happened to

Katie. It would be too harrowing to hear the details; she was your friend," he said kindly. "But her spirit resides with us. Let Robert know, the angels walk with her; she is at peace!"

John promised us, "Angels will guide a walker. Katie's body will be discovered within days. Robert will have his goodbye." But he would go no further than that.

"Are you ready to be obedient and do what we tell you? Are you ready to come under authority?" John asked, with a sudden severity, aiming his questions directly at the five of us. We agreed readily, understanding we were forgiven. The syndicate would continue.

That night, John stayed for a while, gracefully moving forwards from recent horrors to simply spend some time with us, and us with him. Rebuilding a frayed relationship.

It was time to go back to sea. Colin had already refused two ships, as offered by the shipping pool, delaying his departure for almost three weeks. He assured us that this was acceptable; he could get away with that, only suffering loss of money as a consequence. "But three strikes and you're out," he warned. Refuse three ships and the shipping office would place his name at the very end of the list of names awaiting employment. "On the beach," as Colin called it.

"Well, we couldn't have that, my friend," I teased. "Who'd buy me fridge magnets from all over the world."

Colin and I sat companionably in Colin's lounge, both of us relaxing in an armchair, glass of beer always at hand as we chewed the cud. Over the years this scene had been repeated many times. As life moved on, the location changed from time to time, the ever-present being, our friendship, celebrated with a glass of beer on one of Colin's last evenings at home.

Two days earlier, Colin had accepted from the London pool, a container ship, the *Blue Canyon,* heading from the pool of London to Yokohama in Japan.

"Twelve weeks around the Pacific. I'm not sure I can last that long," he said, taking a deep draw from his pint of John Smiths.

"You've done that many a time; you'll do that on your head. You can get yourself one of those new Sony palm tops when you get there," I chided, recognising the familiar moroseness Colin suffered before every trip.

"Ah, I guess I'm getting old. I no longer feel the wanderlust of youth," he countered, with the sincerity and sagacity of twenty-three years of age, looking back on eighteen, as if it were a lifetime before. "And I'll miss Yvette, I truly will! This time she might be it, might be the one. I really think so," he said, sorrow creeping into his voice.

I'd seen Colin have romantic flings many times before. The free-spending seaman on home leave, happy to buy anybody a drink, full of tales of adventures and hardships. Always keen to impress the ladies, Colin had seemed happy to be sowing the oats of youth. Now, it seemed, all this had changed.

To tell the truth, I knew the hardships of seafarers were very few these days. In two days' time, Colin would join his ship to find a large well-furnished cabin, usually maintained by a steward. Satellite television and DVDs were freely available for entertainment and, unless he accepted the occasional month on month off, on the North Sea oil rigs, most ships had a crew bar.

For once, I could sense in my friend's eyes and voice, this time he really was regretting going back to sea. Cupid had fired his arrow. Yvette had moved something at the very centre of his heart, a place previous lovers had failed to enflame.

"You mad fool, what an utter state," I said. "You go off and enjoy yourself. We'll be here for Yvette when you're gone. We'll keep an eye on her. Don't forget, she is still part of the syndicate; we won't ignore her just because you walk up that gangplank." I reached over, playfully punching his shoulder, genuinely pleased for him.

I could feel the anxiety within my friend as he fought his desire to remain by Yvette's side, set against his need to make money, the only way he knew how.

"So how do you feel about going away on Monday? Are you going?" I asked, realising that this really was an inner battle for my buddy.

"I think so," he replied, "but I'm not sure. We've only been together a month; it's all so new and exciting. What happened to Katie has knocked me for six. It was so unexpected!"

"Katie's disappearance was a bolt from the blue. The episode has turned an exciting adventure into a horrific ordeal," I retorted, knowing exactly what he meant.

"I'm scared for Yvette. She's in a foreign land, doesn't know many people. Jerome and his chums aren't playing games! I'm afraid for her," he said, the anguish evident. Colin stood up, going to the kitchen to retrieve another John Smiths.

I waited for him to return. He passed me a bottle of Stella before he settled back into his comfy armchair.

"Thanks, mate," I said, accepting the opened bottle, pouring the cold beer into my glass. "Back to Yvette." I tried to reassure him. "We're here for her, myself, Trish, Sue and David; we won't let anything happen to her."

Colin said, "I know that you're my best friends, but this isn't a playground struggle. Jerome and his ilk are playing for keeps." He spoke warily, finding the right words. "It is something we aren't used to, something we can't comprehend."

There was no denying his words. I thought back to Maurice, mentally picturing him leaping into the darkness. Leaping to his death, his only desire to cause me pain and harm.

"Thanks for keeping an eye on her. I know you're there for us both, but Jerome and his posse are licking their wounds. They've already struck once. There is no doubt they will return! Probably returning with a savagery that we can't even begin to imagine."

I reflected, realising he was right. Colin knew what he was asking when he went away.

"Don't worry, I'll die before I let anything happen to her," I declared, trying to put certainty and assurance into my assertion.

"Besides," he said morosely, "she's a pretty girl; she might have found somebody else by the time I get back! Twelve weeks is a long time."

"It is a long time," I cautioned. "And yes, she is one of the prettiest women I have ever met, while you're one of the ugliest guys she's probably ever met. It is certainly true, she will meet far better-looking guys when you are gone but, tell the truth, has she promised to wait for you."

I grinned, then checked myself, seeing the anxiety forming in my friend's expression. My joke had failed to hit the mark. Colin was indeed in love, and vulnerable. With renewed gravity, I carried on with the effort to pacify my friend. "She has, though, promised to wait. She had the option to wave you goodbye, then get on with her life, looking to meet other men, but she's promised to wait twelve weeks for your return, knowing that you have the chance to misbehave in Japan, and wherever else you go to."

I counselled, "It's obvious to me, the woman's smitten; she has no taste in men whatsoever, but it's plain to see, Yvette's in love with you." Colin half smiled, appreciating the leg pull, but understanding the reassurance intended with it.

"Seriously though, Martyn," he said. "This thing that is happening is way beyond anything I could imagine. This is the last trip for me! The money is good for this one, really good; it will give me a little breathing space, allow me a couple of months to settle down shore-side and get sorted. I'm a cook. I have transferable skills. The money shore-side is crap, but I will be able to work and keep us going, that's if Yvette wants to move in!"

Wow, I thought, one month into the relationship and he is talking moving in together. Colin really did have it bad.

"We'll be there for you, both you and Yvette. Go and enjoy your last trip; don't worry, my friend, I will watch over Yvette," I promised. "After all, it is the will of the Lord and John that you two get together!"

We remained talking sombrely over our beer. Two friends remembering past times from shared history, drinking steadily, never drunk, but never quite sober. Colin checked his wristwatch, moving to draw back the curtains. Way off in the night sky, a hint of colour with the promise of an onrushing dawn. As we had many times before, we'd seen the night off.

A day later we all gathered, wishing Colin a safe journey and speedy return. Unfunny jokes dying in the morning cool, I hugged him goodbye, instructing Yvette, "Drive safely and force him up the gangway, at knifepoint if necessary." I didn't have the heart to warn her to avoid dark, maroon-coloured Jaguars on the journey back.

"They've found Katie," Paul reported over the phone, his voice sounding agitated.

"Calm down," I advised. "Tell me from the beginning, what's happened?" I listened to Paul's description. "A lone walker was out with her dogs in the Shropshire hills, not far from the town of Ludlow. In a remote spot, the dogs became agitated, returning to one spot, whining and trying to get at something partially buried under the bushes. On further investigation, the woman found, I imagine, to her horror, a partially decomposed body, wrapped in polythene sheeting and tarpaulin." Paul paused, allowing me to digest what he had just told me.

Being discovered so far from home, in the opposite direction to her car, the police had taken several days to identify the corpse. Bolty had been summoned to Shropshire to carry out the hardest task of his life: identifying the corpse of his wife. A mutilated corpse, showing evidence of torture. I heaved, wishing anything but that for Bolty, unable to do even the slightest thing to lessen his pain.

"How is he?" I asked, unable to come out with anything better.

"He's here now," Paul informed me. "He's just been returned by the police's victim support unit. Sandra's with him, mostly just holding him. He can't talk right now, tears are plentiful."

We sent our commiserations, but what could we say? I understood the meaning of the phrase. Words just could not express my heartfelt sorrow for Bolty.

Katie was found two days after Colin's departure. To my relief, Yvette had returned with an empty passenger seat and, I guessed, an empty heart. She sought out Trish and me, probably wanting to be closer to Colin by simple association.

The discovery of Katie's body reignited somewhat fiendish fascination by the local television stations. I watched on in dismay as the local news reported, with almost gleeful joy, the ghoulish details of the discovery. Describing, with as much detail as they could get away with, the fiendish ordeal that Katie must have suffered before she died. Feeling slightly sick, I reached for the remote, cutting the reporter's words short with an angry thrust of my thumb.

The police held onto the body for forensic examination; three weeks passed before the five of us travelled up to Oxfordshire for the funeral, undergoing the journey in comparative silence. The police were no further forward in their investigation, and the search for the missing passenger from her last car journey. We knew they never would be. It was just too bizarre a scenario to contemplate.

I certainly wasn't looking forward to the funeral. At twenty-four years old, I had only ever been to one before: my grandmother. That had been emotional enough, even in the event of her natural death from old age. Trish and Sue hadn't even been to one funeral; they were dreading the day, but determined to be there, eager to offer whatever comfort they could to Bolty, however small.

We'd been warned the media and police attention, combined with the emotion of the day and awfulness of her death, were not the ingredients for any sort of respectful memorial and internment. I whispered the word, "Abba, Abba father," yearning to speak to John, craving an angelic presence to protect the day for Bolty.

"I am here," he said, arriving immediately. I asked, "Please protect the day, please ensure that Jerome and his friends are bound, that they can't cause any trouble, not on today of all days." There were no doubts in my mind; if they could manage it, Jerome and his minions would seek to spoil the day. If they had the chance to pour further horror into Bolty's life, then they would, without a single qualm. I searched for the correct words, begging John, "Please prevent this happening, for Bolty's sake, and her parents." But we hadn't needed the words. John knew our desire.

"Do not worry, my friends. The day will be peaceful; evil will be there to wallow in its triumph, but it has been bound in the spiritual realm," John explained. "It can do no harm. Robert is protected. He will grieve in peace."

After that ten second visit, David's spirit returned, replacing John's, as David reclaimed his own body. We continued our journey under the low hanging clouds, driving through a suitably desolate and grey English countryside.

It was almost certainly the worst day in Bolty life. However, we managed to get through it without too much difficulty. The news cameras were present, fortunately keeping their distance while filming the funeral goers as they turned up at the church, dressed in the black of mourning.

The police sent an ambassador to represent them on this sombre occasion, the chief inspector who was leading the investigation. He sat at the back of the church in the next pew to us, silently observing, while maintaining his own council!

Before entering, we sought out Bolty, then Katie's parents, two ageing and unsteady old folk, holding on to each other for scant comfort, completely unable to understand the enormity of what had happened to their precious daughter.

Bolty managed to put on an act for the day. I approached him, giving him a brief hug and gripping his elbow in a show of solidarity, before disengaging. I felt totally unable to perform socially in this abnormal situation, although, the hollow, haunted look, deep in Robert's eyes, dissolved my compassionate and aching heart. Trish and Sue were far more natural, pushing past me to grab him, holding him tightly in a shared bear hug. No words were needed, for what good would they have done?

After this, the day passed swiftly. The church filled up with colleagues and students of Katie, along with many eminent physicists, even a famous TV physicist, well known for his simple easy to understand explanations of the universe and its origins.

I wiped a tear as the coffin passed and again as I listened to the eulogy. I wiped a tear for a woman I'd admired immensely, a woman I barely knew.

During the day, we managed a brief conversation with Paul and Sandra, they informed us, "Bolty's coping, but only just. He's working on autopilot to get him through, falling asleep only when the sleeping pills or whisky kicks in."

David voiced his thoughts. "Hopefully this day will help to draw a line under the whole episode. Once he's got through this, he might be able to begin to climb the hill out of despair. He will need your support though. It's a long hill to climb."

"I hope you're right. Of course, we'll always be there for him. I can't even begin to understand what he is feeling though."

I was relieved when Paul and Sandra moved on, leaving without an appearance from John. This wasn't a day for syndicate activities!

We left the wake early. It was well attended: the university, village and family were all out in force, paying their last respects. So, we left with consolations, sincere and well-intentioned, but meaningless to the grieving recipients. Taking our leave of Bolty, then Katie's parents, we hopped into the car, setting off for home.

An hour down the motorway, David turned to me cheerily, declaring, "Pull over at the next services. There's never enough food at funerals."

"How do you know? You've never been to one," I responded drily, sensing he was trying to lift the mood. "Besides, they don't do hog roasts at funerals, which is what you'd need to be fully satisfied."

"A barbecue at a funeral, now that sounds good. When it's my turn, go for it." He grinned back at me, knowing the mood was lifting. "Pull in, maybe they have hog roast on the menu." I chuckled before turning my attention back to the road.

Pulling into the parking area of the services and finding a space, I noted to myself, since this undertaking began, we'd become far more frequent visitors to this type of roadside catering establishment.

Now we were there, I realised, having only had sausage rolls, sandwiches, and snacks since breakfast, I too was hungry. Leading the way, I resolved to finish the day as unhealthy as it'd begun. I steered the willing group towards a well-known chicken fast-food outlet.

"Bargain bucket, I guess? You guys grab a seat, the bucket is on me." I promised, withdrawing my wallet.

After queuing for service, I arrived at the table armed with fifteen greasy, but very tasty, chicken portions, five bags of French fries, a large bottle of Cola and the salad option for Yvette.

"This'll harden the old arteries," I said, placing the tray down in the centre of the table.

"What did I do wrong?" I joked, noticing a silence around the table.

"Yvette noticed that guy over there at the funeral," Trish warned me, indicating surreptitiously towards a table behind her.

"So, probably on his way home, same as us. The guy's allowed to eat, I guess." I shrugged, looking over, not trying to conceal my interest in my desire to identify who she was talking about. Instantly, I locked eyes with a grim-featured guy, who was staring back at me. I took a sharp intake of breath, momentarily concerned, unsure how to react. The guy glowered at me intently, glaring straight at my face. He was deliberately choosing not to break eye contact, or look away. After what seemed like hours but, in reality, no more than several seconds, I was the one to break the eye contact. There was something unnerving about his stare and directness which caused me to hesitate. "Nothing to worry about. As I said, probably just on his way home like us," I announced, with more bravado than I felt.

"No! He is an evil disciple of Jerome." John appeared without warning. "Do not worry; he is here, but he will only seek to frighten you."

As David returned to us, the guy left his seat. I noticed he was of very short stature; he couldn't have been more than three feet six inches tall. Even so, he was incredibly intimidating. He did not hesitate, walking directly across the floor of the restaurant up to our table.

He placed his hands flat on the tabletop, which nearly made me laugh as he had to reach up to do so. Scowling directly into my eyes, not blinking, "Bastard." He spat the word directly at my face, before he included the rest of the group, turning his scowl in their direction. "Bastards, you're all going to die, same as that bitch Katie!"

If it hadn't been so chilling in context and intensity, I would have laughed at the spectacle of a very small man threatening five people over plates of fried chicken. As it was, he abruptly spun around and marched off, leaving us observing his retreating back in amazed silence. Reaching the door, he disappeared into the night. I dropped the chicken leg back into the box. It no longer tasted as nice. The joy of the treat had been stolen!

CHAPTER FOURTEEN

John turned up one evening while we were relaxing in the flat. He warned firmly, "Be on your guard." John spent an hour, advising, "The threat is still very substantial. The evil disciples of Satan have been stunned by their loss; they seek revenge. But they are also buoyed at being able to inflict so much damage to your protective shield." He reminded us sombrely that there was no room for complacency.

Yvette accepted an invitation to join Trish and myself on a Saturday shopping expedition. We were going to the massive new Mayweather shopping mall in Southampton. We planned ahead. By setting out early, we could make a day of it. Trish and Yvette were keen to devote the whole day to the one hundred and seventy-two shops and restaurants, which this brand new, ultramodern shopping palace boasted.

Trish and Yvette bonded well. Trish was always sociable in company and bubbly Yvette was easy to chat to. I began the journey making an effort to be convivial, ensuring that Yvette felt included. I was acutely aware, I should have done far more to be welcoming towards her over the previous four weeks. I'd made a promise to Colin! We'd tried half-heartedly, but I figured that our history as a group would also make Yvette feel slightly excluded. Fortunately, Trish didn't require my analytical mind to dissect Yvette's actions, and our interactions. Trish was simply happy to be friendly, allowing Yvette the time to assimilate naturally, and at her own pace, into our established group.

The two girls were far too busy gossiping to be interested in me or my chatter. Even my somewhat sexist humour, regarding women and shopping, fell on deaf ears. They enjoyed a catch-up. I gave up, leaning forwards, pushing the button on the radio, turning on the early morning sports show, leaving Trish and Yvette to natter without my inane interruptions.

Covering the miles towards Southampton, Trish found herself fascinated by Yvette's description of her childhood in France, as well as her travels to Spain and Denmark. For her part, Trish shared her own stories of Colin and me, all the mischief and escapades we'd got ourselves involved in growing up.

Listening to these ladies happily chatting, the journey passed smoothly. The M3 motorway became busy as we approached the city. I followed the instructions of the satnav, a computerised voice, directing us towards our destination.

"Glass and concrete, modern, gothic, cathedral monstrosity," I moaned, looking up at the vast intimidating structure towering over me.

"Stop whining and move yourself, you grumpy git," Trish said as she grabbed my hand, tugging me towards the shops!

We were amongst the crowds of eager pilgrims, flocking from the car park towards nirvana. Mine was an opinion, obviously not shared by most of the population.

The place heaved with shoppers, all hurrying, in eager anticipation of spending money before they'd even set eyes on the first shop.

To think I gave up a game of rugby for this, I thought, then mentally chastised myself, instructing myself to cheer up, not to spoil the day for Trish and Yvette. Once I'd resigned myself to the inevitable, I did begin to cheer up. It is no doubt, the array and diversity of shops was impressive, arranged from the big multinational chains, through to small independent one-man outfits.

Trish and Yvette surprised me. Instead of the endless fashion outlets I'd dreaded, they dragged me into the gent's outfitters. Encouraged by Trish and Yvette, I bought a jumper from M&S, then several casual, but brightly coloured, sports shirts from an independent menswear outlet.

Laden down with bags, beginning to dream of a rest and a cup of tea, we wearily exited Zara, a fashion outlet. Pausing on the causeway outside the shop to acquire our bearings, unexpectedly, Trish grabbed my arm, sucking in a short gulp of air. "Is that Anne?" Her eyes searched the crowds on a distant walkway.

"Anne who?" I enquired, then realised Anne meant Anne Giddis, co-conspirator of Jerome and Rosalind. I stared intently, searching the area where Trish indicated, but I couldn't make out any sign of the woman Anne, or Jerome and Rosalind for that matter.

"Probably not, it's almost two months since we last encountered Jerome and his evil gang; besides Anne is very mousey, easy to overlook," I counselled, hoping my confidence was well founded.

Trish turned to Yvette. "What do you think?" But Yvette was unaware of any issues.

She confessed, "I've only seen Jerome and his gang once, at the pub in Watling. I'd have no idea, even if I could see her."

"I know what I saw. It looked like Anne, over on that walkway there, coming out of Monsoon!"

"Are you really sure?" I asked, badgering her.

"Yes, well I think so. Now, come on. It's time we stopped, had a cup of tea." Trish picked up her shopping and headed towards a coffee shop, Yvette and myself following dutifully in her wake.

Revived by a brew, I continued to press the matter. "Come on, Trish, one person in all these thousands, it's pretty unlikely," I announced, waving my arms in the general direction of the crowds of preoccupied shoppers. "Especially Anne, she's unimpressive. I'd have trouble identifying her in a phone box." I laughed, enjoying my own joke.

"Yeah, I guess you're right. It was only a glimpse. Maybe two months without activity has just put my mind on edge," she determined, dismissing the conversation.

Rejuvenating tea drunk, we again threw ourselves into a shopping inspired frenzy. With my purchases completed, I was happy to act as chaperone and bag carrier. Trish and Yvette gorged themselves on coveted and fashionable bargains.

In preparation for the upcoming winter, Yvette was trying on a greenish woollen tweed skirt. I lounged nearby.

I caught a glint of gold, a flash of an earring on a shopper, as he passed the shop. I jerked my head back, looking with a sudden intensity where I'd been lazily contemplating seconds earlier. It was too late; he had gone. I thought he had been tall and dark haired with a roman nose and gold earring! Jerome. But the sighting lasted only a micro-second, too quick to be sure.

Easing towards the entrance of the shop, I looked in the direction he'd been walking, but I couldn't make out anybody who could possibly be Jerome. Turning back, I mentally dismissed the sighting, an over-active imagination induced by Trish's earlier claims.

"Where were you going?" Trish asked, only half-interested, admiring Yvette in the new skirt, expecting me to express an opinion.

"Oh nothing, don't worry about it," I said, turning to Yvette and sticking two thumbs in the air in an appreciative gesture.

It was lunchtime so we made our way towards the American Texas burger restaurant, we'd chosen earlier. The promised flame-grilled, home-made, half-pound steak burgers, with fresh salad and thick cut fries were, we hoped, a world apart from the limp, insipid mass-produced hamburger – the usual preserve of fast-food joints.

We were seated in the faux ranch décor, which sported checked tablecloths and rough cut wood walls, decorated with horns and six shooters. The burger was indeed very good, served by smiling waitresses, dressed as cowgirls. My meal was everything I'd anticipated. Almost worth the small fortune they're charging, I thought.

Reaching for another onion ring from the big sharing platter we'd ordered to accompany our burgers, I glanced casually out of the window. Instantly, I spotted the earring of the man standing motionless, his back to the restaurant window. I froze, arm hovering over the platter.

"What's the matter?" I fell back into my seat, onion rings abandoned. Trish sensed something was wrong.

"Out there, I think he's Jerome," I said, pointing casually towards the tall man sporting an earring. At that precise moment, he chose to walk away, disappearing from view. He hadn't turned towards us, so we were unable to see his features. There was no way of knowing! All I had was an impression, a suspicion that it had been Jerome, standing a mere four metres away. A hunch was enough, the excellent burger turned to sawdust as we lost our appetites.

Three times, during the next two hours, Trish or myself thought we'd caught a glimpse of Jerome, Rosalind or Anne. Always in the far distance, just far enough away to make identification tricky, if not impossible! Dutifully, Yvette followed us, bemused and cautious, unable to recognise Jerome or his gang first-hand, but well aware of the dangers. She well knew the fate of Katie.

I no longer believed that these were mere coincidences. It seemed, after a two-month respite, Jerome and his comrades had re-entered the game as willing participants. A game where, according to John, revenge for Maurice was at the top of their agenda.

We convened over coffee, anxiously discussing the action we should take, continually checking around, expecting another sighting. I attempted calling David, hoping for John or Luke, but there was no reply to my repeated calls. Then we tried Sue, with the same result.

Trish remembered, "Sue and David were taking advantage of the lull in syndicate action; they were planning a city break in Barcelona. I guess they're on the way."

With a feeling of dismay, we realised to get home from Southampton, we would have to drive quite close to their lair in Tufton Gray. We needed a plan that would keep us out of range of Jerome and Rosalind, particularly if they had reinforcements with them.

Remembering the warning, we decided it was a prudent move to cut the shopping trip short and head home, choosing a longer route. "If we follow the motorway towards Portsmouth, then head up, before cutting back on ourselves, we will avoid the village of Tufton Gray totally. I figure this should wrong foot Jerome and co, giving us a chance to escape. Also, as most of the route incorporates major roads and motorways, they will have difficulty in stopping us, even if they correctly guess our intentions."

"Good plan, time we made ourselves scarce," Trish declared, draining her coffee. Gathering together our shopping bags, we headed, along with hundreds of others, towards the lifts, transporting shoppers down into the depths of the car park.

As the doors slid closed, I caught a glimpse of a tall dark shopper with an earring; it was Jerome. A squeeze of my hand alerted me; Trish had also caught sight of him. She leaned sideways, whispering urgent instructions to Yvette. "When we reach the car, we're going to have to make a fast exit from both the car park, then the city; don't hang around when we get out of the lift." Yvette smiled weakly in return.

Five minutes later, the shopping hastily thrown in the boot, all three of us were safely ensconced inside the protective auto. Remaining outwardly calm, I joined the queue of cars heading for the exit barrier. Fortunately, we'd used the machine by the lifts, paying for our parking on the upper shopping level. It was simply a case of inserting the token and making our getaway!

As the car edged forward, I searched my rear-view mirror intently, detecting a dark maroon Jaguar in the harsh fluorescent lighting, edging forwards, several cars behind in the queue waiting to exit the shopping mall.

"They're behind us, about four cars back," I warned Trish and Yvette, seeing no point in trying to withhold the information. Impatiently, we edged slowly forward, three pairs of eyes constantly studying the car behind, tensed for any development! Finally, the barrier released the car in front of us.

"It's time we weren't here; let's skedaddle." I was hoping my edginess wasn't apparent in the tone of my voice.

Once through the barrier, the roads opened up, dual carriageway leading towards motorway, then exit from the city. I braked impulsively, without considering my actions, probably causing the driver behind me to have a moment of panic, before I'd swung the Ford off the dual carriageway at the last moment, taking the first slip road heading back towards the city.

"What are you doing?" Trish yelled in agitation, twisting her head sharply, checking if we were being followed.

I explained, as much for my benefit as Trish and Yvette's. "I reckoned we were out of sight of the Jag following, so I took the first exit, back towards the city; he won't be expecting that. On any major road, we'd find it almost impossible to outrun a determined pursuit from that Jaguar. This way, we have a chance of losing them! By doing the unexpected." As I talked, I continued to drive, taking random exits and turnings, until we were very much lost in a maze of city streets, somewhere deep within the Lordshill district of Southampton!

My two passengers continued to maintain an intense and steadfast observance of the road behind, a vista which remained devoid of threat. Seeing the blue sign, indicating motorway ahead, I relaxed just a little. "That's a sign for the M27. We've escaped; it goes towards Portsmouth. That's our planned route."

Gradually, the tension eased. I'd noticed my grip fastened tightly on the steering wheel and I had to make a conscious effort to ease my muscles, relaxing my hands. Yvette and Trish continued to be watchful, watching the motorway traffic for a car that never appeared. As we drove, the autumnal dusk rushed headlong into darkness.

"Still no sign of them," Yvette announced, relief evident.

Dark night reigned. I drove on relieved, but still harbouring an underlying doubt deep in the pit of my stomach, some unfathomable restlessness which wouldn't surface. It remained a constant misgiving, just beyond reach of my perception.

Maybe the unexpectedness of their appearance had left me feeling so uneasy. I considered the ease in which we'd extracted ourselves from the situation. Above all else, I knew Jerome and co. were relentless. Now they were back, they'd be thirsty for blood. We may have won this round, but I doubted we'd got rid of them for long. Until we knew what their plans were, I knew I was right to be apprehensive.

Another half hour and I'd convinced myself we were actually safe. I voiced my thoughts. "Now we are safe, it would be a good time to eat." A signpost appeared for Farnham. "A perfect place to stop for something to eat," I suggested. "Farnham is a town none of us know; hopefully, we've seen the end of Jerome's evil syndicate, for tonight, anyway."

I drove slowly through the quiet streets, seeking a suitable eatery; the cold damp of an English October evening kept the majority of the town's populous in their warm comfortable homes. Yvette pointed through the windscreen. "Over there, on the other side of the road." She indicated the welcoming lights of a Chinese restaurant just ahead, the *Golden Dragon*.

"That'll do, I take it?" I asked, slowing the car to making sure the restaurant had tables, as well as a takeaway. It did. We were then lucky enough to find a parking space, only twenty metres beyond. "God must love us." I swung the car into the parking slot, eagerly anticipating a feast.

Cliched, oriental music greeted us as we stepped from the drizzle into the warm inviting restaurant. Sporting a faded bow tie, betraying the opulence that the *Golden Dragon* once aspired to, a smiling waiter led us through empty tables, to a table at the rear of the establishment.

"This'll do just nicely." I thanked him, surveying the surrounding tables and my view of the door. "If Jerome or any of his toadies are planning on interrupting our meal, then at least we will have plenty of warning; there's a good view of anybody arriving," I said, plonking myself down on the chair.

Once we'd accepted the lemon-scented hot towels, the waiter passed out menus, leaving us alone to make our selection.

"Chicken and cashew nuts for me, I think, with spring rolls and a pint of lager." Trish handed Yvette the menu, helping herself to a prawn cracker. Yvette ordered a healthy vegetable option, while I stuck with my usual, unimaginative choice. "Spareribs with sweet n sour chicken balls," I said, turning to attract the waiter.

Surreptitiously, I observed Yvette, seated across the table, studying her attentively as she spoke with Trish. Apart from the interrupted Sunday lunch at the Thatched Cottage, today had been her first real interaction with our evil antagonists. I knew she'd looked on, with a horrified fascination, as Katie's disappearance and fate had unravelled on the television screen, but Yvette hadn't been involved, or even close to the action. She'd listened in awe as Colin detailed our night-time mission into enemy territory, but he'd under-emphasised the fate of Maurice, just as I'd made light of it to him. It wasn't something I wished to dwell on.

I quietly contemplated Yvette as she broke a prawn cracker in two, listening to Trish making a point about nuts in a healthy diet. Deep down, I understood, Yvette was my nagging doubt. I'd made a promise to Colin. As yet the syndicate must seem like a big adventure to Yvette; any danger was at a distance and shielded by friends.

Yvette, herself, was a friendly confident girl, but what we were involved in was way beyond bizarre. For her, becoming involved with our syndicate and integrating into a group of friends who'd known each other for years must have been a hugely difficult task. Particularly now

Colin was away at sea. Suddenly I felt guilt at my failure to be more welcoming and protective.

"How did you feel today, once Jerome turned up; did you understand the danger?" I asked, looking at her, trying to both emphasise and convey danger by my tone.

Yvette gave herself a few seconds to ponder, sipping a white wine spritzer. Finally, she replied, "I do not know. It is a danger I do not yet understand, an adventure I'm only just beginning to grasp." Her French accent added delightful flavour to the simple English words.

There was a truth in what she was saying. I'd been there since the beginning, yet I could not claim to understand what was happening and what it all meant. Especially within the context of our modern world. This was a conversation Trish and I had had many times before.

"Do you feel safe?" I asked. "Did you feel safe today?"

"Yes," Yvette replied, "when the two of you are with me, or when David and Sue are with us, then I feel safe."

Trish intervened, asking, "How do you feel when you're on your own in your flat? What do you feel about the syndicate and the dangers then?

"Oh, to me, it is still a thrilling adventure," Yvette said, alternating her gaze between Trish and myself. "I know you have warned me of the dangers, and I have seen the nasty evil cold eyes of Jerome for myself, but the danger is still second-hand, almost like seeing it on a television," she concluded with a half-smile, almost dismissively.

I snatched a sly glimpse towards Trish. My desire was for Yvette to understand the danger we were all in, to make her realise this was a treacherous undertaking we were involved in, one with no guarantees. However, I was hampered by my own internal confusion. Only a few weeks previously, it had all been a game to me too. After Katie and Maurice, I was coming to fully understand the seriousness of our circumstances – the need for constant and total vigilance!

Trish leaned forward, joining the conversation, intuitively understanding my inability to express a danger. I barely understood myself.

"Just promise us that you will call at the first sign of danger!" she said, a note of steel in the request.

"Yes, of course I will," Yvette promised nonchalantly. "But isn't it wonderful to be involved. There is so much more I want to know; however, we do know that we are apostles to the new messiah. We are the luckiest people alive. We will be remembered forever. Isn't it wonderful!" Yvette rhapsodised with the joy of a true evangelist, her features becoming radiant as her imagination explored the future.

"Remember, just call if you feel any anxiety at all," I reminded her, doubtful whether Yvette really understood the threat posed by the enemy.

My words fell away to silence. Yvette wasn't listening, her mind and thoughts were elsewhere, somewhere where there was no danger. I have never been an imaginative person, thoughts of the future and where this was leading were rare for my barren imagination. It was clear, where I majored on the practicality of situation, Yvette allowed her imagination to soar, reaching the sky with the endless possibilities of our journey.

Trish was the first to pick up on Yvette's infectious excitement, putting aside fears for the happier topic – where this was all leading.

The mood lifted as I finally cottoned on, allowing my imagination free rein for once.

"Well, we've been told by John, the new messiah will be born soon; all is about to be revealed to mankind through this messiah, and that we will be numbered highly among his apostles. What a wonderful thought to embrace!" I grinned. The day's troubles behind us, we accompanied the meal with flights of fancy. "Will we travel to Israel?"

"When is it going to happen?"

"Do we know the mother or parents?"

"Are one of us the earthly parents?" Thoughts and fantasies poured out. I had been so absorbed by the dangers of the present that the joy off the future remained elusive! We were safe; we'd successfully eluded the bad guys. Despite slight misgivings deep down, I felt contented when we left the *Golden Dragon*, pleased that Yvette was beginning to feel at home in our company without the need for Colin's presence. I felt we were coming to know her better.

"Why don't you stay with us tonight? Martyn has a spare room!" Trish suggested, looking over her shoulder at Yvette, recalling the angst of the afternoon.

"No, it is alright. I want to go back to my flat. Don't worry, I feel safe there, and I'm feeling tired!" Yvette assured us.

We pulled up outside Yvette's small bedsit, accepting the offer of a coffee. It was our first visit to the bedsit, which was indeed small but meticulously clean, decorated with reminders of her native France, including a small, mass-produced painting of Paris showing the Eiffel tower from afar.

"You know, I still feel a touch uneasy about not insisting she stay with us tonight," I said, once back in the car.

"I know what you mean, but we asked twice, and then there's tomorrow and Monday and every night after that," Trish replied, soothing my fears with realistic pragmatism.

I released the handbrake and pulled away. "True, you're right as always, probably the unexpectedness of this afternoon getting to me," I said, secretly selfishly pleased that I didn't have to share more of the precious time I had with Trish.

After we'd left, Yvette cleared the coffee cups, taking them through to her tiny kitchenette to wash and dry. Even though the day had tired her, she hated mess and refused to leave the washing-up until morning. She ran the water until it ran hot, adding just a tiny dash of washing up liquid to create the foam with which to clean the cups.

As she worked, Yvette allowed her mind to wander. It would be nice if Colin did return home and fulfil his promise to leave the merchant navy, then maybe move in together. I like Colin, Yvette meditated, dreaming of a bright future as she soaped the cups, placing them carefully in the rack to drain.

Yvette gave a jerk, almost dropping the cup into the hot water. A sigh, a human sigh, right next to her ear. She even fancied she'd felt the air move, but that was stupid, how could that happen, she thought, choosing to dismiss the event.

Bang, there was a single thud behind her, coming from the lounge, almost as if a fist had been thumped on the surface of the coffee table, just once. Yvette jumped again, before catching her breath, steadying herself. Cagily she looked through the arched opening, examining the same empty, lifeless room she'd left, just moments before. Yvette relaxed, and released the air from her lungs, not realising until then that she'd been holding her breath.

"Silly, these are small poky flats," she told herself forcefully, speaking out loud to persuade herself of the facts. "It's just a noise from another flat, a trick of acoustics making it seem to originate from close by."

Yvette was tired from a long, enjoyable day. It was important that she fit in with Colin's friends and learn about his past. The secret they'd revealed had thrilled Yvette, who readily accepted the spiritual world in a matter-of-fact way.

Placing milk into the microwave, she decided to have a hot chocolate and a short read, preparing herself for sleep before going to bed.

The cup hardly touched the coffee table when a sudden flicker of movement caught her attention. Barely perceiving it, from the corner of her eye, she had the impression of a dark shadow! Naturally, when she looked round, there was nothing there. Yvette stood motionless, contemplating the past few seconds. She guessed the day may have taken more from her nerves than she'd imagined. Making a swift decision, she turned the television on, killing the sound, seeking comfort from the familiar flickering images on the screen.

Buoyed by the reassurance of the TV, Yvette was able to settle, she read two paragraphs. Again, movement at the periphery of her vision disturbed her. This time, there was substance to her perceptions. She looked up just in time to see a book tilt slowly, then fall from the shelf, where she kept her small library, landing on the floor with a clump. Yvette jumped, giving a small start, a cold shudder ran down her back. This is unbelievable, she reflected. How can this be happening?

Without warning the shelf emptied the rest of her library, eleven books simply launching themselves vigorously from the shelf into space. Some landed on the carpeted floor, a full three feet away from the wall. Some landed close to the cowering Yvette. Emitting a tortured yelp, she launched herself from the chair, fleeing for the safety of her bedroom. She slammed the door behind her, without looking back, hoping and praying for sanctuary, fear induced sweat breaking out. She turned back, facing the door of the room.

Bang, this time the thump was just the other side of the door. "What is it? What do you want?" Yvette stuttered, her voice breaking to a high-pitched squeak. There was no answer. She waited, staring at the door in abject fear. No sound or movement perceptible on the other side.

She was astonished to note her legs had started to tremble. She'd thought this only happened in books, but her legs now felt like rubber.

One minute became two, then three. Plucking up courage, Yvette eased herself closer, placing an ear to the wood, listening for any sounds beyond.

On the other side of the wooden panel, she heard the deeply terrifying sound of rasping breath. Panic overtook, she let out a mournful moan, falling with a bump to the floor. Yvette was trapped; the sweat cooling on her skin made it feel cold and clammy. She shuddered.

In the recesses of her mind, she wished she'd accepted the offer of a bed for the night. Now it was too late, her only phone was on the other side of the door, in the same room as the sounds which were haunting her.

The faintest glimmer of sanity broke through, calming the panic. Understanding that she had to fight to control herself, Yvette decided she would remain in her bedroom until daylight! She knew she would never sleep, but she could remain there in safety, waiting until the dawn came to her rescue. Yvette climbed under the duvet, fully clothed, arms wrapped around her knees; she fought to stop herself from shaking!

A small photo of her parents, hanging on the wall by her bed, flew at her with astonishing force, just missing her head before landing on the floor. Yvette moaned almost inaudibly, unable to find the breath to scream. She turned, gazing with horrified fascination, as a faint eerie glimmer appeared in the corner of the room. Yvette screwed her eyes shut tight, unable to move for terror. When she eventually opened them, the phosphorescent light was still there, seeming to pulsate and shimmer, slowly becoming the faint smoky outline of a being. Yvette felt the faintest gossamer touch on her cheek, as the sigh repeated, right next to her ear.

At last, finding her breath, Yvette screamed. Spurred into action, she threw the quilt away from herself, in the direction of the apparition, her legs tangled in the soft duvet as she fought the bedding to escape from this spirit. She was now desperate to reach the bedroom door.

A knock on the outer door of the flat arrested her panicked flight, bringing her to her senses. With huge relief, Yvette realised somebody had responded to her scream – rescue was at hand. She ran sobbing, flinging open the front door, eager to greet her saviour with profound and eternal gratitude.

Jerome stood on the threshold, his angular good looks framed by the doorway.

"Looks like we're just in time," he said, stepping past Yvette into the lounge. A petrified and bewildered Yvette finally stopped fighting. She fainted, sinking to her knees before crashing to the floor!

The stringent buzz of a phone brought me awake. Realising the phone belonged to Trish and that she was awake to answer, I fell back onto the pillow, rotating to check the bedside clock. It was only half six. Who would call at this time on a Sunday? I turned my back on Trish, hoping to return to my dream.

It was Sue in Barcelona. "Sorry, I forgot you're an hour behind us," Sue told Trish, who'd complained at being woken up. Agitated, Sue continued without preamble. "Luke appeared late last night, but there seems to be a problem. I think there was a battle going on for David," Sue revealed. "David seemed in great distress, almost as if an inner battle was taking place for the possession of his being."

Trish glanced over at me, realising Sue was alone, isolated with David. "Luke appeared briefly and only for a second, saying just one word. It was very faint and he seemed to struggle to pronounce it. The word, danger!" Sue told her sister, the anxiety clear. "After this, David collapsed onto the bed, sleeping through the night; he's still asleep, though he looks comfortable enough. I don't think he is going to wake up anytime soon! The experience frightened me; I got very little sleep. I was too worried about you guys. Katie's disappearance had me imagining all kinds of scenarios. Are you sure you're both okay?

"Yeah, everything's fine here. Martyn is asleep next to me. Sleeping like a baby... with a snoring issue," Trish reassured her sister.

With a magnificent effort of will, Sue had refrained from calling Trish in the middle of the night. "I know it's early over there, but I had to know you were okay, I couldn't wait any longer."

Trish ended the call from her sister, tossing the phone onto the bedside table, then shaking me back into a reluctant wakefulness, dragging me from my blissfully regained sleep.

Quickly Trish imparted the bones of the call, waiting patiently as I assembled my senses from a sleep-soaked mind.

"So, Luke said *danger,* and nothing else?" I stated the obvious, apprehension already beginning to burden my heart. "This is very worrying, Luke and John have a good track record of warnings when there is danger, even if the danger itself can't be avoided."

"Yeah," Trish agreed, "and there seemed to be some kind of spiritual fight surrounding, or within David. Luke had difficulty materialising. Sue thought he was fitting at first," Trish told me, increasing my worries tenfold.

"Is Sue okay?" I asked, suddenly fearful that she was on her own with David, abroad.

"She seemed to be, but she sounded nervous," Trish assured me. David's still asleep; it's Sue who's lacking sleep because she was worried about us," she added.

The possibility of regaining my own sleep had vanished. I rose to make tea and toast while we decided what to do with the warning!

"Trouble is, one word, *danger*, it's just too generalised," I pondered, chewing a mouthful of buttered toast and marmalade. "We need to speak to John or Luke, find out exactly what is happening. When he's had time to wake up, I'm going to call David, use the *Abba* trigger word," I warned Trish.

"Are you sure that's safe; remember, Sue is on her own with David."

"I can't think of anything else to do. If there's danger, we need to have some idea what it is, or where it is," I asserted, for lack of a better option.

"I agree there, but Sue is alone. What if the evil one appears?"

"Remember what John told us, the evil one is bound in the spiritual; when she is alone with him, she should be safe, the evil one may well be prowling but I think he is bound. That is why he didn't materialise last night, the best he could do it seems is try and stop Luke coming through."

"She's, my sister. If anything manifests, she'll be terrified on her own."

I understood where Trish was coming from, but I was devoid of any other ideas. "Text her, tell her to go down for breakfast just before we call," I suggested. "If she leaves him a note to meet her at the table, it's bound to be

David. The evil one certainly wouldn't manifest openly, in a restaurant."

Giving David another hour in bed to enjoy the lie in I'd lost, I called his mobile, getting a reply on the third buzz.

"Martyn, what are you doing phoning so early," David answered, cautiously. "Did you forget we were coming to Spain for a city break?"

"Sure, I hope the sun is shining," I replied, abruptly! "Abba."

"Yeah, it's lovely. We even managed a small swim in the med, yesterday. Not for too long, but it was just about warm enough," he retorted, no response to the trigger.

"Abba," I said again, dropping all pretence at conversation.

"Food here is great, but did you want anything in particular?" he answered, again ignoring the trigger word I'd dropped into the conversation. Twice more I tried, but I was talking to deaf ears; there was no response from our spiritual counsellors! David ended the call none the wiser, with promises of duty free and recommendations for the hotel. My plea for direct spiritual intervention, which, I'd casually dropped into the exchange, had gone unheeded, by John and Luke.

I cooked our own breakfast then, unsure what to do next. We'd got used to John and Luke's spiritual support and guidance. This time it hadn't materialised.

"Thinking about yesterday's events, I guess we need to check on Yvette and the Oxford lot," Trish suggested. "We need to come up with a plan of action."

We stole a half hour, eating a proper breakfast, salvaging just a little of our Sunday morning before disturbing our friends. Firstly, Trish called Yvette, staring fixedly at the phone as it remained unanswered.

"Not to worry. It's not even half eight, the girl's probably asleep," I said as lightly as I could muster.

I then disrupted Paul and Sandra's breakfast. "Hope I didn't wake you? We've had another warning!"

"We've been up for hours; cows don't milk themselves you know," Sandra answered smugly, sounding glib, a line I guess she's used many times before!

"Save me from born again farmers," I muttered, just loud enough for her to hear.

"Puts your breakfast on the plate though, doesn't it?" Sandra wasn't the least offended by my quip. Then she became serious. "Tell me what's happened."

"Sue had a one-word warning, the word *danger*," I told her.

Sandra was instantly concerned. "We're okay, grumpy guts is eating his breakfast opposite me; the last we saw of Bolty was last night. He was here, left to have a quiet evening, the telly and a bottle is my guess. It is his routine these days but who can blame him!" Sandra's concern for her friend was evident. "I'll give him a quick call, make sure all is okay. I'll call you back in a mo!"

"Did you hear that? Everything seems okay there. Sandra's just checking on Bolty." I looked over at Trish, who was trying Yvette for a second time.

Sandra rang back after a few minutes later. "I woke Bolty, who is alive and well, apart from another severe hangover; he's got to come to terms with Katie's death. His drinking is a shame, but I can't blame him, anybody would," she concluded, honestly.

"Still no answer, I think we'd best go around to Yvette's, see for ourselves," Trish said, a touch of consternation in her voice.

"Is her phone actually ringing," I asked Trish, reaching for my jacket and shoes, hoping that this panic could be solved quickly.

Yvette lived in a large block of flats, which had seen better days. There was no answer to our knocking. Standing in the hallway as I waited outside her door, I realised there was a constant background noise, even early on a Sunday morning. Distant yells, bangs and rattles could be heard. This was the type of place where the occupants kept to themselves.

We stayed there for ten minutes, thumping repeatedly on Yvette's door, until a neighbour poked his head out from his own door, unkempt hair and a scowl identifying his irritation at this interruption to his Sunday morning.

"She obviously ain't there mate; she ain't answering her door!" he said tetchily, cockney accent revealing east end origins.

"When did you last see her? Did you see her last night?" I demanded impatiently. Deeply concerned for Yvette, I was in no mood to placate anybody.

"Dunno, probably last night. We heard a couple of bangs and a shout, might have been her, but that ain't nuffink unusual for this place. Come back later," he said, firmly closing his door, leaving us alone in the empty corridor.

Yvette stirred, listening to the slap of the water on the side of the boat, wondering what the noise was and why she was rocking steadily side to side, in a far from gentle manner.

In the darkness, Yvette gradually became aware of the underlying pain: arms, legs and all her limbs ached terribly. She tried to move her hands, hoping to get some feeling back into them.

Experiencing the sharp burning in her wrists, it registered that her hands were tied behind her back. The chair she was seated on was keeping her upright. She tried moving her legs, then feet, discovering they were tied tightly to the chair, some kind of thin and very strong rope, which cut into her skin, generating knife-like agony. Yvette recognised the continual rocking and bouncing motion of the ocean and realised she was a prisoner, abandoned on a ship, somewhere out at sea.

The last thing she remembered was fear; that and screaming for help in her flat. Nausea rose as she gradually understood her predicament. Yvette dry retched, then vomited, suddenly glad of the fact she wasn't gagged, but slowly realising she wasn't gagged for a reason. She was too far away from any hope of rescue. Forlornly she grasped reality; she was isolated, beyond deliverance.

Terrified, in the darkness, Yvette vomited again, feeling the warm bile splatter across her jeans. The acrid smell rose to her nostrils, blending with a faint smell of paint, which she now recognisable as the background odour. She fought the urge to vomit a third time, willing herself to try and remain calm, wanting to investigate the surroundings.

Twisting as far as possible, Yvette became aware that there was a circular patch of slightly lighter darkness in the bulkhead behind her. She assumed that this was a window or porthole. Therefore, it was night-time. As she studied, she thought she could detect just a faint hint of amplified light, or lessening of the darkness. Over the next twenty minutes, Yvette witnessed sunrise, revealing a small porthole in the bulkhead, which was dusty and streaked with grime. The weak, pallid daylight the porthole afforded brought with it slight cheer, just a glimmer of hope, occasioned by the arriving light.

Yvette remained immobilised, tied to the chair for a further two hours. She used the time to fight desperately against her binds, fighting to give herself a chance, trying to improve her outlook. She only succeeded in digging the rope deeper into her wrists and ankles, causing further excruciating pain in an already desperate situation. Blood dribbled down her wrists, dripping with an almost hollow sound onto the metallic deck.

Once daylight arrived fully, Yvette found she was in some kind of store onboard a ship. Paint cans and mops were stacked haphazardly against the bulkhead and all around her. The chair she was secured to was bolted to the deck.

Every now and then Yvette could hear the sounds of people moving about on the deck above, or striding past the door of her prison. She tried yelling, croaking frantically, making as much noise as possible, but no rescue came. They either didn't hear or, more likely, they'd been ordered to leave her there.

Finally, her energy drained, a raging thirst and agonising pains emanating from her wrists and ankles, Yvette slumped in defeat.

Sometime later, she lifted her head, listening to footsteps approaching closer; they stopped outside the door. She heard a scrape as a key turned in the lock. The cabin door started to swing open, swamping the gloomy store with bright light from beyond.

"Ah sleeping beauty is awake." A smiling, almost jovial, Jerome, stepped over the threshold into the cabin, followed closely by the poisonous Rosalind and the equally lethal Anne Geddis.

"This is my favourite bit, when they are helpless, and I have full reign to do my worst. I love that bit." He spoke to his two cohorts before turning back to Yvette.

"What a pickle you're in," he said, leering down at his stricken prisoner.

Yvette tried to stare back defiantly at her captors, but tearstained and dishevelled, with hair knotted, her face smeared with blood, dirt, snot and vomit, she failed to reveal that defiance in her eyes.

Confronted by three arrogant and supremely confident adversaries, Yvette felt the last of her will failing. She began to whimper, tears streaking the dirt on her cheeks, the last of her bravado dissolved.

"Ah, glad to see you understand the hopelessness of your situation. I'll tell you what I'm going to do for you. I'm going to let you have another few hours to contemplate what these ladies want to do to you, Especially Anne here; she has a lover to avenge, though I'm sure she's looking forward to your fate just for the pleasure of having you at her mercy." Jerome turned around, abruptly departing with a cheery, "Bye, coming ladies?"

Leaning towards the prisoner, Anne whispered in a theatrical growl, "It'll wait, the anticipation will do you good. I'm really looking forward to this!" The cabin door slammed shut, leaving Yvette, snivelling quietly in the gloom.

Trish and I had seated ourselves at the kitchen table. "What do we do now? If she's not answering her phone, then I don't know what to do!"

"Too many similarities to Katie; this is not looking good." Trish sounded as concerned as I.

"I don't even know anywhere she might have gone; I know so little about her and her friends."

"I know a little, but most of the time she spent getting to know Colin. Even yesterday, I didn't really ask her about her life."

I warned, "I'm not calling Colin to ask him where she might have gone, not yet anyway. The poor man would be scared shitless. He's not due in Japan for over a week; it would destroy him if I contacted him now."

"I understand that, but I feel so helpless with nothing to do; something isn't right, I'm sure of it."

"I know, we can't even go and kick the door in at Tufton Gray."

"Shame," Trish sounded as if she meant it. "All we can do is wait, see if she turns up for work tomorrow, make our plans from there!"

"Yeah, nothing else we can do without David, or John to call upon," I agreed, standing up to fill the kettle.

Throughout the morning and into the afternoon, we constantly tried calling her mobile, to no avail. The calls were now straight through to the provider, informing us with a computer-generated message, "This phone is turned off, please try later."

Twice more that day, we drove around to Yvette's bedsit, pounding on the door until the angry neighbours told us to leave.

I went to bed, knowing I wouldn't sleep a wink, no matter how far I'd run before bedtime. Deep in the pit of my stomach, I felt queasy. I knew Yvette's disappearance could only mean one thing: I'd failed my best friend, and I would have to face him and tell him.

We were up and organised by six in the morning, but it didn't do any good as Yvette wasn't due to start working until eight. At five past the hour, I phoned Jackson Brothers, the builder's merchant where Yvette was employed. My call was answered by a polite gentleman who briefly informed me, "Yvette hasn't arrived yet; call back in half an hour."

Half an hour later, Trish called, asking to speak to Yvette. "Sorry love, she's not turned up today! No call, no nothing, caused a right mess here too. I've had to come out of the office to serve the front desk," snapped the guy, who was probably a Jackson brother.

Unable to do anything further, I gave up for the moment and went to work. Mid-morning, when I called, Trish suggested tentatively, "I guess it's time to inform the police. Yvette is a missing person."

"Yes, you're right, though no good will come from it if Jerome is involved. I think she's gone forever," I predicted.

"It's all we can do. I'll meet you outside the police station just after one." Trish hung up before I had chance to reply.

The interview took all of my lunch hour, and a little more. We'd begun by informing the desk sergeant, "A friend of ours has gone missing; we need to report a missing person." Dutifully he recorded as many relevant details that we could possibly remember.

"Can you come through into the interview room. I'll get one of the detectives to come and have a word, take some more notes."

We sat in the small inhospitable interview room, waiting nervously for twenty minutes. Finally, one of the two detectives who had interviewed me about Katie's disappearance pushed open the door, looking harassed, paper cup of coffee in one hand, notepad and pen in the other.

Flopping onto his chair he looked me over slowly. "I know you!" he said, making it sound as if it were a crime, simply to be known to the police.

"I'm DC Thomas Lawton. I'm told you've reported a missing person."

"Yes," we replied in unison, eager to get the search underway. Prompted by Detective Constable Lawton, supported by the occasional interjection by myself, Trish began to reveal all she knew of Yvette and her movements from Saturday.

Asking the occasional question, DC Lawton scribbled furiously, eager to capture every word uttered.

"So, to be sure I've got this right," he said. "Notwithstanding the regularity with which you pair have been involved in a missing person's case; you don't know the lady in question very well. But you last saw her on Saturday, and she hasn't reported for work this morning?"

"And she wasn't answering her phone or front door yesterday," I responded.

"Well, that's maybe because she's ill," he suggested, reaching for the coffee.

"She'd have to have been dead with the noise we made," I barked, instantly realising the inappropriate nature of my comment, against our own expectations of Yvette's probable fate, and our proximity to Katie's disappearance.

"In that case, given the propensity you pair have to be on the periphery of such cases, you really would have some questions to answer," he retorted, placing the coffee cup on the table and staring at us with renewed interest.

"Is it likely we would take the time out of our day to report her missing if we were involved," I said, becoming terse with exasperation.

"Ever heard of a smoke screen?" he countered quickly. "Perfect cover," he muttered, to himself.

However riled he felt, I could see the thought of getting close to an important case piqued DC Lawton's professional interest.

"OK, probably nothing much in it, but I will ask the area squad car to investigate. If we get no answer at her door, we will find the landlord and request permission to enter. In the meantime, we'll keep you informed, so don't leave the country," he joked sourly, fixing us with an icy glower.

Yvette awoke with a start, realising that the pain in her swollen and tender wrists and a raging thirst had roused her. The cabin had a palpable smell of fear and vomit; she'd no idea how long she'd been in there since Jerome had left her, hours earlier.

Helpless and bedraggled, she contemplated her fate. Her throat was parched, hurting from lack of water, her tongue sticking painfully to the roof of her mouth, eyes gummed from salty tears. Yvette barely detected, light had gone from the porthole, night had returned. The boat still rocked interminably on the lumpy sea, greatly adding to her appalling discomfort. Yvette's head lolled, as the hopelessness of her situation penetrated her lethargic brain.

She never heard the footsteps approaching along the corridor, or the key turning in the lock. The first she knew was a harsh explosion of fluorescent lighting as the cabin was invaded with a harsh unforgiving light.

"Ah, my little pumpkin, what have they done to you." Jerome stepped over the threshold and into the cabin alone, holding out to Yvette a seductive beaker of clean fresh water. Of the two women, there was no sign.

Jerome moved forwards, tilting the beaker towards her, allowing Yvette two brief sips of the coveted liquid, before jerking the water away from her parched lips, sadistically depriving Yvette of her most prized desire.

"Not yet my little sweet," Jerome continued, grabbing and yanking Yvette's dishevelled hair backwards, away from the precious liquid.

Yvette tried to shout, croaking, begging for the treasured water, but her mouth was too sore and dry, even after two sips. Her lips swollen and parched, she jerked her arms against the bonds, whimpering, trying to reach the water, anything to ease her parched, vomit-saturated mouth.

"All in good time! First, this is what Anne and Rosalind want to do to you." Jerome leant forward, whispering in her ear, explaining slowly, in graphic, horrifying detail, the things they'd planned for Yvette. He went on, detailing some of the details of Katie's gruesome torture and her painful death. A crushed, traumatised Yvette recognised the two women were even crueller than Jerome.

"There is another way though," said Jerome, moving forward once more, gently lifting the beaker to Yvette's despairing mouth. Tenderly holding her head steady, he held the beaker to her lips. Yvette drank greedily, attempting to drain the beaker in as few seconds as possible.

"There is another way," he repeated.

In her desire to get at the water, Yvette wasn't listening. She continued gulping, desperate to get as much of the cherished liquid as possible.

Realising that too much water would fill her with resolve again, Jerome yanked Yvette's head backwards, away from the water. He poured the water onto the deck in a slow and deliberate action, cruelly holding the beaker just out of reach. He smiled in cruel and vindictive satisfaction at Yvette's wretched cries.

He told her, "You must walk away from your friends in England, serve us. That is, if we were to ask you. Thing is, you are in no position to bargain; we have your passport and we've emptied your flat. Nobody is going to rescue you, or even miss you!" Taking heartless pleasure in the pain he was causing, he continued. "You can feed the fish or follow me and do all that I ask. You would go to Haiti; our friends in the mountains will gladly look after a white woman like you. But there is no escape from there. Don't even think about it. We offer no second chance; just a painful death awaits you, now, or in the future. It is your choice! As much water as you want, then a comfortable journey to the Caribbean, followed by a retreat to serve. Or you can give pleasure to Anne and Rosalind. They have a real and dreadful desire to cause excruciating and intolerable pain.

"I can protect you from Anne. She is desperate to make somebody pay for Maurice. She'll hate me if I stop her from touching you, but I can do it, just one word from you.

I will return in the morning," he said flatly, turning towards the door, clicking the light off as he left. Once again Yvette was plunged into darkness, terrified and alone. She began to shake uncontrollably, a familiar sick feeling rising. Yvette vomited, wasting the precious water she'd drunk. She knew she was beaten!

On the Monday, David and Sue flew home from Barcelona, arriving at Gatwick in the early afternoon. As soon as work was done for the day, I rushed over and collected Trish from her office. We set off for Richard and Lynda's, where David and Sue had just returned after their short holiday. They didn't even have time to settle with a cup of tea before we were knocking at the door, sharing our fears for Yvette.

David guessed why we were there. He understood that we were desperate to speak to John. Willingly they followed us to the flat. Sue had primed David of all that had occurred on the Saturday in the hotel; David was aware, danger lurked somewhere.

We'd done our best, trying to give them space to enjoy the break, but Sue had spent a terrible two days, mindful something was very wrong, unaware that Yvette was now missing.

"Poor Colin," she kept repeating, putting words to my fears which I was keeping supressed. "Poor Yvette."

At last, John responded to the trigger word "Abba," appearing as soon as he was called upon.

"I am here, my friends. I understand why you have summoned me."

"What's happened to Yvette? Where is she?" I demanded, not waiting for him to finish speaking.

"There is nothing you can do. Yvette is out of reach. You cannot save her," he countered, turning towards me. "This is a direct consequence of your foray into the house at Tufton Gray. They sought revenge! Without your actions, Yvette would be at home, waiting for Colin," John told me, with a finality that made me feel personally responsible. His choice of words left me with no outlet for blame but myself. We'd tweaked the tail of the serpent and it had turned and bitten us.

I rounded on John, fear and frustration overtaking natural caution. "Is that why you refuse to tell us where Yvette is, because we might go and find her?"

"No, we know where Yvette is; you cannot reach her."

"So, you refuse to let us try!" I retorted, experiencing desperation within the helplessness.

John snapped back. "You shall learn to obey me. Your interference has cost lives!"

I recognised a real anger in his dealings with us: an anger at our failure to do what we were ordered. He was angry at us for making our own decisions!

I should have backed down but, at that moment, I was in no mood to appease. I was too scared. "If you protected when you promised, then we wouldn't have needed to try." I barked, almost forgetting who I was talking to.

"We do warn and protect. We sent angels to protect Trish from the dog. You must obey me!" John declared, his own anger not abating!

"Martyn, sit down and shut up. This isn't doing any good at all," Trish said, cutting through my anxiety with her blunt and forthright pragmatism. I sank back onto the sofa sighing, mumbling under my breath, "What's the use?"

While I glowered, John revealed to us all, "Yvette really is out of reach. She is being transported abroad, a prisoner on a large private motor yacht. Her possessions have been cleared from the flat, along with her passport. When the authorities investigate, they will assume Yvette is simply another itinerant traveller who became bored, fell out of love and moved on."

"Your enemies planned this well," John told us. "There will be no evidence that she has been taken. It will be assumed she has just moved on to another country. The woman, Anne Geddes, is a very good impersonator. They chose a suitable port. Yvette's passport has been recorded as leaving the country. With no CCTV, this will be enough for the authorities," he conceded.

"Poor Yvette, poor Colin." Distressed by the enormity of it all, Sue shook her head sadly, a slow tear running down her cheek, her eyes betraying bewilderment.

John continued with his explanation, divulging that the spiritual forces of darkness had indeed combined and co-ordinated their efforts. "Satan fought a fierce battle for the possession of David's body, he can't manifest to Sue, but that didn't stop him trying to possess David. It would have been too dangerous for Sue if I'd tried to warn you of the jeopardy to Yvette. When we tried, Satan fought us off. It was too late for Yvette. We had to protect Sue!"

John wasn't finished. "Again, you chose to travel for a holiday without our permission," he said, rounding on Sue, not waiting for a response before generalising.

"You must carry on with the syndicate! But for you, Yvette is no longer part of the syndicate. You must put her behind you." He turned to me. "Martyn, you are tasked with contacting Colin, telling him what has happened." With those unwelcome words, John vacated David's body, returning a bewildered David to us.

While Sue and Trish updated David, I sat quietly contemplating. In some deep way that I couldn't analyse, I felt something had changed, something I didn't understand and couldn't guess at. But something felt different to me!

Colin was the name that preoccupied each one of us. Colin our friend, my friend from school days. I'd persuaded him to return to sea for one last trip with the promise: *Don't worry, my friend, I will watch over Yvette*! I had said those very words over a month earlier, but now I'd failed my friend.

Why didn't I insist? I tormented myself, remembering how easy it had been for Yvette to dismiss the suggestion that she stay with us that night. I hadn't insisted. I was selfishly pleased when she refused; now she was missing. We'd had enough warnings during the day: Jerome and his malignant clique were once again active. Given the option, I'd ignored my gut feelings of danger, instead choosing the easiest, most selfish pathway!

Now it was too late! Yvette was gone, and I would have to face my friend, call him and tell him I had failed Yvette in my most important duty of all.

Three days later, DC Lawton paid an evening visit to the flat. Taking a sip of the coffee I'd just made him, seated comfortably on the sofa, he assured us, "The police are taking the disappearance of Yvette seriously. Very seriously indeed." He scrutinised us intently. Unashamedly he was blatantly dissecting our every movement, hoping for some clue which would feed his natural suspicions about a couple now loosely involved in two mysterious disappearances!

"However, we've spoken to Yvette's landlady; her rent is paid a full month in advance. When she opened the flat up there was no sign off Yvette. All her possessions have been removed. There was no sign of a struggle or any wrongdoing!" he concluded lamely.

DC Lawton warned, "Yvette had already mentioned to the landlady that she may be moving on in the future. As far as we are concerned, there is no evidence of any crime, slightly unusual to pay rent then leave, but not a crime. In fact, the UK border agency has a listing for Yvette's passport, leaving the country from West Bay harbour in Dorset, on a yacht. We are of the opinion she simply got fed up, or got a better offer and decided to move on, possibly to avoid further dealings with your friend. It's not an unusual way to leave a lover," he concluded, regretting missing out on a big murder case.

"But surely she would have informed us if she was moving on," Trish responded. "She was with us all Saturday."

"You've known Yvette less than three months. You yourselves admit to knowing very little about her and her past, just that she's started a relationship with your friend Colin, who, you say, is in love with her. Do you think it's likely Yvette would have told his best friends she was leaving him? In my opinion, this isn't unusual for these nomadic types. They make friendships, then move on leaving it all behind when they get bored with the job, or people." DC Lawton concluded, snapping his notebook shut.

He sighed, seemingly realising he was talking himself out of any chance of a big investigation. Due to the lack of funds and resources within the force, any gut feeling he had would have to be shelved.

The detective constable left, thanking us for our hospitality, loosely promising, "We'll advise you if any information comes to light. We did contact the border control in Tenerife, which was the stated destination of the yacht. If it docks and she's not on board, they will inform us."

The missing person case wasn't closed, just not top priority.

I knew the *Blue Canyon* was due to dock in the port of Yokohama on Monday 29th October so I decided to contact Colin then. What to tell him and how much information to reveal to a helpless Colin had been the foundation of many hours of argument and discussion. Ultimately Colin contacted me first.

"Hi Martyn, how goes it? I'm worried about Yvette. Is she OK?"

Briefly Colin explained, "We've been in touch via email. It's quite easy these days; most ships have a satellite connection. We've been swapping a couple of emails a week, right up to last Saturday. Then she suddenly stopped." Colin sounded baffled. "Last email I had said she was going out shopping for the day in Southampton, with you and Trish. Did that happen?" he asked.

"Yes, it happened. We went shopping. Where are you, Colin? I think you'd better sit down; you see, Yvette's disappeared!" There was no easy way to break the news. Quickly deciding to leave out John's confirmation of Jerome and his ghouls, I explained, "She disappeared on Saturday night, didn't turn up for work on the Monday. We were worried. We got the police to check on her and they found her room had been cleared out."

"What does John say about it?" Colin asked bluntly, cutting me short as I tried desperately to reassure, where reassurance was impossible.

"John said that she was no longer a member of the syndicate," I informed him, sidestepping John's confirmation that Jerome and his deadly gang were to blame.

I warned Colin, "The police have investigated. They failed to find any significant evidence to support further investigation, for now! They explained that this happens all the time with nomadic types like Yvette." I was hoping that Colin would choose this scenario of Yvette moving on, over the much more upsetting possibilities he must be currently contemplating.

"I'm coming home. I'll book the first available flight from Tokyo," Colin announced, determination adding finality to the statement.

"There is nothing you can do here. She's simply disappeared," I interjected, knowing that, if the situation were reversed, there was no way on earth that I would do anything other than what Colin proposed to do!

"You must do what you think is right; just call me with your flight details if you're coming. I'll pick you up from the airport," I assured him, feeling huge sadness for my old friend, yet, unable to fully understand the pain he must be feeling. I knew it would get no easier for him when he came home.

Thirty-six hours later, Colin arrived at Heathrow, landing at nine in the morning, bedraggled and exhausted, after forty-eight angst-filled hours without sleep.

"Hi." Colin briefly hugged Trish and me before, following us without further comment. Safely seated in the car, he demanded the whole story. "Tell me from your last sightings of Yvette, what happened on the Saturday. What was she like?"

We revealed all, trying to keep our description as factual and plain as possible, avoiding the use of adjectives wherever practicable.

"Saturday was a good day, that is until Jerome turned up; we managed to give him the slip. We lost him in Southampton and then came home, stopping for dinner on the way."

"Jerome might have followed you. How long was it between your last sighting of him and leaving Yvette?" he asked.

"A good few hours! We had dinner in Farnham. When we took her home, she made us a hot drink; then she refused a bed at my place, so we left her. I thought it was over for the day. Jerome had gone."

Colin changed tack. "What did John have to say?"

"We didn't see John until David came back from Barcelona, two days after. Sue had warned us there was some issues and danger, but she didn't get anything specific. At the time, there seemed to be a battle for his body."

"What did he say when you did speak to him," Colin asked, in a small voice.

"I'm sorry, mate, there is no easy way to say this," I said. "He confirmed that Yvette has been targeted by Jerome. Also, John flatly forbade us permission to visit Tufton Gray." In a feeble attempt to reassure him, I reiterated, "John hasn't said she is dead, only she has left the syndicate. The police have evidence that Yvette has left the country; she could still be alive."

"So she knew Jerome and his comrades were about, yet she refused the offer of your guest room. That's it; she's gone!" he said, without inflexion.

"We did ask her a couple of times," Trish told him quickly, knowing how badly I was feeling about my failure to protect Yvette.

Driving home from Heathrow, we considered the inevitable. Tears for Colin and Yvette weren't far from the surface. Their one chance at love together had been cruelly snatched away. Before they'd even had a chance to begin.

CHAPTER FIFTEEN

We dropped a distraught and exhausted Colin at the door of his flat. I could see that Trish, like me, badly wanted to stay, to be there for him, but there was nothing we could do. Colin voiced a desire to be left alone. "Go, I need to sleep, just leave me." So we left him, returning to work, promising to return later.

That evening, I'd arranged for David and Sue to join us. I hoped John would put in an appearance. He would know how best to handle Colin's grief. First Katie, now Yvette; it's getting closer and closer, I thought!

I couldn't let my friend down a second time. I desperately wanted to be there for him. Straight after work, I sought him out, correctly surmising, even with the lack of sleep and accompanying jet lag that, in his distress, he would only manage a few hours. Colin actually managed four hours before waking, vacantly staring into space until I arrived. This was how I found him. I had to knock three times. I'd considered using my own key, but finally Colin padded to the door, letting me in, before returning to vacuous contemplation.

"Let me cook you some food? Trish, Sue and David will be here soon," I coaxed my reluctant friend. Once I arrived, he began to relax slightly, responding slowly to my inane chatter and questions while I prepared a meal.

"Tell me again, Martyn. What did John say about her capture?" he asked unexpectedly, deflecting me from an attempt at forced joviality.

"I think it best he tells you himself, hopefully tonight. John wouldn't reveal how they did it, or where she was, just that the spiritual forces of darkness were co-ordinated and prepared, that they were seeking revenge for Maurice," I finished, searching in my own mind for some level of justification for our failure.

"How did you feel after encountering them on Saturday? Did it frighten Yvette?" he asked, seemingly curious to understand.

"No, I don't think so; she didn't seem afraid. We'd managed to give them the slip and, anyway, I'm not sure she completely understood the implications and dangers. She hasn't been involved as long as the rest of us; she seemed in good mood. Yvette seemed to me to be focused on the positive side of events."

"I know, she was positive, a glass half full type of girl. It really thrilled her when we told her about John and Luke, even with the dark stuff. I just wish she'd accepted your offer," he said softly, his voice catching, tears not far away.

At that moment the doorbell rang, releasing me from any further difficult questioning.

David, Trish and Sue filed into the room Trish and Sue made a beeline for Colin, to comfort him in the only way they knew how. They both hugged him, holding him tightly, demonstrating they were there for him, not needing words to express their concern for their friend.

Surrounded by the compassion of his friends, Colin made a conscious effort to perk up, accepting, with a small smile, the offered cottage pie and salad that I'd been preparing.

"Thanks, mate."

The room settled down. Colin and I ate our meals, concentrating on the food, while the others kept conversation light and general.

Finishing his meal, handing the plate to a waiting Sue, Colin decided to confront the overriding expectation of the evening. "Do you think John is going to show up tonight?" he asked David directly, without preamble.

"I am here already." David's eyes flashed and his demeanour changed, signifying the arrival of John's spirit into our presence.

"We understand how you are feeling; you are distraught from the loss of Yvette in your life, but there is nothing you can do to change this! You will never meet her again in this lifetime," John informed Colin, in a somewhat harsh tone.

"Why didn't you and the angels do more to protect her?" Colin demanded in response, echoing the same question I'd put to John a week earlier.

"That is because the dangers were too great. If we'd revealed ourselves through David, then the danger to Sue would have been very great. We couldn't prevent Satan striking without the loss of Sue and David," he told us.

"So, there's nothing we can do to get her back?" Colin asked, his shoulders slumping, defeat and despair evidenced by his voice.

"No, there is nothing you can do. At present, there is great danger to you all! The prince of darkness, the evil one, has trained his disciples not to hesitate in situations where they can inflict pain and sorrow. They will continue to push forwards, wanting to initiate greater devastation, to maximise their gains by causing further disruption."

John warned, "Jerome desires to attack again while you are confused and disorientated. He plans to hammer a wedge into the gap he's already created."

"What are they going to do?" we blurted out in unison, dismay in our voices.

"We do not know specific details yet; we only warn you of the tactics of their battle! Be assured, they will continue attacking, wanting to destroy you one by one," John warned a rapidly subdued gathering.

"What about all the protection you promised?" I demanded, suddenly belligerent. I was becoming agitated at the level of danger, while we remained helpless.

"As you are aware, Katie was the first; we feared too much interaction between yourselves and Paul's syndicate. We think they intend to attack Robert, or Paul and Sandra, removing your defences, before attacking you, the main prize. The protecting angels are there for you, but they will not interfere with human choice," he replied, with chilling indifference.

The next night, Colin lay in bed trying to sleep. Despite the herbal tablets he'd bought, he knew there would be no chance of sleep that night. Every time his eyes closed, his mind's eye conjured a picture of Yvette. His beloved Yvette, who he would never see again!

He felt hugely frustrated by his helplessness. To be told who was responsible for the disappearance and...

Abruptly, Colin slammed the brakes on his imagination, unable and unwilling to allow his mind to visualise the consequences for Yvette. There was nothing he could do; he could never get her back.

A month ago, the future had been so bright, Colin had almost felt the need for shades. Yvette, a new life, a new direction, the syndicate. When he'd woken up, he felt he needed to pinch himself, ensuring it was all real. But now this future was gone, and the walls of his bedroom were closing in. The opportunity had slipped through his fingers like sand on a beach, and there was absolutely nothing he could do about it. With an anguished yelp, Colin jerked upright in the dark, reaching out and switching on the bedside lamp. Climbing out of bed, he padded to the kitchen, looking for a drink.

Nearly two in the morning, over six hours of the night left, not the slightest chance he would sleep a wink. Out of the blue, Colin decided he would go for a drive, just to clear his mind, try and anesthetise the pain of loss he was feeling, a pain that couldn't be eased.

He drove aimlessly for over an hour, not knowing or caring where he was headed, simply turning every time an opening occurred. *Tufton Gray, 2 miles* – the road sign was upon him and past before he realised. He pulled over to the side of the road, pausing to ponder. He was on a minor country road. When he extinguished his headlights, there was only a meagre moonlight with which to see by. Colin was surprised to find himself there; he knew the village of Tufton Gray was only twenty five miles from his flat, but he hadn't planned on visiting. His subconscious had simply taken him in that direction, unbidden.

Colin's mind was jumping, his thoughts drifting back to the appearance of John and the words he'd used. He tried to recall if John had issued a specific warning to him about not approaching the village of Tufton Gray, in particular, the house of Jerome!

Starting the car, Colin drove through the village as quietly as possible, tyres crunching softly on the tarmac. In the dark, Colin felt the silent menace from each lifeless house that he passed. His heart beating wildly, Colin imagined himself deep in enemy territory. Eventually, he passed the last dwelling of the village, no wild lights or frenzied chase to characterise his fears.

Instantly he recognised the track where we'd hidden the car on our previous incursion. Instinctively he turned the steering wheel, not realising, or even understanding what it was he was planning. Once hidden by the trees, Colin allowed himself a few minutes for his heart to settle. Time which provided an opportunity to scheme. He had no agenda, no specific idea what it was he wanted to do here. I'll just take a look, Colin thought, opening the car door.

The journey across the fields, then through the woods to the perimeter wall, was only about a mile. If I'm not pretending to be in the SAS, I could be in and out within forty minutes, just to have another look, he promised himself.

Colin's breath formed clouds in the cold November night air as he set out across the fields. At least the sub-zero temperatures solidified the ground, making it firm, if somewhat rocky to walk across. Ahead appeared the dim outline of the woods, closer than he was expecting. Keeping low, proceeding as quietly as possible, Colin moved on determinedly, all the while anticipating the unexpected! Skirting the base of the wall, he listened to the normal sounds of night, hooting of distant owls, sounds of nocturnal animals foraging. Finally, he reached the oak tree, finding, with relief, it was still possible to shin far enough into the branches to see over the wall. Hiding amongst the foliage for twenty minutes, Colin waited, detecting no sign of any Doberman dogs, or any activity in the house. All remained dark and brooding in the chill night!

In the darkness on the drive, he could just make out a dark shadow, Jaguar shaped. A car which seemed, to Colin's fuzzy mind, to be announcing their invincibility, their superiority to the world. In Colin's tired mind, a seed of an idea began to germinate slowly.

It had taken less that forty minutes to return to his VW Golf and back. Colin was a meticulous person; he planned for as many eventualities as he could imagine. In the boot of the Golf, Colin kept a cardboard box for emergencies. An empty cola bottle filled with water, just in case; a petrol canister with an emergency gallon; a tow rope, and as many tools as he envisaged needing in an emergency. It had been an act of a moment, to prepare for his raid. Emptying the water from the plastic bottle onto the ground, he replaced it with the petrol. He took an oily rag used for cleaning hands; a lighter, which was there for who knows what; the tow rope and torch, just in case. Carefully, Colin made his way back through the woods to the now familiar oak tree. Another twenty minutes of watching passed, still no unusual sounds or sights to disturb his mission.

On the summit of the wall, he gently eased himself into a seated position, waiting for several minutes, then dropping the end of the knotted escape rope down into enemy territory! He secured the rope to the overhanging branch, before climbing down, crouching on the lawn. He waited patiently at the base of the wall, watching for movement, cradling the plastic bottle to his chest. Nothing disturbed the night except for the distant hoot of an owl, hunting in the dark.

Moving as carefully as possible, he crossed the immaculate lawn at a crouch. The anticipated sudden outburst of barking, announcing his presence, failed to materialise. Colin was lucky. If anybody was watching, the bulk of the car blocked the view from the house. He reached the rear of the car with no burst of harsh security lighting to expose his presence.

Colin rested briefly, taking stock of the situation, allowing the tense muscles in his arms and legs to relax. He waited until his breathing and heart rate approached normality.

He crouched there, concealed by the Jaguar, holding a plastic bottle of petrol, a cloth fuse and a lighter in his pocket.

Colin's conscience began the debate with his hurting heart; did he have the guts to finish what he'd started?

As he deliberated, John's words kept repeating in his battered mind. *Jerome intends to attack again!* It was too much for Colin's sleep-deprived brain. To him, the Jaguar embodied the evil threat that Jerome represented.

"Strike hard, fast, and first," he muttered to himself, making a decision, unscrewing the cap from the bottle.

He emptied half of the petrol under the rear of the car, just beneath the petrol tank. Colin made a river of fuel, running towards the car and the bottle, which he'd laid in the pool of petrol. A cloth fuse, soaked in petrol, ran through the neck of the bottle to the fuel inside, but it wouldn't have mattered; there was enough petrol puddled around the bottle to melt the thin plastic, which would then add its contents to the growing flames.

Colin sparked the lighter, quickly holding it to the trail of fuel, acting before his resolve failed, watching the hungry flame scurry towards the car and waiting lake of petrol. Colin ran, not bothering to look behind, to see the results of his carefully planned handiwork.

Once in the safety of the branches, he paused, searching the scene of his crime, hearing a soft whump in the distance as the bulk of the fuel caught alight. Quickly the rear quarter of the majestic motor became immersed in flames. From afar, Colin watched cavorting flames with a callous and cold satisfaction. The fire grew steadily, flames dancing around the night, like a whirling dervish.

Lights appeared at the first-floor windows; he saw one flung open. A white face emerged briefly, before disappearing inside again. Seconds later, the front door was flung open. Firstly, Jerome appeared, dressed in a dark dressing gown and pyjamas, followed only seconds later by Rosalind, then Anne, all three jerking to a halt by the door. They realised the flames were now too fierce. The fire grew rapidly, scorching and blistering the exposed paintwork with its intensity, quickly running out of control, devouring the resplendent motorcar with an insatiable appetite!

Jerome looked up, staring into the night, scanning the crown of the wall and tree line beyond. With the light created by the fiercely burning car, Colin felt sure that he was hidden in the shadows, sure that he couldn't be seen.

But Jerome suddenly froze, focusing on the area where Colin hid. Jerome's eyes narrowed as he searched the darkness. Eyes which seemed to be staring directly at Colin!

"Time I wasn't here," Colin warned himself, grabbing the branch, lowering himself to the ground and safety beyond the wall. Out of direct eyeline, Colin allowed himself a moment to relax: no dogs, unprepared and not dressed. It had been a piece of cake, he thought, turning away from the wall.

Barely had he travelled ten metres into the woods when it came for him. A slight movement at the periphery of his vision, then, freakishly, filling his eyesight, an open-mouthed demon, a screeching phantom face roared in to attack him, filling Colin's head with demonical shrieking.

"Arrrhhh," Colin fell backwards in absolute terror but, when he looked, the demon had gone. He sprang up in a panic and began to run. Crashing through the bushes, he fell forwards, twisting, scrabbling on hands and knees across the frosty ground, desperately trying to put as much distance as possible between himself and the ghoul!

He only managed a few metres before it came again, this time from the opposite direction, once more screaming close up, right into his face. He was petrified. It engulfed his vision, filling his every sense with pure blind panic and terror. Colin crashed backwards, ripping his jacket on an unseen branch. Stumbling, he tripped over a root, tumbling down a gradual slope. Crashing into the trunk of a tree, he came to a halt with an unexpected, shuddering jolt. He felt a wave of dizziness as the air was expelled from his lungs.

Lying for several seconds in the mud and mulch, there was no let up. Colin's head filled with screeching and movement all around. Launching himself to his feet, he dragged his bruised and scratched body away from that terrible place, not knowing, nor caring where he was heading.

Disorientated by fear and darkness, Colin staggered and lurched onwards, the screams and mocking apparitions from the darkness, all encompassing, relentlessly pursuing him from all directions. Unseeing in his panic, Colin stumbled forwards, running into another tree, smashing his face and forehead into the unforgiving trunk. He fell backwards, stunned, experiencing an immediate warm sensation on his cheek. Dazed, he touched his cheek, then forehead, assessing the damage. His fingers came away, wet and sticky, as the warm blood oozed from the unseen cut!

STOP, it's in your mind! Colin fought a frantic inner battle, determined to take control of the situation. He fought panic, wrestling with his terrified emotions. The screaming, yelling, ethereal apparitions continued all around. Deep within the recess of his panicked mind, Colin dimwittedly understood they weren't attacking him physically.

"It's in my mind; these aren't real!" Colin shouted into the night sky, wanting them to stop, wanting them to go away. "Leave me alone. You can't hurt me. You're figments; you're not real!" Colin comforted himself by shouting defiantly as the demonic apparitions attacked, desperately trying to regain control, to slow his rapid and panicky breathing.

He took a deep calming lungful of cold night air. Closing his eyes tightly, he waited as his body slowly relaxed. The panic gradually subsided; he started to feel better. His breathing and heartbeat began to slow; the screams in his head receded into the background. Colin opened his eyes, looked around, only seeing the trees of the woods. Movement within the trees caused Colin to flinch, but he grappled and subdued his reactions. He remained rooted to the spot, staring belligerently at the appearance of the apparition until it faded from view.

Orientating himself by the orange glow in the sky, and dappled moonlight filtering through the branches, he could work out in which direction the car lay. The terrible noise and demonic movements remained with him, accompanying his journey through the woods, but with control of his mind and fears, they began to subside!

With noisy chittering all around, Colin resolutely walked on towards his car.

***

After Colin's revelation of his adventure, the cause of the deep purple, swollen gash on his forehead. I was not amused. I lost it for a moment. Red-faced, I yelled, "You fucking idiot; you absolute idiot."

We'd gathered the night after, listening agog as a sheepish and embarrassed Colin recounted his tale. He'd returned home to sleep. Waking and feeling refreshed after eight hours of slumber, Colin realised, the previous evening's expedition probably wasn't the best idea he'd ever had.

"Sorry, I just wasn't thinking. I was tired and hurting. I'm fed up with being on the receiving end. You heard John; they aren't going to let up. I know this will rile them, so I shouldn't have done it, but it's done now, can't be undone," he said, looking shamefaced at the floor.

David spoke, not bothering to be diplomatic. "Forget it! Martyn, when was the last day you never made a single mistake? Besides, they deserved it!"

"Yeah, try telling John that; it's OK for you, never having to be on the end of his wrath." I sighed, exasperated, beginning to relax. Of course, David was right. We'd gone charging off to Tufton Gray once already, and twice I'd punched Jerome, so who was I to judge regarding indiscreet reactions.

"Fair enough, you're right. I'm sorry, Colin, I overreacted. I can't even begin to guess how you're feeling right now, so I shouldn't judge. Even so, you can face John alone, that's if he shows up tonight," I said, absolving myself from any involvement.

John failed to show that evening. We waited with anticipation every time David spoke, but John never appeared, almost as if John had forgiven Colin, due to the mitigating circumstances of fatigue, and grief.

The next evening, up in Oxfordshire, three days after Halloween, Paul and Sandra prepared for a rare night out: a Halloween fancy dress party, being held at the *Thatched Cottage*. In reality, dressing up for Halloween wasn't something which attracted either Paul or Sandra, but it was a chance for a good night out, a time to enjoy some fun with their friends and neighbours. As he attached the fake bolt to his neck, Paul was just sorry that Bolty had once again refused the chance of a night out.

"It would have done Rob good, a night out!"

"Yeah, he could have stayed here. And got drunk in the company of friends, instead of just the bottle!" Sandra applied the green face make-up, which complemented exactly the ghoulish eye mascara already applied.

"Perfect, my darling, you get better looking each day," Paul teased, easily ducking the cushion thrown in response.

"Do you think there's any danger tonight?" Sandra asked, instinctively becoming serious as she remembered the warning that Sue had relayed during their weekly telephone conversation.

"Hopefully not, but we can't be too careful: best be on our guard and alert," Paul replied, sticking a fake scar to his forehead. "For sure, Colin certainly stirred the hornets' nest."

"Do you feel okay celebrating Halloween, with what it represents and all that?" Sandra asked.

"Maybe we should ask John next time he appears! All I know is that it's a bit of fun, and at this time of year we need a bit of cheering up. Especially this year," he said, becoming sombre for a second, remembering Katie and Yvette.

Sandra completed her outfit, aiming a mock curtsy at her husband as she placed on her head the black witch's hat that she'd made from scraps.

"Perfect, if you weren't already married, I'd ask you to marry me all over again," Paul said, smiling broadly at his wife.

"And if you weren't such an ugly toad, I'd accept." Sandra grinned happily, anticipating an evening away from the worries of the farm and syndicate and wishing in her heart that their friend Robert could join them.

That evening, *Thatched Cottage* was packed, full of friends and strangers, all eager to grab a moment of escapism and festivity. Sandra and Paul were nowhere near the most elaborately dressed that evening. They had utilised old clothing and improvisation to fashion rudimentary costumes. Here, it seemed, enticed by the offer of meagre prizes, and the prospect of local fame, a large proportion of the village had gone to town on their costumes, buying especially for the event.

Gracefully easing an Egyptian mummy of indiscriminate sex to one side, Paul edged towards the crowded bar, catching the attention of Stan the landlord.

"Usual gin and tonic?" he shouted over his shoulder towards Sandra, who'd followed him through the throng. "Seems quite busy," he yelled through the din, looking beyond Sandra, wondering what a Margaret Thatcher was doing at a Halloween fancy dress party. Maybe, he concluded, certainly some would agree!

Paul and Sandra circulated, meeting friends and neighbouring farmers, all eager to talk livestock through the din. Andy Baker stopped for a chat before drifting away towards the bar, having never quite grasped the argument that Paul expounded on the desirability for cross bred herds giving increased milk yield!

The evening wore on; they'd pre-planned, deciding to make a night of it. Sandra and Paul needed a break. This was their chance to let their hair down, to forget about all that was happening in their lives!

After several drinks, Paul failed to notice the pub's new barmaid slip a small amount of white powder into their glasses, before pouring his and Sandra's drinks.

The evening progressed nicely, ending with a raucous singsong, after Vlad the Impaler had received the award for the most frightening character in history!

"Take me home; take me home please, I'm feeling tired." Sandra tugged her husband's sleeve, dragging his attention away from a rowdy rugby song he was in the middle of singing.

"I want to go home; I'm tired," she said, leaning forward to rest her forehead on her husband's shoulder.

Paul, too, recognised his exhaustion. "OK, love, I'm totally shattered! Maybe we did need a break, just a chance to let our hair down, relax. It could be the release of tension causing us to feel so tired. Time to go I think." It took moments for the taxi company to be contacted and the time of their pick up to be brought forward.

Sandra fell asleep during the taxi ride, her head cradled gently in the nape of her husband's neck. A gentle smile playing across her features, she relaxed in her secure and tranquil haven.

"Let's get you off to bed." Paul hoped he could stay awake long enough to get his wife up the stairs, then settled in the big brass bed, which served as their shared sanctuary, their respite from the world beyond. It was obvious to Paul; the stress and strain had built up beyond realisation.

Accompanying the release the evening brought, the alcohol had taken a far greater toll than usual. All we can do now, he thought, wearily climbing the stairs, is sleep it off, get up tomorrow, hopefully feeling refreshed. In his exhaustion, Paul failed to notice he'd left the main door to the farmhouse unlocked! It wouldn't have mattered if he'd remembered to lock the door, it just made Jerome's task easier.

Twenty minutes after the last light in the farmhouse was extinguished, two shadows detached themselves from the side of the barn. Dressed head to foot in black, including black balaclavas, Jerome and his accompanying henchman watched and waited in silence.

"What was that stuff Maxine put in their drinks?" the henchman whispered, concerned that Paul and Sandra might wake up once they'd entered the farm.

"Don't worry," Jerome replied. "It's herbal, a wonderful plant found in Haiti; the powdered plant reacts well with alcohol to induce sleep. And if the authorities become suspicious, it's almost undetectable. Even if it is detected, they are going to assume that these two were taking drugs," he stated.

Jerome tested the door, to his surprise finding the farmhouse door unlocked. "Good, saves me a job," he murmured, moving forward cautiously.

Taking extreme care to move evenly and quietly, the two entered the silent farmhouse, waiting in the kitchen for their eyes to become accustomed to the darkness. They remained their frozen, until they could discern objects about them. Moving from room to room, Jerome searched for, and found, two smoke detectors: one in the kitchen, one at the top of the stairs. Reaching up to open and remove the batteries, he replaced them with duds from his trouser pockets.

As the battery was disconnected, one of the smoke detectors let out a single, loud, high-pitched beep. The two intruders instantly froze, becoming lifeless shadows in the darkness, expecting the light to appear beneath the bedroom door, but nothing happened. After a full minute Jerome relaxed, realising they remained undetected.

Jerome had planned his mission well, arriving prepared. Two candles were placed in strategic positions, one on a small table at the foot of the wooden stairs, and one in the kitchen close to a linen cupboard. Flammable cloth was then distributed around the candles in judicious positions, specifically placed to create the maximum spread of flame, a vigorous uptake for the fire. Jerome was clever; there would be no use of accelerant here. "Too easy to detect by the fire investigation teams," he'd told his accomplice. He knew these days they used dogs to detect the minutest trace of accelerant. Jerome had to satisfy himself with the carefully positioned plastic bottle of sunflower oil in the kitchen, placed adjacent to both the candle and linen cupboard. A small canister of lighter fuel was then positioned on the table by the foot of the stairs, put there to give the impression it had been used to fill a lighter, with which to light candles!

Carefully retracing their steps, Jerome ensured that everything was set; the trap was laid. He flicked the lighter, sparking a small flame, waiting for several seconds for a reaction in the bedroom. No sound or movement stirred the night. Jerome lit the white household candle, placing it on its side, observing with macabre intensity as the flame flickered in the night, touching, then finally igniting the white cotton cloth which covered the table.

They repeated the process in the kitchen, warily noting the light of the flickering flames coming from the stairway. With a splash of oil to speed it on its way, Jerome again ignited the candle, watching gleefully as the flame slowly caught, then gathered pace. It sought out the flammable materials that Jerome had carefully arranged around the candle.

"That should do it," he instructed his companion. "They came home, lit some candles in a daft romantic moment, then went to bed pissed, forgetting all about them."

Cautiously closing the farmhouse door behind him, Jerome and his partner made their way across the farmyard, careful to remain in the shadows as much as possible. They crossed a field to the silent Range Rover, hidden beneath the trees. Once safe, they waited, observing in silence as the orange glow grew in the night sky, signalling the success of their plan.

Paul opened his eyes with a start, wondering what it was that had woken him. Jerking his head from the pillow, he groaned; his head was thumping, filled with a thousand tiny hammers. Suddenly Paul noticed the smell, the horrible acrid smell of smoke and fire. Immediately becoming fully alert, he listened intently, hearing the crackling of flames. At the same time, he saw the tiny dancing light beneath the door as the fire forged forward.

"Wake up, wake up, we're on fire!" Feeling the smoke beginning to fill his lungs, sensing that the fire was already out of control, Paul reached over, roughly shaking his wife by the shoulder, desperate to wake her!

"What's up? What's happening?" Sandra was still half asleep, refusing to wake up and face their dilemma. Already she was beginning to succumb to the toxic smoke and fumes drifting unseen through the air.

Quickly, Paul moved across the room, placing a flat hand on the wooden door. He jerked his hand away; the ferocious heat instantly burnt his palm, skin charring, then blistering, beginning to flake off within a second of him touching the door.

It was very clear there was no way out down the stairs. Fully awake now, sheer necessity subduing the effects of the drink and drugs in his system, Paul turned back to look at his wife, feeling the radiating heat from the door behind him as he did so.

Sandra had fallen back onto the bed, eyes wide and staring, but she seemed lethargic, uncomprehending to the peril that stalked them!

Paul knew that the door wouldn't hold much longer. He had to fight against the desire to stop, to lay down and rest. Induced by smoke inhalation, a craving for sleep, threatened to overcome him, as it appeared to be doing with Sandra!

The bedroom window was their only option. "Window," Paul shouted at his wife, raising his voice over the muffled roar beyond the door, thankfully seeing movement as Sandra reacted to the danger. She dragged herself from the bed with careful and methodical movements, staggering towards the darker patch of wall, which was the window frame. Reaching the window before Paul, Sandra didn't wait. Summoning up the last of her resolve, she grabbed the nearest heavy object, a large bedside lamp, which she hurled at the window, as hard as her wearied body could manage. The throw was true, hitting square on, shattering the glass with a crash. Paul heard the sound above the roaring of the raging fire.

Wrapping her hand with the curtain and clearing the frame of shards, Sandra positioned herself on the frame. Turning to her husband to shout, "I love you," she prepared to throw herself out of the window towards the garden and safety.

Sandra didn't get a chance to finish the words; in an instant, with a gigantic whooshing noise, the door gave way, ripping wide open. The hungry flames, eager to feed on the fresh supply of oxygen that the shattered window offered, leapt forward in a single motion. Sandra fell forwards into the room, landing on Paul in the dark smoke.

Instantly, she felt a searing pain; the inferno burnt the skin from her face. Her hair disappeared in that first moment. The pain was intense and beyond. Sandra felt the flesh on her hands and torso begin to tighten, then char. She gritted her teeth; the first flush of pain became agony.

Below her, Paul pushed, urgently willing her to move. Through the fog of confused thoughts, Sandra still realised the necessity for action. Sluggishly, she dragged herself towards where she thought the window frame was, all the while feeling the excruciating agony of movement. Driven by a hunger for the oxygen her lungs coveted, Sandra reached out desperately, feeling the presence of the window ledge, as backward resistance of movement, rather than a touch from an already burnt and clawed hand!

From below and behind, Sandra felt a forceful shove. Paul, gathering up the remainder of his strength, pushed once, as hard as he could, catapulting his wife through the aperture, into the darkness.

Landing with a thud in a muddy flower bed, Sandra opened her eyes, expecting to see the shape of her husband following her. Before he had the time to emerge, her eyes rolled up into her head. Sandra lost consciousness!

Paul fell backwards, collapsing onto the floor. He'd used the very last of his strength to push his wife out through the window. Dimly he was aware of his skin blistering, the flesh falling away from the bone. He looked on at this phenomenon with a curiosity, almost as if it were happening to somebody else. Paul felt tired, so very tired; he wanted to lie down and sleep. Everything became slow; the pain faded to a memory. There was something important that he needed to do, in a hurry, but he couldn't remember what. "I'll remember in a second. Just need to rest a little before I move again," he croaked, recalling, with an inward smile, his wife's declaration of love, only seconds earlier!

I replaced the phone, careful to ensure it had been turned off before meticulously positioning it at the very centre of the small table where I usually kept it, while I collected my shattered thoughts. It was Sunday evening and we had gathered at the flat: me, Trish, David, Sue and Colin. I noticed the conversation had ceased. Simply by observing my reactions to the call, they knew that something was very wrong.

"That was Bolty. The farm caught fire. Paul is dead. Sandra is in intensive therapy with third-degree burns!" I advised, in a whisper, fighting to control my emotions. I saw Trish's hands shoot up to cover her open jaw. Sue's eyes were wide with horror. The four remained speechless, shocked, unable to find the words to articulate a reaction to such appalling news! After an eternity, I gathered myself and spoke again, hearing sharp intakes of breath as I relayed the details, Bolty had just supplied. When I finished, I looked up, seeing damp eyes staring back, knowing I wasn't too far from tears. I fought to control my emotions.

"There is little else Bolty knows: the fire investigators will begin their investigation in the morning. They fought the fire throughout the night, after a neighbour noticed the glow in the sky. Bolty thinks it started just after they returned from a night out, but he thinks there may have been foul play. He said there was nothing in the farmhouse to cause a fire," I reported.

After taking a moment to compose myself, I continued. "Sandra is lying unconscious in the ITU unit of the John Radcliffe hospital, in Oxford. She has severe, third-degree burns to her face and hands, as well as burns on the trachea and the inside of her lungs. It's too early to know if she will survive." We sat there, mostly in silence, for the rest of the evening, unable to speak or express our horror and grief at this latest incursion into our lives.

Colin, who had his own troubles, awoke the next day. He had been home for only four days; time he was using to try and realign his confused and shattered life. That was when he felt able to concentrate on anything other than the loss of Yvette. Now the plight of Sandra had been added to his worries. Sandra, who was lying helpless in a hospital bed, just a few miles away, fully reliant on the professionalism and expertise of the health professionals who cared for her very life.

Sandra was his first thought that morning. It never stops, he thought. It just keeps coming in waves; we have no chance to recover from one attack before the next arrives. Like a tsunami. And what use is the promise of John, he thought. Promises of protection, but never forthcoming, he told himself angrily, forgetting Basingstoke. It was a subdued Colin who went down to the foyer to collect his post. He descended the three flights slowly, unable to gather the enthusiasm to jog, or bound, as he would normally do. Inside his box, he found a small parcel, wrapped up well, only just small enough to fit through the letter box. The parcel was addressed by his forename, *Colin*, no surname, no address; obviously, it had been delivered by hand.

Instinctively, but with alarm bells beginning to sound, Colin ripped off the plain wrappings, discovering inside the gaudy, enticing packaging of a diecast toy car accompanied by a box of matches. Turning it over, Colin found himself holding a model of the Jaguar he'd set alight, four nights previously. It was even the same deep maroon colour. Colin checked, feeling nauseous, knowing the significance of what he held.

Initially, we monitored Sandra from afar, mostly second hand, via Bolty. The very smallest crumb of comfort was that the crisis helped Bolty to move forward. He'd advised us that Sandra's younger sister, and her husband, were a constant at the hospital. From what he told us, it didn't seem that Bolty was able to visit the hospital much himself, but then what did it matter, Sandra remained unconscious, fighting for her life.

After the first week, there was the first little bit of good news. Bolty reported, the burns in her lungs and trachea had been successfully drained. Sandra still hovered between consciousness and oblivion, but we were informed that they were now hopeful that Sandra would live. Next day, Sue sent flowers from us all, not knowing if flowers were allowed in the ITU unit where Sandra remained, but that felt of little importance.

Gradually Bolty reported little daily improvements, a tiny movement in her hands and limbs, her eyes opening, her first words. He told us she was in unimaginable pain, dosed daily with high-strength opiates, but the improvements continued to come.

We cried collectively when he reported, "Sandra's been informed of Paul's death." It was totally understandable when he advised on the next call that it had put her progress back by several weeks.

After the fire, we waited patiently for John to appear. We were confused and traumatised and we needed the comfort and wisdom that only he, or Luke, could deliver. But we were forced to wait for nearly a week.

Finally, John appeared, six days after the fire, telling us, "The angels hold Sandra; her soul is in the arms of Jesus;

he holds her tightly." After this brief reassurance, John changed topic, warning us, "Do not expect a visit from myself or Luke for a while; the dangers are immense. Satan watches and roars, waiting for his chance to finish his work, to destroy your syndicate, once and for all. In the supernatural realm you are now constantly surrounded by angels, for your protection." But he cautioned, "We can't appear for some time, my appearance, or Luke's, will initiate such a spiritual battle, David may not survive."

Resigned, we each said goodbye to John, then Luke, knowing that it would be some time before we spoke again, wondering what dangers the interim period held.

November became December, then January. In delight, Bolty reported, "Sandra is now out of danger! She is in a specialist burns unit." Her skin, it seemed, had over twenty per cent third-degree burns. Sandra would be hideously disfigured for the rest of her life, but at least she was alive.

Promptly we made plans and set off for Oxford. When we got there, they advised us Sandra didn't want visitors but, even so, she did allow Sue in for a few minutes, just the once. Taking our flowers and greetings from us all, Sue disappeared inside the ward. Sandra begged Sue not to visit her again, to let her continue with the rest of her life without further contact.

A week later, in his quiet Scottish accent, Bolty reported, "The fire investigators have found no evidence of foul play; they've put the fire down to an accident with candles, following a drunken night out." A version of events that Sandra never challenged.

CHAPTER SIXTEEN

Luke reappeared in the February. We'd used the three months since the fire as a quiet time of rest and recovery. John and Luke were good to their word; we saw nothing of them, and I guess the angels had done their job well as there'd been no sign of Jerome, or his devotees, not since the diecast Jaguar was delivered to Colin.

Via Robert, we kept in constant touch with Sandra's progress. He told us that, under a famous plastic surgeon, she was beginning reconstructive surgery, though the difference he could make would only be cosmetic. Sandra would still be disfigured for the rest of her life!

Bolty confirmed Sandra wished us to stay away, not to contact her again. Although saddened, I completely understood why. Despite her voluntary involvement, Sandra had paid a terrible price for her participation in this adventure.

On the first Sunday of February, myself, Trish, Sue and David were playing Trivial Pursuit, all relaxing in the flat, when we noticed the flash deep within David's eyes; in a trice we were talking to Luke.

"We've been some time, my friends, although I have been observing you. I know you are all well."

"Luke," we spoke together, rushing our words, delighted our friend was back; we could begin again.

Luke continued. "It was necessary for us to allow you time of recovery. Satan made too many inroads into your protective network. The Oxfordshire syndicate of Sandra and Paul is no more. Satan has his victory for now, but we have raised a syndicate in the city of Nottingham. Jerome's evil syndicate do not know they exist yet." Luke went on. "They will continue training and, when they have completed this, we will bring them to this area for your protection."

I asked, "Are we safe from the evil syndicate at the moment?"

"When we do not use the body of David, or the calling table as conduits for communication, then you are safe!" It is the communication between us that alerts them to your activities. Satan and his evil angels roam the world; they know when we are in contact. They will tell Jerome of this visit, very soon."

"So, we're in danger now?" Sue said, immediately concerned for our safety.

"Not tonight, they have no time to mobilise," he assured her. "Since November they have been drunk on their success; at the moment they hold little threat for you, but they will seek to mobilise when they know we are communicating."

Luke ordered us to collect Colin. "You are to be honoured, our Lord himself will appear to you, through the vessel of David."

Luke advised, "You will each be given a private audience with the spirit of the Lord. He has a spiritual name which is unknown to mankind; that name is Voytec. You must bow and call him my Lord," Luke warned.

Excitedly, I bounded up the stairs, three at a time, hammering on Colin's door, demanding he join us immediately.

"Luke's back; we have a special audience," I blurted out happily. Colin swiftly closed his laptop, where he'd been working, and hurriedly followed me down the stairs to join the rest of the group.

Trish was already in conference. Luke had commandeered the second bedroom. Trish had volunteered to be first, to be given a private audience with Voytec. She returned, several minutes after we'd arrived. Flushed and excited, I could see in Trish the demeanour and joy of the thrill she'd experienced, by being at the epicentre of such an awesome privilege!

Sue followed her sister, nervously entering the room, hands clasped before her in a servile manner. Before the door closed on their private audience, I saw Sue bob her head in a bow.

Sue remained inside for an interminable twenty minutes, while I paced up and down, keen for my turn to arrive. Eventually the door opened, and Sue joined us, a serene expression upon her face. A calm seemed to emit from her very soul! I had no time to ask her for details. Sue motioned for me to enter. I took a deep breath, entering the room she had just vacated.

"Come in, Martyn, my son, sit down." He signalled for me to sit opposite him. We'd become adept at recognising the differences when we had a visitation; this wasn't Luke or John, of that, I was sure. I could tell this at a glance, the mannerisms and body language were vastly different.

"Voytec," I said, in awe, bobbing my head once, quickly.

"You must call me your Lord," he said, in a humble voice, but with a firmness which I found quite surprising.

"Sorry... Lord." I remembered the Lord at the last moment, then waited for him to speak again.

"I have viewed you from afar; you perform well, you are strong and protective. That is what I want from you. I have chosen to bless you. I am lord of all; how would you choose to be blessed?" His statement knocked the wind from my sails. I hadn't expected that, and I had no idea how to answer. As far as I was concerned, I had everything I wanted in life, Trish, a good job, the syndicate coupled with an exciting future, what more could I want? I asked myself, before finally blurting out, "A happy marriage to Trish, and good health... Please, Lord."

"It will be granted to you," Voytec promised. "The only thing I ask in return is your complete obedience to myself, and what I ask of you."

This didn't seem a bad deal to me, I thought. Several times we'd mucked up by charging off on our own initiative. I guessed it could be no less of a disaster if we did what was asked of us.

After Voytec left, John returned to the vessel that was David, spending the evening, before warning, "It remains dangerous in the spiritual realm. You will only receive the barest, and most essential communications for a foreseeable time, until the spiritual battle subsides, and the Nottingham syndicate are ready."

For three days a week, Lynda used to give her time to an animal charity shop in town. She managed the donations, ensuring the smooth running of the shop, maximising profits for the feeding of lost and stray cats and dogs. It was something that Lynda enjoyed greatly; she got to meet people and make friends among the other staff.

Thursday morning Lynda jumped out of bed as usual, looking forward to her final day of the week. She didn't need to be at the shop until ten, mid-morning, so there was no rush. She got ready, then left for the short drive into town, anticipating the challenges of another day.

Turning out of the driveway, Lynda failed to notice the green Mini Cooper parked across the road, condensation fogging the windows on a cold morning. There was no need to notice the Mini; Lynda was going into town, a normal working day at the shop.

The occupant of the Mini leaned forward, picking a mobile off the dashboard. He made a ten second call, before starting the motor, slamming the car into gear. It pushed away from the kerb rapidly; the motor gunned forward catching then tailing an unconcerned Lynda, before overtaking her on the approach to the ring road.

"Fool," Lynda said out loud, as the racing green Mini shot past her, driving far too fast for the icy February conditions. Once past Lynda, the Mini slowed, staying just ahead of her Fiat 500, as they approached the junction for the Newton industrial estate, a huge industrial complex on the south side of town. The district which provided most of the manufacturing jobs in our small town!

"What's he doing now?" Lynda grumbled to herself as the Mini reduced speed even further. "He overtakes me, then holds me up," Lynda complained, leaning over, wondering if there was another car in front of the Mini, one she hadn't noticed.

At the last second, she saw it, hearing the screech at the same moment. From her right-hand side, out of nowhere, thundered a huge tipper truck, brakes screaming in agony. The truck instantly and completely filled her vision, as it bore down relentlessly on the small Fiat.

With a huge, sickening crash accompanied by the grating of tearing metal, the truck hit Lynda's small Fiat just forwards of the driving compartment, spinning the car out of control, onto the pavement. The car smashed into the wall of a small factory unit, situated opposite the entrance to the trading estate.

Barely aware, Lynda heard the sickening crack of a bone as her leg snapped in two places. The break brought no pain, only numbness, the pain would come later. Her whole world slowed to a crawl; Lynda began to pick out individual sounds as the metal ripped and tore apart, like a bean can in a crusher.

Abruptly, the car ceased its momentum, coming to a juddering halt in a tangle of wreckage. Within her cocoon, Lynda remained conscious, listening to the creaks and groans as the twisted wreck began to settle. Suddenly pain began to wash through her body, mind-numbing agony, which robbed her of conscious thought. Her vision began to close in. Lynda was in a dark tunnel, falling backwards into a black world. She saw a sea of stars all around, swaying and swirling within the advancing darkness. Slowly Lynda closed her eyes, sinking deeper into darkness, falling into unconsciousness!

"Trish, Trish, it's Mum. She's had a crash. She's in hospital." Trish recognised the stricken voice of her sister on the phone.

"Calm down! What exactly do you know, is she badly hurt?" Trish tried hard to focus, fighting to keep the rising panic out of her own voice. A small part of her subconscious mind abstractly began to wonder, was this connected to Luke and John's reappearance ten days earlier? Sue took a series of deep breaths, calming herself enough to communicate to her sister all she'd been told by the manager of the shop, where their mother worked.

After getting no response at Lynda's home address, the police had phoned the number called work, on Lynda's smartphone. They'd informed Lynda's boss, Gordon Lee, that a large lorry had failed to stop, due to black ice on the road. It had driven straight through the junction, ploughing into Lynda's car. Not wanting to deliver such horrible news with a blind phone call, the police asked Gordon for location details of Lynda's family. Gordon promised he would contact Lynda's family to deliver the bad news in person.

"I don't know the details, but dad told me she is in a bad way," Sue informed her. "Gordon went to see Dad as his office. He conveyed the bad news face to face." Richard had asked him to notify Sue, and asked her to contact Trish, while he made his way to the hospital, ten miles away.

"Dad said he will send a taxi to pick us both up. He said we weren't to drive when in shock." Trish was amazed at the clear thinking of her father; even in such adverse moments as these, he remained level-headed.

Ten minutes later, Trish had just had enough time to let her boss Paul know she was leaving, when Sue arrived, sitting in the back of a taxi. Ashen faced, the two girls fell into each other's arms, wanting the comfort of shared distress.

"Trish, Sue, over here." Richard stood in the waiting area, identifying himself to his two daughters with a wave. They rushed over to their father, hugging, before disengaging to hear the latest news of Lynda from a pale and shaken Richard.

"She has a broken leg, crushed ribs, a punctured lung and a swollen brain lining, the meninges, which may be serious," Richard warned the two girls. "We have to wait. She is in the operating theatre now; they're setting her leg, trying to re-inflate your mum's lungs."

Richard had to glare fixedly at the wall behind his two daughters, knowing, if he were to look them in the eyes, he might break down and start sobbing.

Worried, they sat as a group, waiting for seven hours while Lynda underwent the surgery to reflate her punctured lung; then they set her shattered leg.

Trish and Sue called myself and David late in the afternoon, informing us of the accident and Lynda's current plight. The call left me feeling empty, desolate. Lynda was such a wonderful cheerful person, why did it have to happen to her?

Immediately I arranged to collect David from his office; we rushed to the hospital, eager to be there, unable to do anything but offer a comforting presence.

"What's happening? How is she?" I demanded, as soon as Trish and I disengaged from each other's arms. A tearful Trish told us, "The hospital has advised us, the major problem is the swelling of Mum's brain – it's called the meninges. They say fluid is still causing pressure on her brain. The surgeon's warned there might be an unseen injury. They might need to operate again, to relieve the pressure on her brain." Trish gulped, tears trickling down her cheek. I pulled her close, not having any other answer.

David and I took it in turns. Firstly, I accompanied Trish to the hospital's canteen, leaving Sue and David with Richard. Then Trish and I stayed, making brave conversation, while Sue and David ate. Valiantly, we tried to cajole Richard into eating, but he was unable to stomach more than a cup of tea; a sandwich remained untouched on the table beside him. Flatly, he refused to leave the waiting room.

At ten o'clock in the evening, the surgeon found us in the waiting room. We followed the weary surgeon to his little office, eager to hear any news.

"The pressure on her brain is growing too quickly; there is an unseen leak of blood. We are going to have to operate again," he said sombrely, directing his remarks towards Richard. "We require your formal permission but, frankly, we have no choice," he counselled, before softening his approach. "The chances for Lynda are good if we can operate soon enough and stop the leak. Frankly, it's not good having to operate again, so soon, but I don't think we have a choice."

"Yes, please operate, how long before we know?" Richard asked, looking around at his daughters.

"You'll not get any news for at least four to six hours, but that really is just a guess," the neurosurgeon replied, before departing to begin the process of trying to save Lynda's life!

"I just can't stay all night," David blurted out. "I have to be at Slumbertron at nine tomorrow morning. Mr Yakamoto is flying overnight from Japan. I have a meeting with him at nine!"

We all turned, seeing David's tormented features as he realised he was trapped between inflexible working commitments and a vital personal situation!

Appreciating David's dilemma, I considered all options. "I can drop David home, then I'll come back to wait," I suggested, giving Trish's hand a squeeze.

Richard spoke. "No! you stay at home, get some sleep. I'll be here all night. Trish and Sue can get a taxi home once we've had some news."

Understanding it was primarily a family crisis, Richard was offering an escape option to both of us. I desperately wanted to be there for Trish. I could see from their facial expressions, Trish and Sue wanted us to be there with them. But, I think, Richard was trying to be fair to me and David; we both had work commitments the next day. I figured also, it would probably comfort Richard to wait in the loving, undiluted company of his two daughters.

With evident regret, Trish waved us off, promising to text me as soon as they had any news at all.

Richard and the two girls remained in the now empty waiting area, contemplating the minute hand of the universal white-faced wall clock, moving forwards as if running through treacle. At times it seemed to slow to almost nothing, but ultimately the minutes turned to hours. Coffees were drunk, sandwiches unwrapped to be left uneaten, as they waited forlornly, desperate for the slightest scrap of news. Eventually, in the early hours, at 2.58am, the door to the hospital waiting area finally opened. The same surgeon who'd met with them earlier entered, looking frazzled but still dressed in fresh, if somewhat creased, un-ironed, surgeons' greens.

"Good news, I'm pleased to say," he informed the family. "We found a leaking blood vessel. We cauterised that and then we managed to reduce the swelling, ease the pressure on her brain. We think she will pull through now. She is recovering from the operation and will be unconscious for several hours in ITU but, for now, we believe the worst has passed," he explained cheerfully, to an incredibly relieved father and daughters.

Richard collapsed onto the nearest chair, feeling like the weight of the world had just been lifted from his shoulders. Trish and Sue both yelped with joy, then burst into tears, as the burden lifted. They hugged their father, both crying and laughing at the same time, conscious that a crisis point had passed.

"Hopefully, it's all downhill now; you two get home, let Toby out. I'm going to wait here until she regains consciousness." In the crisis Trish and Sue had both forgotten the needs of the dog. Naturally they wanted to remain with Richard but now they appreciated the necessity of letting the dog out. Sue agreed to her father's suggestion.

"Okay, call us the second you hear anything. We'll use the free phone by the main entrance, order a taxi from there."

Trish and Sue waited with their father a moment longer, taking the time to text me and David, before once more hugging their father tightly and kissing him goodbye. They departed along the deserted corridors, towards the main entrance of the hospital.

"There's no need to call for a taxi," Trish told her sister. "There's one over there, with its light on." She waved her hand in the direction of the taxi, watching with relief as the engine roared into life. The taxi nudged forwards towards the hospital entrance.

In the dark, both girls failed to notice the phone number on the side of the taxi wasn't from a local firm. If they had stopped to think, they would have noticed the name of the taxi firm on display was completely unknown in our town. It might have registered but the two girls were tired; all they wanted was to get home and rest! The driver kept his head down, turning away from the hospital's CCTV.

"Martyn, it's for you, a Richard Cummings." Stephen held the phone towards me, causing immediate consternation when I realised who it was. The previous night I'd eventually fallen asleep after Trish's good-news text. Now what was the problem? Why was Richard calling me at work? I hurried to take the call, beginning to worry!

"Hi Martyn, it's Richard. Have you heard from Trish or Sue?" Instantly my anxiety level hit ultra-high!

"No," I replied anxiously, "last I saw of either of them was last night at the hospital with you."

"They never came home last night. I've just got here from the hospital. There is no evidence that Trish and

Sue came home. I was hoping that they went to you instead."

My level of foreboding rose another notch, reaching 9.9 on a scale of one to ten. It was very unusual for Trish and Sue to go off the radar like this. I promised Richard I'd try David and other friends and get back to him as soon as possible.

He lifted my spirits only slightly, letting me know, "The good news is Lynda is now out of danger; they say she is beginning the slow road to recovery."

I phoned David directly who, unsurprisingly, knew nothing of the girls' whereabouts. Immediately, he was as concerned as I was. We agreed to meet at once, both of us full of misgivings, anxious to seek answers as quickly as possible!

It wasn't the time to worry about the dangers involved. As soon as we met, I used the trigger word, "Abba," not caring about risks and John's warnings.

Instantaneously, John arrived. Without greeting, he warned, "You have no time to lose. Trish and Sue have been captured by Jerome and Rosalind! They are being held at Tufton Gray, but only for a short while. Jerome intends to move them soon; he has evil plans!"

"Can we go and rescue them today, now?" I asked, not really caring about the answer. I was going after them immediately, no matter what.

"You can," he informed me, "but you need support. Jerome has combined with another group of Satan's worshippers. You will be outnumbered, even with Colin and Robert."

John's warning made sense; there was no point in charging in, just to fail.

John returned David to me. Quickly, I explained the details to him, before phoning Colin, who instantly agreed to drop everything and join us on a rescue mission.

I was surprised but pleased. After calling him, Bolty appeared just as keen to accompany us, agreeing to meet us at a service station en route. "I'll bring some tools and other bits; we may need them," he told me in parting.

We met Colin at the flat, hurriedly preparing for battle. Fortunately, I'd kept the short wooden axe handle from our previous mission. It made an excellent club. This was no time to be squeamish; it'll do just fine, I thought! With the addition of dark clothing and a torch, I was ready. Colin and David, also suitably attired, were prepared for battle, both favouring vicious looking wooden clubs.

We set off for the service station and our meeting with Bolty. Without drawing attention to myself by speeding, I drove as fast as I dared, frantic to get to Trish.

John didn't require the trigger; during the journey, he appeared without warning, updating us to the circumstances surrounding Trish and Sue's whereabouts.

"They've moved Trish and Sue from the village," John reported. "Trish and Sue are still prisoners, but they are being moved. Jerome and Rosalind are transporting them to Somerset, to a location called Underhill Woods." My blood ran cold as John said grimly, "Jerome and his evil comrades have abducted them to perform a ritual sacrifice. He's always wanted to carry out a human sacrifice; now his master, Satan, has given him permission."

After this terrible news, it took several minutes to be able to concentrate thoughts. We carried on, in bleak silence, towards our meeting with Robert.

Bolty was already there, waiting for us in the café. Quickly we told him of the rapidly changing circumstances surrounding the whereabouts of the two girls.

"We can go on to Somerset from here. I've borrowed a Renault Scenic people carrier, so we'll all fit in; there's room for Trish and Sue when we find them, let's go!" The sergeant's training took over, Bolty took command. He stood, walking out of the restaurant to the car, not waiting to see if we followed him.

Underhill Woods registered on the sat-nav; we were able to continue on our mission, filled with an intense determination to recover the two girls, release them from the deadly clutches of evil. Bolty drove steadily west on the motorway. Outside, the rain came down in brief but heavy showers, as the traffic built up into the early evening rush hour. Hidden behind the low-lying rainclouds, the sunset caught up, overtaking us as we drove!

"Underhill Woods has an entry showing on the internet," Colin announced. "It is situated on the coast at the edge of Exmoor, high on a hill overlooking the Somerset town of Bracken Castle. A place of remote natural beauty, accessible by a single road, nicknamed heartbreak hill, which is flanked by three-hundred-foot cliffs, dropping down to the ocean," he reported, reading the entry from the screen of his smart phone.

"Best we make plans for when we arrive," I said, hoping John would appear, intervene and lead us into the battle this time. John failed to materialise.

Just after eight in the evening, Bolty pulled off the road, allowing the car to glide the last few feet across a darkened car park. With mixed emotions, I noticed the silent brooding, brand new, maroon Jaguar, parked on the other side of the car park. Next to the Jag sat a Range Rover; then two other cars. I realised we were outnumbered, but we had God on our side. God and desperation!

Silently and resolutely, we prepared for battle, ensuring all clothing was darkened, face and hands muddied up, weapons at the ready.

"Ready?" I whispered, taking a last quick glance towards David, beseeching in prayer for John to appear, to lead us into war.

"Yes, let's go," David responded from the gloom.

"Wait a moment and keep watch," Bolty instructed, disappearing into the dark. Running at a crouch towards the Jaguar, he knelt, reaching under the front wheel arch. He spent several minutes carrying out some unknown task, helped by the occasional flash of a torch.

"Another skill they taught me in the army was a little bit about explosives," he explained on returning. "I've improvised, using one of Paul's bullets. I've placed a small charge into the tread of a tyre. If they decide to chase us, as soon as the percussion cap detonates, then the tyre should blow; hopefully that should prevent any chase," he announced nonchalantly.

I wondered why he hadn't just let their tyres down, but, I figured, with casual indifference, they deserved everything they got!

Trish and Sue were terrified. Jerome, Rosalind, Anne and another man they did not recognise held them prisoner throughout the day. They had been brutally tied up, then locked in the cellar of the house at Tufton Gray. The shock, closely followed by fear, began when the taxi driver pulled over in a remote lay-by. Jerome appeared out of the darkened night, gripping a knife in his hand. Opening the car door, he'd threatened the astonished Trish and Sue. They were bound and gagged, before being bundled into the boot of the taxi, followed by a bumpy drive into captivity, then a blindfolded walk as they were bundled into their cellar prison.

During the day, they'd been tied to chairs. Chairs that were bolted to the floor of a gym. A gym they'd recognised from our previous descriptions!

Apart from the discomfort and distress of imprisonment, there'd been no physical torture to suffer. However, the mental cruelty was huge. Anne had delighted in recounting, in the minutest detail, the tortures she claimed to have previously inflicted on Katie and Yvette.

Anne and Rosalind triumphantly briefed the petrified girls. "This is Valentine's Day. Jerome and ourselves are going to sacrifice a love offering to the master, Satan."

Trish and Sue began to whimper and shiver hysterically as the evil Rosalind took cold-hearted pleasure from the meticulous description of violation and abuse, she intended to inflict, when Jerome and his clique finally had the opportunity to gorge on Trish and Sue's suffering. Grabbing Trish's hair, yanking her head close, she snarled dramatically, "You should be pleased; you'll be with your God tonight. You'll have a martyr's send off."

Slowly, we made our way into the woods, the four of us in single file. Eyes continually searched through the darkness, looking for a sign off movement or any glimmer of illumination in the night sky.

"Over there." Behind me, Bolty indicated just the faintest glow of orange light in the distance, reflected against the low-hanging cloud cover.

Straining to concentrate, I agreed. "It might be man-made. A light or it could be a fire, possibly in a valley, or a dip in the terrain." Careful to make as little sound as possible, we edged towards the light, gingerly, at a crouch, appropriating mud from the damp and slimy forest floor as we moved. As we got nearer, the light grew in strength, giving off just enough illumination for us to see where we were placing our hands. Moving closer, I knew I'd been right. The flickering fire was situated in a natural depression of the ground, affording some concealment for the participants of the evil scene, which now presented itself, twenty feet below!

Illuminated by the dancing firelight, I could make out several people milling around a clearing in the dell beneath us. I counted them, ensuring I remained hidden from their sight. There were at least seven people moving around, seemingly randomly, but all focused on two figures spread eagled over two short tree trunks. The prisoners' wrists and ankles were tied to stakes, hammered into the ground. From a distance I couldn't establish identities of the victims, but it didn't require an Einstein to work it out.

"Hold it, wait!" Colin whispered in a theatrical tone, putting out a restraining hand, impeding my momentum, correctly anticipating I might charge forwards without stopping to take stock.

Listening, we heard chanting coming from the protagonists participating in the bizarre ritual. We couldn't discern the words, but I guessed they were calling on their fiendish master to appear, accept their ghastly offering.

I watched mesmerised, unable to react, as the leader, probably Jerome, bent down towards the ground at his feet, lifting something high into the air. He held it in both hands, at full arm's length, high above his head. The sputtering firelight highlighted this terrible scene. He paused for several seconds, calling into the night to his master, before slamming the object down hard, aiming with full force at the head of one of his spread-eagled victims.

"Noooo…" The long, drawn out shriek of anguish came from just behind me, the yell dying out to nothing. David brushed past me, running wildly through the trees towards the clearing.

The evil leader jerked to a stop, twisting, searching the foliage where the unexpected commotion had erupted, only yards away from him. There wasn't a second to waste. I leapt forwards following David, sensing Colin and Bolty react and follow me. I crashed through the muddy undergrowth, slipping once on the damp ground.

David burst past the last bush and into the clearing. As he arrived, he met one of the Satanic followers, who'd turned to confront him. Unthinking, David swung his wooden club, hard and fast. I heard the dull thud; the club caught the Satanist just behind the ear, causing him to crash to earth in an instant.

Pandemonium erupted, shouting and yelling echoed through the night. David was joined by the three of us, wildly swinging our clubs at anything that moved.

We were outnumbered. In the dim firelight, I realised, from the shadows and movement, we were faced by more than the seven I'd originally estimated. But we had surprise and resolve on our side.

In the clearing that night, I truly understood the meaning of the word berserker, as describes the ancient fighting warriors. I would have faced a battalion if necessary.

By the light of the fire, I saw a quick flash of steel; a knife was jabbed towards me. Distantly, I felt a sharp pain in the left forearm, before twisting, slamming my axe handle down hard, with brutal force, onto the knife carrying hand. The dark shape screamed, which I cut short with a hard, sharp jab of my fist to the throat of my unknown assailant, who disappeared backwards, into the fray.

As I turned, searching for my next target, Colin and Bolty pushed past. In the dark I heard a short female scream, abruptly curtailed, as Colin, or Bolty failed to differentiate in a lust for retribution.

A threatening figure came at me in the darkness. I screamed defiance at the hostile shape, springing forwards in the same motion. Catching a movement at the last moment, I twisted my head sideways, just in time to feel a heavy object glance off my left temple, crashing into my shoulder. With the jolting impact, I saw stars. My legs gave momentarily before I instinctively rammed my elbow sideways, connecting with the head of my attacker. His forward momentum took him slightly beyond me, before my trusty axe handle caught him a weighty blow behind the ear. Without a sound, he collapsed like a sack of potatoes. I turned prepared, but the original foe from the frontal attack, had melted into the darkness.

In an instant it was all over. What was left of Jerome's evil band evaporated into the night, dragging three unconscious forms between them. We stopped, gasping for breath, unsure what to do now we'd disengaged from the enemy. We didn't interfere as the Satanists collected their wounded and skulked off, slinking deeper into the shadowy darkness.

I turned, seeing David bent over and weeping, holding the still form of Sue, who lay unmoving on the ground. Poor sweet Sue, who lay with a horrendous jagged hole in her skull. A hole from which blood seeped freely, soaking the ground beneath her.

Also lying over a fallen tree next to her sister, spread eagled and tied to stakes at all four corners, my own dear, adorable, Trish; her clothes and skin were muddy and slick with blood – Sue's blood, which was splattered across the clearing. Trish, her eyes wide open, was staring vaguely into space, making not a single sound!

"Come on, they won't take long to regroup; there's enough of them. We'd better get out of here." Bolty was the first to regain composure, instantly planning our retreat.

"We can't, this has gone too far, we have to call the police," I shouted angrily, staring towards Sue, where David still knelt, cradling her bloodied head in his arms.

Colin drifted over to David, kneeling beside his friend, taking Sue's limp wrist in his hands. I studied him, sitting motionless for several seconds, until he turned towards me, shaking his head dejectedly.

Realising the need to summon help, I spoke urgently. "Has anybody got reception?" I asked, checking my phone, finding no signal. Bolty, David and Colin confirmed we were in a mobile black spot; there was no phone signal!

I was certain that we now needed the authorities involved; it was a murder. We couldn't move Sue's body from the crime scene.

"Can you guys stay here?" I asked Colin and David. "Bolty and I will drive towards the town until we get a signal. We'll take Trish with us! We'll be back as soon as possible, as soon as the police are on the way," I reassured them, knowing they would be thinking of a return of the bad guys.

Reluctantly, Colin agreed, begging, "Come back as soon as possible."

There was no need to ask. I could see there was no way that David would leave Sue alone in those woods, not even for a second.

"Before we go, we'd best agree the minimum ground rules for responding to the forthcoming questioning," Bolty interjected, displaying some sound thinking.

Quickly, we agreed. I would claim that Trish had managed to call me on a mobile, telling me they had been kidnapped and were heading for Underhill Woods. We'd found it on the internet and followed, wanting to know for sure that Trish and Sue were there. I would claim that Trish had been stalked by Jerome for some months: when the police investigated further, the episodes at Supertramp's and the Thatched Cottage would help to prove this. We agreed on our stories, knowing they would sound lame to an investigator, but the truth was even more unbelievable.

Bolty, Trish and I set off from the clearing, feeling and hearing the first pattering of raindrops, striking the leaves at the top of the canopy, it quickly intensified into a downpour.

As we'd started from the clearing, Trish pulled silently towards her sister, her facial expression stricken with distress at the idea of leaving her sibling. I'd guided her onwards, leading her away from a scene of destruction and horror which would haunt us for life.

The pair of us steered Trish through the woods towards the car. I held her hand tightly, talking to her, encouraging her all the way, but she never made a voluntary movement, or a single sound; it was as if the mute button had been pressed.

When we reached it, the Renault was the only car in the parking area, standing alone among the rapidly forming puddles. Quickly we steered Trish to the car, now thankful that Bolty hadn't let the tyres of the Jaguar down. Maybe we should have hidden the Renault, I thought, but when we'd first arrived, it hadn't occurred to me.

With a savage twist of the key, Bolty started the engine, gunning the motor just once, before selecting the gear and sprinting for the exit. Turning right from the car park, he followed the coastal road down the steep hill towards the town of Bracken Castle, three miles away.

When we'd first arrived, just over an hour earlier, I'd realised why this was known locally as heartbreak hill. A long steep climb, rocks on one side and a steep drop to the ocean on the other. The road climbed nearly three-hundred feet to the top of the hill and *Underhill Woods, beauty spot.*

Bolty was driving swiftly, in a hurry to complete our mission and return to our friends, but then I noticed, in the side mirror, the headlights of a car rapidly approaching us!

"Behind." I motioned to Bolty, keeping my voice sotto, unsure how much Trish would hear, or understand.

"I've seen them. Don't they ever stop coming." Grimly, he tightened his grip on the steering wheel, as the headlights approached to within feet of our car.

"Hang on," Bolty warned. "It's still a couple of miles to Bracken Castle." The two cars touched with a jolt and grinding screech of twisting metal. I held Trish's hand tightly, but it was as if nothing had happened; she never flinched in the slightest.

Again, the chasing car edged closer to our tail. In the mirror, I thought I recognised the shape of a Jaguar, before it touched, and the metallic crunch came again. I felt the rear of our car shudder before Bolty, fighting hard to steady the car, regained control. "Bastard," he muttered.

Twisting my neck savagely to search behind, I stared at the Jaguar, again it began to inch closer.

At that moment, something changed. At first, I didn't recognise it; maybe I saw a puff of smoke or heard a faint thud through the uproar as the tyre burst, or maybe I'm deceiving myself, but as I watched, the Jaguar seemed to twitch. Suddenly, it careered across the road, towards the steel barrier protecting the road from the rocks that were rising up into the darkness above. The racing car met the steel barrier with a diagonal blow. The car smashed hard into this unmovable obstacle with a deep crump that shook the ground, before bouncing away, across the road, unable to arrest its momentum. Bolty and I stared open mouthed. In our wake, the Jaguar slewed across the wet greasy surface, hitting the opposite crash barrier full on, ripping a post from the soft wet ground, teetering towards the vertical drop and the cliffs below. With a ripping noise, the barrier gave way, parting with the sound of tortured metal, as the heavy, speeding Jaguar forced its way through the protective barrier. The maroon car swayed once on the cliff edge, before disappearing over the side into the night, with an abruptness that was both relief, and shock at the same time.

"Shit... did you see that?" Bolty slammed the brakes on, screeching to a halt. Hurriedly we flung ourselves from of the car, dashing back up the road to the still groaning gap in the crash barrier.

Dazed and speechless, we stood motionless, staring into the rainy darkness. There was no ball of flame or scene of carnage; the only sign was the set of muddy tyre tracks cut into the grass verge, leading away from the twisted wreckage of the crash barriers to the cliff edge. Of the scene in the darkness below, there was no sight nor sound, just the distant wind and waves striking the rocky shore!

"Come quickly, we need ambulance and police; there's been a ritual, sacrificial murder!" I don't suppose the emergency operator had received many calls like that one, but she handled it with consummate professionalism, even if there was just a little incredulity in her tone!

"Caller, hold the line please, an ambulance has been despatched; it will be with you shortly."

As succinctly as possible, I passed on as many details as I could, finally being warned, "The ambulance may take twenty minutes, but the police will be with you shortly, sir."

Unexpectedly, feeling the weight of everything bearing down on my shoulders, I felt incredibly weary and drained. Only then did I notice the increasing pain in my arm, the aches throughout my body. I looked down, trying to focus my confused thoughts on the blood-soaked sleeve of my jacket.

"Come on, mate. Let's get back to David and Colin," I said, leaning on the car for support. "Police are on their way!"

"I simply don't believe you!" The detective stood over me, fists balled and resting on the table between us. Already I had been in police custody for nearly twelve hours; this was my second interview. Elsewhere in the police station, Colin, Bolty and David were undergoing similar interrogations.

"It's true," I declared, staring at the two detectives facing me. "I had a phone call from Trish telling me she had been kidnapped and was being taken to Underhill Woods." We followed to find out if it was true."

"And the kidnappers just let her out to make a phone call; pitiful, my mother could do better," he sneered, spraying spittle across my cheek, his face just inches from mine.

"Ask Trish," I said, hoping for the first time that she was still mute, for now.

"And you've no idea how Mr Jerome Brendon-Smythe and Ms Rosalind Brendon-Smythe happened to be killed in a car which mysteriously crashed through a barrier and down a one-hundred-and-fifty-foot cliff," he said, voice weighed down with saccharine soaked incredulity. "Two people who live just twenty miles from you."

"I knew they were there. We chased them away from the woods. Jerome's been stalking Trish for the past eight months but we'd no idea about the witchcraft and sacrifice! Last we saw of Jerome was in the woods. I don't even know who Rosalind is, let alone if she was there," I answered. "It was pretty dark in there."

Having got an extension from the courts, they pushed us all for a full forty-eight hours. We kept ourselves sane, reminding ourselves, we were indeed innocent; we'd done nothing wrong. But it was a terrible time for us all; the detectives who questioned me didn't believe a word I told them.

They'd checked out the stalking claim, which bore the weight of testimony, from Trish's workmates and Stan, the pub landlord, but that only brought a rash of questions to why we hadn't already reported the stalking, particularly after Katies disappearance. Despite our relentless protestations, the investigators failed to believe we were innocent of all crime.

"What do you say to this?" The lead investigator slapped a newspaper on the table before me. That day's copy of the *Moon*, Britain's leading red top tabloid newspaper, known for its sensationalist reporting. In massive block copy, the day's headline read, *Human Sacrifice as Satanic Cults Clash*. In smaller typeface, *Three dead*. Slowly I picked up the newspaper, reading the front-page article in full, before responding to the detective, who'd waited patiently while I read.

"It's all crap, well most of it," I told him, spinning the newspaper back across the table. "We had no idea that this guy was in a cult, not until yesterday when he kidnapped Trish and Sue from outside a hospital where their mother lies in intensive therapy," I stated with emphasis. "Until then we were just hoping it would go away, all this."

And, of course, you know nothing about Katie Bolt and Yvette Sanchez he said, yelling into my face, willing me to make an error.

"No, Katie's husband Robert was with us in Somerset. We all have alibis for Katie's disappearance. If Jerome was involved with her disappearance, then I know nothing. But the police yourselves reported that Yvette had left the country under her own passport. Why aren't you asking these questions of Jerome's friends," I replied, in frustration.

"Because Jerome and his sister are dead, and any friends they may, or may not have had, have disappeared. You are our only link to the truth of the matter," he replied frankly.

I suggested that he would be better advised to direct his resources into finding Jerome's friends, but that only led to another four hours lying on my bunk in the cell.

Finally, the police had to admit, there was not enough evidence to hold us in custody. As testified by the four of us, the murder of Susan Cummings was believed to have been carried out by Jerome Brendon-Smythe, now deceased. This was supported by Sue's blood and DNA found on Jerome and Rosalind's clothing, his skin oils and DNA on the rock used as a murder weapon. Any further information regarding the crash and subsequent death of Jerome and his sister Rosalind in a road traffic accident was unforthcoming. There seemed to be no witnesses, and the rain had washed away any evidence.

The detective told me, "There's not enough evidence to prove the tyre of the Jag burst due to an explosive device within the tread of the tyre. But we've seen Robert Bolt's army record and we're going to be watching you."

I believe it was the fact that the police knew Underhill Woods had previously been used by cults, to carry out animal sacrifices that swayed them into believing we were largely innocent victims, caught up in a torrent of horror. I'm sure they did not believe our claims about our arrival at the woods, but there was now enough evidence at the crime scene, and Tufton Gray, to implicate Jerome for the murder. They even began to investigate the house at Tufton Gray, looking for clues to Katie's murder!

Bowing to our requests for anonymity, we were released in the early hours of the morning, one at a time, from the back entrance of Taunton police station. Seeking to avoid the braying press-pack waiting outside the front entrance for their sensationalist story, I sneaked away through the dark deserted streets, making it to the train station just in time to catch the first train out of there.

CHAPTER SEVENTEEN

I met up with Colin and David, two days after we were released from Taunton police station, Once together, there was no celebration of survival, rather resignation, a subdued acceptance that our lives had changed forever.

I hugged David, holding him tightly for several seconds, communicating my sympathy as best I could. We'd all had a terrible few days, none more so than David.

I revealed the latest news of Trish. "She remains catatonic, unable to speak, the unit where she has been taken, near Taunton, have diagnosed post traumatic shock. Her doctors think she'll take an awfully long time before recovering any power of speech. They've warned there is a chance Trish might not recover at all," I told them, feeling the weight of such a possibility bearing down on my heart.

We knew the investigation wasn't finished; the police wanted answers, answers we couldn't give them. We also needed answers, answers from John or Luke. After all the assurances we'd been given, I wanted to know what had gone wrong in the spiritual world, how had such devastation been allowed to happen?

Following our release, we knew that we were under a great deal of scrutiny, both from the press and the police, who we knew were paying close attention to our every movement.

"It's a good job that they haven't bugged our flats. The arrival of John or Luke would cause many raised eyebrows," Colin joked. But all the same, we decided to de-camp to Colin's flat. It was on a higher floor, less susceptible to directional microphones.

Also, after our release we were greatly concerned by the continued presence of tabloid journalists. The sensationalist headlines about satanic wars and sacrificial murders continued for a couple of days. We'd all been approached by reporters, searching for a story. Fortunately for us, though not Richard, most of the rat-pack camped outside Richard's driveway, bombarding him with questions whenever he returned from visiting Lynda or Trish.

It was providential for us all when another major news story erupted elsewhere in the country, a couple of days after our return. Richard woke up to find the rat-pack had decamped for pastures new.

Aided by the surprise factor, I think we'd got off lightly in the fighting. Considering how outnumbered we were, it could have been far worse. But it remained unknown how many of the opposition were truly dedicated to their cause, or even how deeply they were involved.

I ended up with a deep stab wound in the left forearm, just above the wrist. Waiting for the police to arrive. I'd found my sleeve black from the blood. Fortunately, before placing me in the cells, the police took me to Taunton Musgrove hospital for treatment, six stitches.

Now, two days later, Colin exhibited, for our inspection, a couple of massive black and blue bruises on his shoulder and stomach, indicating the area where he'd been struck with some kind of club. Like me, Colin claimed not to have noticed until after the battle.

David sported a single black eye, but we knew his suffering was greatest of us all. During a phone call, Bolty reported several bruises and grazes. Overall, I think we'd been extremely lucky to walk away from the confrontation.

In anticipation, we waited for John's arrival. Once more he appeared without warning, commandeering David's body in an instant. Eyes flashing, accompanied by the perceptible change in body posture.

"John?" I began, seeking confirmation.

"Martyn, Colin," your father is sorry for your losses. We are sorry that Sue had to die!

"You're sorry?" I countered. I felt so empty of emotion that I was unsure if I felt angry or just defeated. If it was anger, then where could we aim our anger? At John, who'd appeared at our own instigation, offering tribulation and adventure in the service of the Lord, but only if we chose to follow. Or could I be angry at Jerome, who'd paid a just price for the carnage he'd brought to our life. I flopped back into my seat, unable to complete the sentence.

"Yes, we are sorry, but we never offered anything other than trials and hardship in our service," John countered.

"I guess it's all over then," Colin replied, without emotion.

"Why do you say this?" John asked, sounding genuinely puzzled.

"You said that we were in a syndicate of six; there are only three of us left. What good would we be for the forthcoming arrival of a new messiah?" I replied. We were both incredulous at the ease with which John could move on from the loss of our comrades.

"But you have already served well. Jerome and his faction have been identified and defeated. You have removed the opposition and opened the way for the new messiah to come into this world, a messiah to draw mankind to himself, to serenade the end to time," he told us.

"It sure was a heavy price to pay, particularly for Sue, Yvette, Trish, Katie, Sandra and Paul," Colin said, caustically, the regret of his voice echoing my own feelings.

Unexpectedly, John rounded angrily on us both, glaring. Almost shouting, he retorted. "Do you not realise how blessed you are to have me here in your flat, a visitor from the heavens. You should be flat on your face worshipping me, not moaning about how hard it is. Every prophet in history has had to pay a heavy price, as you call it, for the privilege of being chosen. It is not the end of your dream; this is just the beginning. It will get harder yet! You weren't promised an easy time. I warned you in the beginning how difficult and dangerous this was going to be. Why are you so surprised when this turns out to be the case? If you, and mankind in general, weren't so arrogant, unwilling to obey my words and commands, then the price you pay is a consequence of the choices you make," he declared, leaving us both stunned by the level of vehemence in his voice.

I felt aggrieved at John for speaking in this manner. I believed we'd just been through an intense, horrendous ordeal on his behalf, now John berated us for it.

"We were just saying that the experience has taken a lot from us all," I snapped back in response. Beginning to bite.

"It took far more from Sue," John informed me curtly, "but Sue and Katie's selfless sacrifice has now removed Jerome from opposition. Jerome, with his friends, sought to destroy your syndicate; they have been stopped. Your friends are indeed in the company of angels. But the work will continue; the new messiah must be given to the world. There is no longer a threat. We can now use David freely as a vessel of communication; it is no longer dangerous," he assured us.

John remained another hour, describing how the pathway had been opened up between the spiritual and earthly worlds by the destruction of the evil syndicate.

"Anne Giddes has disappeared, but we promise, she poses no threat on her own." John left, assuring us that we could call on him or Luke at any time. It was now safe for them to appear. "But, if you so desire," he promised, "you may take time for rest and recovery."

Two weeks later, dear, sweet, loving, caring Sue was cremated. Our friend Sue, who, for everyone she met, only had compassion and love in her heart. Sue, who'd warned veraciously of the dangers of intruding into the spiritual realm. We cremated her at a packed crematorium, on a cold and wet Thursday afternoon. She'd died, aged just twenty-five years old. I helped carry the coffin, my arm around my friend David's shoulder; the tears flowed freely on such an emotional day.

Lynda was beginning to recover, physically at least. She was pushed in a wheelchair by her husband, a bright silk headscarf protecting the operation site. Both parents were almost broken in half by the unforeseen and senseless destruction within their family.

Trish wasn't at the funeral. Once the ambulance arrived at Underhill Woods, Trish had been hospitalised, initially in a secure unit. A week later, they'd transferred her to another unit, much closer to home. Close enough for Richard to visit each evening after visiting his wife.

I'd visited as soon as she was transferred. They warned me, "Trish has suffered extremely severe, post traumatic shock syndrome. It's two weeks since the attack and she is still unable to utter a word." The kindly medical staff tried to reassure me. "This might be normal; she could recover with time, maybe even lead a normal life, but for now, Trish's mind has retreated within itself. Almost like a computer, the brain is switching itself to safe mode, just to keep her functioning."

I do know, when I was eventually allowed to visit her, as they ushered me into the ward, Trish's immediate reaction was to shy away from me, almost as if I were an infectious disease carrier. It's not as if she didn't know me; she was frightened in my presence. I stayed two minutes before they gently shepherded me out of there. Afterwards, the head psychologist sympathetically suggested, "Maybe Trish isn't quite ready for visitors just yet. We hoped your face might give her something of a lift, but it seems it was the opposite. Martyn, we will keep you informed of her progress, but please do not return until she has recovered enough to want to see you. It could set any recovery back again."

Just prior to Sue's funeral, Lynda was allowed home from hospital. The funeral had been delayed specifically to allow Lynda to attend. Richard waited before telling her of the abduction of their daughters and the subsequent murder of Sue. Naturally, Lynda imploded with grief, unable to comprehend what Richard was trying to tell her frail and unbelieving mind.

After my disastrous visit to Trish, I'd begun to visit the home of Richard and Lynda every couple of days. I needed to be kept informed of her progress. Also, it gave me a small feeling of closeness to Trish, just knowing I was talking to her parents.

Usually, I would visit just after they'd returned from the unit, where Trish would accept them without reaction, as she sat in silence.

Solemnly, Richard informed me, "There is still no change in Trish's prognosis. She remains unresponsive although, occasionally, caused by an unknown trigger, fearful reactions and distress surfaces. That very day," Richard counselled," She became almost inconsolable when a piece appeared on the local news about the round table in Winchester!"

The doctors were now convinced, Trish was there for the long term; it was possible, or even probable, that she would never fully recover. Her trauma may have been too great. They'd suggested to Richard that any recovery may only be partial.

"Thing is, Martyn, we'd like to have a little chat with you." Richard spoke to me, glancing significantly towards Lynda, who'd just entered the dining room, still in her wheelchair. With an ominous feeling, I sat where I was directed, perching on the edge of the dinning-room chair, seated opposite Richard and Lynda, waiting for them to speak.

"We don't know what has been happening over the past year, but we would like you to stop coming around here, and please refrain from any contact with Trish." He'd begun with the thunderbolt. Richard held Lynda's hand, seeking mutual support for their difficult task, both determined to protect their remaining daughter from any perceived threat!

My mouth fell open in disbelief; here I was, the only tenuous link I had to Trish being unceremoniously ripped from my grasp.

"But why?" I stuttered, knowing the answer, accepting their motives, even as I asked the question.

"We've no idea what's been happening, or whether you're involved in a cult. We knew that you guys were traipsing all over the country with Trish and Sue; we didn't want to ask. Trish and Sue were old enough to make their own choices," he said bitterly. "But this past few weeks, Sue and Trish, then newspaper men camped on our drive, screaming questions about satanic cults and murderous conflicts. It's simply too much for us. We've lost our eldest daughter whilst trying to recover from Lynda's accident," he explained gently.

Richard forged onwards with what was no doubt a prepared speech. "We don't blame you; we don't even want to know what it was all about; I suspect it might be too difficult for us to hear at this time, but I think it is right that you and David don't visit this house again. Please don't make any attempt to contact Trish. If she recovers and wants to see you, then we will accept this, but until then, please don't come here, or try and contact her in the unit."

Briefly I considered confessing all that had happened over the previous months, immediately rejecting the thought as unrealistic. Though devastated, deep down I applauded Richard's courage. In his shoes, I hoped I would have the courage to do the same. I glanced at Lynda, wanting a reprieve.

"Please," Lynda begged. With her one-word appeal, she destroyed my last remnants of hope!

"I think it is best you leave now. Please do us the honour of respecting our request." Richard stood up, speaking with finality, moving towards the door. "I'm sorry it's come to this; please tell David of our wishes," Richard said, as he closed the door firmly on another chapter of my life.

I drove home in shock, unable to digest what had just happened. Deep down I'd unrealistically expected Trish to recover, things to return to normal. I'd lived the past weeks in denial, now, forced to face the reality that Trish was no longer part of my life. I went to bed and cried myself to sleep, unable to comprehend a future without her!

For me, the loss of Trish from my life was the last straw. I found I couldn't think straight or concentrate on anything. At regular intervals, I began to break down in tears, or I'd simply find myself staring into the middle distance, my mind a blank. I believe, over the next few days, I tried to go on normally, going to work as usual. But five days after Richard's bombshell, after a breakdown at my drawing board, Steven, my boss, ordered me to go home and make an appointment to see a doctor.

At that time a visit to the doctor's was rare. After sitting in the surgery for twenty minutes, explaining my current difficulties to a sympathetic but harassed looking doctor, he quietly wrote out a sick note, advising me that I was suffering from my own traumatic breakdown. I was advised, "From what you've told me, it's likely that you will need several months of rest and recuperation before you can recover sufficiently to face the world. I'll write a note for the first four weeks," he told me, with a kindly smile.

For the first two weeks of trauma, I was unable to relate with anybody. I would sit alone in an empty flat, staring at the blank walls or the television screen, ignoring all visitors and phone calls. My workplace was great, sending flowers, promising to hold the job open for as long as I needed.

Colin and David both tried, but to begin with, I was unwilling to interact, even with my closest friends. I found I desperately wanted and needed my own company.

After about two weeks, I'd moved forwards slightly, able to fill my days with long country walks. It was springtime and the blustery weather did me much good. Wrapped up against the wind and the chill, I walked for many solitary hours, finding solace in nature and the awakening countryside.

Unlike Trish, whom I monitored through word of mouth, I gradually began to climb out of the valley of despair. Walking and contemplation, my closest companions, assisting me in my efforts to endure each day, as best I could!

Slowly, Colin and David had been allowed back into my life. Many evenings we would sit as a threesome in a pub, or the flat, aimlessly talking about whatever. Each of us treading carefully, wary of accidently blundering onto another's pain and hurt!

Eventually, John began to appear again, visiting regularly, sometimes spending the majority of the evening with us, sharing general conversation. At first, I was unsure how to handle this. I knew John's visits could be dangerous for me; they'd been the root of our grief, but John seemed unconcerned.

During these visits, he failed to mention the future, or the times which lay ahead. He deprived David of our company, but seemed happy to enjoy it himself, teaching us about the structure of the spiritual realm and its interaction with mankind.

By mid-April, I was managing huge eight-hour long walks. I found the solitary thinking time would do me good. Several times a week, after checking the BBC weather forecast, I would prepare my small rucksack with a day's provisions, then set off. Sometimes with a plan, but more often with just an expectation of a day's walking.

One Tuesday evening, I'd prepared the rucksack for the next day. My plan was to drive to a designated walk. The day dawned clear and bright, bringing with it a breezy chill, the type of April day I was becoming used to.

The walking was excellent, described in my *Walks of Great Britain,* as easy to moderate in difficulty. I'd parked in a remote spot, intending to complete the fourteen-mile circular walk. The bracing, blustery winds, coupled with the weak, but cheerful, April sunshine felt like a tonic. I noticed, for the first time in a long while, I almost felt good about being where I was. I wasn't able to look into the future yet, but I was far in advance of where I'd been for the past two months!

Eight miles into the walk, and the distant pub hove into view. It was mentioned in the guidebook, I carried. *The Blacksmiths Arms, a welcoming and comfortable place to take a breather. Providing a selection of excellent, real ales and a reliable snack or bar menu.* Instantly, the limp ham and tomato sandwiches, I knew were waiting at the bottom of the rucksack, lost their appeal. I'd completed more than half of the fourteen miles, building a thirst on the way. Quickly I considered my options, deciding I'd earnt it. I could afford to stop for a beer, maybe even two, and something more appealing than soggy foil wrapped sandwiches.

For early afternoon, the bar appeared empty, but I guess most of the trade came at the weekends and later in the summer. Empty was perfect for me. I marched to the bar, ordering a pint of Bishops Trumpet, *an award-winning real ale*, as the advertising slogan promised. Taking time to choose, while appreciatively sipping the pint, I ordered a cheese ploughman's from the unhurried, laconic barmaid, before working my way towards the beer garden. Exiting through the French doors, I searched for a seat, somewhere out of the chilly wind, but still bathed in the bright April sunshine!

"You look somewhat troubled; are you okay?" I looked up, silently cursing. The only other patron in the pub seemed to be an extrovert, wanting interaction. Briefly I considered telling him to go away, leave me to the lunch I'd nearly finished, but this stranger continued talking before I had a chance to react.

"If I had my Jesus hat on, I would tell you that Jesus is the answer but usually that's the prompt for a swift retreat by yourself, so I won't. Besides there is nothing worse than a preaching Christian," he informed me, sitting down uninvited, opposite me.

"I lose so many potential friends that way. Instead of weighty theology, the least I can do is buy you another pint and spend ten minutes talking about the lovely weather we're having and the great walking," he said, attracting the attention of the disinterested barmaid, listlessly engaged in drying pint glasses.

Eventually, having accepted a fresh pint, I ditched the idea of telling him to get lost, deciding that I had to begin to interact at some time. Maybe, I decided, a complete stranger who was too talkative was the best option. I could sit back, let the conversation flow over my head, unnoticed.

"Anyway, you're way off track. I feel fine, and I believe in Jesus," I declared, thinking about the reverend William Dean, wondering if this was going to end as badly.

"Good," he replied. "I don't need to do all that Jesus loves you bit, so off-putting for the non-Christian majority. I'm Jeff King," he announced, holding out a hand. "Fellow walker, and fellow Christian, it seems." Jeff raised his eyebrows, waiting while I introduced myself.

"I might be a Christian, but I'm certainly not loved by Jesus at the moment," I assured him, "even if I do feel okay in today's sun!"

"Ah, life gets in the way. Sometimes it just helps to talk it through with somebody who has no vested interest. Wanna try?" he asked, taking a deep draught of his foaming pint, leaving a ridiculous foam moustache, which he didn't seem to care about.

"I tried once before, with a vicar; it was a total waste of time."

"That's because it's his job; so many of them can't think outside the box. No pressure, drink your pint and leave if you want, but it might help to unload your troubles, knowing that we will never meet again," he said, with a small friendly half-smile.

I considered it; I could feel the urge to tell him to get lost rising within me. But then I thought, he's right, a total stranger who I will never meet again. The perfect recipient of my woes, and if I got the same reaction as with the reverend Billy, then I'd know I was on the way to insanity; I decided, I'd just have to risk it.

Starting at the crux, I began. "Do you believe in spirits and Satan?" I asked, gazing straight into his blue, quizzical eyes, wanting to gauge his reaction.

"Of course, that's what it's all about, the spiritual battle against the devil's evil forces." Jeff hadn't batted an eyelid. Calculating, I quickly decided to tell our whole tale, only leaving some of the self-incriminating details out. Jeff sat back and made himself comfortable, pint in hand, patient expression on his face. He allowed me free rein to talk, relate our tale at my own pace, Jeff only imputing an occasional "hmmm," or asking a pertinent question, when it seemed relevant. Having finished, I sat back, waiting for Jeff to speak. The telling had taken nearly an hour; my third pint was now drained, the empty glass on the table before me.

Finally, Jeff spoke, taking his time, choosing the words carefully. "That's a very frightening tale you've just revealed. Can I see the tattoo that appeared on you?" he asked, nodding towards my thigh.

I twisted in my chair, lifting my shorts, showing him the tattoo; by then I'd forgotten about it. It had almost become part of me. "Hmm interesting, but this is not a Christian tattoo," he said. "The eye signifies the eye of Horace, ancient Egypt, which is always portrayed in the Bible as evil. The tattoo you described on your girlfriend's leg, I think, signifies the ancient religion of wicca, but I may be wrong."

I waited for more revelations, not daring to speak. "I can't tell you what to do with this information; only you and your friends can decide, but there are several observations I would like to make, for you to think about, that is if you're willing?" he said, glancing up and waiting for my approval.

I agreed, keen for him to continue.

"Firstly, there was no apostle Luke in the Bible, the gospels of Luke and Mark were written around the time, by contemporaries of Jesus, but they were not of the original twelve disciples. Secondly, have you considered the significance of the apple smell, which you tell me appeared to you all, at some time or other. This is an aroma which signifies Adam and Eve, the fall of mankind. But most importantly, the Bible doesn't reveal a new messiah; it's very specific! There is only one messiah, Jesus: The Bible says he will return to Earth as himself. Without this promise, then Christianity might as well not exist; it's the central promise of the religion," he instructed.

"But John said the Bible was written by man," I countered, beginning to feel on very shaky ground indeed.

"The Bible was written by man, but it was inspired by God; don't ask me to explain some of the harder text. Sometimes where Christians are concerned, mankind's judgement seems to swamp God's love at times!" he responded, "but think about it, if the Bible isn't one hundred per cent the inspired work of God, then we might as well give up as Christians. I look at it like this, there's a spiritual world. In our modern world, mankind is constantly seeking, of mediums, or superstitions, even the horoscope in your daily paper, but then, we deny God, saying he doesn't exist. However, still blaming him for everything that is bad in this world.

Think of it like this, we both agree there is a spiritual world, right?" Jeff halted, waiting for me to agree to the existence of a spiritual world. "Well, imagine this, I think of the spiritual world being the fifth dimension; you have one, two and three, the spatial ones, four is time and the spiritual dimension is the fifth dimension. I think the sixth dimension is the truth within that spiritual world! A truth that accepts the spiritual realm is divergent, not always from the right source; spirits may be different to how they appear, even if you think of them as benign. There is one way you can test it, the spirit you know as John, that is," he revealed.

"How's that?" I asked, feeling slightly nauseous by the turn of events.

"The Bible is very clear. God has given all authority to the Lord Jesus; your spirit has to acknowledge Jesus as his Lord. Your spirit has to state quite simply, *Jesus is my Lord*."

"Even if it were a fake, this spirit," I asked, "could it not just say the words."

Jeff promised me, "No, I have no idea how it works in the spiritual, but in the name of Jesus you have full authority. I believe in spirits because it's the cornerstone of my religion. I know this works, so unless your spirit, who claims to be John, can accept Jesus as his Lord and saviour, then I'm afraid it is a fake, a lying demonic spirit."

There was nowhere else for me to go with the conversation. I began to believe, just a little, and with this belief, I felt a great lifting begin within.

"Can you come and tell my friend Colin what you have just told me?" I asked him.

Jeff politely refused, saying, "I need to be back home to the wife and kids for tea." So we swapped phone numbers, Jeff promising to be around if required.

Later that evening, Colin and I shared a takeaway Chinese meal, while I recounted the events of my day, the revelation I'd received over lunch. As I explained what I'd learnt as best I could, I saw the light of understanding in Colin's eyes.

"What do we do now?" Colin asked, reaching across me, choosing another salt and pepper rib. "It's not as if it were a picnic that's gone wrong; people have died."

This was a question that I'd pondered myself, while completing the final six miles of the walk.

"I think we'd best wait until John appears, ask him to acknowledge the Lord Jesus as his saviour, shouldn't be too hard. After all, he claims to have been his disciple when Jesus walked the earth," I replied.

I cleared the remains of the Chinese away while Colin phoned David, inviting him around. We both felt unsure, nervous about the evening. We'd both known David since we were ten years old, at junior school. This thing had dominated all of our lives for over a year, costing a great deal for all involved, including David. The possible outcome to our planned experiment didn't bear thinking about.

David arrived, encouraged by the prospect of an evening away from the noisy and boisterous family home. Opening the door, greeting David, I had to make the mental distinction between the spirit which could manifest and David, my close friend since school days.

Fortunately, we didn't have long to wait; the spirit, known as John, wasted little time before the characteristic flicker of the eyes and change in body posture alerted us the spirit was with us. I took the lead with our questioning. "John?" I asked.

"Greetings, my friends, you are recovering well, Martyn. We will soon move on with your syndicate's work," he said, looking at both of us when he spoke.

"Before we do, can we ask you a question?" Colin interjected.

"That is why we spend time together; we teach and answer your questions, which is why I am the teacher, you are my pupils!"

"Good! So, when you were on the earth, you followed Jesus right? Can you now tell us that Jesus is your Lord?" I noticed that Colin had spontaneously become more assertive with John, failing to complete the request with a please.

"I am your teacher; you will do what I tell you. You must obey my voice. You have seen the consequences of failure?"

"Yes," Colin said, "but Jesus was your Lord, you followed him here on Earth; we're simply asking you to acknowledge that Jesus Christ is your Lord." Colin sounded reasonable, but there was a steely finality in the demand he'd made.

I joined the conversation. "It's quite simple. We feel hugely let down by you, and God. To get here there has been a massive price to pay. If you want us to continue, then I want to know that you worship the same Lord Jesus as we think we're following. It can't be that difficult if you were his disciple," I told him.

"David lost Sue as part of that price. If you want to avoid the consequences, then you have to obey me," he demanded tersely, not meeting our eyes.

"David paid the price, but David isn't you! Only after we hear you say, Jesus Christ is my Lord." I commanded, understanding that a not so subtle change was taking place.

"I will not worship him." We saw his lip curl as he spat the words out, the predominant emotion in his eyes turned to hatred. This time there was no specific moment where we recognised the battle within before a switch between the spirit of John and an evil spirit.

With an unexpectedness which was frightening, he became a snarling, ferocious angry beast. The eyeballs rolled upwards into his head. I saw his back arch as the beast manipulated David's body. The teeth were revealed as his top lip receded. His hands became claws, he sprang towards us, seemingly intent on clawing at our faces. We fell back from his onslaught. I noticed the same sulphurous smell in the room. The fear induced in Colin and me exploded, quickly becoming terror as we hurriedly backed away from this evil beast.

Distantly my mind cottoned on; we'd been supplied with an answer, a weapon for this battle. I remembered the words of the guy I'd met earlier, Jeff.

"In the name of Jesus, I take authority. I tell you to leave." The snarling beast occupying our friend's body flinched, halting in its pursuit of Colin and myself.

"In the name of Jesus, go," we both repeated, seeing another definite flinch when we recited the words at the snarling, but now stationary fiend.

"In Jesus's name go!" The beast started to fall back, edging away from us, as if our words were spiritual mace, sprayed towards an attacker. We began to ease forward, gaining confidence through our authority over this beast. In a split second it, and David, were gone. It turned and walked away, quickly opening the door, departing without a word, leaving two very confused but relieved guys behind. The nightmare was over!

EPILOGUE

In the end, it turned out we weren't involved in a Hollywood style good versus evil battle – just a sea of evil of which we were, unbeknownst, submerged somewhere in the middle. That was the last time I saw David. He went home, told his mother and family that he was leaving to find himself. The very next day he left, getting on a coach to who knows where. If he did contact his family again, then we never heard about it.

I truly believe that David's body was commandeered by an entity from another realm; what this was and where it came from, I have no idea. Call it a malevolent and manipulative demon if you like, who knows. But I do know that David was unable to carry off the act. I had known him for far too long to believe that he was capable of such destruction, deliberately.

Also, I have to believe, David knew nothing about the entity which possessed him. When I realise the mayhem that was caused, the lives lost and destroyed across the few short months, I have to believe that my friend David did not know what he was really possessed by, or what it was capable of, through him. But sadly, I realise it was David who announced to his family, he was leaving. It was as David he walked to the station and got on the bus.

What the connection was between David's and Paul's group, or Jerome's evil empire, I have no idea. If they knew we were being duped or were just other groups deceived by the same spirit, and fighting for their own cause, I do not know and, to be honest, I don't really care anymore. I've never been back to Tufton Gray, and I have no intention of going!

I occasionally see Trish now. They were fortunate that Richard and Lynda were wealthy enough to bring Trish home, cared for in loving surroundings.

In time Richard and Lynda mellowed a little. They are now happy for me to occasionally see Trish, but nothing remained the same. Trish is happy in her own enclosed world; she doesn't really recognise me, or want to interact when I go around. I belong to another world, another part of Trish's life: a part of life where Trish's brain simply refuses to visit.

After that night, I never saw Bolty again. I hope he recovered and lived a happy life. Somehow, I doubt it!

Sandra still lives on the farm; it is now managed by her younger sister and her family. The last I heard Sandra lived a reclusive life, simply getting by.

That Saturday was the last we saw of Yvette; sometimes I like to daydream that she escaped and started a new life somewhere else in the world, but we never found out. I just pray she survived somehow, but my doubts are big.

I still see Colin quite a lot, but things have never been quite the same between us. The ease which we used to share has been tarnished, just a little, by the wedge that was driven in when Yvette disappeared. Fortunately, the gap between us never grew larger. Since it happened, Colin has never mentioned my failure to protect Yvette, not once! It is probably something within me rather than Colin but, deep down, I know that I failed him. From this I couldn't recover.

Colin himself never went back to sea; instead, he carried on with his computer studies, got a degree and now works for a mobile phone company in the south. Colin eventually met and married a lady called Laura. They met at work, I think, and now have, as far as I know, a happy family life with three children. We meet up occasionally for a beer, and a chat, I think he is happy with his life, but when I was the best man at his wedding, I never saw that intense gleam in his eyes, the joy of love which I'd recognised the night before he shipped out on his last trip to sea.

As for me, I sold up and moved on, about six months after David left. There was nothing left for me in that town. I got a new job and moved to the Midlands. I never married, or even sought a relationship. Trish was the one for me and if not her, then never. I live a very quiet life now. Gradually, I drifted into attending church; I figured that if it was a demon, then I should give God a try, and I am happy in my own way.

But of the bright futures we all envisaged that cold winter's evening when we started on the Ouija board, they were gone – our futures all faded to dust!